$24

DISCARD

‖‖‖ ‖ ‖ ‖‖‖‖‖ ‖‖‖ ‖ ‖‖‖‖‖ ‖‖‖
D1563691

AND THE WORD WAS

AND
THE
WORD
WAS

[a novel]

Bruce Bauman

Other Press · New York

An excerpt of this work appeared, in a slightly different form, in the first issue of
Black Clock magazine.

Production Editor: Robert D. Hack

Text design: Natalya Balnova

This book was set in Melior by Alpha Graphics of Pittsfield, NH.

10 9 8 7 6 5 4 3 2 1

Library of Congress Cataloging-in-Publication Data

Bauman, Bruce

  And the word was / by Bruce Bauman.

    p. cm

  ISBN 1-59051-141-7 (alk. paper)

    1. Manhattan (New York, N.Y.)–Fiction. 2. Murder victims' families–
Fiction. 3. Jewish philosophers–Fiction. 4. Americans–India–Fiction. 5. Loss
(Psychology)–Fiction. 6. Separated people–Fiction. 7. Sons–Death–Fiction.
8. Physicians–Fiction. 9. India–Fiction. I. Title.

  PS3602.A955A84 2005

  813'.6–dc22

                                     2004013623

To my mother, my father, and Suzan

I would like to thank the following for their support: the Virginia Center for the Creative Arts, Sweetbriar, Virginia; the UNESCO/Aschberg Foundation, Paris, France; the Sanskriti Foundation, New Delhi, India; the Jewish Communal Fund, New York, New York; and the 18th Street Arts Complex, Santa Monica, California.

And Abraham lifted up his eyes, and looked up, and behold behind him a ram caught in the thicket by his horns. And Abraham, offered him up for a burnt-offering in the stead of his son.

—*GENESIS*

Prince Prahlad, son of King Hiranyakashipu, refused to give up worship to god Vishnu. The King with his sister Holi, who was immune to death by fire, conspired against Prahlad. Holi took Prahlad in her arms and entered a blazing furnace; yet it was Holi who was burnt to ashes by divine intervention, while Prahlad survived unscathed.

—Ancient Hindu myth

1

MY NAME IS Downs. I am a Jew. Whether or not that is essential to the story I am about to tell only you will be able to judge. Maybe you could read through my whole tale and never know until—kabbalah-krishna-kaboom—comes the HollywoodBollywood car-crash denouement and my dilemma is, at last, resolved. But I am no trickster, so it is best I tell you in the beginning.

2

I LIVED ALONE. In New Delhi. Before moving there, I lived my whole life, thirty-nine years, in New York City. Please, no Second Avenue New Deli Borsht-Belt and famed, Holy Cow bagel chip jokes. I've heard them all.

I did not choose Delhi because I was a Pepsi-Generation hippie turned dyspepsia-generation yuppie, who long ago got stoned and laid to the ragas of Ravi Shankar and yearned for the gloried conquests of youth; no, his music bored me into stupefaction; I did not choose Delhi because I was a midlife-crisis New Ager with a self-indulgent belief that I'd find a drive-thru guru who would instantly end my emptiness and infuse me with internal peace; no, because I must've set a record when I was, ever so politely, asked by the enlightened Desiree Prana (born Rene Kerstein of Roslyn, Long Island) never to come back to her yoga class because I disruptively murmured "shit" and "fuck" every time I couldn't contort my body into Gumbyesque position; I did not choose Delhi because I craved Indian food and hung out in the dingy restaurants on East 6th Street; nope, because even the odor of curry upset my delicate digestive system. I did not choose Delhi because I was infatuated by the literature, the art, or the movies; I knew almost nothing of the Indian arts. I did not choose India because I wanted to conquer the languages of Hindi, Urdu, Punjabi, or any of the hundreds of other languages and dialects spoken by over one billion people; no, I wanted to be deaf to the world around me. I did not choose Delhi because of my lustful desire to experiment with the innumerable sexual entanglements of the Kama Sutra; I almost never expected to have sex again after I left New York. Nor did I choose Delhi because of my mystical belief in the reincarnations of Hinduism.

I chose Delhi because it was so foreign and far away. Because I knew almost no one, and no one well at all. And no one knew me. But most of all, I chose Delhi because I no longer believed in god.

3

3

I am, therefore god cannot be. The death camps existed, therefore god cannot be. God as creator, thus his existence, as are all of our existences, was an error. We are either a mistake of a god gone mad or a universe that randomly stumbled into life.

—Levi Furstenblum,
from *MYSTICAL MISTAKES*, published in 1975

4

I WAS BORN Neil Downs. Thankfully, my
mother didn't listen to the wishes of her mother, the last observant person in our family, and name me Chaim. My mother
said I never acted or looked like a Chaim, or either one of them
for that matter.

My father's eyes were hazel, his hair dark, curly brown,
which he slicked back in a nineteen forties, Sinatra-style pom-
padour. My mother's eyes were blue-green, her hair straight and
light brown. They both had tawny skin. I am a genetic freak,
reaching back to the muck of my recessive gene pool, against all
odds, that found their European ancestors in a pair of Cossack
and Aryan interlopers, for I have wavy blond hair, blue eyes, and
fair skin. And I married a blond-haired, green-eyed, alabaster-
skinned WASP with the three names of Sarah Brockton Roberts.
And, we had a blond-haired and blue-eyed son: Barry Castor
Downs. We named him Barry, as is the Jewish tradition, for my
father Ben, who died from a combination of life-exhaustion and
cancer a year before his grandson's birth. From the beginning,
my son was no Barry, always Castor.

The day he was born was the happiest day of my life. Better than becoming a doctor, losing my virginity, smoking pot or doing downs, meeting Sarah, making love to Sarah, falling in love with Sarah.

To us, Castor, a breech baby, was special and grew more special with each passing day. To him, and only him, I gave my unconditional love. Only Castor—amidst the smells of pain and death squashed under the odors of toxic cleansers; the pillars of lies that the diseased must tell themselves and that we pretenders to knowledge of sickness and death reinforce; the blasphemy of blackened eyes and broken hearts of beat-up wives; the sadomasochistic bruises of abusive lovers; the shriveled arms and deteriorating insides of streetwalking junkies; the wealthy cokeheads with paranoid delusions of sudden heart attacks; the foolhardy twenty-somethings who tested their mortality by rollerblading at break-bone speeds; the uninsured poor who came in for a cold and left with the surety they had TB; the loneliness addicts who came to me as a last resort to cure the incurable ills of life—among the simple sadnesses of everyday existence in the emergency room where I worked at St. Vincent's Hospital in downtown Manhattan—only my son gave me faith in the future of humanity. In god.

5

THE ONE PERSON I knew in New Delhi was
Charlie Bedrosian, who also happened to be the U.S. Ambassador to India. I met Charlie not because we buddied up as non-Brahmins at Columbia—we found out some time after we met that he was there twenty years before me. We were middle-class guys trying to climb, the best way we knew how, the ladders of the American caste system.

Charlie epitomized the unvarnished intelligence and real-politic patriotism of the first generation of Foreign Service bureaucrats who earned their promotions on merit, not family clout and white male pedigree. Charlie served all over Asia: Vietnam before the war ended, India during the early seventies, Indonesia when the CIA aided in the murder of thousands of Timorese. Now, nearing sixty, he sought and received his last, short-term plum assignment before retirement where he would reap the rewards of the many favors he'd done for "friends" in the entrepreneurial world he'd helped keep in order. Then India and Pakistan restarted their nuclear arms race and Washington prolonged his tenure, which gave his second wife, Chrystie, who, at best tolerated India, time and an excuse to begin shtupping the compound doctor. Soon, Charlie wished he'd taken the offer of a sweet Caribbean island posting.

We met years before when I was doing my residency at Lenox Hill Hospital on the Upper East Side. Charlie and his first wife, Jane, rushed in to the ER with his oldest son, Chuckie, who'd OD'd on cocaine, Seconal, and alcohol. They'd found him nearly comatose on the bathroom floor of his room at the Stanhope Hotel, where the family was staying while vacationing in New York. Chuckie's heart was minutes from arrest; minutes from going down and never coming back. They carried Chuckie into a waiting limo and made it to the ER in less than three minutes. Iris Jones, the head triage nurse, no slouch in the intimidation department, usually guarded the entrance from waiting room to examining room. Charlie was inside in seconds. Iris ran to find me, "There's a guy out there who's as scary as anyone who ever came here with a gun." His presence, a never quite handsome baked-straw complexion of a face that had seen plenty of death and a voice not loud, but demanding, said this is a man with whom one did not fuck around. "My son is choking on his vomit. He needs attention. Now!" Chuckie was aspirating so we sucked out his oral cavity, got his heart going, and he came out of it without any loss of mental or physical power, if not any greater awareness of his instability.

"I'll never forget this," Charlie assured, almost as a warning. And he didn't. I received holiday cards and notes of new postings. He called when he visited New York, and sometimes he booked a tennis court at the bubble on Eighth Avenue and we'd play a few sets. We went to dinner a couple of times, but despite Charlie's easygoing, good-guy social veneer, gusto of a laugh, and ambassadorial congeniality, our minuscule areas of mutual interest and differing political views, after the weather-family nontalk, left us with a wide gap of nothing to say. Still, Charlie kept tabs on me. He couldn't help himself; he was a spook wearing an ambassador's suit. I didn't consider him a true friend, so I'd decided to wait until I arrived in Delhi, and then see if I wanted to contact him. I already had my visa, booked a room at a small hotel, and gotten all of my shots and other requirements when he called me.

"Downs! Bedrosian. You're coming to India you ungrateful Commie bastard." I didn't mention that I was no more of a Commie or a bastard than he was. "You didn't contact me? I'm so deeply hurt." His tone dripped of mockery.

"Charlie, how'd you know?"

"C'mon. Got you flagged. Your visa came through my office."

Knowing Charlie, this did not surprise me; it made sense the second he said it. "It's not a vacation. I'm coming to . . . well . . . I don't know why I'm coming. But I'll be there a few months."

"This is your lucky day. I need you to work for me. We need a new doctor at the embassy."

I didn't believe in luck anymore, and if I did, luck like working for the U.S. government I could do without. "I don't really want a job right now."

"This'll be a cakewalk for you. And the doctor I got now is a shit and I'm going to can his ass."

"I'm not a specialist in exotic medicine."

"You'll read a few books and wing it." He then coughed and cursed under his breath, before saying loudly and dryly, "Chrystie is getting a little too chummy with the pisspot." I'd never met Chrystie. "Smartass will be doing time in AIDS, Angola by next week."

I didn't answer. I didn't understand how he could be so matter-of-fact about AIDS, his wife's possible duplicity, or his own. He screwed around on Jane for years before he traded her in for Chrystie.

"You there? Downs, I said" he paused, "I need you. And you'll need my help. This town is a computer chip wrapped inside a sari stuffed with a Sanskrit surprise." That sounded like Charlie giving me one of his oft-used, cocktail party lines. "These people believe in reincarnation but this place is hell on people who've never been here before. It'll eat you alive without my help."

"I'm a big boy. And I told you, I don't need a job for now."

"But you do. Try it for awhile. If you don't like it, then quit."

I had no will to fight him. "OK." Right, I told myself, I could quit.

"Good. You coming alone?" He already knew the answer to that question.

"Yes." I volunteered no more information.

"OK. I was so sorry . . . did you get my . . ."

"Thanks, yes." I tried my best to be welcoming, but also to stop the conversation there.

"Just so you know, I understand."

He didn't understand. Not for one millisecond, but what good would telling him that do?

In another two weeks, Charlie, as he promised, had no trouble pulling strings to get me the job and moving the other doctor to Angola. My new tickets and information books in hand, I was packed and gone.

I arrived at one a.m. in the midst of the August heat and humidity at the tail end of the monsoon season, at the former RAF base that is now Indira Gandhi International Airport. The jet finally approached this home to millions—a city bathed not in the brightness of an electric nighttime but dotted, it seemed, with tiny comets of light that, as we came closer, I realized were bonfires sparkling across the city.

Charlie had changed my visa category so his men met me and shuttled me through the diplomatic line. Outside, the dark petals of pollution hit me within seconds; I wiped my forehead with my hand. Black soot already dusted my face. All around me, natives and newcomers coughed. Sucking in the Delhi air is akin to choking on hits of a giant carbon monoxide-filled hookah. Before I climbed into the waiting car, two beggars moved within one foot of me. Another two greeted me with spit gobs that landed close to my shoes. Others grabbed for my bags to put them in the trunk of the car offering, "We help, help." The unblinking officers shooed them all away. There were colleagues, and even friends, who'd bet the degeneration would have me back in the USA in one day. How wrong. The dirt and disorder suited me just fine.

I sat stone-faced and terrified as we drove through teeming streets of obvious poverty toward my new home reserved for the Foreign Service doctors in the wealthy area of Hauz Khas. We turned off the main road and passed through two arm-guarded gates to get to the complex of streets that housed many embassy personnel. I thought about the advice of Matt Silverman, a good friend since childhood. He was loyal as hell, but if we met now, most probably we'd pass each other without looking past our outward appearances. By his own admission he'd become a hard-edged, slippery, and successful dealmaker who, after a factory visit to India, came back with two exaggerated, imperialistic insights. "First, The Discount Theory goes double for Americans in India and is to be used literally. If they offer you something for ten bucks don't pay more than five. Max."

Matt usually based his Discount Theory on the amount of bullshit spewed in the world, not only the amount of money

11

involved. He gave everyone a discount on the degree of truth in their story. From 10 percent to 99.5 percent. It was a damn good theory to use for those of us without built-in BS detectors.

"And," he held his breath before issuing his second cynical proclamation, "don't go all shocked flaccid liberal on me, but it's no different from here, only more so. Everyone takes *schvartz-gelt*. The whole system is based on bribery. And best of all, it's expected for you to have 'people.'" He gave me his sendoff advice, "So, get yourself lots of people, I would. You'll love it. Life is cheap and servants cheaper. It's like California, where even the people have people."

"Matt," I protested, "I don't want or need help to fix my breakfast and iron my T-shirts."

"Sure, you don't. You'll see."

I saw. I didn't even have to hire my own people. We drove inside seven-foot-high brown stucco walls and up the driveway that led to the marble and mortar structure that was my new home. Two Indian men greeted me, Vishnu and Chandon. I believed I'd politely ask them to leave in a matter of days.

They unloaded my bags and led me to my new home—a three-bedroom, one-level house that was atypically furnished in an odd mix of Indian and American styles. Lavish Indian rugs covered the marble floors. Two antique couches sat L-shaped in a sunken living room with a handmade coffee table in front of them. Along the large wall stood hand-carved bookshelves with a large TV in the center surrounded by English-language books, both paper and hardbound. On the other cement walls hung Indian miniatures and American landscapes. Chandon told me there were three bedrooms because the embassy staffers often came with their families. I asked him to show me to the master bedroom, which he did. It had a double bed with marble bed stand, two wooden dressers, big closets, and blank walls with a near-empty built-in bookcase. Two large windows were closed with dark green silk curtains drawn. The house was immaculate.

Chandon turned on the ceiling fan and a long-tailed gecko scrambled across the ceiling, looked down, stopped, and took residence directly above the bed. Waving my hands in the air, I tried to urge him away. Amused, yet aware I better get used to them, Chandon and Vishnu good humoredly tried to move him to the adjacent bathroom—to no avail. I motioned to forget it and they started to unpack for me. I stopped them. I had my own sense of order and chaos and wasn't sure I was even ready to unpack.

In a combination of sign language and high-pitched and syllabically upside-down (to an American), musically ca- denced broken English (which far exceeded my Hindi, which was nonexistent), they bid me, "Sleep night. We have tea for you, when you no sleep," which I did for fourteen hours—the longest I'd slept in months. Late that afternoon, I showered and dressed and had some toast and tea before heading to my office. I automatically started to get into the front seat of the Ambassador, a large round-topped, off-white nineteen fifties- like Pontiac. Chandon shook his head and opened the door to the back seat. Inside, I gripped the strap above the rear window. I soon found out working seat belts were a rarity in most Delhi cars. Chandon sped the car through unfamiliar daytime Delhi street life. I wanted to scream "Stop!" as he whipped past a bright blue, hand-painted bus smudged with dirt with the request to "Please Horn" painted on the rear that meant honk loud and often, put pedal to the metal, and pass at your own risk. In that one ride I saw more beggars in one block than any tough-on-crime American politico could ar- rest in a lifetime, and a deathly decapitation in the midst of

13

the car-scooter-rickshaw-bus-crammed streets that everyone ignored. I finally breathed freely when we reached my office at the American Embassy complex in Chanakyapuri, the area in Delhi that housed most of the embassies.

The nurse who I'd be working with had already left for the day. I was checking out the office equipment when Charlie, wearing a red-and white-checked shirt, open collar, no tie, tan slacks—the picture of a relaxed man—sauntered in and clapped my shoulder. Right behind him sashayed Chrystie and an Indian woman in her mid-to-late twenties dressed in an olive-green sari and sandals, who strode with a confident and proud posture that gave her an immediately larger presence than her five-foot three-inch height.

Chrystie dressed as if she were living in Georgetown rather than India. Her posture and walk, almost a prance, in shorts revealing her legs, flouncing bleach-blond hair, a tight tank-top emphasizing her silicone-enhanced breasts, an immediate and conscious dismissive stare that taunted "Ha, you can't have me," disrespected every basic Indian custom.

She reached to shake my hand. I felt her eyes taking my measure. Not sexually. Politically. This was no Jane he'd married. I shook her hand firmly while uttering a noncommittal, "Nice to meet you," and then I felt the instinct to hug Charlie, which, when I felt him pull back, seemed to surprise the hell out of him.

Charlie apologized because my nurse hadn't waited for me. "Your men speak limited English and they don't know the best stores or restaurants. Holika," he said and pointed to the Indian woman, who looked resolutely into my eyes, "will help you find what you need outside of what they got here. Help you get acclimated to the Indian way of doing life."

Holika smiled a smile that beguiled with an inscrutability that could hide four thousand years of collective wisdom or a studied silence signifying not very much at all. I couldn't tell which. "And Doctor, you can tell me the secrets of New York. I have only visited. Someday I will live there." Her oval brown eyes, peering out from her face of copper complexion, fixed on me, ignoring Charlie and Chrystie. I nodded, not sure how to respond. She bobbed her head from side-to-side and that set in motion the swaying of her torrent of braided, waist-length black hair. "I must go to meet my uncle." She spoke with an Etonesque Anglo-Indian accent that told everyone, even a newcomer like me, of her upper-class status. "I look forward to helping you. Please do call."

"I will," I lied. I had no desire to call or ask anyone for any more help.

She and Charlie shook hands, while Chrystie made a motion in the air with her hands that they should call each other.

After she was beyond hearing distance Charlie leaned toward me, "Her uncle is Vijay Pillai."

"Not a clue."

"Well, here's one: he's one of the richest, most powerful men in India. In some ways more powerful than the government. He made his money years ago in exporting textiles, pottery, and terra cotta items, and he wisely founded Indya Petrochemicals. As a favor to Vijay I let Holika act as a 'liaison' between her people and us. Call her if you want. If you don't want to . . ." He shrugged and tilted his head to the left. "But he's a great connection for you."

Connection for what? I wanted to be disconnected. That's why I was in India.

Charlie kept talking. "But the only way she's going to New York anytime soon is on her honeymoon. Her marriage is being arranged to Smacka Abhitraj."

Chrystie, repressing a laugh, interrupted, "It's pronounced Samack, or better yet, if you can say it with a slight sh, like

Shamack, but it's spelled S-a-m-a-k-a. You'd think our big diplomat would know that."

"She takes a few Hindi lessons," Charlie half-sneered, before finishing with me. "Well, you know who he is, right?"

I nodded. I'd read all about him in *Time* magazine. He was a thirty-three-year-old information technology billionaire based in Bangalore, the Indian Silicon Valley.

"Vijay has no kids of his own and Holika's brother and sister are still not married, so she's on her way to a baby-making career, just like Uncle Vijay wants."

I had no interest in her baby-making future.

Charlie detailed my duties. After another day or two of rest, I would start my normal work schedule, 9 a.m. to 5 p.m., four days a week, and 9 to 12 on Friday. An orderly brought me a cell phone so the embassy could always reach me in an emergency. My superior was Paul Schlipssi, "the admin" who ran the administration office on weekdays, but I didn't really have to answer to anyone. Two military doctors saw to the military personnel and would take over for me on weekends. If there was a serious emergency, they'd call me. One of them was always on duty at the compound.

Chrystie said she would bring their young daughter, Heather, in for a checkup because she suffered from asthma. As they were preparing to leave, Charlie asked me what should have been an innocuous question:

"Is there anything else I can do?"

"I'd like to find out if Levi Furstenblum still lives here."

Charlie looked flummoxed. Chrystie, who had moved closer to the door, straightened her posture and leaned her head slightly forward. "He's a Holocaust survivor who wrote one creepy book in the 1950s, then disappeared." Chrystie smiled and held her breath for a fraction of a second. I didn't need to interject that Furstenblum also wrote a second, less renowned book in the 1970s. "I read it in college but have never forgotten it," she shivered as she spoke.

"See why I married her?" In a sense, this was true. Chrystie's breeding was implicit with the cultural and social panache that Jane, and for that matter Charlie, lacked and never cared about acquiring for herself. As Charlie made it to the top echelons of the diplomatic corps, Chrystie was the model, if utilitarian, choice for Charlie, who bluntly chided Chrystie as his "Wallet wife, cause without my wallet, I have no wife."

"I heard he lives in New Delhi," I said. I'd been taken with Furstenblum's books for years. Even *before*, I often read his work at home, alone in my room, after one more inexplicable day of patients and families enduring pain and illness that seemed beyond reason and left me feeling so inadequate. Furstenblum was perhaps the only person in Delhi, no, in the entire world, I now wanted to meet. I wanted to know how he survived the death of his first wife and only child in Auschwitz. How he made sense of this world and continued to go on.

"Call my secretary," Charlie said, "and if he's here, she'll find him. Sure there isn't anyone else I could introduce you to?" He meant women. He did not glance at Chrystie. She inhaled, sucked in her cheeks and then she exhaled deeply, but she said nothing.

I wanted to stay as far away from their war as I could. "No. No one."

Charlie walked past Chrystie on his way out and patted the butt of her white shorts.

17

6

18

When Adolf Hitler won the Nobel Peace Prize, fifty years ago in 1946, my mother, father, sisters, and I listened with rapture to the ceremonies on the radio and then watched them on the weekend newsreels like everyone else who lived in Munich. My father, who was a Munich policeman, never seemed happier as we celebrated this bold man of peace, The Fuhrer who saved Europe from world war and solved the problem of the Jews.

—Levi Furstenblum,
from his novella, CHAMBERS OF COMMERCE, written in 1951

7

AFTER ONE WEEK I felt at home in Delhi with its stench, poverty, pitiless look in the eyes of the privileged, and hunger in the belly of the outlawed, but very much alive, Untouchable class, and most everyone's necessary blindness to unimaginable chaos and energy. A city on the verge of complete and total collapse of the social order suited my unstable inner self. A city where mansions are surrounded by fifteen-foot-high stone and cement walls with tents, dirt patches with glass shards hidden like mortars, barbed wire, and gun-toting guards, and the tents housing uncountable numbers of ruptured bodies hug the walls on the lawns of those mansions. Where Disneyesque elephants, pick-pocketing monkeys, skeletal cows, casually drop their feces, greet you and parade freely down the street. Where one-armed children pound the windows of taxies, limousines, and even the ricketiest of three-wheeled motorized rickshaws begging for a single cent. Where there's as much dust and pollution per square inch as anywhere else on earth. Where the air is filled with an unstoppable hum of life to a symphony of honking horns, rousing music, and indecipherable voices. Where sumptuous dinners can be infested with parasites for which no scientist has ever found a name. Where a raucous dream of salvation presages no fear of the unknown future. Where gorgeous coal-eyed, sari-garbed woman blithely strut barefoot through cyber cafes. Where disease floats in the air like kites without strings over the Ganges, and where the mosquito bite kills as easily as the thrust knife. And where the winter sunrise feels like inner peace must come and the summer midday heat assures release in death and eventual nothingness. Where thousands have come to conquer and all have left, in the end, defeated by a culture as old and tired and young and vibrant as any on this planet. Here, I felt at home. In India, my sorrows were met with a nod and not an ounce of false pity from anyone, because I had let my son die.

8

I WENT TO Delhi to be alone. Not to find my-
self, but to lose myself. To get away from bad history. To be
where no one recognized my face. My name. To forget about
Sarah. To bury all memories of Castor.

In those first weeks, in a useless attempt to keep my inner
self in check, I kept to a low-level basic regimen. I worked at
the embassy. In my free time I walked through the thriving markets beside shrines and temples, in the new areas of Delhi built
within the last fifty years, and the claustrophobic, grimly sunless
cupola-like streets of ages-old Delhi that reeked of the burning
dung of despair. I carried a can of mace in fear of the roaming,
wild, and often rabid dogs. I kept a wary eye on the too-human
looking monkeys, who stealthily lurked on the roofs of Delhi's
grimmest structures and who were rumored to toss objects on
the innocents below. I avoided walking under the teetering,
illegal power lines with mangled wires that looked like hundreds of venomous, tongue-flicking snakes slithering up a tree
after a flood. I usually got ripped off because, despite Matt's
advice, I didn't want to know how to bargain yet. I slept badly

and ate sparsely. I read. Books, no newspapers or magazines. I never opened my laptop to check email. I had cable TV, which I did not watch. In the darkness of my insomnia I tried to find my way to sleep with flights of fantasy to Sarah, old girlfriends, shamefully to Chrystie—and to Holika and making her come and come again.

It took some time for my body to adjust to the time change, the food (the embassy staff brought water to the complex), the thousands of contradictions of Indian life where people sit lotus style on chairs, hands flouncing at cyber cafes, cursing because the connection takes an extra nanosecond while calmly accepting that ordering one cup of tea can take hours. I rarely ate outside the compound or my home. I took B$_{12}$ and acidophilus pills to avoid Delhi Belly because I am no fan of curd or yogurt. I spoke more to Vishnu and Chandon, who resonated with kindness, than to anyone else.

Vishnu, with the usual moustache, thin and small-boned, no bigger than five-five, spoke slightly better English than the younger Chandon, who came from the north of India near Nepal. Chandon, only twenty-three, stockier, more Mongol-looking, bounced with youthful energy, forever trying to teach me Hindi: each day teaching me a very basic word: sugar: *cheeni*; tea: *chai*; good: *accha*; thank you: *dhanyavaad*; please: *kripa*.

At the compound, most treated me with benign indifference, which was fine with me. My nurse was a Marine. Nice woman with the unfortunate name of Donna Dickman. We had very little in common, chatting mainly about home and life in India. She didn't like Chrystie at all. It was during a consciously loud discussion between one of the military doctors and her that I overheard the details of the attaché's story about Chrystie moaning "turn me on" to the previous doctor. I wasn't much into that gossip, and they were more careful after I loudly closed the door to my office.

The Indians, all of whom spoke at least rudimentary English, were deferential, but they saw their own doctor. My patients were compound Americans, tourists who called and had clout, and influential Indians.

After two weeks, I began to see the city with my eyes more open. Amidst fragrances of perfume, incense, and the stench of open sewers, the splendid colors of the fabrics and city flora of orange and green and yellow, and sounds of ever-present honking horns and clattering Hindi tongues, the young children stood out. Everywhere, I felt their energy. From the beggars to the little boys and girls of the private schools and the mothers, fathers, and grandparents with their sons and daughters. Each day at the same intersection, one beggar girl, six or seven years old, thrust her painted red and pink face against the car window. With her few words of English, "Ha-lo, money, please mister, food, yes," her sharp features, beneath her scruffy hair and tattered boy's clothes, she possessed a sense of dignity, a worldliness greater than most adults and so-called high-class people. I wanted to scoop her up in my arms, kidnap her into my car, reclaim her innocence, and give her the love I could no longer give to Castor. It was a silly and damn superior feeling on my part. I couldn't help myself. Each morning, as she scampered up to the car, and against the advice of almost everyone, I gave her money, maybe the equivalent of a quarter. I began to wait, hope for her gaze of expectation as my car approached—and I recognized, ever so dimly, her hope in that gaze—and my heart broke again. She bowed her head not so much in appreciation, but demurely. Demure is right because she had a consciousness of her physicality no child should have, a knowledge that I think scared her. I gave my alms, and she sped to another guilt-ridden "customer."

One morning, after weeks of this budding new ritual, the intersection we usually took was blocked for repairs, which would take months to finish, and we took a new route to work. A week after we started taking the detour, one lunchtime, Chandon drove me as close as possible to the intersection. The girl was nowhere in sight. Chandon asked the vendors and other beggars if they knew her. Knew where she might be. Everyone shrugged. Even if they knew, they weren't telling. She was gone. Who knows why or where? These children disappear and no one ever gives a damn. Other children replaced her at other streets, and I wanted to ignore them but I couldn't—they all reminded me of Castor.

My mother, Zohar, doted on Castor as she had never doted on me. He was the answer to her prayers for an obedient son. Yes, I was Mr. Big Shot Doctor. Big deal. I'd failed her as a son. Never acknowledged her strength. Never been good enough. And I had married "out." Not that she or my father ever said a word. It came through in the flickering glance at Yom Kippur, when so unreligiously, instead of fasting and repenting, we gorged ourselves and then settled in the den to watch television. Yet, Sarah was not one of "us." When Sarah became pregnant, we agreed the child would be raised Jewish, whatever that meant. Then came Castor, who would keep the family spirit alive. Her spirit alive. For when he smiled, and my mother smiled back, it was my mother's smile. Not mine, not Sarah's, my father's, or Sarah's mother or father. Sad-lipped and burdened by an unknown ghost, he was hers as much as he was Sarah's and mine. For that, she loved me as she never loved me before.

She had wanted me to become a lawyer to retaliate against an unfair world. To get back what my father had lost. My father, a reticent tinkerer of a man, spent hours in his little lamp

store, Lighten Up, on Third Avenue at 92nd Street, by the
YWHA. For years, he played with his "inventions," which my
mother routinely patented. Everyone except my mother thought
he was a crackpot who preferred tinkering about, alone in his
back room, to dealing with the customers. One evening, when
I was still a young child, and my mother told and retold this
story, he came home grinning, an infrequent occurrence, holding a contraption between his hands, "This gizmo acts as an
electronic converting device and can save money and energy
on lamps, TVs, you name it." He called it The Gypswitch. My
mother, as usual, patented the idea. Someone in the patent office got wind of the invention, presumably a spy on the pay-
roll of the electronics giant General Dynastic, as we always
called it in our house. When I was a kid my father used to tell
me this joke: Why'd the moron salute the refrigerator? Because
it was a *General* Dynastic.

25

Well, the moron wasn't so stupid. Because when the rep-
resentatives from General Dynastic contacted my father about
his "little invention, which may be of no use at all," they bar-
gained hard, steamrolling my mother and a cousin we used as
a lawyer into selling the patent for $75, 000. It was either sell
or they make other arrangements. Which meant steal it and let
my parents sue them. Seventy-five thousand was a pretty hefty
sum back then. Hefty enough that we moved from Queens to a
nice apartment building on the Upper East Side of Manhattan.
But The Gypswitch was no "little invention." It was soon found
in electric appliances around the world. "It made the *gonifs*
richer," my mother, with breathless vitriol railed, "and no one
stops the bastards from stealing millions of dollars from us
while your father, he sits back there stooped over more inventions, the lawyers tell me 'Don't worry,' and they ask me for
more money, when I thought this case was contingency and the

fat *bulvon* corrupt judge sits there half asleep and you, you, I need your help in this lawsuit so I want you to become a lawyer and get me justice."

She wanted me to undo the bargain. Get the money my father deserved. She'd point her polished red fingernail at me as if it were my fault. "This is America. How could they do that?" And I would say, "That *is* America, it was always America. Your America is a lie." I thought of my college history professor using his faux sonorous TV voice, who would say, "This was the *radical sixties*, we were at war at home and in the streets and in a far-off country and in our own homes." Well, actually it was years later and my mother, and even a Korean War vet like my dad had been against the Vietnam War from the mid-sixties. That didn't matter. My father and I took turns as her personal flypaper where whatever we said turned out to be an insult that she got stuck on for hours. She never appreciated my "sarcastic tone" and I'd get a barrelful of guilt-mongering, "Help me do something. I didn't kill myself in that store so you could go to college and live a nice life for this!" What "this" was remained unspecified, but I knew, she wanted me to be the savior son. I, despite all they had done for me, could not carry that cross.

Instead, I went to medical school and she was proud but still she withheld. I married a soon-to-be successful and independent-minded artist in Sarah and she was proud, but still she withheld. Then came Castor, whom she loved as she never loved anyone else.

She relished coming to our Chelsea apartment from her Upper East Side home so she could sit with her "baby," even changing his diapers. As he grew, Sarah and I relied more and more on my mom's help. She picked him up from day care, taught him nursery rhymes and how to read, took him to Central Park, the zoo, movies. And it was she, not Sarah or I, who first noticed his precocity. She who insisted, not, she claimed, out of grandmotherly ego, that our boy was a genius, not in the overused hyperbole of the adjective-challenged media, but rather a boy of uncommon abilities.

At first, I was afraid to believe it. Then I had to. When he was four, he, Matt Silverman, and I were watching the Yankee game on TV. Castor had already grasped the fundamentals of baseball, which are primarily mathematical. Matt and I were sitting on the sofa yapping about the batting average that Tony Gwynn, the future Hall of Famer, would need to maintain a lifetime batting average of .330 if he played another five years and continued to decline at the same rate. From the floor, where Castor sat keeping a scorecard of the game, a soft voice wafted up, ".319. Dad, he needs to hit .319." I did a "Yeah, sure, kid" double take. "Let me see how you did that." I reached for the paper he used. He tilted his head up, almost apologetically; he couldn't show me because he'd done it in his head. I couldn't figure it out without a paper and pen. Not even without a calculator. But .319 it was.

So, my mother turned out—so smugly—to be right. And he became, was still, always as much her baby, as he was ours.

My mother, because we were already in debt—I was still doing my residency and Sarah was working at Pearl Paint for minimum wage—paid to send him to Dalton, a private school on the Upper East Side. Sarah and I favored a public school, but the system was unprepared for him. They'd coddle him at Dalton; he was a prize. But Sarah carried a deeper, personal animosity to private school. She suffered through three years in a Chicago boarding school. Still, Dalton seemed, and we looked at other schools, the best for him, and it was blocks from my mother's apartment. The school treated him well, gave him a good education, let him skip only two grades, and did not showcase him as a toy.

When he was to enter ninth grade, to please us, he switched to Stuyvesant High School, a special public school that one has to apply to. I had attended the old Stuyvesant. The up-to-date building, a ten-story complex built in 1992 in Battery Park City with ultramodern facilities, was closer to our apartment and closer to the Hebrew school he had started attending. Stuyvesant was filled with multiethnic, regular kids who didn't spend summers on "The Cape" or The Hamptons or in European tennis camps. The teachers were the best in the city. The computers, science, and math labs equaled those of Dalton. Stuyvesant was more in keeping with our notion of America, where everyone should get the same fair shake. If you got accepted there, and the competition was much more difficult than when I attended, it was based on your abilities, not who you knew or what kind of donation your family could make.

We worried about taking Castor away from his Dalton friends, but in skipping grades, he had made new friends. His closest friend, Drew, lived down the block from us in Chelsea, was Castor's age, attended Hebrew school, and watched and played sports with him.

Castor took the admission test, passed with no problems, and then visited Stuyvesant three times. Then we sat down for a family powwow. Without my mother.

Castor, clear-eyed with his complex mix of adult genius and emotional twelve-year-old insecurities, spoke with his usual soft clarity. "I want to switch, but Dad, I know that Mommoms," his pet name for my mother, "wants me to stay in Dalton. And you don't seem to care if I go to Hebrew school."

I was all set to interrupt in my Father Knows Best style, but Sarah stopped me with a flinty glance. She anticipated what he was going to say: no matter what my mother thought, he was Sarah's son.

Castor had agreed to go to the Chelsea Reformed Hebrew School for the single purpose of getting Bar Mitzvahed. We had thought long and hard about his religious education. I despised Hebrew school when I was a child, and the time it took from my hours of freedom. I was no fan of my teachers either, but in the end, years later, I was glad I'd gone. Sarah, who had agreed years before, was as much against organized religion as she was against private school. But my mother wanted this desperately.

Castor said, "So, how about I try Stuyvesant? I guess I can always switch back."

He was right about that, or if not, another private school would take him.

29

"I'll stay in Hebrew school for Mommoms' sake. But, if I feel like it, I can quit right after the Bar Mitzvah."

He reached the decision with such maturity that, again, he scared me. I, even then, was never so, so Solomonic.

The beautiful task of confirming my mother's worst fears fell on me. I couldn't ask Castor to do it, though I thought about it. Sarah nobly wanted no part of this guilt-giving session. I popped a Valium before telling her. I was right to be ready: her accusatory tones came blasting forth. For a woman barely five feet tall, when she let loose I had visions of rattling chandeliers in apartments three floors away. "You're taking my baby's care away!" She so mellifluously yelled when I told her what we were thinking. Her eyes blinked and lips quivered as she gave me her soup-mix look—a blend of contempt, anger, and concern.

"Maybe I shouldn't have closed the store. Maybe I'll move to Florida, my friends are all moving there or are dead. And you and Sarah and my baby don't need me anymore."

"Ma," I girded myself, "we need you as much as ever. Castor needs you as much as ever. He loves you so much." She didn't respond but I read her mind: Then why is he doing this to me? Leaving me? "Ma, do you want to sell your place and move downtown?" Now retired and with the store closed, she had much too much time to fill contemplating betrayals and failed lawsuits.

"No, my friends are all up here and I have my routine."

I closed my eyes hoping to hide my exasperation but I was thinking, You just said your friends were dead or in Florida.

"You'll still see him all the time. And us too. We'll come every Sunday. You can come any time and we have the extra room for you to stay over. We call you every day."

I fought a losing battle, but to her I had won the war, we had taken control of our son's schooling. He was no longer a baby, but a boy on the way to manhood.

I left that day feeling washed out and thinking, Somehow I should have handled the whole situation better. I still think I should have.

After surviving, if not flourishing, without my father for over a decade, the lawsuit finally and permanently lost, hope for redemption crushed in a maze of papers and words she did not understand; her baby growing up and now miles away, one late Friday afternoon, she took Castor to the movies and then to the coffee shop on East 86th Street and Lexington, where the waiters knew my mom and fixed Castor an extra-sweet vanilla egg cream to go with his burger and fries, then she kissed him goodbye, put him in a taxi, and pushed some money into his hand. And she slowly walked back to her apartment, stopping to buy a pack of cigarettes and a bottle of Diet Pepsi, then bidding her friendly "goodnight" to the doorman, checking the mail, taking the elevator upstairs, mechanically turning on the

TV to "Law and Order" reruns, never bothering to undress or remove her makeup, so exhausted she was, she lay down on her bed and died in her sleep.

Consumed with guilt and sadness, I spent many weeks hugging my son to my chest as he and I cried and cried as we'd never cried before.

9

ONE DAY, AS I prepared to leave at around five thirty, I was told Charlie wanted to see me in the library. I crossed the football field-sized lawn to the semiprivate offices of the official staff.

A young officer left me alone in the room with the door open. I started checking out the book collection when I heard a presence hovering at the doorway. I turned and saw Holika leaning with a Lauren Bacall-like aloofness against the doorframe, smoking a filtered cigarette.

"You staring at me for a reason?" I asked.

"So friendly you are today. But yes, Charlie said you were here and asked me to say hello and I became entranced by your look of the Diasporic Jew."

"What's that mean?"

"Lost and wandering far away from home and searching for answers in books."

"Lost, but not looking for answers."

She bobbed her head skeptically and stepped into the room, dressed not in the traditional sari but in tight, claret-colored silk pants and a blue velvet top with short sleeves. She stopped about two feet away from me. "So you say."

"And you, you're a disbeliever then?" I tweaked her.

"In the words of men, belief is the opium of manmasters."

"This from the sayings of Mahatmamiss Holika-ji?"

"That's Holika to you," she tilted her head upward and sensually inhaled and exhaled the smoke from her cigarette.

"OK, Holika to me, how do you know I'm a Jew?"

"Charlie and Chrystie."

I felt an inner sigh of relief. "What else did the fun couple of New Delhi tell you?"

"Charlie thinks you are a great doctor. I feel he does not think you like him very much and I think that bothers him. And you have the worst tennis form and the fastest feet and hands."

"All that nonsense and nothing else?"

She paused, "Yes, that you are very sad and lonely."

"Don't believe everything you hear."

"How about what I see?"

"The hand is quicker than the eye and I have quick hands."

She forcefully put out her cigarette in a ceramic ashtray. Her glance and broad smile seemed like a dare to play on. "And what did you ask about me?"

"Who says I asked?"

"Ask, told . . . always something is said." She said with a sense of certainty and she was right.

"That you're Vijay Pillai's niece and you're engaged to marry Samaka Abhitraj."

"In India, it is best not to believe everything that you hear."

"So, you are not engaged?"

"Not to him. Not to anyone."

"Bang, bang goes the hammer. One nail in the knee." I flexed my knee as if it hurt.

33

"Is that why you did not call me? Afraid?"

"No and yes, I didn't know if it was sincere or your duty on the welcoming committee."

"It was sincere then. Now . . ." She bobbed her head in the motion of a buoy floating on the soft waves of an ocean, a look I was becoming familiar with from many other Indians, the meaning of which I never learned to decipher.

"And now?"

"Now is forever in the past." She flashed an enigmatic closed-lipped smile. "Think of the future."

"Then we'll play again?"

"That is your choice." I didn't have a clever answer and she seemed impatient. "Where are those quick feet now?"

"Wounded. And I've been out of this game for some time. Not sure I want back in."

"You must. And there are many ways to recovery. I must go. My driver is waiting. Ta-ta for now."

She waved and left the room. I went back to being a Diasporic Jew looking at books until Charlie showed up about ten minutes later. He called out from the hallway, "Hey buddy, be there in a second."

He stood in profile talking to Hal Burden, former Secretary of Defense and now CEO of Environ Enterprises, one of the largest energy conglomerates in the world. On television Burden appeared like some cartoon caricature: blubbery and vastly overweight with a belly that plunged southward toward his tiny feet covered by polished cowboy boots. A history of heart problems made his breathing wispy and belabored. This muffinish body was topped off by a few curlicues of blond hair on his otherwise balding head, and thin, sneering red lips that saturated the TV screen against his ultra-pale skin. In person, even without hearing the exact words of his confident sinister whisper of a voice, his presence loomed large and fierce and didn't seem comic at all.

They shook hands and then Burden took off. I watched Charlie's gait ease from a stiff march into a stroll and, as he entered the library, his face muscles loosened as he shifted from the stern emissary of American power to the genial Uncle Charlie, ambassador of good will.

"I hope you don't mind that I didn't introduce you." He assumed correctly that I would recognize Burden. "His plane is waiting."

"No problem."

"You see Holika?"

"For a few minutes." I nodded.

"Good. Give her a call. Got this for you." He stuck a piece of paper with Levi Furstenblum's number and address in my shirt pocket. "He lives in Lajpat Nagar."

Perfect. The government built the neighborhood of Lajpat Nagar specifically for Hindus who fled from Pakistan after the Partition of India in 1947. Furstenblum would live among outcastes in their own land.

"Thanks." Although I so much wanted to see him—I'd been rereading his works at night when I couldn't sleep—I doubted I had the chutzpah to call him or just drop in. Still, I was glad to have it.

As if reading my hesitancy, Charlie then said, "He also goes to the Jewish temple on Humayun Road near the Taj Hotel."

No way, I thought, that Furstenblum, this man of lost faith would still go to temple. That I had to see.

"So, how is everything going?" A young soldier brought in a whiskey for Charlie. I didn't want anything.

"As well as can be expected."

"Nobody bothering you?"

Holika had bothered me, but not in the way he meant or I wanted to explore. "No, and for that I thank you."

"I didn't get where I am by not knowing when to shut the fuck up." Charlie pointed to the French-style wooden terrace doors. We stepped outside. "This goes no further."

"Scout's honor." I held up my hand, anticipating some inner secret of impending Indian–Pakistani upheaval for which I needed to be ready.

"What do you know about that get-it-up pill? And I mean the real one." He couldn't even say the word.

"Viagra, not Erecto." Erecto was the Indian knockoff version. Often, the Indian pharmaceutical companies didn't pay any attention to American patents and knocked off expensive drugs. Mostly it was OK but not always. "It works. I believe it's safe."

"Can you, um, get me some . . . surreptitiously?"

"Without a trace."

"You know, the Indians would call it karma." He stopped me before I interrupted him and explained that a man of his age should expect such things. "Yeah yeah, Neil. I've been no saint. I can't afford another divorce, and hell, she's a great lay and needs to be fucked. Often. And I want it to be by me. I know you've had your troubles but finding out your wife is . . . fuck it . . . I know the 'How many doctors does it take to screw a light bulb in an ambassador's wife?' jokes are out there."

"I haven't heard any," I lied. Even in my relative obscurity and desire not to, I'd heard them.

Charlie finished his drink in one long gulp. It was the prevailing belief that Chrystie was a brat at best, and had married him for his position and money, which made her something more or less than a brat. I never believed it was that simple. I felt lousy for Charlie.

Here he was verging on retirement and a long-planned life of serving on corporation boards, collecting fat checks, and playing golf. He'd seen his teeth go yellow, his hair turn gray and thin, his belly get larger and doughy, and now, his dick go limp. Nobody, especially his kids, gave a damn that he climbed out of the scummy streets of Buffalo, that he'd made it to the top of his profession. Nobody but Jane, his first wife who he'd dumped for a second-rate looker who could pull off the good manners and breeding schtick, and who had expectations, which included living in New York or DC, not India. I believed Charlie had seen too much to fool his inner self.

"You'll be in touch?"

"Soon," I reassured him.

We shook hands. Charlie left the library.

10

38

THE NEXT DAY I called the temple and spoke to the aged Rabbi Judah, who, in broken English said, "Yes, sometimes, please, Levi attends services."

Although I told him that I was not religious, had never been religious, and that all I wanted was to meet Furstenblum, the rabbi, in his high-pitched Indian-English accent and enthusiastic voice coyly pleaded with me to come on the following Friday night. Their congregation was so tiny that he needed every man just to get the required ten men for a minyan. I said I would come soon, but maybe not that Friday.

I found the courage a few Fridays later. I arrived a little early and mistakenly opened the blue gate to the Jewish Cemetery adjacent to the temple. I froze. The smell of curry and incense and wood burning over open pits in the back of the cemetery hit me from a small tent-village of Indian squatters with naked toddlers and stray dogs wandering around. A huge color TV perched on a bench, playing a Hindi "beach blanket"–style movie, and a father and son kicked a tattered soccer ball. The adults stared at me with their bony faces. I sensed their apprehension. Was I the Jew cop come to chase them away for sacrilegiously defaming the dead? Although Hindus cremate their dead, and cemeteries are rare in Delhi, they understand the sanctity of honoring the dead. A burst of hot wind swirled dust and garbage into the air and a tin can smashed into the headstone of a Rachel Mulemet, aged ten, daughter of Moishe and Ruth. Before that it was as if I'd blocked out the headstones. I was thrown into a dust storm world of dream memory—so odd what we chose to remember and forget in the midst of pain—of Castor and our arguments after my mother died about his finishing Hebrew school. Sensing my guilt, like any normal pubescent child, he gave me hell. He dabbed the blade with the incisive tones of his deepening voice. "I am only doing this for Mommoms cause she's watching me and I promised." He'd look at me sulkily.

"I know," I would answer, my voice curt, exhausted from hours in the ER. "That's the best of reasons."

He would stop and twirl the curls of his hair with his small hands, "I know that you and Ma don't care because you never go to temple."

My precocious genius had cornered me. He seemed all too ready to assume my mother's mantle of chief guiltmonger.

"Toss the football when you're done?" I would offer as he trudged to his room. He ignored me, but later he would come out of his room carrying the mini–rubber football and we would go to the long, narrow hallway and throw the ball for hours. He struggled mightily. Unlike physics, which came so effortlessly to him while most of us stared at equations in perplexity, making a nimble catch or swiping an errant throw remained elusively mystifying to him. His hand–eye coordination, as he so frankly put it, "stunk." Still, he tried and tried. I played down his inability. And Sarah, who had nothing but disgust for the

overdeveloped muscles of steroid mooks and their inflated sala-
ries and self-important status in a society that worshiped them,
became pissed off at me for his feeling of inadequacy. I lamely
blamed his friends, society, anybody but me. She scoffed with a
simple "Bullshit!" and urged me to stop watching and listening to "the drones" who broadcast the games. But I couldn't
resist the pull of receding time, becoming friends with my son,
tracking his mood swings as we watched TV, becoming upset
as the Knicks got creamed. Or as he jumped in the air giddily
(and clumsily) and slapped high five as the Yankees paraded
off to another World Championship. Sarah couldn't wait to get
me alone. "Castor is only ten, but you, Mr. Big Shot Doctor,"
her cadences rising and falling as had my mother's when uttering that almost condemning phrase, "you acted like such a
child. I thought you were different." Her father, who had left
her and her mother early on, and her three stepfathers had been
hard-drinking, rough-and-tumble football fanatics. I never
drank much, I was certainly not rough and tumble, but I was a
good ol' American sports' sublimator.

The Indian father miskicked the soccer ball, it rolled toward
me, and I picked it up and tossed it back. The boy hopped over
the headstone of Rachel buried in the polluted graveyard soil.
Was Rachel as sweet as my son? Was she so tired and innocent
and worldly at ten? Had her disease made her wise? Did she
melt her father's heart when she whispered, "Daddy, let's play"?
Did she look so forlorn, feeling time so precious, when her
parents argued in front of her? Did she crick her neck and arch
her eyes like her mom when she was disappointed in her father? Did Rachel's parents stay awake when she fell ill with the
simplest cold because she always seemed frail? Did she, like Castor, move too fast through life? And did her father, sick to his
stomach, look insane as I know I looked when friends—yes,

friends—explained her death, "It is destiny, god's will." I'd rant to myself, trying to remain polite and in control, "Fuck destiny. Any god that could do this to my child, fuck him too." Yet, still they gave Rachel a Jewish burial, as we had buried Castor, blessed by a rabbi, in the ground now, beside his grandmother. I shut the gate with my dry eyes closed, for I had shed all of my tears.

My mind shut down. I stared out the window, almost unaware of where I was as Vishnu drove me home. Home to find a telegram from Sarah:

> Neil, I have emailed you, called the embassy. Finally they gave me your home address. Please, please contact me if only to say you are alive. I've said it a thousand times and will keep saying it until you answer me. I'm sorry. I will have to live with this until I die. I love you, I always loved you. Sarah.

41

Sorry. Yes, sorry that on the afternoon when Castor lay dying, she lay beneath Jeremy Riegle, while she still "loved" me.

Yes, I was sorry, too, that with all my dignity stripped, I still had not told her that our son had died asking not for me, but pleading for the loving touch of his mother. To hear his mother's voice—one last time.

11

The fundamental question is not whether god is dead, that out of pity for mankind he suicided himself as Nietzsche fervently believed, as to enable us to accept and endure the eternal recurrence to overcome our weakness, instead of embracing the nihilism dominating the culture around him. Nietzsche's question and answer were those of an optimist. Dostoevsky, with his ferocious and lovely pessimistic Russian heart, posed the question, which informs all of his work, and which must first be answered: What happens when there is no god? Unfortunately, we found out—Hitler, Stalin, Dachau, Auschwitz, Treblinka, the Gulags, Hiroshima and Nagasaki, and the nuclear explosions and mass murders to come. For they will surely come.

—from *MYSTICAL MISTAKES*

12

A FEW WEEKS later, Rabbi Judah called me.
He didn't pile on the guilt and ask why I hadn't showed up.

"I want to tell you, please, Levi is coming this week."

"You sure?" I'd been the victim of too many religious ploys to accept his word on faith.

"As sure as one can be with Levi."

"I'll see you then."

"*Tov*," he said, which means "good" in Hebrew.

The service started at six-thirty and would be over by seven-thirty. Not enough time to be too torturous, I hoped.

Next to the cemetery alongside a long blue wall creaked a rusty iron gate, which opened into the temple grounds. An aged, petite, kindly woman with one front tooth greeted me. She pointed toward the temple building. A plaque on the wall detailed the history and noted the many benefactors who contributed to the building's construction in 1954. Before that the congregation met in people's homes. The woman took my hand and led me to the back of the courtyard, where the rabbi had his office next to a library and seminar room.

The rabbi, who appeared to be in his seventies, also missing some front teeth, barely five-three and Indian in every possible outward way except for the yarmulke on his head, grinned, pleased with himself because I had come. Each person usually increased the congregation by ten, perhaps twenty percent; there were no more than a dozen permanent Jewish families left in Delhi.

Rabbi Judah, in a stunning mist of languages (English, Hebrew, Hindi) explained in one long sentence, as if he stopped I might run away, handed me a book, which detailed the history of the Jews in India, pointed with his withered finger to the word *peacock*, which designated the Jews who had arrived in India before the time of King Solomon, because peacocks are indigenous to India and the word *peacock* appears in the Bible and has the same root as the original Sanskrit and Tamil languages and now most Indian Jews had gone to Israel. He stopped for one breath and I asked him to explain the swastika sign, which I'd glimpsed all over town.

"Please, you must understand, *Emmis*, I tell you truth, the Indians never persecuted us in any of our communities. Only the invading Portuguese or Moslems.

"The swastika, maybe it was an Aryan sign brought here thousands of years ago, or maybe a Vedic sign from before the Aryans took and misused it. To an Indian it's a good luck sign—*swasti* means auspicious, good deed—it is often found on the hands of Ganesha, the popular elephant god." And, he rushed, with his fluttering short legs, over to a wooden table and on a piece of scrap paper drew the Indian swastika . . .

卐

and then the German.

卍

"Look closely at it. It is the reverse of Hitler's swastika. Long before Hitler, the reverse swastika was an omen of bad luck to an Indian."

Two teenagers peeked in on us. It was time to start the service.

We walked back into the temple as I thought about signs and symbols and words and their continuous evolution; how one hundred years before I'd never have thought for a second about the millennia years old symbol, which now caused a tightening of my spine each time I saw it.

In the intervening minutes, a crowd had assembled. The grin on Rabbi Judah's face said this was a larger crowd than usual. I got a charge seeing the array of Jews. Rabbi Judah introduced us all quite formally. I was "Dr. Downs." I met the black assistant ambassador from Angola and his kids, a Russian émigré couple, the son and granddaughter of the rabbi (his wife and daughter were out of town), two young men in Delhi from the U.S. on business, a South African investment banker, two couples from the Israeli Embassy, a French couple both of whom were journalists, the husband worked for the Agence French Presse and his wife for the international edition of *Time*, plus regular "Indian" members of the congregation. Two curious German tourists came in late and sat in the back row. Three Indian Jewish teenagers without their parents slipped in and out during the service. And Levi Furstenblum, whom the rabbi did not introduce to anyone, and who sat alone in the back, in a side corner of the room.

I recognized him immediately. Now eighty-two years old, gripping a wooden-handled cane, each step achingly taken. The brutally fierce and formidable face of too much hell-brought wisdom that stared out from the back cover photo of his books remained unchanged by the passage of time, and a life that never again fell sway to the leisurely vicissitudes of hope.

He was larger-framed than I imagined and roughly my height, five-foot ten, but unlike me, large boned. A brown sport coat and open-collared wrinkled shirt shlumped on his body. His bald head was topped by a hastily placed yarmulke. His facial skin was reddish and crinkled. A straight, but fleshy, nose with nostrils that twitched from smelling too much pain and death. He wore gold-framed, green-tinted glasses all during the evening ceremony. I expected wisdom at least and hoped for kindness and forgiveness to come from him. But no, his presence emanated magisterial anger. Almost a menace. I watched him as often as I could without seeming intrusive. There was no way I'd find the courage to introduce myself. He did not sing or pray during the service, only sat or stood in complete silence. Not even mumbling, "Amen."

When it came time for the Kaddish, the prayer for the dead, the rabbi counted the house—for once, and only once, I was glad that women didn't count in the needed ten "Jewish men" for the minyan. It didn't matter; there were more than ten of us. I sank in my chair. I did not want to make the choice of standing, signaling that I was in mourning. One of the American businessmen stood and I hesitated, almost stood, but stayed seated. My hands gripped the sides of my chair. No way could I find it in my heart to pray for the soul of my son to a god in whom I did not believe.

Singing "Dayenu," usually sung only on Passover, had somehow become part of the Indian service. It was an unintended comic highlight with so many accents and differing Hebrew pronunciations, Rabbi Judah said the Kiddush prayer over the wine and then the crowd mingled. The Frenchman, Olivier Donneaux, who worked for the Agence French Presse, asked me if we had not met before, because I looked familiar. "No," I said, we hadn't, "but you know, it's because we all look alike." I exaggeratedly scanned the room. "Yes," he replied, "it's me with my big nose and I am not even born a Jew. It is my wife who is born Jewish." He laughed a robust deep-throated Gallic laugh, and pointed to an attractive redheaded woman who talked with the Angolan. I felt Rabbi Judah tugging at the edges of my sport jacket. He led me away and introduced me to Furstenblum as "Dr. Downs, who very much wants to meet you."

Levi stayed seated, not even reaching to shake my awaiting hand. He looked and spoke to me with an "Oh, no, not another fool come to seek banal wisdom and an autographed book" weariness.

"A nice Jewish doctor?" With his still evident Germanic-Jewish accent, though he had spent his early life in Prague, and the needle of his satirical question, he took all advantages away from me, which deprived me of any seriousness. "And your wife?" Ever perceptive, he spotted the wedding band, which I had never taken off. "A shiksa?"

"Of course."

"That's why she's not here?"

"We're separated."

"Children?"

"Not anymore."

"When?"

"May."

"And you didn't stand for Kaddish?" There was more curiosity in his voice than sympathy.

"I couldn't."

Suddenly, he wet his lips with his tongue. He heaved a sigh. "I must go." He stood up, pressing with both hands against the knob of his cane. "You want me to tell you how I have lived.

47

You want me to tell you a lie and this I cannot do." He took off his glasses and held them in both hands as he gripped the knob of his cane. He waited so I could see the pure coldness in the eyes of the man who wrote the words that had caused so much controversy: "There is something dirty about all those who survived the death camps, no matter if they were German, Gypsy, homosexual, Communist, or Jew. Only those of us with the most vicious inhuman instincts survived. All those survivors who announce their profound wisdom or remorse or forgiveness are liars."

That courageous bluntness is how *he* survived, first the small camp of Terezin outside Prague and then Auschwitz. How he survived the death of all of his loved ones. How he survived the death of his wife Leah and daughter Ottla while he remained helpless to save them. How he lived for over fifty years after the death camps. How he foresaw the twisting of unspeakable horror into a pale justification for the behaviors of mankind. I could never imagine being inside his head, living with his demons.

He waited. I felt like he was scrutinizing me; I felt he could read my mind as his being told me that he had an absolute lack of caring about me. "Mr. Downs, you are a doctor, you know more than I do about saving lives. I only know about death. I never saved any life but my own."

13

Hitler gazed out at the adoring crowd. Nodding. Stroking his mous-
tache with his fingers. His tight-lipped smile of satisfaction, satis-
faction for us all.

The Jews mobbed him with adoration as had the Germans and
Austrians and French. He saved them all. Many had scoffed when
he made his first offer of a homeland in the countryside outside
Munich—and more—he would pay them to leave their homes in
all other parts of Germany. But the offer was sincere. He paid them
fair value for their homes. Soon Jews from all over Germany came
by foot, by car, by the trainload. Then the Germans led by the Fuhrer
and his men helped build this new homeland for the Jews.

The day that Dachau officially became an independent domain
was a great day for Germany and a greater day for all of Europe,
but the greatest of all was for Hitler—the best friend the Jews ever
had.

When the other European nations saw how well Germany's
Jews adjusted to their new country, that the German economy had
recovered from its depression once the Jews were gone, they too
wanted to solve their Jewish problem. They approached the Fuhrer.

Bruce Bauman

He said, with his open heart, "Of course, they are welcome. But they must be paid for their homes and land."

A system with which all countries from France, the Netherlands, Austria, Poland, the Balkans, and Czechoslovakia complied. Only England and Russia refused to help their Jews.

Soon, all the Jews of Europe, paid in full for their belongings, which they left behind, by funds from not only their own countries but with the aid of the generous German people, came streaming by the trainloads. First thousands, then hundreds of thousands, and then millions danced into the new land of milk and honey, of "the chosen people."

—from *CHAMBERS OF COMMERCE*

14

THE NEXT FRIDAY evening Vishnu drove us about half an hour south to where the state of Delhi ends, just before Haryana. We arrived at the farm of Vijay Pillai, for a pilgrimage of a slightly different sort: a birthday party/early Thanksgiving dinner for Charlie. Situated on a twenty-acre estate, maybe three acres of "farming" were done as a tax dodge because farmers don't pay real-estate taxes. Even ardent nationalists like Pillai hated paying taxes. We drove through gated, high-walled communities with armed guards everywhere. No poor people camping out in this neighborhood of what my mother would have lovingly called the "muckiest of the muckymucky." Vishnu drove down another private road almost a mile until we came to another gate, where a procession of cars were already parked with the drivers sleeping, milling around listening to the radio or sneaking drinks.

I deep-breathed, flashed my invitation, and went inside the gate. There were two hundred invited guests and I think they all showed up. The Indian and many Western women in their hand-embroidered saris seemed like the human flashing of a peacock's fanned tail preening around acres of land with five two-story guest houses situated in far corners, with the main, marble-palatial home in the center of the star-shaped compound. Gardens, pools, and stone and pewter bowls filled with flowers abounded, using up much-needed water.

At least thirty men cooked and served a mix of Indian food and rarely found American food: turkey, stuffing, mutton burgers, corn, crispy french fries, and apple pie. The Indian food consisted of traditional chicken tikka and shrimp tandori kabobs; vegetable curries like *Sag paneer*—a great spinach dish; *alu vindaloo*—potatoes in tomato sauce; onion *bhaji*; three different kinds of rice; garlic and regular naan breads; buffalo cheese; dahl; yogurt; *gulab jamun*—honey-dipped milk balls; and ginger ice cream.

Seating at one of the twenty tables was open. Men served trays with glasses of beer, rum, whiskey, vodka, Bloody Marys, Cokes, bottled water, and fine wines.

Around the outdoor, Greek-style theater with ten-foot-high terra cotta horses and other assorted animals, fountains spouted water from various portals. Twenty-five gas-heated lamps dotted the outdoor eating area and took the nip out of the air.

A small crowd circled Pillai. Tall, a touch over six feet, and lithe (he practiced yoga a half hour every day) and dapper in tailor-made Indian off-white pants, off-white silk pajama shirt, and darker brown vest, neatly cut white hair and trimmed beard framed his oval, light-brown face, dominated by a broad, slightly reddish nose. He greeted friends and foes alike with the classic "*Namaste*," palms pressed together at his chest. His head slightly tilted down, his presence yearned to achieve the Gandhiesque. He came to national prominence first, not for his money-making abilities, but when he was jailed in 1975 during Indira Gandhi's reign of martial law in what the Indians call the Emergency. During this period Gandhi suspended the Constitution, censored the press, and imprisoned her enemies. After the Emergency ended, almost all prisoners of any stripe were given amnesty. Upon his release Pillai gave a speech in which he espoused the necessity of passive resistance in the face of all enemies, internal and external, who threatened India's democracy. The speech solidified his reputation as a national figure, a position he never relinquished. With this image of him in my head, and his all-enveloping eyes, his aura seemed more fearsome than beatific.

His understanding of English was total, but in public he often spoke only Hindi, always with a translator/bodyguard by his side.

Also by his side proudly stood his nephew Ratish, Holika's younger brother. Burly, five-foot four, with slicked back, oiled hair, a beak nose, no moustache, and pinprick eyes behind glasses, he strutted beside his uncle, aware of his anointing as the patriarchal heir to the family heritage. I'd met him briefly when he came by the embassy compound to get some minor cuts and bruises mended after he'd had one of his many car accidents. He often preferred to drive himself, leaving his driver at home. With his supercilious and boisterous laugh, he narrated how he almost killed an old man trying to cross the street. The old man refused to stop and so did Ratish until the last possible second. "Do pedestrians have so many rights in the States as they do here?"

I shook my head and answered, "Nowhere that I know of do pedestrians have fewer rights than here."

"Boy . . ."

Boy, I thought, did this guy get lucky, because Pillai had no children of his own. Pillai's childless marriage to his wife, Deva, with whom he rarely spoke and never appeared in public,

53

was the grist for scores of malicious rumors. Some said that she lived alone, a prisoner in one of his many houses. Sometimes they would share the same house, but never the same bed. The rumor mill claimed that he banished Deva because she couldn't have children, but for reasons of conscience he refused to divorce her. Whispering campaigns by his enemies and neutrals—he had few true friends, only allies—abounded. Rumors not worth repeating. But whatever the truth, Ratish and Holika, with tremors of some mega-deal among Pillai, Abhitraj, and Environ rocking the biz world, aside from a conjoining of fortunes through marriage, would, one day, control billions of dollars.

As I wandered around, Chrystie, dressed in a one-piece black sleeveless dress with plunging V-neckline, emerged from the house surrounded by revelers. I eked my way toward her. She spotted me, sped up, touched my shoulder, and kissed me on the cheek. "I'm so glad you decided to come out of your bunker. We never see you."

I had no answer. I couldn't say, That's because you never invite me. I never see you unless you come to the office unannounced for your ongoing case of amebic "pets" or when you bring in Heather for regular checkups.

Instead, I mumbled, "I met Levi Furstenblum last week."

"Oh, you must tell me about him some time." Then she smiled winsomely and introduced me to a gaggle of people with Indian, American, British, and German accents. I didn't remember one name. With them was Holika. Despite her pure silk, semitranslucent sari, her hair combed down to her waist, a heavy coat of facial makeup, more rouge and darker lipstick, a tiny ring through her right nostril, and her flamboyant public smile and laugh, her eyes looked frazzled. She reached out and we shook hands, almost as if our flirtatious dance in the library had never happened. Holika politely introduced me to a startlingly thin woman named Tracee.

Charlie hustled out of the main house and hurried over to me. I'd already given him his birthday present and he was one grateful "stand-up" guy and happy man. So, I assumed, Chrystie was again a satisfied woman.

In seconds, other guests needed their cheeks kissed and backs slapped. I nudged at Holika's hand for her to stay behind. She sneered with a practiced imperceptibility that Indian women have mastered over the centuries to counteract the phallocratic and condescending attitudes. She stepped toward me and stood between her friend Tracee and me.

"Now you want to talk to me? I am currently indisposed toward you for not calling me." Despite the previously charming opposite up-down pitch and cadence of her English, no linguistics degree was needed to hear she wasn't kidding.

"Things are hard for me now and . . . and you're engaged."

"I told you I am *not* engaged," Holika stated firmly.

My tone defensive, I continued. "I am wounded. Really." I held up my two palms. "All I got left after our last encounter."

"Cannot play."

Samaka Abhitraj stood timidly, slightly stoop-shouldered under a banyan tree twenty feet away. Holika's back was to him, and over her shoulder I saw his glance, his roundish eyes behind wire-framed glasses, despite the circle of people surrounding him, never straying from her for more than a few seconds. With his pleasant and attractive face with thick lips, straight, black, early-Beatle mop-top haircut, his presence was at worst unassuming, not at all like the media image of him as "The Barracuda Boy" of the Indian IT world.

"Can I change your disposal by asking if you're free for dinner tomorrow night?" I mumbled without emotion, as if I were asking her the time.

She said in a low but clear voice, "I would very much like to show you Nehru University. James Roberson, the American scholar, is here to give a lecture at 4:30 tomorrow. Meet me there."

I started to protest that Nehru is huge, but only nodded knowing that I was choiceless if I wanted to see her. She formally held out her hand and said loud and clear, "My pleasure to see you again. Please, would you come meet Samaka?"

"Of course," I said politely. Yet feeling paralyzed and awkward, I didn't make a move.

"You must come now."

Reprimanded, I marched over and Holika introduced us.

"I hear that you are an excellent physician and diagnostician," his voice floated out softly with an understated equanimity.

"Thank you," I said rather nimbly, my social graces again on display.

"Why don't you get some food?"

Samaka saved me from further embarrassment and I shuffled off to the buffet tables. After I'd stocked up my plate, I stood alone wondering where to sit. Not far away I recognized a table full of embassy personnel. Although everyone had been cordial—with one or two exceptions— I felt no great kinship. I also didn't feel bold enough to intrude on their cliquishness. Close to me, at a large round table, sat a giggling and loudly talking group of well-dressed Indian women, many of them beautiful, unmarried, and in their twenties. At least three of them talked on cellular phones while simultaneously talking to their tablemates and smoking cigarettes. I was astounded at how many Indian upper-class and caste women, young and old, smoked. Holika's youngest sister, Alka, whom I'd met briefly at the compound with Chrystie one afternoon, sat with them. I not-so-furtively watched their youthful frivolity, both enchanting and disturbing, until I heard a voice calling out, "Dr. Downs." Olivier, the Frenchman, who had been at the temple the previous Friday, waved at me. It didn't surprise me to see him and his wife, who sat beside him. I learned long ago in New York, after so many "chance" meetings, that all major cities are small towns inside a bigger space. "Please sit with us." I noticed Tracee, who had been with Holika, sitting at the same table.

Both hoping to get the hell out of there without having to talk to someone and glad to see a familiar face, I decided to take the vacant seat beside Olivier. The table was not far from where Holika and Samaka entertained more guests.

57

Olivier politely introduced me to everyone at the table.

"We were just commenting how the Internet will make newspapers and magazines, as we know them, extinct in twenty or thirty years. And they will talk out loud, so no one will read at all. Books will not have to be burned by the fascists, it'll happen naturally."

"Not for me. I love the feel of the paper when I read." Tracee spoke with an indeterminable accent. She rubbed a paper napkin between her bony fingers. Stylishly dressed in a light-blue pants suit, I wondered what her connection was to Holika. "Paper gives the words life and who gives a shit about twenty years from now. Twenty minutes from now is tough enough for me."

"Tracee, it is a game. Play along. You are in your late twenties, hmm—I stop there—young, yes, but too old, and you write about food and we all have to eat." No doubt, this was a mischievous inside joke and I was on the outs. Tracee shook her head and pushed her plate full of hardly eaten food toward

Olivier, who pushed it back toward her and then turned to me.

"And what of you, Doctor? What about your profession in thirty years?"

I caught Holika's eye watching me handle the questioning. "Me? By your standards, I'm already archaic. And I'm going backward. I gave up newspapers for books." Except for one dour guy who had been introduced as "Ahn-drew from Oxford," everyone was a bit drunk and in a jovial mood. Everyone but him laughed or attempted to smile knowingly.

"No, no, I mean medicine," Olivier Donneaux said, prodding me to join in.

"People will still be taking it," I deadpanned, and made eye contact with Holika as Samaka touched her shoulder and she turned to talk with another group of people. I lost all energy and answered blandly. "The return of the house call through the Internet. Soon blood samples, x-rays, somehow will all be diagnosed online. Medicine sent."

"You're on the right track but too far behind the curve," interrupted the dour Oxfordian, who managed to speak in the specific English manner that comes through the nose while the speaker seems to have stopped breathing. "What you all think, sorry to say, is so pedestrian—we will be outdated as a species. Soon. In the full spectrum of evolution it will be miraculously quick, chips will be implanted in us at birth, then natural selection will take over and they will be as natural to us as a thumb. We will be born with them. All information processed immediately. We won't need newspapers or doctors. That is the future."

His insight seemed all too appropriate, and without irony, in a country that felt like *Blade Runner* meets *National Geographic* in a head-on collision.

"That's not my future." My obligatory appearance noted and my stomach full, and with the indeterminate ache suddenly resurfacing, I decided to excuse myself. "I have to be going. My future is a hot date with Ms. Djuna Barnes." I got up and bid them goodbye.

"*Nightwood*, a great book," said Olivier, my new French friend, who decided to stand up and accompany me. He leaned close to me and spoke in a manner of a long-lost best friend, "I tell you last week, you look familiar. You said your name was Downs."

"Because it is."

"Yes, you are Dr. Neil Downs. I think of your first name after. You are the doctor with a boy killed in that catastrophe in that New York high school. We must talk about it."

59

I clenched my jaw. My fists. I closed my eyes, and attempted to meditate away my anger.

"Please, I know it is you. I am sorrow for your tragedy."

Meditation failed. "Fuck your sorrow." Never before had I felt such hatred, such violence toward someone who had really done nothing to me. "Come on." I poked him in the chest with the bent knuckles of my right hand. "Let's talk." I slowed my pace deliberately as we passed Chrystie and Charlie who sat with Pillai, his translator, and Hal Burden and some other American business heavyweights. I ducked my head and made no eye contact with any of them and ran past the gate and outside the stone wall with men toting their rifles. Suddenly I whipped around, lost in madness, and grabbed him around his throat and thrust him against the stone wall.

The drivers and guards silently watched us. They would never interfere.

"Listen, you parasite, you or your wife or that magazine she works for print one word about my wife, I swear I will beat you to such a pulp that they'll be using you for newsprint. I begged you motherfuckers to give my wife and me privacy, which is all we had left, and you couldn't do that. Now, *I am begging you*: Please don't."

I let go. He waited until I was near my car and spit at me, "You crazy fuck, man, big American shit doctor, who you think you are?"

I did not turn around.

15

CHARLIE HAD PROTECTED me for as long as he could. Now my secret, the reason behind the reasons I had come to India, was about to come gushing out in the disingenuous tongues of gossip.

My son had not died of a terminal disease, been run over by a drunk driver, taken an overdose of drugs, or been slain by his own hand.

No, on a seemingly ordinary Thursday in mid-May, an hour before going to Hebrew school, three and a half hours before I was to leave the ER to meet him for a night of pizza and watching the Knicks playoff game, because Sarah was attending an opening at her gallery, he and hundreds of other students rushed or ambled or dawdled into the sunny spring daylight after another day at Stuyvesant High School. Waiting outside were Bobby Skirpan, Rusty Kickham, Mitch Tabaldi, and Linda Graper. How well I have come to know those names repeated in my head like an evil mantra. They screamed at their fellow students "Niggers, Jews, and Spics—prepare to die!" "Fuck the chinks!" over and over as 400 bullets rocketed and ricocheted from their automatic weapons. When the carnage on West Street ended, twenty-one people lay dead, thirty-three wounded, and my son, Castor, lay atop the body of Mary Sweedlow, his unrequited fantasy of lust, with two bullets lodged in his failing body.

16

AS I HAD fled to Delhi, Sarah took to hiding in
the inconspicuous town of Prescott, Arizona, to be near her
mother, Romey, and where Sarah spent a peaceful two years of
her turbulent childhood. Romey, with the maternal instincts of
the rattlesnake who gives birth and quickly moves on, divorced
and remarried three more times, moving Sarah in a modern
wagon train from Chicago to Prescott to San Francisco. When
Sarah was fifteen she caught Mr. Romey Number Three mastur-
bating in her bed with her bra draped over "his hand and his
thing." Sarah ran from the house, jumped on her motorbike, and
didn't come home for three days. In the end, Romey blamed
Sarah because she cut school that day, never thinking Number
Three would've left work early. Romey gave her hell and packed
her off to boarding school instead of tossing the pervert out on
the spot. Sarah's generosity of heart, how she forgave Romey for
picking some creepy guy over her, is one of the many reasons
why I loved her. Sometimes, when they fought in front of me, I
wanted to ask Romey how she discarded her own daughter like
used underwear, but Sarah refused to let me. She simply said,

her hurt only given away by the slight nervous tic of her twitching neck, "She's my mother. I accept her and *all* her faults. Until you, I had no one else."

Which was true, Sarah had no father to seek and give comfort. After fading into the American wilderness of rootless ex-husbands, her father died when she was thirteen. It was only after she graduated from college that she and her paternal half-brother, who had never been welcoming, established a relationship. An adjunct professor of archeology at Arizona State University, he lived in Chandler, right outside Phoenix. Romey spent winters in Scottsdale, so ideally Sarah would have a glimmer of support.

I was afraid to send Sarah an email. I no longer trusted its safety. I had received too many nasty invasions from people calling themselves "Xtian Death" and "Four Horsemen." I needed to warn her. I owed her that. And I missed her. For over fourteen years she was my confidante. My truest friend. We had shared so much, were still inextricably bound in our loss and mourning.

They were twelve and a half hours behind because, as a measure of independence, with the 82½ parallel splitting the country down the middle, India chose to be on a half-hour schedule when almost all the rest of the world rounded off to the nearest hour.

Her phone rang and rang until the machine picked up with the canned voice, "Please leave a message." I called out and she picked up.

"Neil?"

I imagined her smell; the sweet fragrance of her sweat as we made love, her white-skinned breasts enlarging as she inhaled, her throat going taut, her hair twisted and tangled. What I once called the purity of her soul-smell.

"Finally, you called."

"Yeah," I heaved a sigh, releasing the claustrophobic air of guilt and anger, which continually welled in my chest. "Some journalists found me here. One works for the international edition of *Time*."

"Oh." I imagined the twitch in her neck, which always started when she was nervous, acting up. "I hoped you were calling to wish me an early Thanksgiving."

"I have almost another week. You OK? Still taking the antidepressants and calling Debbie?" Debbie was her therapist.

"Yes, and still crying a lot. Thank god for Debbie and the drugs. She saved me from losing my mind. I talk to her all the time."

"That's good. Painting at all?"

"Not much. I canceled my next show. Barbara was fine about it." Sarah trusted her dealer, Barbara Kugliani to be an exception to the rule of art dealer's being heartless. "*The Enquirer*'s started bugging Barbara. They want to know why it took me so long . . ."

She didn't complete the sentence. She didn't have to. Neither of us wanted to relive aloud her missing hours.

"Neil, I really hoped you were calling to say you were coming home."

"I have no home."

"You do with me."

"That home doesn't exist anymore."

"It can again, I promise. I'm so lonely, Neil."

I didn't answer.

"Have you met someone?"

"Many people."

"Neil, you know what I mean."

"No."

"Tell me beneath your hate that you don't love me anymore and I will never ask you again."

I couldn't and she knew it. I sidestepped answering by asking a dull question. "Are you going to your brother's or mother's for Thanksgiving?"

"Not sure. My mother's been the evil Romey lately."

I let that pass. Romey had never been anything but civil to me, never exhibiting any more interest in me than she had in anyone except her husbands. Over the years I kept my feelings to myself as best I could, until after the murder, when, despite my anger at Sarah, my own desire, and my eventual flight, Romey announced she was leaving New York the day after Castor's funeral. She and I talked and she stayed for five more days, giving an outward show of support, but she remained frighteningly impassive, never visibly shedding one tear for her dead grandson or the pain in her daughter's heart.

"I was invited to this artist's, landscape painter. But she has kids and so do her friends."

So did her half-brother. She couldn't go to either place. "Sarah, I will think about a visit."

I heard her tears, her nose clogging up. "OK, Neil. I have to go. Please call me."

"I will." I hung up, suddenly mad at myself. I wanted to be cold. Hard. Instead, I was hurt and guilty and I cried for her. Her pain. Knowing she lay sobbing alone in that vapid little town. And then I thought of her with Riegle while I tried frantically to save our son's life and I hated myself for hating her again and less awful for loving her still.

Then I jerked off.

17

RELEASE, BUT NO relief. As I had for so many nights, I relived The Call. The afternoon. At 3:39—I know because every TV station in America reported the exact time— we received a call that there'd been another psychotic group of teenagers who lost their minds and blew half their former classmates to bits. This time it was no rural school in Arkansas or Colorado, but right in Manhattan. All the hospitals in the area would be receiving the wounded. My mind did a hop, skip and giant leap over the unthinkable: that the school might be Stuyvesant. That my son might be one of the wounded.

I was head of the ER. I called on every available doctor, intern, and resident in the hospital. Ordered more nurses. Made sure we had extra fresh frozen plasma. Stationed all the extra beds. I called in all available surgeons. We were ready. Within minutes the ambulances screeched in with the paramedics in states of panic like I'd never seen. I directed who to do what to whom. Blood spouted and leaked from the children's shredded bodies. Their howls pierced and echoed throughout the halls. For this brutality, there was no preparation. Parents already clamored in the waiting room wanting to KNOW! And so, desperately, quietly, did I. But I had lives to save, and then one of the stretchers barreled in and I saw Castor. My boy.

I heard the paramedic's voice—"multiple bullet wounds— one to the chest cavity, bp dropping rapidly, heart taching at 130 . . ."

The first patient you have who dies is forever marked on you. Mine was a fifty-four-year old woman named Elise Rosenberg. She came to the hospital for minor arm surgery, which went fine. A blood clot had formed and then went to her heart while she was in recovery. Everyone warns you of the first-death trauma. Doesn't help. You think about quitting. If there's something you did wrong. You can't understand the harrowing fragility of life resting in your hands until it happens. How a patient or family member's life is forever changed by the delivery of unforgiving news; how fast the promise of tomorrow can end; that time is merciless. And so begins an emotional hardening and denial. There is no other way to survive. I was no different, never confronting the possibility that "it" could happen to my child, my wife . . . Although deep inside I had imagined and repressed many horrors, you know the day of reckoning will, one day, inevitably come.

When mine came, shock took over. It's astounding how much pressure and pain the body and emotions can absorb. Suddenly time slowed, a long tape delay to my brain, which blocked the message: my son is dying. I didn't, couldn't fail now. I couldn't. I touched his arm pretending to find his fading pulse. I told one of the residents to prep him for immediate surgery in the OR. I didn't dare tell anyone he was my son. I moved onto the other children and two teachers who lay bleeding, moaning, struggling for their lives. I detailed who and what and in what order things should be done. This was my job. I had trained all my professional life for the Big Emergency.

Quietly, I asked one of the volunteers to call my wife at home, studio, cell phone, and tell her to get to the hospital right away. She did not ask why.

The signal came that Castor was prepped and ready. I chose to operate on him, for if he died then I would blame no one, only myself. I prayed to the god of Abraham and Isaac and all gods to help me spare my son's life. He was conscious and I whispered in his ear, "I love you" and he whispered back in his last seconds of consciousness, "Where's mom? Can I see her?" I bent over and kissed him and hugged him. And then, as I attempted to remove the bullet from his chest cavity . . . A voice penetrated saying aloud what I knew, "Stop, he's gone." I clenched my jaw, my arms and hands cradled him, and I held my breath until someone, I don't remember who, removed him. I felt like my insides were collapsing—my life was disappearing with his life.

I still don't know how I continued that day. It's as if someone else took over my body. I worked until all who we could save were saved. Two more children died that day in my emergency room. One of them named Bobby Skirpan. Eleven others, who were seriously wounded, survived.

Finally, I asked a nurse to bring in Sarah, who arrived hours too late. I went into my office. I stared at her red eyes and beaten face. From each of us came no words. Only silence.

Then I broke down.

18

STILL UNABLE TO sleep, I was reading when my cell phone rang. This probably meant medical emergency. I exhaled, fearing the unimaginable.

"Neil, it's Chrystie, I'm on the way back into town with Tracee. She fainted. She's revived now, but I think she needs to see you. You met her tonight. Very pretty, fine features. Half-Indian, half-American. The food critic."

"Oh, yeah. You said she's conscious?"

"But weak. She has a problem when she drinks because she doesn't eat much. She's anorexic."

"OK. I'll be at my office in fifteen, twenty minutes."

I didn't want to wake Chandon, who was asleep outside in the servant's small room, so I called a taxi.

I got to my office and they were already there. No Charlie. Tracee's heart and blood pressure were fine. Her pulse was thready. Her tongue showed signs of deep dehydration. Chrystie helped her into a gown and onto a table in one of the examining rooms.

"I'm going to hook you up to an IV with dextrose solution, potassium, and other minerals."

"How about punching it up with some liquid Demerol?"

"First, I need to take a blood test."

She flinched. Her complexion blanched. "I hate needles and I will faint again. I really need a tranquilizer."

"And I really need to see just how low your nutrients are."

She bowed her head in acquiescence. I put on a pair of surgical gloves, took her blood, and then inserted the IV.

"That was almost painless."

"Almost? Now rest. I'll be in the next room."

Chrystie and I walked into my office. She reeked of alcohol but seemed perfectly in control of her senses. She balanced her weight between her hips and inhaled as if she wanted to say something. Nothing came out but an exhale of whiskey breath. She mustered a flat, "Good night."

"Don't worry, she'll be fine if she starts eating."

She scrunched her eyebrows. I shrugged. She left and I sent the blood work over to the International Hospital with one of the Indians who was always on duty. I lay down on one of the couches in the waiting room.

Six hours later, the messenger awakened me when Tracee's blood tests came back. I called over to the lab to double-check the results. They were sure. I tiptoed into the examining room. Tracee was still asleep. I needed to take out the IV before it started to back up. She didn't need another bag.

I nudged her awake and unhooked the IV. She let out a pipsqueak "Ow." She was slightly dizzy, so I helped her to the bathroom, where she dressed and called out, "Can you get me a driver to the Hyatt Regency?"

"Is that where you live?"

"I want to go for a swim." She walked out from the bathroom under her own power. "They have a nice pool."

Her flippancy surprised me and I must've looked bug-eyed stupid.

"I live there part time. It's the only easy way for a single woman not living with her family. I have an apartment in New York. I'm going there next week. I do a food column for Cosmo: 'Tracee (double e) Murkagee's Art of Anorexic Cooking.'" She laughed and against my will, so did I. "I *do* write a column on food for them."

"One of the embassy drivers will take you. First . . ." I reached out and pointed to my office. I held her blood test results in my left hand, "First, Tracee, we should talk. Please, come sit in my office."

"Uh-oh. Bad news comes in sit-down talks in offices. But since I don't work for you, you can't be firing me. So, I can eat. Really, I can."

"It's not that."

She sighed and suddenly looked much older. Her body became concave, her face almost magically falling, surrendering to gravity. "I don't have to sit and we don't have to talk. I know. I am HIV positive. How did you suspect? How did you know?"

"I didn't. The tests are routine here." Not only were they routine, they used the newest and fastest test.

She eyed me suspiciously. We stood in the suspended animation of the examining room. "Ethically I won't, can't, tell a soul. You have to help yourself. Soon. I'm assuming you're not taking any medication either."

She looked at me as if to say, Why should I?

"There are many drugs that can prolong your life. Please stop drinking and smoking. Get a damn good diet. Eat. Exercise, for Christ's sake."

She ignored me. I leaned over a table and wrote down the name of a doctor I knew in New York. "He's terrific. He isn't closed to alternatives or anything."

She snatched the paper without looking at it. "You want to know how I got it?" Her eyes suddenly teared-up; empty of the spark of life and filled with the dread of oncoming death.

I didn't. Still, it was best to let her talk.

"My husband. Half Indian, half white American from a wealthy family. Big deal in the art world. He worked for galleries and museums as their Asian expert. Blue chip, all the way. I thought he was a good mix of cultures like me. Nobody warned me, and I was too blind to see that he was a perfect candidate for a secret life of the dickhead variety. What a hypocrite. Idiot that I was I was honest with him and told him I'd slept with a few guys. What was I thinking? He'd get drunk and call me a 'whore' and 'slut.' Then this." She pointed to her vagina. "Every time that shit got five feet away from me he took up with cheap hookers. He's dead, so I'll shut up." She spoke without self-pity, only self-loathing.

"You did nothing wrong. Life is just . . . well, it's fucking unfair." I didn't like my platitude. "Once, in the ER in New York I had a patient, a famous comedian, I can't say who, he almost died from freebasing cocaine. We pulled him out of it. Later, I got a call from him." I attempted to insert TV-style animation in my voice. "He said, 'Thanks doc, that night I realized I better be careful and enjoy whatever time I got left cause I'm gonna be dead a billion fucking years, forever!'"

"Most un–Hindu-like attitude." She managed a small laugh. "Besides, I enjoyed myself. Sort of. Would you believe I never had an orgasm? And I tried."

I'd gotten used to confessions of the most intimate sort in the ER from people I'd met for ten minutes and might never see again. I'd lost the ability to absorb, be genuinely compassionate and move on. It was one more reason I couldn't work there anymore.

"Too much sex and not enough food, the irony of my life. God is a very funny person with a sick sense of humor."

I wanted to hug her and comfort her and say, It's gonna be fine. But it wasn't and I couldn't.

"Don't look so sad," she was trying to console *me*. "You are very caring, despite what they say."

"And what do *they* say?"

"That you are angry."

"They are right."

"Yes, but with justice."

"Justice—a word that often now means just the opposite."

"Maybe, but be quiet and listen. After you left last night there was a row between Chrystie and Charlie. Olivier began complaining about how he could take you but you surprised him."

"Now, you do look upset." I gritted my teeth. "Chrystie told Charlie she wanted you fired for hitting one of her guests. Charlie said over his dead body and he'd even help you beat the shit out of Olivier. They were both drunk. That's when my flair for the dramatic intervened, and Chrystie got upset with me."

I didn't give a shit about the job and Charlie kept proving to be a better friend than I thought. "I applaud your timing. But why did she get upset with you? I don't get Chrystie."

"Getting is Chrystie's job. She is not so complicated. She wants, she gets, or she gets mad."

"She was nice enough to bring you here."

"She intends to move to New York and I know many people she would want to know. She has great pretensions to live up to." Her eyelids drooped in fatigue.

"OK, time for you to go. Please rest and eat. Call me if you have a problem. Drink water. Eat. No caffeine. But get some help. You can live a long life if you—"

"Please, no more advice." She leaned over and her lips parted wistfully. "You *are* cute—before—too bad we did not meet before."

I laughed at her mix of stoicism and goofiness. "Before, I was a faithfully married man."

I took her arm, she was still weak, and escorted her outside to an awaiting car and then I went home.

19

When I was a young man I was guided by Wittgenstein's statement, "The limits of my language mean the limits of my world." I was full of myself and decided my world would have no limits. Words were the key to existence, to my relations to others, to my love for my soon-to-be wife, to my fellow scientists, to the link between god and me.

Then language became my demon. Language gave the despicable heralds of a terrible mankind, the vehicle to despoil every living human being worth a damn.

And then words became the delivered message that said there could be no god.

I wished, no longer a believer, that words and language had never existed.

I have lived with words that have not enlightened as I had hoped as a young man, but the screams of pain and sorrow. The words I have most often heard are not the words of god but of god denied. The screams of Ottla, my three-year-old daughter. How I wish I had been deaf. My wife and child mute. Instead, eternally I hear my wife's plea for help. Her gasps of pain. And finally the last words she spoke, as I sat there tied to the chair with my back, so smart those Nazis, turned away from her, as they defiled her. I could only imagine her face, imagine their brutal perversion as I heard her last words, "Forgive me, Levi."

"Forgive me, Leah," were the words she never heard me speak.

—from MYSTICAL MISTAKES

20

WHEN I GOT there, Vishnu gave me the message that Levi Furstenblum had called. He was having lunch at precisely 2:30 at the Indian International Center on Lohdi Road. If I wanted to meet him, I shouldn't call back, just show up. Or not. If I did show up, I need only tell the host to lead me to his table.

My body sagged with exhaustion, but there was no way I was missing this opportunity. I took a short nap before Vishnu drove me over to the center, which is a cultural hub for the elite of Delhi with a fine library, restaurant, and living quarters, all of which you must be a member, or accompanied by a member, to use.

I arrived precisely on time. Furstenblum was easing himself into a chair at a nearly isolated corner table by a window inside the first-floor dining room. He spotted me walking behind the host and waved his cane.

"I thought you would come." No happy hello from him. Only a stark expression and eyes hidden behind tinted glasses. "Please, sit down."

I was nervous and felt tremors in my hands as I sat down and spoke at the same time. "I was out late and then had an emergency and I am supposed to meet someone at a lecture at Nehru University at 4:30, so forgive me if I seem . . ."

"Roberson's lecture?"

"Yes. You know his work?"

"We're kindred minds of a sort. Not in politics. I am meta-political," he stated this sentiment with a challenging growl. I didn't question his assertion. "In his true calling he is a modern Kabbalist, for when you are a Roberson, what is linguistics but a searching for god in words? But his quest is futile."

I thought I understood what he was telling me, yet wondered if he wanted me to question him. I'd wanted this chance but was too scared right then to take it. I continued in the same verbal plane. "Are you going to his lecture?"

"It is on politics. I said I am meta-political." His condescension was palpable as he shook his head and frowned. "He called me yesterday. Perhaps we will meet." Delhi was getting to be too damn small a place. "We speak via email." It surprised me that Furstenblum had email. But why wouldn't he? Unlike most of us, he probably understood how it worked. "Besides, there will be too many people. My hearing aid is no good for groups." He pointed to his ears. I saw a tiny hearing aid tucked in each ear. "Come. As good Jews, let us get serious." He handed me the menu. "The Moghul chicken is excellent, though I am partial to the fish and chips."

We ordered and then he got to the reason why he had called.

"Judah corrected my misimpression that you were here as a tourist. You work as a doctor at the embassy, but you are not Foreign Service or in the military?"

"No."

"So, tell me, why are you here?"

I thought about being flip, even provocative—feeling embarrassed by my deep reverence for him—but decided to just say the truth. "I'm running away."

"Yes, this seems like a good place for that. I cannot run and could not run when I came, the Nazis saw to that." He spoke both literally and figuratively and seemed to be talking about himself while slyly talking about me. "I could not return to Prague for the friends I had were either not friends or dead. I tried America. Much too prosperous and self-satisfied. And soulless. Then I went to Israel. My friend Schneerman persuaded me to go there. You've heard of the great Rebbe?" Not reverence, but amusement lilted from his voice as he pronounced this title of honor. "To whom I am ineluctably bound because we survived summer camp together."

Adolph Schneerman, born into a wealthy and assimilated German-Jewish family of whom he alone survived Auschwitz, immigrated to Israel, where he'd become a noted Kabbalist and head of a renowned sect of Orthodox Jews.

"I know the headline stuff."

"As do most. He is more complex than his reputation and his *farbissener kop* belie. Before you judge from the headlines you should know that every day for two years he lamented, 'What did we do to deserve this?' Of course there was no answer. But when he survives, he thinks somehow he is Yahweh's special envoy. So he leapt into total and absolute faith of his messiah's eventual return. Which led him to his answer that those in the camps deserved to die for past sins as now do the Palestinians." Schneerman's proclamation made headlines in Israel and caused tremors in religious communities around the world. It made him a pariah in many of those communities. "He and I will never agree on his repugnant beliefs. Never. But I understand how he came to these beliefs."

The waiter brought the food and we started to eat. I did not know his custom, so I remained quiet until he got halfway through his fish and chips, when he spoke again. His mind keen, he picked up exactly where we left off.

"I had to leave Israel after a disheartening experience in a bank in Tel Aviv. I was waiting on line when a Yemenite Jew screamed at a European Jew, 'Hitler should have gotten you all.' I could not stay in another place with so much hate and bigotry. I remain angry. But I am beyond hate."

"But there is plenty of bigotry here with the caste system and the problems between Hindus and Moslems."

"Yes, but I found a certain quiet here. So, in a sense, I, too, was running away." He did not smile at his admission. "I did not understand Hindi. Even fewer spoke English then. I found it easy to be foreign." I understood exactly what he meant. "And then I met Hannah, a Jew, oddly enough—her family fled Germany in the thirties and went to Iraq. In the fifties, they came here. In the sixties, the rest went to Israel. Hannah stayed with me. She died two years ago."

He recited this matter-of-factly while drinking his beer. I wanted to say "sorry" or something, but his presence forbade any gratuitous offerings.

"Why do you still go to temple?" I asked.

"Because I am a Jew and whether I believe in Yahweh or not, the Germans and the Czechs and the French all proved my Jewishness. And," he spoke with an uncommon, Tevya-like zestful irony, "they need a tenth for the minyan."

I had read his books and seen him in the temple, and this didn't jibe. Feeling a bit bolder I voiced my skepticism. "I don't know if I can accept that answer."

He gave out a muffled, almost encouraging laugh. I felt OK about challenging him. Then he bowed his head, slid his glasses slightly down his nose and gazed at me above the frame. "I go because I need to look in the eyes of those who believed as I once believed. Because you cannot run away."

"And in my eyes?"

He stared in my eyes but did not answer my question. "You know that when I was a student I was a physicist?"

"Yes, you wrote a little bit about that in *Mystical Mistakes.*"

"Correct. And I thought I was much better than I was. I theorized that I alone could reconcile the seeming irreconcilable contradiction between Heisenberg and Einstein."

He had written about that with great humor. He answered Einstein's declaration that "God does not play dice" with his own challenge "Yahwehna make a bet?" As far as I knew Einstein never accepted.

"I even had a name for my theorem before I had a solution: the Furstenblum Paradox. Through the beauty of math I believed I would find my god. Before I found the solution, came another solution and my world was taken apart." Because of his abilities as a physicist, the Nazis had offered to spare the lives of his wife and child if he had aided their weapons program. He had refused. He believed the Nazis would kill them either way. "And I came to a completely different conclusion about god in any form."

I listened, awed by the almost wrath-like self-analysis without any forgiveness for the hubris of youth or the impossibility of his choices.

"Now, something happened to you and the question arose that all of us face, some very simply, some very abstractly. And the question is always, in one form or another, this: How much must you love god to accept Auschwitz? Or whatever happened to you? To accept that god exists after that? There is only one answer to that question. The answer you have come to. And then you must find another answer."

His surety of my torment left me too intimidated to ask more questions. He finished his food. "I am tired. My knees hurt." I could see the pain as he crossed and uncrossed his legs.

"There are surgeries and medications that might help you. They are expensive but something could be arranged."

"I have money. I made sure the Germans paid me. And my books, though not big sellers have never been out of print in twenty-five languages."

His voice and words said he did not want to mend his knees, end that pain.

He paid the bill. I knew better than to protest. I thanked him for his generosity and I meant not only in buying me lunch. As we walked slowly outside, he told me that he came there every Saturday after going to Bahrisons, the bookstore at Khan Market. "Join me anytime," he offered.

Despite my despair, I was flattered and pleased and said I would, and offered to give him a ride, but he said he had his own driver. "Why shouldn't I?" He gave me a stern, tight-lipped nod in response to my look of surprise. "If you don't want me to renege on my offer, you must understand that I wrote and I speak from my essence. I was not and I am still not a good person, but people like you don't want to believe that I wasn't a sweet-souled mensh before Auschwitz or that I didn't metamorphose into a nice *boychik* after." He spit out the word "nice" with such bite that I shivered. Even at his decrepit age, with his aching, crumbling knees, I thought this man would kill me for a last piece of bread.

21

When man appears before the Throne of Judgment, the first question he is asked is not, "Have you believed in God?" or "Have you prayed or performed ritual acts?" but "Have you dealt honorably or faithfully in all your dealings with your fellowmen?"

—*THE TALMUD*

Soon the Jews began building homes and new chemical factories and experimental facilities for new medicines and medical treatments. Some German doctors visited, even assisted in the experiments and were immensely impressed with what the Jews were doing inside the medical offices they built in Dachau. They promised huge rewards from these experiments in the future.

We saw the films of the new community of the men in their beards and women in their long, black dresses going to pray and then to work. The less religious moneymakers and traders built up their new city-state. The Jews were finally ending their stateless wandering around Europe. Because of the brilliance of the Fuhrer, they were all finally together in one place. . . .

And so too the economies of the countries of Europe flourished. Using these new resources, everyone begin to thrive. Unemployment went down. Inflation went down. Because of the master plan, the Fuhrer's final solution to save the Jews, to solve the Jewish problem, which had plagued Europe for centuries, was in place for lasting peace in Europe. For this accomplishment, the Fuhrer happily accepted the Nobel Peace Prize from the Nobel Prize–winning Norwegian writer, Knut Hamsun. A photo of Hamsun, with his bearish smile, welcoming the Fuhrer to Oslo hung on my wall.

And then came the greatest shock to all of us.

Suddenly, even inside our home in Munich, we began to smell horrid fumes sweeping in from over the border, which was only ten miles away. At first, we ignored it. Eichmann and Himmler investigated and claimed it was the Jews right to do within their lands whatever they chose. They were experimenting with new technologies of power, a new gas, Zyklon B, which would make them a self-sufficient energy state and financially stable. My father seemed worried. But not the Fuhrer. During his radio broadcast, he reassured us that all was well. "Trust me," he said, "the Jews will act honorably and live up to their part of the bargain."

Then came the dirty dishonor of what they had done to themselves. Of how they betrayed the Fuhrer's hope for the Jews. My father, who was one of the policemen chosen to investigate, told us before we saw the unimaginable photographs of the devastation. He came home a shattered man. He couldn't understand why six million (six million!) people would kill themselves in mass suicide. And to starve themselves like that! If they needed help, we would have given bread. Soup.

But killing themselves with such monstrous gas—we couldn't understand. I was a teenager and did not comprehend why they chose to meet their god. I cried and cried at the madness and my father's sadness. He spoke to me of what he'd seen and happened for many months. So hurt he was, he never talked to me of it again.

He could never comprehend such mass societal insanity. Such calculated taking of life. So like the Jews to be so orderly and quiet, he said. Still it is not comprehensible. No one, not the most intellectual of men or wisest of philosophers or the most spiritual priests and reverends could explain it.

Simply, even after all these years, I have one explanation: the Jews were to blame. No one else. They killed themselves by their own hands of their own free will. We did all that we could to save them. It was their choice to meet their god, who did not stop or save them.

—from *CHAMBERS OF COMMERCE*

22

VISHNU HAD TROUBLE finding the right
building in the sprawling mass that is Nehru University. Built
on the small hills of Delhi, set off from the noise of the streets
but not immune to the pollution and dirt, graffiti slogans of left-
wing groups and Communists marked the peeling walls. And
with groups of people congregating, sitting on the grass, standing, smoking cigarettes in huddled circles, it felt vibrant, en-
ergetic, although it's said to be calm in comparison to the fiery
uprisings before and during the time of the Emergency.

We found the sociology building. It was fetid-smelling,
badly ventilated, and had dimly lit halls. Torn loose-leaf paper
with the jottings of hope, and empty cans and cigarette butts
tossed in garbage buckets lined the hallways.

Roberson, Texas-born, taught linguistics at Princeton, already in the midst of reading his paper on globalization, was
equally infamous for his contrary view that the U.S. was not
a democracy—in essence had never been a democracy—but
had been a budding republic at one time and was now a
postmodern Darwinian plutocracy. I'd heard him speak and

read his pieces on linguistics on the radio. Virtually no American mainstream newspaper, magazine, or TV station printed his political pieces. They found their way into small magazines and local radio stations, or lectures given in more welcoming countries.

There were over three hundred people jammed into the room. I spotted Holika sitting in an aisle seat. She didn't turn to see me, as had others. I felt more than marginally conspicuous. Roberson was the only other non-Indian face in the room. I stood in the back among a group of other latecomers, who also couldn't find a place on the floor.

Roberson presented a lucid case for why we now lived in an era where elections are a sham. The ruling elite controlled information and wealth with a combination of the nuclear sledgehammer and linguistic subtly that George Orwell never imagined. Roberson unexpectedly quoted the conservative English philosopher Bill Black's contention that "democracy is incompatible with the free market." This, he said, was a mangling of language, because it was truly an unfree market controlled by a corporate and political elite. Black's fear, and Roberson's hope, was that the masses will figure this out and find a new form of democracy with new media.

He sedately ended his lecture and I made my way over to Holika, who in blue jeans, black T-shirt, and denim jacket, soft dabs of makeup, her hair tied back in a ponytail, barely resembled the same woman of the night before. She spoke with a group of friends. I waited until she caught my eye and she made a motion toward me with her eyes and she stepped toward me and away from the group.

"Sorry I came in late. I had to meet with someone for lunch. Levi Furstenblum," I announced with childlike pride. I felt sure she would know who he was and I was right.

"A dear friend of mine loved his work. How do you know him?"

I didn't want to go into too much detail so I just said, "Charlie set it up."

"Neil, you look tired. Are you OK?" She asked, not meaning to give offense.

"I was up much of the night with Tracee, that friend of Chrystie's." I did not add that the lunch with Levi was helpful in a way I couldn't yet define as well as emotionally exhausting.

"Yes, of course. She is my friend, too. I have known her since childhood. How is she?"

"Fine, for now."

The crowd thinned and we filed out of the small auditorium. "What did you think of your Mr. Roberson?"

"Why is he mine? I refuse to take responsibility for 300 million Americans any more than you would one billion Indians." I answered defensively. After talking with Levi I wanted to avoid any serious discussion.

"Easy, doctor."

"Sorry. To answer your first question, I don't know about the no-democracy angle, but the harangue on how the media catches a story and becomes obsessed with nonissues to keep the public diverted, that hit a nerve."

"Yes, I imagine." She veered her glance away, but her statement told me that she knew.

"I'm surprised that you liked him."

"Who said I did? Maybe I am spying on the enemy."

"Holika, I saw you, you agreed with him."

"Watching me, were you?" she said with a snake-eyed stare and a giggle. "Let us take some tea so I can watch you." She held her right hand up and out as if she were going to take my

89

hand, but instead just pointed down the dirt pathway to the teahouse.

"No dinner?"

"Tea first," she insisted in a soft voice.

"Is this a test?"

"Yes," she said as she undid the band holding her ponytail and shook out her hair which grazed my shoulder, "but you cannot study."

As many people nodded "hello" in her direction and she calmly smiled back, we crossed over terrain, a wind-littered, dry-dirt landscape dotted with shrubbery that felt like a Western movie set. At the teahouse, I bought us two teas and we sat outside on two wobbly wooden chairs that looked out into the city's haze. It was the first time we sat together almost leisurely. I studied her face, which was not classically beautiful; her nose had a slight bump; her dark eyes slightly too close together; her chin came up a bit short. Yet, it all worked so well with the elegance in her presence, her carriage. No doubt, she was aware of her sway over people. Perhaps she was older than I thought. I was never good at guessing ages. I knew better than to ask her age or tease her about her few gray hairs.

"What would Samaka or your uncle say about your attending this lecture?"

"About the same, though for different reasons, as my having tea with you."

"Disapproval then?" I asked.

"Absolutely. And jealousy. Poor Shmuck, that is what I call him," she laughed. The correct pronunciation did make the words sound similar. "He loves me but he has a vision of me that is only a silhouette of who I am. He has only a vague clue of what he will be taking on if I let him." She sighed and laughed at the same time, while bobbing her head, which ended with an abrupt "hmm," then smiled at me while again shaking out her hair. "You see, I know some Jewish words."

"You know what shmuck means?"

"Loser."

"No. Yiddish for penis, like dick or cock. From the German, I think, for *shmuck*, which means jewels."

She nodded. She could take it from there. "Am I here as a serious jester for your affections or a tour stop on the welcoming committee?"

"That is quite a bold question considering that you are the one who is presently married."

"Separated and getting more separated by the day."

"What is your wife's name?"

"Why do you want to know?" I remained ever cautious about discussing Sarah with anyone.

"Curiosity." She finished her tea and waited for my answer.

"Sarah." I said barely audibly.

"Good name. Saraswati is the goddess of knowledge who protects the arts. She is exceptionally beautiful and loyal to her husband."

Two out of three ain't bad, but that last one . . . I thought and sipped my tea before giving a censored answer. "Well, this Sarah is an old WASP name." Her Pilgrim ancestors probably knew the biblical story of Sarai, who changed her name when she married Abraham and started the tradition of the name Sarah, but Sarah's parents were far removed from any Bible class when they named her. "I prefer not to talk about her. It is too serious. And I *was* in a good mood."

"You will be again. You know that there are Hindu theories of maya, where life is lived under the veil of illusion." She stopped. She was about to trespass onto forbidden territory and she knew it.

"Holika, I don't want to sound like a jerk but I don't believe in any god or gods that you must pray to. None. And my loss is no illusion—veiled or unveiled." I was not ready to speak of him yet.

"I am so sorry. I feel like I can talk with you, but I see we do not know each other well enough for this discussion."

"Yes, but are we going to? Or is this an illusion? Are we sitting here?"

"Yes, we are. And yes, I think we will. But I must disappear for now."

"N-*ow*?" My voice went high-pitched.

She giggled girlishly before answering. "I am meeting some friends for dinner."

"I guess I failed the test. Or was it fixed?"

"Fixed. If I had told you, you might have pouted or been less than yourself. I did decide we should meet again. I will call you in your office this week."

23

WHEN I WAS in my mid-twenties there was a TV show, "The Last Degree," about the pressurized life at an unnamed Ivy League law school. The show starred Steven Hansen, who has since faded from the scene, a blond, whose hair curled at its ends, and who, with the exception of his turned-up and my straight nose, bore an amazing resemblance to me. Even I saw it in our similar body language. More than a few times, his fans asked or stared at me until they determined, unluckily, they were mistaken. Once, when Sarah and I checked into a hotel for a conference in Orlando, the hotel clerks thought for sure I was Hansen. Soon there was a ruckus in the lobby and busboys and clerks were sticking papers in my hand wanting autographs. It became a damned family joke because only my brusque New York accent finally convinced them that I was really a doctor.

That slim brush with fame told me how much I cherished my anonymity. Even in the self-contained world of medicine, where the stars are research doctors, I was content to do my job in the anonymity of the ER.

Not so Sarah. She wanted recognition as a famous artist, and knew she would gain it as soon as she came to New York. While she was still a student at the Art Institute of Chicago, Jeremy Riegle, at the height of his fame, gave a guest lecture to Sarah's class. Sarah was one of the star students in both talent and beauty; Riegle made sure he met her. Soon Sarah found herself in his bed. She foolishly thought she had seduced him. They had a three-night stand. He gave her his notorious rap: "Come to New York, I'll help you. And you will renew my inspiration." Her ego and naïveté at all-time highs, she fell for his snow job. She called him two months later before she came in for her Easter break. He invited her to come to see him, an invitation that she misinterpreted. She flew into town and went directly to his loft, where, hocus-pocus, he fucked her one more time. And then he fucked her over. When she awoke in the morning, she found a note. "Please, take your time. Have breakfast. I had to drive out to the Hamptons to be with a friend. Let yourself out and leave the number where you're staying and we'll get together again before you leave."

Sarah found out that he had seduced hundreds of women. If they suited him and they agreed, he brought them into his stable of assistants and occasional bed partners. Stunned and in denial that someone could treat her like just another "street fuck," Sarah chose not to call him and make her own way.

Years later, when her career started to do well, the art world being so small, they met again. He did not remember that he had taken a painting of hers for his "collection," did not remember her name, and barely recognized her face. As she gained minimal recognition between SoHo and Chelsea, he helped her out. He included her in a show he curated, and wrote an essay for a catalog for her first solo show. I thought this was some form of redemption for Sarah's mistake. That he truly believed in her work.

This limited art success had not garnered her real fame, no worldwide recognition.

But now, unknown to us, as I continued operating and the gurney rolled my son to the hospital morgue, we were suddenly gaining worldwide "fame" without having any control over our names or our fates. From the Net to local and cable TV, I was becoming known as "Dr. Neil Downs, who worked heroically through the tragic murder of his son, Barry Castor Downs. In the waiting room, his wife Sarah Brockton Roberts, a well-regarded New York artist, stood courageously with the other parents of the fallen."

While Sarah and I crumbled, side by side on the soft leather couch in my office, TVs throughout the hospital and the world showed film of the carnage. Through the locked door came a most unwanted message, "Neil, it's Shana." Shana Armstrong was the assistant operations officer of the hospital.

"Bad time, Shane."

"I know. But there is a mob of press and we have to get you out of here unless you want to hold a press conference."

Hell no, was she nuts? I didn't want to talk to the press. Not to anyone. Including Shana.

Thus began a new nightmare. One that happened to others. Never to me. One that happened to those who lusted after fame and recognition after murdering their children, lying to save a killer's ass, having their wangs cut off, or sucking a president's cock.

Sarah and I drank some bottled water and cleansed our faces with alcohol swipes that I had in my office. Ray Esperenza, the besieged hospital PR director, who also acted as a liaison between the administration and staff, and was also someone I considered a friend, along with two security guards, successfully hustled us into an ambulance through a corridor exit. When the ambulance pulled down our block a mob of reporters and satellite trucks surrounded the front door to our apartment building. And a new insanity began. The ambulance driver took us to the safety of my friend Matt Silverman's house in Rye.

That next morning, before I had finished my coffee, Ray called me on the phone and implored me to give a statement, which we issued. "Sarah and I ask that you let us mourn in peace. We thank all of those who have already sent cards, flowers, telegrams, and emails. We appreciate more than words can convey these outpourings of love and support. We ask that instead of flowers, that you send all donations to your favorite charity in Castor's name.

"Once again, we send our deepest thanks for your expressions of love and support."

That didn't end it. Ray, who knew me well—we played racquetball together and had taken Castor and his kids to Knicks and Yankees games—did his best to deflect all attention from us. In the next few days we discovered who our friends were and just how much information you could find out about anyone. The papers, the magazines, the television, and the scandal creeps went berserk. We found these "facts" published in the papers or on the Net: my college records, photos of Sarah and Castor, Castor and myself from times I could barely remember—all given or sold by people we had trusted and some from those we didn't remember. There were interviews with Castor's schoolmates and teachers. His IQ and school records. Evaluations of my performance from college onwards. I heard I was a great doctor or a hack who couldn't even open his own practice. My run-ins with the higher-ups about the uninsured and a paper I'd written in college about the benefits of a nonprofit, single-payer health system, excerpts from letters of protest for the way hospitals hounded stricken patients for payment were cited. They mentioned my father as inventor of the Gypswitch. They traced Sarah's pedigree as a descendent of Revolutionary War hero Mawbridge Brockton. Her gallery let the magazines use photos of her work. *People* did a special little spread with photos the gallery had in their files. *USA Today* ran bios of all the murdered children, and then copies of the speeches at the masses or ceremonies.

We received calls through intermediaries at Matt's house from all the major networks. A college acquaintance who worked on "Nightline" called Matt and begged him for an interview. The *New York Times* ran front-page pictures and then a supposedly investigative story on ER rooms in New York, focusing on mine, and how we handled the crisis.

All of this came out in one fashion or another: We were members of the ACLU and Common Cause. I'd served two three-month stints with Doctors Without Borders. We had signed petitions and Sarah had donated paintings to organizations hoping to ban all guns. They wanted us as spokespeople, but only said so through a television spokesperson, and never contacted us directly.

Celebrity-news programs like "Xtra" and "Inside Edition" ran stories on the killing and did profiles of us all with a peculiar slant. We never watched them, but we heard. Friends taped them for us in case, in some less frenzied future, we wanted to relive our celebrity status.

We were told that one radio blowhard gave this commentary. "It is so sad and tragic what happened to Dr. and Mrs. Downs, but if it is true that Mrs. Downs had an abortion, I wonder if they regret that now." Sarah had no abortion that I knew about.

One aspiring mayoral candidate used film of the shooting in an ad saying this would never happen in his city.

The Policemen's Benevolent Association recorded two videos using the shooting. One for the younger set used Pearl Jam's "Jeremy" on the sound track. For the older set, they used Elton John's "Funeral for a Friend." Both were used without permission as a come-on. Twenty-five bucks for the video and a sticker for your car.

This charade of gossip and salacious fascination with the killers, the dead, and their families, passing for news, continued unabated, and still goes on.

98

The loneliness of so many who wrote us at the hospital, the gallery, or just "New York City," frightened and saddened me. We both received offers of dates, marriage proposals, yes, marriage proposals, sexual orgies, love mail, and, of course, hate mail.

Then came unending sources of information and explanations for the behavior of the four "misunderstood and disturbed teens." Mitch Tabaldi and Rusty Kickham attended Stuyvesant for two years, making the long trek from Howard Beach, Queens. Neither had done well either academically or socially. Kickham, who was to star on the soccer team, never went to practice and quit the team after his first year. Tabaldi had been disciplined for bringing a gun onto school grounds, which resulted in his being "asked" to leave Stuyvesant after his junior year. Kickham, his only real friend in the school, left with him. Not long after, Bobby Skirpan, Tabaldi, and Kickham, who'd been friends since kindergarten formulated their murderous scheme. Linda Graper was Kickham's girlfriend. All the words and analysis spewing out of the TV and the Internet could never truly explain why four middle-class kids turned into cold-blooded killers.

The vilest of all was a Web site/CD-Rom game. I didn't check my email for weeks after the murder, and then, when I did, I found information on a game called "Genius Kill," in which the player decided which "Jewface genius" or "nigger" he hates most and then kills him or her as they leave Stuyvesant. Then the player got points for killing more kids than Skirpan, Tabaldi, Kickham, and Graper. I knew all about this game because someone calling himself "Xtian Death" sent it to me on my email. They had shot Castor fifty more times and, as he wrote to me, "Jew dock, you never saved him. Not once."

My belief, my faith in some repository dignity of humanity plummeted.

99

We spent the next three days bunkered with Matt and his wife and two kids as the TV trucks with their satellite dishes practically barricaded his house. Matt, slippery and conniving as he was, proved an invaluable friend. He arranged for the burial service and dealt with the rabbi of Castor's temple.

He explained to the principal that Sarah and I could not attend the mass memorial at Stuyvesant, where not only students and teachers who knew the murdered and now martyred, but also mayors and senators and governors and limelight seekers eulogized the children they never knew.

After three days, on Monday morning, the time came to bury my son. I barely noticed the sunny, seventy-five-degree winds of spring in New York. I wish I could say we had a beautiful ceremony with heartfelt eulogies for a hundred friends and family. But no, we chose to skip the service and go straight to the cemetery in Queens. I hoped the press and public would leave us alone to mourn in peace. But no. Outside the cemetery was a braying pack of journalists. Once inside the cemetery we carried my son's casket in silence from the hearse and placed it into the ground beside his Mommoms. When the rabbi hymned his prayer, and, after some mumbled "Amen," the only sound I heard was that of uninhibited sobbing as I threw the first and last shovels of the dust whence he came onto his final home. In that moment of internal solitude and grief for us and peace for Castor, there should have been silence, but above us whirred the blades of a helicopter with someone snapping pictures of the suddenly ubiquitous face of Sarah Brockton Roberts as she wept hysterically.

In that moment—when I felt almost like jumping into the grave beside my son, and I knew Sarah did too, so out of our minds were we that we clung to each other fearing that if we let go we'd disintegrate into the pain—the thought that saved me was a realization that I must flee America.

That evening, Sarah numbed herself with tranquilizers, which did not stem the flow of tears, and then finally we were alone in the extra bedroom of Matt's home. I couldn't keep quiet any longer. My son was dead and my heart broken beyond repair; this was the time to ask the question that would seal our fate.

We had not made love since before his death. And I needed to make love to Sarah that night, to feel myself inside her, to feel as if I lived somewhere real, that I could survive in some less horrific future if we could make love and life again. But that was the Sarah who had been my faithful wife, my love, my soul mate. Inside her, I had never felt alone.

"Sarah . . . Where . . ."

"Do we have to do this now?" She had been waiting for that question. She pushed herself off the bed and tugged at the strings of her nightgown. Her neck began to twitch. Fast. Her faced twisted.

"I have to, yes." I stayed seated on the bed.

Because the papers found out she did not arrive until four hours after the initial call went out for her, we gave the story that she was at various openings and galleries, one step ahead of the search party. They'd never uncovered the truth about her whereabouts. Thankfully.

"Neil . . ." Her body drooped into sadness and she started crying. Different tears from those she had wept for Castor, tears of guilt and remorse instead of the purity of loss. "I was with Jeremy."

"*With* him?"

"Neil, it's so complicated and I don't even know how to explain what . . . We have lost so much more than one child. More than Castor."

Yes, I thought, we have. She came to me and needed me to hug her, and I did. But as we held each other, my arms had no strength. "Harder, hold me," she whispered. "Harder" in Sarah's world indicated forgiveness. I tried. I wanted to. I couldn't. Yes, we had lost more than just Castor, I thought, we had lost each other. My last inner reserves of love, of belief in anything seemed to evaporate against my conscious will, not just from the ineffable place where we find love and heart and our souls, but even from my physical being. She felt my arms go weak and she fell away from me and she stared at me and I closed my eyes—and she knew.

That night we did not sleep together. We never stayed one night alone in the same room again.

In the moment when we needed most to be one, we were two—far apart, and alone in our own suffering. In that moment, from her and for her, despite the weight of my guilt that somehow I was at fault, I was gone.

24

I SPENT ALL Monday and Tuesday waiting for calls from Charlie or Chrystie or some repercussions from Friday night's near-fight with Monsieur Donneaux. None came. Nurse Donna told me Charlie had flown off on embassy business and wouldn't be back until late Tuesday or Wednesday in time for his Thanksgiving Day dinners. There were numerous dinners, private and official, and now for sure I would not attend any of them.

The call I wanted was from Holika. I couldn't call her. It didn't come. What I did receive was a handwritten, hand-delivered note from Cécile Donneaux.

> Dear Mr. Downs,
>
> I am writing to apologize for the behavior of my husband, Olivier, on Friday of last week. It was most unfortunate that he did not speak with me before he talked to you. I can only say that we will not break your confidence, or approach you about this subject again.
>
> I hope you will forgive him. I hope we see you again at temple.
>
> Sincerely,
>
> Cécile Donneaux

Embarrassed by the whole conflagration, I called and left a brief message on the machine. It didn't matter anyway. It was only a matter of time before the press would find me.

Then, just after five on Tuesday, the phone rang. It was Matt. The operator knew he was safe to pass through to me.

His voice spit out in his usual fast pace even at 7:30 a.m. New York time. "Yo, bro, listen, I got an idea for us to take advantage of your situation in India."

"Matt, I'm not in the mood."

"C'mon. Play along. Money is good and this is about money. Now, what does India have more of than almost any other country?"

"OK, Socrates, I give up. What?"

"Over . . . one . . . billion. . . ."

"People."

"Exactly."

"And people die. And what do American medical schools and research hospitals have a dire shortage of?"

"Corpses to do experiments?"

"Smarter and smarter. Dead bodies, man, that's the ticket. You think you could start researching this so when I come visit . . ."

"You are one sick motherfucker."

"No, I am a committed capo-nihilist looking to make megabucks. I'm too old for computers and too thick anyway, so I'm just hustling to make my nut to retire in style. Hey, what's the U.S. got more of than any other country? I'll answer for ya. Lawyers."

Not one month after Castor was buried, the parents of Bobby Skirpan, the leader of the kids who murdered my son, filed a civil lawsuit against St. Vincent's Hospital and me. They claimed that I had neglected their son in favor of Castor and the sons and daughters of those their son had murdered in cold blood.

It was a depraved fantasy. That day I didn't know his name, much less that he was a killer and racist, when I ordered each person to be taken care of in the order I thought best.

My lawyers (Oy, I hate that phrase), I mean the lawyers of the hospital, asked for a summary dismissal.

"Neil, dismissal denied. They asked for an extension and the judge gave it to them. They already asked to depose you."

"Man, can't they . . . this is sick."

"Your lawyer guys will be calling you soon. There's another one gonna handle this now."

I'd dealt with four different lawyers already. Although Matt urged me to hire my own lawyers, I'd decided to let the hospital lawyers represent me for now.

"Matt, gimme the numbers."

"They said fifty-fifty chance of success. With the lawyer discount, you're fucked."

In Matt's Discount Theory, lawyers had the least credibility of anyone except politicians with law degrees. You could only believe 0.5 percent of what they said.

We made plans to speak soon, and I hung up the phone. A little later, as I was going over some paperwork, Holika, unannounced, knocked on my door and waltzed in with her hair up, dressed in a one-piece cotton gray sleeveless dress, with a dark-red cashmere shawl wrapped around her brown shoulders. Until I saw Indian women in shawls, I always associated shawls with Russian babushkas slumped over a stove in a dark kitchen. Holika wore her shawl like a cape; a weapon of the toreador taunting her bull. "Charlie told me you were usually done by now."

"He's back?"

"Yes, just this afternoon. I took tea with Chrystie, the British ambassador's wife and the third and youngest Mrs. Hal Burden." She waited a beat before she tweaked me. "You Americans have invented a new form of legal polygamy for men." She curled her nose and giggled. "I felt the inspiration that you would be most pleased to see me."

"Most pleased since I just had an awful day. Please don't say I look it."

The phone rang again. The operator said it was another long-distance call from the States. She thought it was the lawyers. She put them through.

Holika sat in the chair in front of my desk.

"I gotta deal with this."

She smiled, "No problem. Take your time. I am not going anywhere else tonight."

I heard the phone click. "Hello, you there?"

"Please hold for Bunny Lemaster."

"Who?" This was a familiar name, but no one I'd spoken to before.

"Neil, this is Bunny Lemaster of DWI—Distinguished Writers International—once a screenwriters and authors agency and now the largest arts entertainment agency in the world calling from our New York office." The voice, craggy and assertive, sounded lousy, laden with cigarette smoke and breath spray. Suddenly, dingdong, I remembered why the name sounded familiar. The tabloid media and the *New York Times* tabbed Bunny Lemaster as the most powerful agent in the "entertainment arts." Lemaster's name, when attached to a "project"— books, movies, TV programs, you name it—made the project golden.

Two books and at least one TV movie were in development about the killings. Sarah and I decided to let people do or say whatever they wanted. We'd never participate in such farces. Others had tried to talk to me through friends, the hospital, but no one had found me in India.

"Listen, some people may cower or celebrate at your call. I am not . . ."

"Please, Neil, let us not make rash decisions in haste," Lemaster coolly interrupted me with the pitch already in place and shifted into a speaking voice, not sophisticated and haughty, but with the street-corner charm of the local Queens drug dealer. "I am not so crass as everyone says, and don't be in such a rush to brush me off. Wait until you hear who I have sitting here, the Oscar-winning actor Fred Henry and Emmy award-winning writer Ally Sendar and they want to do a project

on how America now thrives so vicariously through the tragedies of others and you handled the terror with such savoir faire."

"Savoir fare-well," I sighed, and put down the phone.

Holika circled to the back of my desk, stood behind me and rubbed my temples. "About your son?" I nodded as her small hands gently caressed my head and then she leaned over and whispered, "Come, we must go to some place quiet. Safe without a phone to disturb you."

Safe, yes safe. How I needed to hear those words.

Holika rubbed my temples for another minute before she stopped, picked up the phone, and started dialing. "I'm calling the Taj Palace Hotel." She handed me the receiver. "Get a room. If it is booked, tell them you are calling at the behest of Charlie and Chrystie. There's always a saved room."

I did as she asked, and then she gave me more instructions. I told Chandon to take the car home and gave him and Vishnu the night off. I'd take a taxi to the hotel. Holika had given her driver the night off as well.

"Do you always think so fast or did you have all this planned?" I asked.

"I think fast and sometimes act fast and sometimes slow and . . . Do not jump to any conclusions. I will see you in an hour or so. Order something festive."

I took a taxi, checked into a fine room, and ordered champagne and smoked salmon. I hadn't had salmon since I'd landed in India.

When she arrived around 7:30 and before I opened the bottle, she made a call on her cell phone. "Uncle, it is me, I will not be coming tonight. Preeya is feeling down so I am going to stay with her for awhile."

Holika lived in the duality between ancient traditions and the unstoppable rush to modernity. Like so many Indian families, in the villages and the cities, all the generations lived together in one home. "Home" meant one of the houses in the Ashoka Road compound owned by Uncle Vijay, the patriarch of the family. Holika's father, mother, brother, and younger sister lived in the second largest house.

She said goodbye and clicked off the phone. "These days my Uncle starts drinking every night around seven and soon he forgets everything. By tomorrow, he will not remember I did not come. And Preeya, who is a trusted friend whom you must meet some time, knows how to back me up and I will see her tomorrow. We are working on something together."

"What?"

"Something we do for India and women's rights," she said perfunctorily, and kicked off her shoes and curled up on the comfy blue velvet love seat and its three oversized silk pillows. I opened the champagne and poured us each a glass. "Come, sit." She patted the love seat and I sat down. Her head rested on the pillows and her legs relaxed over my lap. We toasted wordlessly. I caressed her bare legs with my left hand. She sat up a bit and I thought that was a sign to stop. She moved her legs as if I should continue. "Please, it feels good. But you must tell me about your son." She wasn't prying or being voyeuristic. She wanted to understand.

"What do you know?"

"Does it matter? Only what the papers and magazines wrote. I do not care about that. Just talk to me."

"It won't be very amusing."

"You have amused me before and I am sure you will again."

For the first time since he had died, I spoke of Castor.

"I feel his missing presence every day. All the time. Even before, waiting for you, I turned on the TV to ESPN—I used to joke with Castor that it should be called the Extra Sensory Perception Network because they had the results so fast—they were advertising their Thanksgiving pre-game show for the football doubleheader. I had to turn it off. Every year I tried to get off work on Thanksgiving so we could watch together. The Lions and then the Cowboys." It didn't matter that football was as foreign to her as cricket was to me. I rambled on and on. Not making much sense, but that day I realized it was the future that I had lost and missed as much as the past. I could live in the images of what was. I could only imagine the images of what was not, never to be. Sarah and I would never see Castor get Bar Mitzvahed, graduate high school, run off to college as we held our nerves in check in fear for his safety, console him after his heart got broken, get married, make crummy life decisions, go off to travel abroad by himself. Never see him have children. I would miss so many little pleasures and torments of life. I would never again think, I am the proud father of Castor Downs.

Finally, tired and tipsy and teary-eyed, I ran out of confessional gas.

"I have never loved anyone as much as you love Castor and Sarah."

"Sarah? I hardly mentioned her."

"You did not say her name once, but she is everywhere by her absence. It is almost as if you are mourning for her, too, but she is not dead. You do not have to pretend that for me."

I remembered that self-assured and unreadable smile I first saw in my office when we were introduced, unaware of what she hid behind it. That night the smile became less inscrutable and filled with compassionate wisdom.

"And what is that? And what of you?"

"There will be time for me." She squirmed around in the love seat and placed her head on my lap. Her eyes now glinting, sucking out my sadness, then I bent over and kissed her and I lost myself in her mouth, her hair. When we came up for air, she sat up.

"Are you prepared?"

I was dumbfounded and for a second, unsure of what she meant. Her swirling tongue reached out of her mouth to her upper lip, and her eyes waited, giggled at me. It had been years since I needed to worry about that question. "No," I said numbly.

"Men," she spit out the word and shook her head, "you are the same all over."

25

110 HOLIKA DRESSED AND left in the middle of the night, while I floated pleasantly in the cusp between sleep and waking, vaguely hearing her assurance that she'd call later that day. Then she picked up the pillow covering my head and leaned close to my right ear. "You will remember not to call my house." Her sister Alka or her brother Ratish often picked up the phone and listened in and I was not yet privileged with her cell phone number.

I tucked the pillow back over my head and fell asleep.

In the morning after a leisurely breakfast of tea and doughnuts in the pastry café located in the lobby, which with the exceptions of the few touches of marble and gold, swirling Hindi symbols carved in the walls, could've been a five-star hotel in Anywhere, AmericaWorld. I left the hotel, walked almost jauntily down the long driveway, a sanctuary path leading into the streets of New Delhi. I jogged across the street and cut through a gas station filled with rickshaws and taxis and cows. Like life in New York, where I barely noticed the thousands of leashed dogs (and we treated scores of dog bites in the

ER) and rats and their shit, I'd become blithely accustomed to the cows and their dung.

I crossed over Humayun Road and went to the Jewish cemetery about three hundred yards down the block, where I stealthily opened the blue gate. The street-families sat outside their tents beside warm fires, preparing for their low labor jobs or begging. The children readied for their ragpicking and maybe, if they were lucky, attending a school for a few hours before resuming their stations for afternoon rush hour begging. I smelled bread cooking over an open dung and wood fire and heard the TV playing with electricity siphoned from the temple. The squatters stared warily at me. I wandered deeper into the cemetery, over a mound of graves beyond the tents. The dogs began to bark; I reached for my mace. Two young boys held them back. One spindly legged young man dressed only in his undershorts and scruffy white T-shirt approached me. "You are Jew?"

I nodded.

"No worry, please come, we watch cemetery for you."

"Thank you." I thought he wanted money and I reached into my pocket to give him some rupees. He waved me off.

Among the newer graves, I spotted the headstone of Hannah Furstenblum, Levi's second wife. I picked up some small stones and placed one on her gravestone. The Jewish tradition of leaving stones rather than flowers on graves dates back thousands of years. Stones became the sign of visitation because they represent a sense of permanence. The Talmudic rabbis thought flowers, which soon wilt and die, were too close to pagan customs. They also calculated with their secret formulas that the soul might hang around for awhile, doing what, the rabbis couldn't say (enjoying a last nosh?), before it took off for destinies elsewhere. They used the same reasoning for the year-long wait to unveil the permanent headstone.

At the front of the cemetery, I placed three small pebbles on the headstone of young Rachel Mulemet. I said no prayer for Rachel, only mouthed soundlessly that I, at least, remembered her.

I started back toward the Taj to catch a taxi home, but in the middle of Humayun Road, mixed in with the cacophony of sputtering engines and clanging horns, was a circling crowd. I saw a woman lying on the ground cradling a child. A man, it turned out to be her husband, head cupped in hands, stood shaking and talking in Hindi. Others yanked at the woman's sari that had gotten caught in the spokes of the scooter, which had flipped out of control. I yelled "Doctor, doctor" and a man grabbed my arm and pulled me through the crowd. Blood oozed from the woman's skull. I knelt down, took off my jean jacket and used it as a pillow and a tourniquet. A young guy appeared with a rather intimidating-looking knife, and sliced the cloth of her sari so her body came free. A woman gently took the baby from the mother's arms. In the snarled traffic someone found an empty taxi, by the time an ambulance showed up we could all be dead. The driver hesitated when he saw who I wanted to put in his taxi. Knowing how cab drivers worked in New York, I waved a five-hundred rupee note in his face. With help, we lifted her into the back of the taxi. The husband, sensing the potential loss of his most needed possession, managed to start his scooter and followed the taxi to the compound.

At the embassy gate, the guard recognized me; he too hesitated before I yelled to let us through. We stopped outside my office and two Marines helped the woman into the examining room. Her husband halted, afraid to enter. I waved him in and spoke authoritatively, though he didn't understand, that it was safe for him to enter. I did a thorough exam. There were no signs of internal bleeding or severe edema. I took x-rays. All revealed nothing serious, only a mild concussion. I put in eight stitches. I wrapped her twisted knee in an ace bandage. The baby seemed physically unharmed.

I called in one of the Indian assistants and asked him to explain to the woman that she should wear a helmet; especially if she were going to ride sidesaddle with a child in her arms. He laughed and explained to me that the law, after a series of revisions to accommodate the Sikhs on religious grounds and women who claimed helmets would ruin their appearance, applied only to non-Sikh Indian men. I asked him to tell her to wear one anyway. Then we called a taxi and I paid the driver to take her to their home; no riding on the scooter yet. They didn't have a phone but I gave them my number and said they should call from one of the thousands of STDs—public phone stands, not sexually transmitted diseases—located all over Delhi, if she got a headache or felt any other side effects.

An hour later Paul Schlipssi, "the admin," and my ostensible boss, who fashioned himself a no-nonsense guy, marched into my office. His step mirrored the erect, stiff-necked gait of a military man, although like so many of his bombs-away ilk, he had dodged the draft during Vietnam by staying in college forever. He declined my offer to sit, preferring to stare down at me with his brown eyes attempting to look tough, as if that would make me feel inferior.

"Listen, Downs." He didn't like me because I was not Foreign Service or military, and I was a pet of Charlie's. "You have a list of people who get treated in this office, no one else without my permission. You've already allowed too many Americans of no account to come here." He leaned over the desk and placed the computer print out of the list on my desk, deliberately turning it until it faced me.

113

"Sure." Donna had already warned me that I'd permitted more nonlist people to come to the embassy than had the previous doctors.

"And next time you want to play 'save the Indians' take her to AIIMS or NDP." AIIMS and NDP were the two largest public hospitals in Delhi. "Treating the low-caste or homeless Indians is trouble. The Indian authorities do not appreciate our beneficence. You have heard about that German doctor?"

I nodded. Dr. Henreich Blaumer, after he retired from his practice in Frankfurt, moved to India and began his own street clinic in Connaught Place, the showcase tourist center of Delhi, peopled with thousands of beggars, whom he began to treat free of charge. The authorities didn't appreciate his interference and arrested him twice, and they kept him in jail for pederasty, of which he was innocent. After years of resistance, they gave him tacit permission to practice if he kept a low profile.

"I'm a doctor first and your employee second." I stood up so we faced each other eye to eye. "I don't care what you or the Indian authorities have to say. I was trained to help people. To save lives and minimize pain. You have your job and this is mine. If I can't help someone bleeding on the street, I'm outta here."

Even Schlipssi wasn't that callous. He nodded. "Just be judicious in the use of your abilities and the magnanimity of your heart."

26

I HAD LOST the three loves of my life: my son,
my wife, and my job. I could never bring back my son. The Sarah
who I knew was gone forever. Then there was my work in the
ER. The one time I needed to lose myself in work and sublimate
my pain, my work became my pain. I couldn't go immediately
back into St. Vincent's. Not come within blocks. Some of the
nurses and staffers cleared out the office for me. I never opened
the boxes. I could not look at the pictures of Castor, and of Sarah
and me. We stored the boxes in the apartment.

We had very little turnover in my ER among the nurses, the
orderlies, the volunteers, and the security guards. It was a second home to many of us, where we laughed at the absurdities
of life, shot the breeze about sports and movies and politics and
family weirdness. Where trust was a necessity with illness and
fear surrounding us. Trust enabled the entire staff to work with
grace and calm during the immediacy of the ordeal and its af-
termath, though a spare few spoke to the tabloids. Some, too
haunted by the enormity of blood and death, moved to other
hospitals or private practices, or left medicine altogether.

It was more than Hippocratic devotion, but for years I thrived on meeting thousands of people who passed through the ER, and unlike the TV hype, most did not have serious life-threatening illnesses. We acted with a cool determination and not with sweaty, soap operatics. The patients all had stories, faces, and languages, and they would fade in and out of the hospital. I would often feel a tinge of regret that I would not forge bonds with my patients. I reassured myself that most of my doctor friends in private practice had mostly superficial, one-time-a-year, let-me-review-your-chart relationships with their patients. Some patients I'm sure I would've loved talking to at length. Others would've been forgotten the second they left my office. I owned no burning desire to specialize in onco-logical evaluations, gastrointestinal investigations, or ventricle incisions. Instead, I got off on the immediate gratitude of the patients I helped.

After Castor's murder, I didn't want to hear their stories. Or for them to hear mine. I didn't want to help anyone with tales of my sorrow while I felt so bathed in bitterness.

I had lost all faith in myself as a doctor. So had others.

Two days after the shivah, the Jewish period of mourning that we observed for three days, instead of the official seven, at Matt's house, Ray Esperenza called. He'd never expected that his job would include managing a crisis this severe. He told me that the hospital was hiring a professional firm, which was fine with him. I thought this call was one of friendship.

"Neil, when are you . . . are you moving back to Chelsea?" Ray was a pretty effusive guy, and that is why he was so good at his job managing hospital egos, but his voice sounded detached.

"Don't know, Ray, it's too soon." I wasn't sure where we, or more precisely I, would be staying. Sarah's and my impend-ing separation was none of anyone's business.

"OK, then, I'll come up there." Apparently, whatever he had to tell me couldn't wait. I thought the hospital brass wanted to offer special gratitude for my work.

Ray arrived the next day with flowers in hand for Sarah. I took them into the kitchen and brought him a can of Coke. He looked ghastly; his shirt stained with sweat and it wasn't that hot. He got straight to the point of his visit. "We all know what you did was valorous, damn heroic. But," he sipped the Coke, "and I don't agree, Neil," he began to have trouble breathing, and he began crushing the still half-full can, "the board of directors thinks it's in your best interest to take some time off. They mean a long time off."

"They're firing me?" If I hadn't still been in shock, this would have sent me there.

"Not exactly, but yeah, dammit, they prefer that you don't come back."

"But I have a contr—" I didn't finish my sentence. Ray, unable to look me in the eye, cupped his hands on his sagging jowls and told me any discussion was futile. I didn't bother to ask why. I couldn't take any more devastation.

They made an offer to pay the remaining three years of my salary if I agreed not to show up. Ever. I didn't agree or disagree.

Matt and a lawyer friend of his stepped in to negotiate for me. They demanded that five years of salary be paid in full up front, and that I would be allowed to take another job. They also secured recommendations and a letter saying that to protect my reputation, it was my choice to move on. The hospital agreed to four years of salary. Matt and the hospital board and their lawyers saw potential lawsuits coming. Matt understood they would need me on their side. Even after Ray's visit, I still naively thought the hospital settled because it was the right thing to do. Matt didn't disabuse me of my notions until

Skirpan's family officially filed their suit. That payoff is why I didn't "need" a job.

For the wrong reasons, Charlie had been right. I needed the embassy job when I first arrived in New Delhi. It served as a buffer between the world outside of me, and stopped me from languishing in the free fall of despair. After helping the Indian woman in the street, for the first time since before . . . , I felt worthwhile. The terrified grimaces of the couple and then their glints of hope broke the frieze of faces in the lost faith of my living death.

Perhaps, if Holika and I had not been together, I would've helped the woman and then let it pass by as another day in the formless, shapeless time that had become my life. During the night as Holika and I merged as one, filling the deep emptiness of longing within ourselves, the shield over an even darker and more protected wound deep inside me began to crack. No matter that she did not intend to make life, I felt life in me. And as we made love, slow and dreamy, her small, strong hands gripped my back pressing for my expanding cock, her praising voice, a luxurious whisper borne on the ancient breaths of the Kama Sutra, urged in the syncopation of breath and words, "Please touch me beyond my body," and the images of Castor and Sarah, who I felt, saw—even waiting for the taste of Sarah when Holika and I first kissed—Sarah's image inside my head as we began, faded and I inhaled and saw only Holika, and when my sperm exploded inside her as she came. The bad air flowed out of me as if I'd been holding my breath for six months. The immense release of the weight of my pain went from falling in on me to falling out, and although this floating above soiled memories didn't last, couldn't last yet, I felt the first lightness of a breath free from despair.

In those moments of lightness, I felt almost like the Neil Downs that I was the moment before I got The Call. It was time to make changes in my everyday Indian life. That meant—as much as trusting my emotions with Holika, for I was clueless where we were heading, if anywhere—finding more work.

All India Institute of Medical Services is the most famous hospital in Delhi. New Delhi Public Hospital is for the down-trodden with conditions ranging from atrocious to OK, where you are sent to die and have a damn good chance of doing so, even if you shouldn't. Dr. Dillip Patel, who I'd never met although he'd worked at Long Island Jewish Hospital in Brook-lyn for years before returning to India, was the medical super-intendent of NDP, as everyone in Delhi commonly calls it. After more than a few phone calls, I got in touch with him.

He spoke with the abrupt irony of a long-term New Yorker, but also the cadences of a native-born Indian.

"Neil Downs? I know that name . . ."

Uh-oh.

"You used to work at St. Vincent's? I am good friends with Casey Freed. I worked under her when I first came to America."

"Really? Casey is a terrific surgeon."

"Yes. Now what can I do for you. Is this about your plea-sure or my business?"

I told him what I was thinking.

"Is a week from Wednesday at 7 o'clock a problem?"

"Not at all." I'd hoped to go sooner, but couldn't object.

"Get here early, take some time and look around first, and then," I thought I heard him suppressing a laugh, "then we will talk."

27

WHILE MOST OF the American staffers rejoiced in having Thanksgiving Day off, I was stricken with the empty terror of aloneness. No matter that I lived thousands of miles from home and that the holiday passed unacknowledged by the billion people surrounding me. Because of my body memory and my sensations, my heart knew it was Thanksgiving. The morning smells of cooking turkey and marshmallow sweet potatoes, the sounds of the parade and baton-swirling babes in miniskirts with off-key bands and football on the television, and the after-dinner hefty belly echoed with the sensations of yearly rituals spent with Castor and Sarah, and before that with my mom and dad. Now, as I desired when I came to Delhi, I was alone. In the morning, still Wednesday night in Arizona, I called Sarah and the voice mail answered. I left my message. "Call me. I need to talk to you about the unveiling." I hated getting innuendo messages; but I still had no sure idea of my plans.

In a display of my Diasporic Jewishness, I went for a pre-sunrise walk in the New Delhi streets. The fall wind had arrived and it was a brisk 55 degrees. The street noise hummed. Even the tent homes along Aurabindo Marg, the main road, remained oddly still. I made my way down the narrow, semipaved and dusty streets past the Aurabindo Market into Hauz Khas Village, where the glitzy shops, galleries, and restaurants weren't close to opening yet. The street ended by the Hauz Khas ruins, a tomb with other smaller buildings overlooking the royal reservoir surrounded by ten-foot stone walls dating from the thirteenth and fourteenth centuries. Now, more of a park than sightseeing stop, it was kept neat and garden-like because of its proximity to the wealthy homes and apartments. As almost everywhere, homeless people lived there, but not nearly as many as I suspected the first time I'd strolled over there. They slept not in tents, which I was told was not allowed, but in straw and mud constructs or makeshift box houses on the grass or on the stone floors of the monuments and tomb.

I stood by the wall that overlooked the dry reservoir bed trying to imagine the life of seven hundred years before. Imagining only reminded me of when Castor, Sarah, and I visited American Indian sites at Telakapakai in Arizona, and we searched the grounds, not to possess but only to touch, for an archaeological memory of the lost and beaten cultures. Unable to find anything more than a few old rocks, later, the three of us bought souvenirs in the refurbished mining town of Jerome.

As the sun rose, I heard Sarah's newly saddened voice hovering inside me.

Sunrises and sunsets filled her with mystical hoo-ha, which inspired her abstract paintings and her belief in humankind. In the cold-aired winter mountain peak sunrises of Vermont and the hallucinogenic colors of an Arizona sunset, she brimmed, content with spiritual uplift. I wondered what she felt sitting alone, gazing out from the top of Thumb Butte in Prescott, what treacherous or vengeful god she saw now.

Behind me, a baby began to cry. I turned and saw the teen-aged child-mother with a bare breast and a baby so small I was sure it was a newborn. I closed my eyes, turned and slipped away. The crying quieted by the suckling on the mother's breasts, but the yelps of hunger pierced too deep and I heard Castor's cries as the doctors prodded and toggled him from Sarah's beautiful vagina. Sarah at first hesitant to breast-feed, vainly fearing it would ruin her figure, then letting him go longer, too long before saying "no more."

Unhappy and ever more diasporic, incapable of escaping my external or internal nightmare, I rushed toward Aurabindo Marg, where the traffic had picked up and I waited, checking to see if it was safe to cross. I looked to my right and was accosted by the six grinning faces of an American sitcom, Big Brother-like from a gigantic billboard. Their series' myopic view of life in New York, where everyone was white, rich, even though they never seemed to work, and didn't have a care except who they dated, was coming to Indian cable TV. From that too, I guess, there was no escape.

Once at the apartment I thought I'd take a Valium and sleep the day away far from poisoned memories and cultural vapidity. Instead Holika awaited me, sitting cross-legged on the couch in the living room, sipping tea that Vishnu had made for her, thumbing through the pages of a new copy of *Mystical Mistakes*. "After you mentioned him, he seemed so important to you, I went and bought his books."

Her perception and her desire to know about him impressed me. I felt the need to say, "Thank you," which I did. She half-smiled, not parting her lips and continued.

"I understand why you wanted to see him. I especially like this passage." She sat up straight and read in a straightforward but determined voice. "'The honest, most difficult leap of faith is to *disbelieve* in god, and to surrender to the mystery of having one life with no return, no salvation, and no final judgment.'"

"It's a good one, but right now I'm having no problem disbelieving but finding faith in the mystery."

"You will. It takes time. I think it is good and very lucky that you have talked to him."

"Me, too." I wanted to say maybe they could meet some time. I didn't feel comfortable making that offer.

"Neil, let us have breakfast and then take a ride."

Holika had not come over that morning particularly because it was Thanksgiving, though she knew I was off from work. We didn't have a sit-down breakfast but picked up some delicious bread and cakes and coffee at the bakery in Hauz Khas Village. Then she drove us over to the Lakshami Temple in the Mandir Marg section of New Delhi. Lakshami is the powerful and popular four-armed female goddess of money and wealth.

Holika had driven by herself. She owned a Maruti, a car made by the Indian government in conjunction with Suzuki. Very few Indian women drove in New Delhi. Hell, I was in no rush to try it. She seemed quite recklessly sure of herself as she negotiated her way. While zipping in between a weaving rickshaw and a moseying cow, she asked me what I knew about the caste system. I said I'd read some. I knew the technicalities of the four major varna or castes—a word the Portuguese used first—and that there were hundreds, maybe thousands of subcastes called *jatis*. The use of Untouchables as a name was banned so they adopted the name Dalit, and any prejudice against them was illegal. I knew there was much dispute on the societal, religious, and historical roles of the caste system. She never interrupted or corrected me.

We parked across the street from the temple and all she said was, "Come." Before entering the temple the Brahmin handed Holika a gold silk scarf to cover her head. We took off our shoes and stepped almost daintily on a red carpet, up and through the sandstone and white marble gates of the temple. She asked me to remain quiet, not to ask too many questions in the temple, and not to give one rupee to anyone. I asked why not. She whispered, "This mafia of Brahmins and Trusts control the money."

We strolled around, reading many of the plaques with inscriptions from the *Vedas*, of battles from the *Bhagavad-Gita*, of the transmigration of the souls from the *Gita*, of the unknowability of the omniscient god from the *Upanishads*. Then she stopped in front of one tablet and leaned her head forward. I carefully read the inscription:

> *For those who are wandering in the world characterized by the veils of birth, death, old age, sickness, and suffering and are caught in the wheel of illusion (maya) characterized by three trends light (*satya*), movement (*rajas*), and darkness (*tamas*), the only way to be saved is to take refuge in god with pure heart.*
>
> —*GITA*

I looked at her, lifting my right eyebrow, understanding why she brought me there and beginning to understand her. Unlike Holika, I was tantalized by the beauty of the structure, the (to me) exotic rituals, the vibrant colors. Her face expressed the same raw frustration I felt when I attended a temple service at home. I wanted to tell her that and more, but she spoke softly with an undercurrent of admonition, "We will talk later."

We walked past scores of people making their offerings. The smell of marigolds and sandalwood dominated the air. As we exited the temple, she gave back the scarf, and the Brahmin, in his orange dhoti, sensed Holika was the wrong person to ask for money, so he focused on me. She stepped between us and said, "We must go."

As we crossed the street to the parked car, I said, "So seriously, unlike our little joust in the library, you too are a total disbeliever."

"I believe in myself, in women. In India. We are a great country. I do not believe in hypocrisies and illusions created by the gods of men." Before I could ask her what she and her friend Preeya were actually working on for the women of India and what her uncle thought of her disbelief, five homeless children saw my face and ran to my side of the car. I reached to give them some rupees. She commanded, "No, do not!"

"Why not?" I was taken aback by the ferocity of her tone and reaction. I understood her reluctance to give the official types money; I felt the same way about the Jewish hierarchy in New York. I'd seen many people react with such callousness to the kids, but I didn't expect it from Holika. "That kid is hungry and that isn't an illusion."

"Please, do not."

I didn't. She started talking to the eldest boy in Hindi. He was about eight or nine and thumbtack thin, with blue-green eyes. They argued, her voice aggressive, his voice brazenly resistant, his visibly cut and scabbed hands waving in disgust. After two minutes, the boy stormed away. We got in the car. A furious Holika slammed her small foot hard on the gas pedal and began to join into the honking madness. When she cooled off, I asked her what that was all about.

125

"I asked him to get in the car and I would take him to a home where he could get food and clothes and off the streets. He refused. He maintained that his life was freer on the street and that I was a rich woman and did not understand."

"Why wouldn't he come?" I was baffled.

"Because he is on something. Maybe glue. Speed. Something. I want to save these kids, and giving them rupees that will be immediately taken away is not the way to do it."

Of course, I'd been so blind. It hadn't registered. What a doctor.

"If you must give them something, give them food and watch them eat it. Their bosses take money from them. That is one reason why I showed you that plaque. Because maya as a philosophical excuse for earthly suffering, and this caste system, which most of the people you meet will tell you is dying away, is not dying. And it must die."

"Not so long ago you said you believed in maya." I said trying to lighten the intensity just a notch.

"No I did not. And we were jesting then."

"Aha, another quantum woman."

"What do you mean by that?"

"Quantum physics has determined that light sometimes acts as a particle and sometimes as a wave. I used to joke around with Sarah, because depending on what she wanted to serve her purposes whether she believed in god or not, karma or not, her right to change her mind or not, she was a quantum woman believing what suited her."

Her shoulders sunk, her cheeks pulled in tightly, she inhaled through her nose as she barely missed hitting a cow lingering on the edge of the road as she pulled down my street and jammed on the brakes too hard, and muttered, "Shit."

"What's wrong? Did I say . . . should I just shut up?" I thought I'd screwed up by mentioning Sarah.

"No, Neil, I know about quantum physics. My husband used to call me the freest of the Free Radicals." Her voice was filled with remorse. She struggled to park the car in an extremely large space, bumping the tires against the sidewalk, then turned off the engine and twisted her torso toward me. Her hands still gripped the steering wheel.

"You must know I sensed right away we shared something deeper." Holika's well-built wall of composure was collapsing, "I promised myself I would tell you today. He died almost ten years ago. It was the hardest time of my life. So, that is why I know, at least, I have empathy for how hard it is for you. His death informs almost everything I do and say, even now."

The subject of her widowhood, even for a liberated, educated woman from Holika's background, was not one for wide public discussion. But this wasn't public; this was private between the two of us. I thought that was all she was going to tell me. It wasn't fair. Or right. Fairness had nothing to do with it. I could feel her ache, but she wouldn't allow me to comfort her as she had comforted me.

"I'm sorry." I made a motion to touch her head. She flinched with her hands and then crossed her arms in an unwelcoming gesture.

"Preeya and I have an appointment with Sharmilla. She runs my Uncle's charities. We are raising money to buy supplies for some villages."

"Can I help?" My question was open-ended.

"No. Not now." She lifted her arm off the steering wheel and started the engine. If she didn't want to talk that was her choice, but I wanted her to trust me. And I knew, no matter our immediate connection, trust takes time.

I stared at her and then away and then at her again. She gazed straight ahead but I could see her jaw quivering. The car engine idled, vibrating the seats ever so slightly.

"Do you know the name of Siddhartha Singh?" She turned forty-five degrees and spoke softly without relaxing her body and hands, which still held the steering wheel as if it were a lifeline.

"No. Should I?"

She inhaled and then her words spit out with turns of anger, regret, and even phrases of lost innocence, not in any linear fashion, but quickly, to get the torture over with fast.

"I wish yes. Siddhartha was from a lower class and caste and the youngest professor at Nehru." I felt her pride in him still. "I was a student. We were married when I was nineteen, eleven years ago now. He was so much older than me—thirty-three," she almost smiled. "It was not an arranged but a true love marriage, so you can imagine my family, especially my Uncle Vijay, was most distraught." Even in the upper castes and classes, the vast majority of marriages are arranged, with the traditional formalities. "Siddhartha was brilliant and with so much vitality. A true Indian nationalist. He led a small group of people who called themselves the Free Radicals. Those who wanted to change my country and make it truly great and free." Her voice trembled. "And then after only two years, he died."

She spoke no more. I leaned over to try to hug her. Her posture refused any tenderness from me. "No, please, I must go." I didn't understand her reticence. I sighed, feeling helpless and unrightfully confused.

"I must go. I will call you tomorrow." She dropped her arms and took my hand in hers. "Neil, I see you are vexed. Later you will understand."

"OK," I squeezed her hand.

"Please, you must go now."

I got out of the car and watched as she pulled away; after all that had happened in those few days, suddenly I was back in time.

28

YHVH
Time

*As a teenager I decided that time—the mortal everydayness of life—
was my enemy. I harbored the arrogant desire to disentangle the
linguistic, mathematical, and metaphysical web that would lead
to a spiritual godhead and defeat everyday time. I imagined that if
god existed, the answers I sought must live in the secrets of YHVH,
the tetragammaton, the mystical four-letter symbol, not yet a word
yet giving birth to all words, signifying the Old Testament Yahweh.
I had faith that the Kabbalistic code, YHVH, the tease of love, the
nom de guerre of god, could be understood, and I, of all people,
could speak the language of god. Of course, I was a fool.*

*Those four letters signifying timelessness, of time beyond
mortal time, are a jester's trick. Cosmic alchemy. I came to understand Time, that one word, was god's fiercest weapon. I understood
how much was given and taken away in time. More than in the ever-
hopeful chimes in the hidden syllables of love. More than in the
self-serving I. Time destroyed and ruled love. Time negated the I.*

Time was the only word fit to do battle with the notion of god. Time was the only word in language not at war with infinity. Time was the god creator's greatest weapon.

My investigations were, even then, more philological than pious. I searched in the meanings of the Torah as a sign, in the alphabet as a code. And I found a fate worse than the eternity of Hell. I found the total exile from god; the reneging of the promise of Kabbalistic reincarnations; the fear of never getting a chance to attend the trial. Worse than the exile from Canaan. The Kabbalah pointed to an exile in a world excluding god.

Upon that full-of-faith precipice of discovery I teetered when the Nazis showed me the way to a place of exile excluding god. I understood that god was the weapon, not time. Time is a gift. During my time in Terezin and Auschwitz I came to understand my *true enemy and the enemy of all of humanity: those barbarians posing as religious paragons who use "god's timelessness" as their most powerful weapon. Consciously or not, they understood time had become finite. And I understood this trick of immortal time is my true enemy.*

—from MYSTICAL MISTAKES

29

BACK IN TIME: Not to the Rashomon moments
of Castor's murder and Sarah's deception. Not to reveling in the
triumph and guilty angst of having sex with a woman other than
Sarah. Nor falling deeper into the abyss of no imminent futures
with Castor. Those obsessive thoughtdreams, and thousands
more, bullied themselves through my head in the next two and
a half days as I cringed in bed or sped to the toilet with a gut-
ripping case of Delhi Belly. This most unphilosophical attack
of diarrhea transported me into the immediacy of elemental
time, when, on Thanksgiving afternoon far from home, this, and
not making love to Holika, signified my official Indian baptism.

Vishnu took a sample in a plastic cup to the International
Clinic, which they analyzed in less than twenty minutes. The
Indian doctors are adept at analyzing all forms of amoebic bac-
teria and parasites, which kills more Indians than almost any
other disease. They correctly prescribe medicines. Unfortunately, many people never got the right medication.

I spent the day in high whimper-and-moan. When Holika
called, I mumbled at Vishnu, "Please ask her not to come over."

I cursed every possible place that I could've picked up the dreaded parasite: some contaminated tea I'd grabbed at a café the evening before. Some "fake" bottled water I bought at the local store. Or maybe, unthinkingly, I'd brushed my teeth with tap water or let slip a droplet from the shower into my mouth.

To keep from dehydrating, I sipped embassy-supplied water mixed with bland-tasting mineral packets. Vishnu, smiling triumphantly, found some Gatorade in the INA market. His smile turned to a frown when I refused to drink *Lhassi*, the milky white concoction of yogurt, salt, and rosewater, the Indian home-remedy for the runs that he made for me. Its smell and taste made me nauseous.

In the vapors of the first night, a 101-degree temperature adding to my delusional state, with the creeping, visceral passing of time I missed my home and suffered hallucinatory tropes of my American innocence dying. Of my barely remembered grandmother happily stirring the mixed greens of her matzo-ball soup and the wispy consternation on my mother's lips as she tried vainly, even using the same fifty-year-old pot, to emulate my grandmother's cooking; of grand games of playground Ringalevio and my father slumping out from the dank claustrophobia of the store's back room and taking me to now-extinct New York City candy stores; as my parents and I vacationed in Montreal and I imagined Wolfe and Montcalm in the Canadian snow, heroes in the French and Indian War who merged into my teenagehood and the unheroes in the wrecked carnage of rice paddies and the limping American behemoth; as Sarah shook her head in dismay as I became emotional while staring at an original copy of the Declaration of Independence as she scoffed at my same watery eyes when we visited the ivy-covered baseball stadium of Chicago, which then seemed as far way as India, and I fulminated over the

uncelebrated May Day Chicago massacre. And I imagined
parochial schoolgirls who would not look at me once they knew
I was an other; until college and Cathy, parochial no more, and
we dreamed our male–female duet in a high-octane jalopy ride
like Ginsberg, Corso, and Cassady flying across the beat up
imagination of Kerouac's America; of the magical mystery
music of the Beatles, who became the stars of Lonely Heart
World, USA; of East Village nights and Mudd Club mornings;
and a fifth anniversary at the Rainbow Room with Sarah sparkling in a cocktail dress and a smile I thought would never
end as we came home tipsy, swilling a 3 a.m. breakfast of
strawberries in champagne while listening to the Fitzgeralds,
Ella on the stereo and Scott from my lips, like a cracked morning in America commercial, as I read to my baby as he slept.
Of our last anniversary at the River Café, where we fretted that
Castor, in no time, would be going off to college, and Sarah
wondered if we should try for another child, and I, looking
forward to enjoying our lives together, traveling, maybe leaving New York, and feeling so content, explained my feelings,
which basically were: No, no way.

Of the day Castor, Sarah, and I drove across the Arizona
desert, which hid conspiratorial bombers and we emerged from
Highway 10 and onto Pacific Coast Highway, and we, even I,
the sunset misser, became engulfed in a sunset of gold—not the
gold of Sutter's Mill or the dyed hair of Louis B. Mayer's
harem—a golden sunset that enchanted Balboa five hundred
years ago. My foot tapped with adrenaline and I pushed harder
on the pedal; the car rushed toward the edge of the physical
America and the beginning of the new, imagined America.
Sarah searched for something on the radio and in an electro-
magnetic epiphany out came the wave-crunching chords of
Dick Dale, the man whose guitar sound is L.A., blasting out

"Hava Nagila." Which jump cut into Lucy, Ricky, Ethel, and Fred singing, "California, Here I Come." And then, in the midst of this vast American panorama of color and money and hope at the end of the twisted manifest destiny, I saw the black-and-white newspaper faces of Oswald, Ray, and Chapman, the isolated, insane assassins wandering through the streets like a single bullet that ricocheted from Kennedy to King to Lennon in a perverted 6-4-3 triple play and then ripped through thousands of others and, and finally . . . landed in my son's back.

The pain in my gut, mirrored in my head, the dream of being home, gone. I missed America no more.

When semi-lucid and bored and waiting for the next expulsion, my guilty conscience nagged, You deserve to suffer for acting like such a hardassed putz to Sarah and betraying her by sleeping with Holika. My left brain answered with a swift, Yeah, but she slept with that asshole Riegle first. So it went for hours while I waited for Sarah's call, which did not come. Logic deserted me, and I thought I'd willed myself sick in some physiological masochism because, at that moment, I would've sworn that somehow, *she knew.* Then I convinced myself I deserved to be sick because Castor had died and I was left alone to give thanks for a life I could barely live. I dismissed those notions of reward and retribution as fairy-dust superstition. What I couldn't dismiss was my guilt toward my dead son, because, no matter how absurd an idea after one night of love making, inside me pounded a traitorous urge to make a child, to replace Castor with a child from inside Holika. To stem the torment and to escape the real-time ache, against my sanguine fantasy wishes, I imagined not only making love to Holika but making a blond-haired, blue-eyed boy with tiny freckles on his forehead and around his slit-like cat-shaped eyes—"go 'way go 'way go 'way," I railed at the unwanted vision—who looked exactly like Sarah.

Unable to flee, I put pillows over and under my head, and like a little child afraid of both the dark and the light, past and future, I curled up in a ball and wished myself to sleep.

30

SUNDAY MORNING AT a little after seven, the phone rang. I answered, though still groggy. Since I received so few calls, I thought it was Sarah. Instead, Holika's voice, despite her question, rushed out with a breathless urgency, rather than modest concern. "Are you feeling better?"

"I dunno. I was sleeping," I grumbled. "But I caught it fast. The meds worked."

"Can you move about?"

"Yeah, I guess. Why? You want to come over?" Passage had slowed considerably.

"Later. Now we need your assistance. My brother Ratish has had another car accident. He is fine, but he hit a girl. I think she is not badly injured. Are you able to meet us at your office?"

I didn't want to go, but it was part of my job, and I wanted to see Holika. Chandon drove me to the compound where the people on duty moved with a hung-over-from-holiday-indulgences languor.

In my outer office, Holika sat on the edge of the leather cushioned sofa holding the hand and caressing the hair of the scruffy, shivering young girl, who she introduced as Ooju, and who seemed more scared than badly injured. Ratish paced in front of them, looking disheveled in his sweat-covered off-white, button-down shirt and baggy tan trousers. His small, bleak eyes peered out nervously behind his glasses, which sat crookedly on his nose. His eyelids twitched open and closed at a frantic speed.

Sensing Ooju's apprehension, I approached her as delicately as I could. Even still, she flinched before I touched her. I whispered, "Ooju, it's OK," and Holika reassured her in a few words in Hindi. She stood not even five feet and weighed maybe eighty-five pounds. I picked her up, cradled her in my arms against my chest, and carried her into the examining room. I asked Holika to change her into a gown. While Ratish and I waited outside, he explained that he was on his way to a meeting, and not speeding or driving recklessly, when the girl appeared from between cars right in front of his car. He hit the brakes and didn't slam into her; he thought he barely grazed her. A group of men and women, who lived in the tents along the side of the road, charged and circled him. He started "freaking out, thinking they might stone or beat me to death." Using his cell phone, he called the police, who – Shazam— with the promise of magic rupees, showed up fast, kept order, and dispersed the crowd.

Holika opened the door and signaled me to begin the examination. Ooju's left leg was swollen and scraped, but I didn't think any bones were broken. "Some of these bruises, I can't be sure, but they don't seem to be from any car accident." To go along with scrapes on her legs and arms, which I cleaned and bandaged, there were lacerations, and what appeared to be burn wounds on her achingly thin wrists and ankles.

Ratish shrugged his shoulders, not uncaring, but in bewilderment.

"Holika, how old is she?" I asked.

"I think eleven. When I spoke to her before she gave me very little information."

"Talk to her. Find out what happened."

Holika spoke to Ratish in Hindi, then he pointed to the outer office and he and I went there to wait.

Ratish took out his cell phone and made a call, again speaking in Hindi. He started to light a cigarette. I shook my head and he stopped. He finished the conversation, hung up, and made sure to look me in the eye.

"Thank you for coming. I heard you had a case of our famous shits."

"Yeah," I nodded. His intense, tightly wound presence did not inspire comfort even while exchanging small talk.

He sucked on the unlit cigarette before talking. "This was not my fault. Truly. I was on my way to give a sunrise talk to some environmental groups on the necessity to clean up and save the Yamuna River. You may have had a touch of the shits, but imagine what the people who drink and wash in that river get?"

I didn't have to imagine: hepatitis, skin diseases, lethal dysentery, lead poisoning from the factory and small-business runoff, and every known and unknown form of cancer.

"We have turned Delhi's lifeline into a sludge pile of waste. I am going to change that."

Wow, I thought, even this me-first solipsist had a compartment of social concern and nationalist determination. "I can't save the river. But don't worry, the girl's not hurt from anything you did."

Holika opened the door and waved us inside. Ooju clung to her side. "I am going to take her to Summit's." Summit ran one of the homes for street kids. "Your suspicions were cor-

139

rect." Holika frowned and her teeth clenched together. "Let us leave it at that."

Holika decided against my taking x-rays of her leg and tests for STDs, TB, or HIV. She understood better than I did how to handle the situation.

As they were leaving I said to Holika, subtly, I hoped, "Please call me later and let me know how she is doing."

Ratish stepped toward me to shake my hand, which I shook back. "This is much appreciated. I understand you did not have to come here." His voice still raspy and macho, but suddenly tinged with sincerity and without its usual sly superiority. "I am having some friends over for dinner before Holika leaves town next week, if you feel up to it, please come. I will let you know the time and day."

Before I could answer, taken aback by the depth of the sting of her leaving without telling me, Holika, still holding Ooju's hand, turned and stepped in front of Ratish so he saw only her back. She spoke with her neck tilted forward and her eyes touched me in ways her hands could not. "Ratish, do not put it like I am leaving forever. I will be gone less than two weeks.

"Neil, now that you are no longer ill and allowing yourself to be disturbed," she tweaked me while communicating with me in a language of old words with new meanings, "I will call you later and look forward to seeing you in less strained circumstances."

31

BACK AT HAUZ Khas, I called Sarah again; no
damn answer. I left another, more urgent message. Exhausted
and still weak, I lay down and took a three-hour nap.

When I awoke Chandon handed me a package that Holika
sent over by messenger, which is an inexpensive method to
supersede the unreliable mail delivery in Delhi. I opened
it with misplaced trepidation for it contained a few articles
and a slim pamphlet with a note clipped to the cover, which
pictured the sculpture of a burning body of indeterminate
gender.

"This might be of interest to you. If I do not call before, I
will see you at your home at eight, tomorrow night. Please make
sure that Vishnu and Chandon are not there. Holika, aka Quantum Woman II."

She was right. Especially after she showed so much interest in Levi I wanted to know more of what made her into the
Holika I knew existed but the depths of which I had only begun
to explore. "The Invisible Burning: The Manifesto of the Free
Radicals," showed me much more of her past and of her diffi-

culties than she than would ever tell me. It was a thirty-two page pamphlet filled with exquisite color abstract and realistic paintings and photomontages accompanied by complementary, impassioned text in English and three languages I didn't understand. The most eerie and beautiful were a mixture of Western installation art and Indian culture shots from a gallery exhibition—found objects like scarves, saris, shoes, all thrashed and cut to show the ravages of society, were placed on walls and hangers.

The first page quoted Bhagat Singh, no relation to Siddhartha but a revolutionary executed by the British: "I have no doubt my country will be one day free. But I am afraid the brown sahibs are going to sit in the chairs the white sahibs will vacate." The manifesto, confrontational in substance and style, condemned the accepted societal and individual practices of mental and physical brutality toward women and lower castes. It called on the emerging educated classes to duly end the caste system, to end a system where it was justified that so many still lived in poverty.

The news and magazine articles discussed the Free Radicals, who took their campaign to the villages and to the major cities, doing ritual burnings to attract attention to their cause and to educate the lower castes. They videotaped interviews with women and men in the villages. The pamphlet, published before Siddhartha's death, said little else about him or the individual Free Radicals except that most of them hailed from the lower castes and classes. This was not a movement for self-aggrandizement but, as the text proclaimed, for the betterment of the nation and the individual.

This gift signaled that Holika, almost a decade after Siddhartha's death remained incapable of articulating aloud her profound, unhealed wounds for someone she loved as deeply as I loved Sarah and Castor. Why she hid her love behind a denial, I was only beginning to comprehend.

The next evening when Holika came by, despite my secret yearnings, I was prepared. I maneuvered her slight body with such airy ease.

Later, we lay naked on our backs in bed sipping tea, listening to a tape of melodic Nepalese music that Chandon had given me. Because Holika had erected interior boundaries that shifted capriciously, or so it seemed, I mentioned, with a curiosity balanced by reluctance, not Siddhartha specifically, but the Free Radicals.

"Thank you for sending the package." She only nodded. I pressed on, ready to stop if she answered again with silence. "It helped."

"Good." Her voice was not terse. This would be a hard conversation.

"They . . . it's so courageous. Do you still agree with what they said and wanted to do?"

"Yes, of course."

"How do you manage to balance your life with Uncle Vijay, going off with Samaka and his crowd, while hanging out with radicals and what you believe?"

"I cloak myself in repentance and say almost nothing provocative." Holika's firm voice came now, not from her throat, but from her rebuilt sturdy interior. "I told you when we first met not to believe everything you hear in India. And not always what you see either."

"Are we back to life being an illusion?"

"In some ways, yes, but a real illusion. I am a spy in my own life. It has taken me years to be trusted again and I tell extremely few people my real agenda."

"Which is?"

"Without sounding grandiose, I am in an extremely fortunate position. Some day, my uncle will pass on, and Ratish, Alka, and I will inherit a great deal of money. I will be in a very strong position to achieve at least my modest goals. I want my country to return to the ideals that its great founders wished for it. If I do nothing more than educate women on the rights of their bodies, then I have succeeded."

She said no more, but I understood she had far greater dreams. Suddenly, the caution and calculation of her speech and her dress, the wariness of her friendships, and her reticence in revealing her whereabouts made complete sense. But a relationship with me, except as an assertion of her independence, did not. I wasn't sure whether I wanted to question that yet.

"Your secrets are safe here."

"Of course, or I would never have been with you and would not be here now." She understood innately she could trust my confidence and that I existed outside her world.

"Now, I am going to the villages for two weeks as a representative of my uncle's nongovernment organization to talk about birth control. But I will talk about much more."

Nongovernment organizations filled the gap vacated by inept state and federal governments and became the most important social institutions in India. They fostered change and gave hope in forms of health, food, and education to the Indian village population.

She placed her teacup on the side table and turned, bent her elbow, and rested her head in her right hand. "I took you to the temple not because I believe, but to show you what those of us who will change India are up against." In the shrine, despite her disbelief, she'd refused to utter a whisper against the religion, as if it still hinted of blasphemy. "But I do believe a pure heart is necessary to live a just life. Siddhartha possessed the purest heart of anyone I have ever met." She closed her eyes. I understood her flight of memory to the unrecoverable past and a future denied. She did not linger long. "You cannot be pure of heart while being a sanctimonious prig and hypocrite. I think you have a pure, if bedeviled, heart."

The phone began to ring. I eyed it as if Sarah's figure might appear like a genie from the receiver. Holika sat up almost playfully. Her eyes did an exaggerated paranoid dart from side to side. There was no sense of jealousy or possessiveness in her. "You can talk. I can go into the living room."

"No, no, I can't. I need to speak with Sarah about when we should do the unveiling of Castor's gravestone. We gotta do a special Jewish ceremony before May. I'm thinking about Christmas, but it may be too soon."

If it were an emergency, my cell phone would start in a second. It didn't.

I sighed. She sat up with her legs crossed lotus style, shook out her mass of hair, and began combing it with her hands. She smiled pensively and subtly began to answer the question of "Why us?" "You are estranged from someone you are still in love with but no longer trust the way a partner needs to be trusted. And it is possible that I will be engaged to someone I love, but am not passionately in love with him the way a partner wants you to be passionately in love."

The phone rang again. I jumped in place. Spooked. This clandestine affair business—and that's what it felt like, even if we were separated—was new to me, and I was no good at it. I talked over the ringing phone.

"If that's true, why are you going to marry Samaka?"

"I told you not to assume that." There was no mistaking the force of her assertion. "But I was at a women's conference last month and a writer, you wouldn't know her, said that many, too many men, still have the mentality of a burner or a scoundrel. I agree. Samaka is neither. He is a good man and he understands what I want to do and supports me." I nodded my head. "And a married woman in India is much less suspicious and has more freedom." I thought I understood her reasoning.

The phone finally stopped ringing.

"Does he have a pure heart?" I asked with impure motives.

She finished combing her hair and tied it back in a long ponytail and did her head bob thingamajig. This time I think it meant my question made her angry. "He loves me purely." She took both of my hands in hers. "This may be hard for you to hear because of where your life is now." My bedeviled heart syncopated faster. "But Samaka is brilliant, open-minded, kind, forward thinking. He comes from the Sudra caste." That was the lowest caste just above the Dalits. "His father had great ambitions for him. He would bring home broken typewriters and Samaka would fix them and sell them and look where he is now. His father changed the family name to Abhitraj. In Hindi *abhita* means fearless and *raj* means to rule. *Samaka* means peacekeeper. Samaka has never forgotten his beginnings or his mission." She looked at me with displeasure for being so impertinent with my question. I still did not understand our boundaries. "And he loves me. And my uncle and father approve and that is important for me now. I know that you denigrate such reasoning."

"Not entirely."

"I too am against arranged marriage, but I arranged this one myself, and in your country more than half of love marriages end in divorce."

"Yeah, I know. I might be entering that exalted second half."

Suddenly, I didn't want to talk any more about Sarah or Samaka. I deflated of good air, and my insides filled once again with bad air of my competing desires: the guilts, hypocrisies and joys and wonder of being with Holika, and the melancholy over all that Sarah and I had lost.

"Please do not look so glum. You smiled so sweetly until now." She massaged my belly with her hands.

"You don't think, saying what you said two minutes ago, it is strange to be here with me?"

"No, because I *choose* to be here now."

"And the question again arises: Why?"

"Stop acting like a silly boy. It does not become you."

I must've looked hurt, although I knew she was right.

"OK, if I must. Quantum physics, attraction of humans is like that of particles that collide and exchange information in a way that defies classic physics, forever linking them. I feel that way sometimes about people, and I feel that way about you."

I couldn't dismiss that theory. No one had ever reduced attraction only to physics but no better explanation came to mind.

"I'd like to have that formula."

"No *man* can ever be trusted with that information. It is too dangerous. Look what you have done with your knowledge."

"I'd rather not."

Her eyes closed and she smiled obliquely. "My father and uncle would severely disapprove." Her lips smacked closed and let out an impish popping noise. "I believe that first day we met that you understood my loss and I understood yours. I see you, and . . . And, you love someone else."

The implication of our impermanence, of her need to express independence wafted in the air between us as we lay there, oddly one together, oddly apart. Maybe fifty years before, we could never have happened, not like this. Holika was from a new India, a new class and breed of independent women and men. Perhaps she would become engaged to Samaka in what was not truly a love relationship and not truly an arranged marriage. In the end, I believed she would go to him. And I, I had no idea where I would end up. My guilt still plagued me, my empathy for Sarah felt crushing, but I also knew I needed to be away, to be separate. To find a place for my loss, to understand the inexplicable of what I had done to Sarah to cause her to lose faith in me, of what my son had done to deserve to die.

"Neil." She turned on her side. "We are good now because we understand the hidden sadness in our hearts." Holika and Matt were the only two people who I'd confided in, not only about Castor, but also about Sarah. "Do you know the famous phrase about the vagaries of the heart from the philosopher Pascal?" I shook my head. "Siddhartha told it to me and I have never forgotten it. 'The heart has reasons that reason cannot know.' You may never know whatever happened between you and Sarah. But you must dig inside her and you. Maybe some day you will understand, maybe you will not. I believe this, and I have done much searching inside myself, what happened with Siddhartha, as brutal as it was, has made me a better person. Harder in some ways, more generous in many others."

"I don't know if that can happen to me. I feel like a worse person. I'm not sure what the hell I'm doing. I obsess on it every damn day. What did I do wrong? What did I miss? And I end up thinking not of Sarah, but of Castor."

She placed her right hand on my eyes and closed the lids and pressed her hand against my head as if to shut out my demons.

"Please, Neil, let us enjoy our time together. The future—I learned ten years ago—is at best unknown and changeable. That is why I am a quantum woman."

I smiled with an inner bleakness.

Holika didn't spend the night. When she left, feeling duplicitous and as if I were being watched, I tiptoed across my room, picked up the phone, and called Sarah. No answer. I tried her brother and left a message on his machine.

I got back in bed. Holika's fresh body smell of mint and saffron penetrated, and for the first time in years, my bed, sheets, pillows, and my body smelled of someone other than Sarah.

The phone rang again in less than ten minutes. I scooted across the room.

"Hello." I said waiting to hear Sarah's voice.

"Neil, I've been calling *you* for hours." Nothing like the accusatory tones of Sarah's mother to instill optimism.

"Romey, what's wrong?"

"Do you mean why am I calling instead of the woman who is still your wife?"

Romey's All-American beauty queen face and figure had allowed her to skate through life. Sarah believed all of Romey's husbands and lovers, whether rich or poor, educated or not, physically or mentally abusive, all possessed two binding qualities: "They got off on fighting with a virago and enjoyed their own and others' misery." I saw that Romey often seemed perplexed by, and jealous of, Sarah's and my happiness and tried to sabotage us. More than once, she offered when Sarah and I argued, "Neil, just give her a good sock across her head." Unwilling to engage with Romey, rarely would I answer. I would shake my head and leave the room, which ended our argument because how could I stay mad at Sarah with her mother so gleeful at our bickering?

Now Romey took unseemly pleasure in taunting me.

"She tried to call you but got no answer. She will call you in a few days. She moved to Santa Fe for awhile."

"Why'd she go there now? Where is she staying?" I felt a sudden chill in my body, a sting in my gut. To hell with my hypocrisy, and I knew I was being a dickhead—I didn't much like that idea, not one damn bit—because Jeremy Riegle owned a ranch in Santa Fe.

"She'll have to tell you the little details."

She paused letting my imagination dwell on her finely tuned phrase of "little details."

"I asked her to stay with me but she insisted on leaving."

"Did the gossipmongers find her?"

"Why are you asking me? If you had stayed in New York and faced up to your failure like a man instead of playing the heroic doctor and running off like a cowardly husband, you'd know where she is and why. I bet you're not even seeing a therapist, if you can find one in *that place.*"

Always unsure of what Sarah told Romey, depending on that day's anger, I didn't know if she knew about Mr. Riegle.

"Here is my new cell phone number, and please don't give it to anyone but Sarah." I gave her the number. "OK, Romey, you tell her to call me anytime."

Mentally exhausted, I got back in bed, watched the geckos scramble across the walls and ceiling, and after I finally fell asleep I awoke within hours, sweating and crying, from the netherworld of a horrific nightmare. A child, Castor in feel, but I never saw his face, only his back, darker haired, maybe even a girl, tugged at my doctor's smock as I raced down the snow-covered streets of Delhi City, New York. Suddenly, the child, still alive, lay atop a burning pyre at the corner of Hauz Khaz and Bowery, pleading, "Daddy let's go, we have to go. You can't stay here or we are going to die. Help me, Daddy. Save me, Daddy," while my mother stood in the grandstand beside the pyre screaming, "Failure, loser, I wish I'd never had a child."

32

152

After denying YHVH, Kabbalah, and the mystics, I searched for significant and slight differences between Yahweh, father of Abraham, and the Christian god, father of Jesus. This is what I concluded.

Yahweh tested Abraham with parricide, which would have Abraham effectively eradicate his heir; thus his, YHVH's, future. If Abraham had sacrificed Isaac, he would have ended his lineage on earth and the Jews would have disappeared before they ever existed, not even leaving a fossil to trace their extinction. God's chosen would have been no more; he would never have seen his son again.

The architects of Christianity improved on this mythical act of parricide. This god sent forth his son to be crucified by the hand of the people. In this vision of heaven the saints and the sinners, even converted Jews, could be saved if they would hear the saving, silent word of their father. This god was secure in the knowledge that he and his son would be one again in heaven.

—from *MYSTICAL MISTAKES*

33

IN THOSE DAYS following Thanksgiving, my life, imperceptibly to me then, slipped from aimless weeks of drifting from one sadness to another, with no discernable distinction in hours or days, to where weeks became rememberable as days and even clear moments. Internally, I still searched obsessively back in time, remembering how Castor hated, absolutely hated, getting his haircut and would give us the silent treatment if Sarah, the only human allowed to touch it, cut it too short. And the one time Sarah decided to take him horseback riding, he bravely got on the horse, which then galloped off away from Sarah and the dude-ranch cowboy. He cried in fear and yelled at Sarah, who blamed me because I convinced him that the only things horses were good for were cowboy movies and betting on at the track. And when he was eight, he decided he was too old to come into our bed and watch TV with us and Sarah tried to lure him back, "C'mon, I'll scratch your back." Leaning to one side, shaking his head, he informed us he'd "outgrown" that attachment and Sarah clutched my arm, forlorn, our son was growing up. So she and I became content cuddling on the couch, watching silly TV sitcoms, holding hands while strolling in Central Park, or looking out upon the city from the River Café. And I wondered, How had our love become so poisoned? I pushed my thoughts out of the past to the future—they suddenly came to New Mexico and inevitably ended with a counting down to Castor's unveiling where the artificially imposed period of mourning should end.

Yet, for the first time since Castor's murder, though it seemed odd, feeling less removed and less sullen, I craved the satisfaction, excitement in the possibilities of working for people who needed my help at New Delhi Public Hospital.

Hundreds, if not thousands of homeless people, living in cardboard and garbage constructs at best, surrounded NDP. They waited for handouts from patients grateful to be alive, for the daily emptying of the hospital refuse, for the tossing of the clothes of the dead, which they rifled through and claimed for their own meager wardrobes or sold.

Chandon declined my offer to come inside and waited in the car, which he parked in a spot reserved for the doctors.

The hospital grounds smelled like, well, shit, filled with excretions, mud, exposed pipes, and sewers. Worst of all, due to a plumbing mismatch in the height of the sewer pipes and hospital drains, the excess runoff seeped right into dirt and soil. If it weren't for the scores of people, I could've easily mistaken the main crumbling building for the barn it was seventy years before, when it housed the U.S. and British cavalry horses. Now, almost six thousand scheduled patients a day and a thousand more in the ER, swarmed into NDP for help.

I entered the hospital through the ER. The smell of disease and detritus pervaded. Beds and cots took up all available space in the halls and corridors. I read the fatigue on the overworked faces of the doctors, nurses, and orderlies.

Most people ignored my presence, but those who didn't gave me a raised eyebrow or a squinting glance somewhere between inquisitiveness and inquisition. Westerners were not often seen in this hospital, where every day those with malaria, typhoid, lost legs, torn limbs, rabies, snake bites, monkey bites, TB, polio, cholera, HIV, and hepatitis B and C, as well as broken-hearted, scorned widows and brides flocked to this hospital. The hospital reeked of death, unlike hospitals in America, which cover the smells of despair and disease with banal art on the walls, new coats of paint, and daily doses of ammonia cleanser. The Indians let the smell of rot pervade, suck into your nose, your eyes. As I walked through the halls, in the faces of the sick and the caregivers, I felt their unhindered faith in a collective mantra: we have survived five thousand years and will survive thousands more. There are more than a billion of us. Let them die who cannot survive— they will be back.

Suddenly the electricity went off for five minutes. This happened frequently in Delhi and could last for hours. The embassy, my home, and the homes of the wealthy and even upper middle classes had their own generators, so we rarely felt the inconveniences and possibly fatal problems of living without electricity. Unfortunately, NDP's generator system was weak and in constant use only in the operating rooms and ICU wing.

Floating in this grayness, amidst a chorus of coughs echoing in the halls, I felt like a clean bronchi inside a giant TB-infected chest cavity.

When the lights came on I needed help because the signs were not well marked. An orderly, who understood some English, took my hand and led me to Patel's office on the second floor. Patel's secretary asked me to wait in the hall. There were no empty chairs, so I stood or leaned against the wall. Patel did not greet me with even a nod as he rushed by five times in the almost half an hour that I waited and watched.

Patel's black hair looked like a bad toupee, falling over, mop-like. He wore black-framed glasses, and the lines on his face leading to his sunken eyes seemed as crisscrossed as Delhi power lines. He sped around talking, never stopping, hunched as if seeking to avoid a random piece of debris that would come zipping toward him and knock him out.

Eventually, he asked me into his cramped office, crammed with files, papers, and assorted paraphernalia. Half the bulbs in the overhead lights were out.

"Sorry about the wait." His tone was flat and unconvincing. He check-marked boxes on a form in front of him on his cluttered desk and still avoided prolonged eye contact.

"No problem," I said.

"So, you want to help me out?" He stared at his dried hands, which played with a ballpoint pen. "How would the director of Metropolitan Hospital," the public and decrepit hospital in Harlem, "react if some Indian doctor called him and showed up saying he wanted to work there?" Finally, he lifted his head, his brown eyes challenged me, and I veered my eyes because the answer would be a loud and derogatory cackle. No way would he be hired. The AMA would jump and scream and never let it happen. Not by accident did the U.S. have fewer doctors per person than any Western country.

The phone rang and Patel spoke impatiently in Hindi.

I mentally prepared my spiel: I understood the difficulty we faced but I was prepared to play the game. I'd done my research during the intervening week and knew they needed doctors desperately and the government had allotted him money for 250 new doctors but each had to be certified by the unions, state, and

federal government bureaucrats and all sorts of oversight com-
mittees. The doctors at the hospital were also threatening a strike
if he hired doctors from out of state. As always, I thought there
was one major way to get around this and all problems in Delhi.

When Patel hung up, he still didn't let me speak. He told
me another story.

"Before I left Brooklyn to come home to India, I took my
family to Disney World. We stayed in what is a respectable
hotel. When we were out eating one night, our room was broken into. Money, clothes, cameras, suitcases, my children's
souvenirs, everything—stolen.

"The hotel said they would compensate me, then they offered almost nothing because they claimed I hadn't properly
locked my terrace door. I refused their offer as an insult. A lawyer friend in New York promised to get me triple what I wanted.
So, I said, 'Please.' And you know what happened?"

I shook my head, afraid to guess. I felt disappointment returning slowly to my gut.

He began repeatedly flicking his wrist, rapping his fingers
against his desk. "The lawyer made a deal with the hotel and I
received not one dollar."

I sighed, "I'm not surprised."

"Of course, you are not. You understand how your country works. I had lived in America for almost a decade when that
happened and I should have seen it coming. Instead, I was incredulous. Both countries are, in my experience, irredeemably
corrupt. It is only in style and form that we differ."

I nodded in complete agreement. He'd given me my opening. "What if I go through the process and offer to work for free?
I have some connections. And," I flashed my ace, "I make a
donation' of a reasonable number to the hospital?"

"There will be a protest. Will you pay a translator to be with you all of the time? And, there are so many people who require 'donations.'"

Almost pleading, my throat tightened, "Can you give me a number?"

"I shall be most un-Indian and be bluntly impolite, there is no number. Normally yes, I would take your offer, but there are consequences beyond money and your connections that I cannot overcome. What if you get sick? Disease is everywhere in this hospital. Do I want to face Mr. and Mrs. Bedrosian?"

"You know them?"

"Well enough that if you gave Mrs. Bedrosian TB," he tapped his head with the knuckles of his left hand, in another religion it would've been accompanied by an "Oy vay," "the wrath of the destroyer would pale in comparison."

We both laughed. Patel had been humoring me. He could never have let me work there.

"Change comes very slow and very fast to India. If there is a change, I will call you."

My interview and hopes for fulfilling work ended right then.

34

ROMEY'S ACCUSATIONS ECHOED in my head as the unmentionable, if not universal, small, personal, unwanted, and feared words that could become truths: her truth that I was a coward hiding in India, a truth that pressed harder and harder against me in those first few weeks in December.

The morning after meeting Patel, the Ambassador car got stuck in a traffic jam behind a bus blowing out diesel fumes, while every car, taxi, and rickshaw from Delhi to the Pakistani border obeyed the blue bus's "Please Horn" sign. I'd taken Holika's advice and stopped giving out money. My daily ration of fruit and bread was already gone when a scrawny woman, with her naked baby tucked against her chest, pawed at the closed window. I wished I were invisible and I could reach out, swipe the baby from her arms, and drive away unseen. Instead, our eyes locked and I saw that she was high, and despite my guilt, I understood a few rupees would do her no good. I tucked my head into my chest and closed my eyes, still feeling her slack-jawed stare of practiced need. Chandon began arguing with her in Hindi. She shook the baby at him. Then the cell phone rang. My heart raced once again hoping to hear Sarah's voice in this wanton game of tease, but a voice that wished it were a cudgel stick pounced out in a harsh and nasal accent.

"Neil Downs, Lee W. Corricelli here."

Yeah, of Karpstein, Forman, and Corricelli. They, I had come to know from papers faxed to me by my lawyers, repre-sented the family of Bobby Skirpan.

"How'd you get this number?"

"That is not of your concern."

Not even Romey would be that nasty, so I figured there was another explanation.

He smugly informed me that he "had been alerted" that I'd made plans for Castor's unveiling, which meant I was coming to New York. Stunned, I didn't answer him with a "yes" or "no" because I needed to talk to Sarah before I made any official plans. I hadn't mentioned any date to "my lawyers." Only Matt, Holika, the cemetery coordinator, and the rabbi knew I was contemplat-ing a Christmas Day unveiling.

I gripped the phone. "How do you justify your existence? Extorting money from dead people."

"I don't think it is in your interest to get personal, Mr. Downs."

"Your clients' kid killed my son, and I shouldn't get per-sonal? I did not kill anyone, unlike the child of your client."

"That is a debatable point that we will determine in court. Have a good day or is it evening there? And I hope to be meet-ing you and your wife soon."

I hung up and slumped down in the car, which hadn't moved ten feet. I felt trapped worse than in a stalled subway car under the East River, rightfully anticipating a dreadful next few days and long nights of hellish phone calls to Judy Ludovicci-Lint and John Linscombe. This was the newest duo from the team of lawyers who'd been assigned to work my end of the case. I needed to talk to them, not only because of this call, but because I hadn't set a date for the unveiling.

Ludovicci-Lint let me know that Karpstein, Forman probably paid off a worker in the cemetery to find out the schedule of the unveiling. They'd also hired a detective who found Sarah in Prescott. I surrendered to my anger and let loose with a few choice epithets at Ludovicci-Lint and Linscombe for not telling me this before. For trying to spare me the ugliness of litigation. How could I explain to them that I was afraid it was not the detective who chased Sarah from Prescott, but her desire to see Riegle? More afraid of what Karpstein, Forman might know.

According to Ludovicci-Lint they'd subpoenaed Sarah, which was way out of line. Normally the request was made through the lawyers. Ludovicci-Lint assured me she would quash it with no problems. It was harassment. This only displayed the dirty, no-holds-barred scare tactics they were ready to use and this aggressive ploy would backfire on Karpstein, Forman when she moved again for a dismissal. She would get an unlimited extension of Sarah's deposition; they would invoke husband/wife privilege, which could exclude her altogether, but they still wanted Sarah to testify. "Sarah will be a perfectly wonderful witness for our side." Ludovicci-Lint spoke in a low register, with accentless, quick bursts. "The aggrieved mother being harassed. Besides," she asked, almost rhetorically, "they can't learn much from Sarah about you, can they?"

"About me? Nothing that that will help them. Nothing." I answered with a flawed truth. If Karpstein, Forman found out about Sarah's whereabouts for those missing hours that would lead to a whole slew of "reasons" for my "choices" in the operating room.

Ludovicci-Lint also delivered an encore of delightful news. The families of the other murdered children and teachers initiated two more civil lawsuits, one against the families of Kickham, Skirpan, Graper, and Tabaldi, and the other against the city and school board for lack of security. This was no damn surprise. Within days of the slaughter the parents of the wounded and dead found letters of solicitation from a score of lawyers in their mailboxes, under their doors, and on their phone machines. I wanted no part of either suit.

The prospect of my sneaking in and out of New York now near zero, I resigned myself to being deposed, not to being exposed.

In the midst of this swirl of conversations and faxes, Charlie called. "Downs, we need to play tennis."

It had been almost a year since I last played, when Castor had begun, unquestionably to please me, to take tennis at Stuyvesant, and we had started hitting the ball on weekends at the court inside the seminary on 10th Avenue, which was associated with St. Vincent's. The summer before we went to an early-round afternoon session of the U.S. Open, which, I think, he enjoyed almost as much as I did. Probably because I did.

As my mind wandered and Charlie talked, a staff person brought in a folder that contained three newswire printouts and handed it to me. "Downs, you have the folder?"

"Yeah, just got it."

"Take a look. We'll talk tomorrow morning at seven at the courts."

I read the printouts. Luisa Torres, mother of fifteen-year-old Elissa Torres, who was killed instantly and never made it to an ER during the massacre, committed suicide three days after being interviewed for a coming *Newsweek* magazine article: "Stuyvesant: Six Months Later."

I'd met Elissa. She belonged to a group of older girls who doted on Castor. I knew her mother as well. Luisa was a single mom who'd worked for years in the Woolworth's on 14th Street. When it closed, she found other low-paying sales jobs. She lived on Avenue B in the gentrifying streets of what she still fondly called Loisada.

Luisa brought Elissa to the ER after Castor told me that Elissa suffered from asthma and wasn't getting the proper care. Like so many people without health insurance, and many of our patients, they used the ER as their primary line of defense against illness. During those visits I learned that Luisa existed for the sake of her daughter's future, which seemed so bright the second she buoyantly stepped through the doors of Stuyvesant High School.

After Luisa spent a lonely Thanksgiving Day, on Friday, after leaving never-answered messages with *Newsweek* staff reporter Julie Earl, and the grievance counselor hired by Stuyvesant, she trudged to the church on Avenue D where she lit a candle for Elissa, after which she went home and poured herself a glass of Jim Beam. Then she took her unregistered .38-caliber revolver, and shot herself once in the heart.

Reading about Luisa scared me. I wanted to call someone, send flowers, do fucking something. I wanted to speak to Sarah.

I wished I knew if Luisa had other family. I didn't want to go online and read about more than I needed to know. Too much evil would surely invade my screen. Luisa's reason for doing the interview baffled me until I thought about her aloneness, her need to speak of Elissa. How speaking aloud brought Elissa to life for those minutes when Ms. Earl treated her as if she were her best friend, as if she cared, as if Elissa were still alive, as if the tragedy could be undone. And then, after Earl faded into her upscale world, Elissa's sweet voice and silly, embarrassed laugh repeated in Luisa's head until it faded to this: Elissa, my Elissa is never coming back. All Luisa's hopes and dreams for her daughter collapsed into a vacant solitude shifting between excruciating pain and feeling almost dead, so she finished the job. And that, I understood.

No matter that Sarah and I always refused to talk to the press; that wouldn't stop them from hunting us down. I thought a follow-up call or a visit to the temple to talk to famille Donneaux might be in order. I thought I'd talk over my options with Charlie.

We met at the club where I felt out of place among its manicured gardens with women kneeling on hands and knees snipping and shaping the flowers with scissors, perfectly swept clay courts, and Victorian Age rules that all players wear whites, which I bought the previous evening.

Charlie pretended that these games meant nothing to him, but he hated losing. I cared less now than ever before. I'd insinuated that a doubles game suited me because I was slowed down from my dysentery and being in lousy shape. "Cut it, I don't want to hear any excuses out of you when I whip your ass," Charlie ordered in his mano-a-mano voice.

Before we started, he stretched and flexed. Despite his growing midsection girth, Charlie kept in damn good shape. I stood rather inertly, feeling brittle. He put his right leg up on the bench and leaned forward to stretch his calf and turned his head to me. "You read the papers I sent over?"

"Yes."

"I fixed it so *Newsweek* and *Time* will not approach you." Charlie was way ahead of me.

"How'd you manage that?"

He finished flexing and opened a new can of balls. He bounced them off his racket. "*Newsweek* will be getting an interview with Hal Burden about Environ's nuclear projects and their benefits to India. And you'll soon be reading an exclusive interview by Madame Donneaux with Indian Prime Minister G. B. Sowat in *Time*." That was a major coup. Sowat was a notoriously tough-to-get interview.

"Charlie, why do I deserve such preferred treatment?"

"Cause you're so cute." He tossed one tennis ball at me, which I caught. He held the other two in his hand and tapped my butt with his racket.

"Come on, Charlie."

"Dammit, Downs, you saved my only son's life."

He eyeballed me up and down with that peculiar American pathetic frown of pity and pathos that made my stomach implode. I gnashed my teeth behind my widening, closed-mouth grimness, because I had no damn answer—and I felt pathetic.

"Let's play, Downs."

No more needed to be said. Charlie played fast. No rest between points. No small talk as we switched sides of the court after the odd games. Charlie played tennis as if it were football: the harder you hit, the better. But like so many macho players, he hit the ball into the net or out as often as he hit a winner. His off-the-court strategic caginess gave way to the impatient foolishness of the Buffalo street kid. He caustically made fun of my style as "girl's tennis," because I used my speed to keep the ball in play instead of slamming away, until he eventually screwed up. He beat me in the first set. Then I found my stroke, got in a mental safety zone, started to hit to the corners with my shots, keeping him on the run, then bringing him into the net, where I could easily lob or pass him—which pissed him off even more. I won the second set.

In the third set I rushed out to a 3-1 lead, and he blistered with anger. Not that I felt sorry for him, that was impossible, because he wanted to win so badly, and he had been so good to me and I needed his goodness. I began to purposefully hit out on my forehand, hit my dink shots into the net. He never doubted his victory. He even let slip a mild boast, "I thought you might get me 'cause of these old legs."

I smiled benignly like a good loser and he patted me on the shoulder with an aging, avuncular pride as we headed to the showers and then ate breakfast in the club with other embassy and official types. During breakfast, I realized that for much of the hour and a half I actually had fun with my endorphins exploding. We planned to play again soon.

Outside, while waiting for our separate cars, I decided to mention the two other favors I wanted from Charlie and that I'd been too intimidated to broach before. The first was less threatening. In the midst of the hubbub of the last few days, Levi had called when I wasn't there and asked Donna if he could come in for a consultation about his knees. Initially, having never heard of him, she said no. Since the to-do with the Indian couple and Schlipssi, Donna was under "no bend" orders to get *his* permission for any nonemergency, nonauthorized list cases. Levi was on no list. Schlipssi certified his denial. I felt too embarrassed, because I hadn't yet taken up his offer to meet for lunch, to call Levi back until I had good news.

"Consider him your new patient."

"I'd also like to do some research on someone—and I need your guidance."

"I'm listening." His car pulled up. He opened the back door.

"Siddhartha Singh."

He raised his eyebrows, his control and tact steadfastly back in place, he chose his words carefully, "I'll take care of it, but don't push your friendship too far." I wondered if he meant my friendship with him, or if he suspected that Holika and I were trysting the night away and not simply visiting Hindu temples.

Then, it seemed, he abruptly changed subjects with a question that superficially expressed compassionate curiosity, but in Charlie-speak was no question at all. "Hey, how did you enjoy your foray into the world of New Delhi Public Hospital?"

"H . . . how . . . ," I stuttered and stopped because I hadn't told him about my meeting. That reinforced my fear that Charlie kept tabs on everyone and every action, even of a nonpolitical entity like me that transpired in his circle and outside, too. I felt like a dope for not realizing that Charlie, or one of his assistants probably, had spoken to Patel on my behalf. "Not much. And even less as I think about it now."

"Yeah, it's a sinkhole over there, and I've warned you, you need to be careful where you step in Delhi."

35

SARAH AND I met when she was twenty-six and I was twenty-four, when Matt dragged me along to a summer rooftop party in SoHo given by a group of artists, one of whom we knew from undergrad school. Sarah intended to come with the guy she'd been dating, and meet up with a group of friends. Earlier that evening they had a tiff, which progressed into an official breakup after she decided he lacked serious-contender credentials. He decided to go home. So she came to the party alone, and instead of her friends, she met me. I soon learned that finding a replacement boyfriend so quickly fit into her routine state of her affairs; she'd never gone half an hour between boyfriends since she began "dating" at the age of sixteen. Despite my initial trepidation over her impulsive, self-assured assertiveness, from the moment we committed to each other on a windy beach on Orient Point on the eastern tip of Long Island, Sarah *never* gave me reason to doubt her love. Never gave me one reason to feel jealous. If men flirted with her in front of me, she blew them off instantly. If some art amoeba began doing his version of the locomotion, she brought me along to lunch or a gallery hop and that ended that. And I never gave her a reason to doubt me, though, early on, she often searched for clues about patients, nurses, or the few female interns and residents, never admitting her jealousies, which led to some inane arguments. Thankfully, Debbie, though no strict Freudian, worked with Sarah—the girl with a father who physically and emotionally abandoned her, a mother who emotionally abandoned her and physically discarded her to benefit her own selfish needs. And Sarah grew into a secure woman who found in me a partner of unquestioned loyalty who would never abandon her, until . . .

So, quite consciously fearing those long-ago patterns were repressed but not dead, my defenses were as high as my hypocrisy when Sarah finally called.

Immediately, I heard the quivering tightness in her chest as she spoke my name, "Neil?"

"Hey!" I yelled joyously. "Finally."

"Yeah, it's been tough. After that fat bully found me and shoved his ugly hand in my face as I was leaving the gym on Whiskey Row," that's what the locals called the town square in Prescott, "I had to get out. I tried to call you but you didn't answer and I had to leave fast." She spoke speedily as if trying to justify why she hadn't called me back.

"You in Santa Fe?" I tried to sound nonchalant but my breathing became labored and I coughed to cover my nerves.

"You OK?"

"Yeah, it's the Delhi pollution. Not like Santa Fe."

"Yes, it's so clean and clear. I've always loved it here and it seems safe. For now."

She didn't volunteer exactly where or with whom she was staying and I didn't ask.

We talked about Luisa Torres, and her voice turned taciturn, so I shifted subjects, trying hard to make her laugh, regaling her with my failed exploits with Patel at NDP and of Charlie's ego on the tennis court, but the laughter chirped out forced and the lighter mood felt frail. I tried to tell her about Levi, whom she knew I idolized, but she dismissed it with a brusque "That's nice." This transparent window between us let in refracted light and hid much of what we each did not know.

Sarah had spoken to the lawyer who handled her art business dealings. He compared Karpstein, Forman's in-your-face tactics to the lowest form of lawyering. He suggested she hire her own representation if Ludovicci-Lint refused or failed to get her out of testifying.

170   "Please, Neil, I can't live that day out loud again. I can't." Even more forcefully than her words, the lament of her voice begged not to face her questioners.

"They have to listen to me."

"You hope." Even before the hospital's graceless behavior and the new lawsuits, Sarah didn't have much faith in the class of lawyers and business people whom she endearingly called corpo-rapers. "So, what do you think for . . ." she could not, had not yet uttered the name "Castor" aloud, "the unveiling?" Again, I imagined her neck twitching anxiously. Her skin contracting so tautly that her veins and arteries thrust out looking like constricted straws.

This question was loaded with so many other questions, questions too soon asked and without answers, possibilities and lost possibilities that I couldn't yet accept, and imaginings I couldn't suppress—and in that instant I chucked my prepared answers about the unveiling. "Easter, Easter Sunday. Everyone will be too preoccupied with themselves to care about us."

"Oh," the falling hope in her lowered voice was palpable. "I thought maybe that you were coming during Christmas and New Year's."

"I thought about Christmas, but it's too soon." I spit out my words too fast and without forethought. "I'm not done mourning and I want to make sure I figure this shit out with the lawsuit and you know I always had big problems with those holidays."

"Sometimes you liked New Year's."

"Sometimes, but not this year."

"Don't you have any time off?"

Inside that question, she posed the real question, "Can we meet?" and my guilty silence obscured the truth that I had loved spending New Year's with Sarah. Not this New Year's as I pictured her strolling along in the red dust and in the brisk air that whips with the comfort of need, and I saw her hand-in-hand with Riegle.

My pause lasted too long and the despair of our lies by silence became verbalized taunts and admissions seeking blood. With the precise vector of words and emotional pitch she proved her power to still hurt me and make me feel like an asshole in one swift sally of verbal projectiles.

"Neil, I came here because I told you I was lonely and I feel so broken, my heart, my nerves, and you were so distant when we talked." Her voice, instead of fragile, popped out in short cadences of certainty that she chose right by moving to Santa Fe. I saw her; her disappointment hiding in her twitching neck and tightened jaw turning angry, bringing out her fortitude.

I did not answer. She repeated herself. "You sounded so distant, far away, like you were never coming back and I felt so lonely."

"I understand," I said, "I'm lonely too."

"You're still alone?" Her bluntness surprised her, "I mean . . ."

"Yeah, Sarah, still alone." I thought for seconds about the comfort I'd gotten from Holika, but whose elusive presence and my belief that I was no more than a foreign interlude before she eventually committed to Samaka left me chillingly alone. "By myself with a future of more . . ."

My words, though both true and untrue, bristled not so much with hypocrisy but with a deeper untruth, that by keeping Holika my secret, I hoped to hurt Sarah more if she believed I remained alone. Jealousy would drive her further into self-justification and I wanted to remain the victim, wanted her to feel traitorous for running to Riegle, whose name she had not even mentioned. I thought the old Sarah would see through the transparency of my words, but not this Sarah.

172

"Neil, what I did was indefensible, stupid, deceitful—almost anything you can think of I will accept. I've condemned myself, but *I did not kill Castor.* I can't blame myself for that and you can't either. Just as I can't blame you because he died in *your ER.*"

She stopped. Her words drilled through me: the image of Castor limp on the operating table, bleeding, *dying*, while my hands . . . no. I, Dr. Neil Downs, failed to save him, my son. This memory that haunted me every damn day, almost every waking hour since that moment, for the first time was said aloud by my wife, the mother of my son.

Silence from both of us filled the space between Delhi and Santa Fe. Suddenly, tears of unbearable sadness for our dead son.

This space between us widened beyond the physicality of thousands of miles with these new accusations, hers spoken and mine silent, and there was no mending the wounds. Not then.

I waited and wished we had not talked about this until we were face to face, but it was too late and so I lied aloud. "Sarah, I don't blame you and I certainly don't blame myself."

"Are you sure?"

"Yes." I felt shitty again and wanted to be able to reach and hold and reassure her with my touch. Instead, I hoped the emotion in my voice could console her. "Yes, I'm sure."

"Do you miss me? Because even when I'm hating you and I know you're hating me, I miss you. Is that sick?" She didn't wait for an answer. "I *need* to talk when I can see you, to explain things I never got a chance to explain to you in person."

"I know but it's so complicated and I miss you too, and I'm afraid." I stopped, censored myself. I didn't know if what I missed was a past or future Sarah. The present Sarah disappeared into the past the second my words flowed out of my unconscious creation of language to consciousness, and our nuanced, secret pact in the meaning of words and actions, which she once understood as had no one else, seemed lost.

"Neil, I'm afraid, too, but the longer you wait the more afraid I get." She let those words hang, penetrate almost as a threat, not as an ultimatum, simply Sarah reacting to her inner self, a woman no longer youthfully impulsive, but a woman of action. "I hate this, this purgatory."

She was flailing, falling away from me and I couldn't let her. "I promise I'll think of something. I will."

"Neil, what'd you say? I couldn't hear you."

So terrified of my own words, I'd spoken too softly. I repeated myself. Said I would call her soon on her new cell phone number and hung up still aching for her body, her smell, her companionship, her hand gripping my arm for comfort as we slept, her caress of my hair, her lips waiting for my kiss, kissing my cock, my head between her legs, my tongue caressing her soft, silky vagina, but I could not take refuge in fantasy sex. Feeling the guilt of my lies and hypocrisy and pain of fevered jealousies, I climbed to the roof of the house and stared into the starless, miasmic, and darkening sky of a suddenly blacked-out New Delhi.

In the not far distance I heard sirens and sniffed the smoke dissipating into the already unclean air. The lights in the nearby homes with generators sputtered on like low wattage fireflies. Chandon turned on our generator and came up with a flashlight to fetch me. Instead of going down and staying inside we brought up a kerosene lamp, which almost all houses had for just these occasions, and two Kingfisher beers.

At first he'd hesitated drinking with me, it went against Indian class and caste propriety, so I made a deal. He would teach me Hindi while we shared a beer or two. That night as we held our Hindi lesson on the roof, Chandon gazed out with his accepting-of-life gleam and uttered my favorite phrase: *Ye hai India*, a catchall expression which meant, This is India.

As he swilled his beer, the ambivalent waves of desire and repulsion roiling my gut, I murmured, "Tell me this one: cowardly husband."

36

Still, amongst all this tragedy, it is even more tragic what happened to our great leader. The Fuhrer, a hero of Olympian stature, who had acted so honorably to his fellowmen, with his empathy and compassion for the Jews, joined his brothers in whatever heaven they are all entered, by taking his life, and that of his wife Eva, with his own hand.

And now, as I write this, when the new century dawns, after so many years of trying to understand, I still do not understand WHY the Jews suicided themselves. Even less, do I understand why there are those who blame the Fuhrer and the German people for what happened to the Jews.

They came to their new nation willingly. They rejoiced at their hope from freedom from their oppressors. We have the proof. The photographs. The films. Their words. Their god abandoned them. They did it to themselves. No one else. My father was there. He knew. He saw. He wept. And he told the truth. And now I have told you the truth.

—from *CHAMBER OF COMMERCE*

37

THE CITY ELECTRICITY remained off all night in my neighborhood. The local streets were still closed the next morning and a worse than usual traffic jam ensued, so I arrived almost half an hour late at Chanayakapuri. A researcher, who impressed me as a spy and who needed a simple blood test for his high cholesterol, paced in the corridor outside my office. Waiting in the outer office was a woman who worked with the cultural attaché. She suffered from ulcerative colitis and had an appointment for a flexible sigmoidoscopy. In two adjacent chairs sat a woman and her teenage daughter talking in waiting-room quiet tones to each other, neither of whom I knew, but who received the Schlipssi OK. The daughter had an infected spider bite on her leg that needed to be drained. On the cushioned sofa, peeking out from behind *The Times of India*, eyes unseeable behind dark glasses, sat Levi Furstenblum.

After getting Charlie's OK, I called Levi and asked him to come in the afternoon when it was less busy. Obviously, he didn't listen.

"There was a fire in my neighborhood," I said as I went straight to Levi. His presence forbade any grand or even formal welcoming. "I have to take care of these people first."

"I can wait. I have my newspapers," which he rustled in the air. As he did I spotted the two headlines—"Bollywood Hot Bods" and beside that, "Woman Dies in Kitchen Electrical Fire." Underneath were photos of one actor, one actress, and another of a street close to my home.

"That's the one," I managed to say both rather feebly and a bit too emphatically as I pointed to the newspaper. No one reacted in any special fashion and I started the day's business.

It took over an hour before I got to Levi. He'd fallen while walking in his apartment and bruised himself; he'd become more worried that his bones were deteriorating faster now. Life in a wheelchair did not suit him.

I, not Donna, accompanied him into the examining room. He scoffed when I asked if he needed help changing into his gown. I left the room. When I returned, Levi almost snarled. He looked quite miserable. The sleeves on the gown flowed around the chaffed skin of his arms. I came closer to take his blood pressure and I saw the numbers.

"Another gift I couldn't return." My eyes, against my will, flashed away. Levi said, voice without rancor, "You haven't seen this before?"

"Yeah, a long time ago. One of my Hebrew School teachers, but he always wore long-sleeved shirts, even in the hot weather."

Poor Mr. Hershkovitz. I'd caught him by accident in the seedy Hebrew School bathroom one afternoon when he had his sleeves rolled up as he washed his face. He bowed his head as I gawked like an idiot at his incredibly muscular forearms marred by those numbers. We had not liked each other. I'd been a troublemaker, he a cranky disciplinarian. After that day, I became a model student of quietness, if not studiousness.

"Too bad for him." Levi's past was his future, and he possessed no shame. With his burial, he would unashamedly take the signature of earthly depravity to his grave. Which would be, judging by the results of his EKG, blood pressure, chest x-ray, and complete blood chemistry, some time in the not-so-near future for he was in remarkably good health. After the exam we sat in my office. He sat stiffly in a slightly worn tan leather-cushioned chair. I sat behind my desk in a leather swivel chair. My desk exemplified my personal chaos with papers disseminated in no order. Donna tried to keep the files in order for her sake as well as mine, but it was a futile attempt.

Levi scanned the small room and saw I had in no way personalized it with pictures, paintings, diplomas, or knickknacks. It looked pretty much the way I found it.

I told him I felt confident he would survive the long recovery of double knee replacement surgery. The x-rays showed a complete degradation of the bone and I imagined he had almost no cartilage, which would make the operation difficult, but still manageable.

I offered to call Privat Hospital where he could get MRIs of each knee, as well as a bone density test, after which we'd then meet. He agreed. He asked me for pain pills. "The pain is more formidable than ever and I am no masochist." Tylenol with codeine was not strong enough, made him sweat, and gave him constipation. I wrote scrips for Darvocet and Vicodin. He nodded as I warned him to get the drugs from specific hospitals or pharmacies. Although you could get almost any drug with a prescription from any street pharmacy and most were straight, some knowingly and some not gave out dummies or potentially dangerous versions of the drugs. I handed him the prescriptions and he took them from me. "Be careful with them," I warned again. He nodded and his hand shook slightly, but *he* noticed *my* nerves. "Are you having more unsettling problems? Today you seem, perhaps more visibly tormented than before."

"Do I really seem worse than before?"

"Yes, pale with that unmistakable ache of incompleteness that is not visible but can be seen." There was the note of the mystical in Levi's insight, but he was right.

"I've been talking to my wife and making plans for my son's unveiling instead of his Bar Mitzvah." I stared at the floor. Suddenly, I felt the heavy sadness of unwanted tears but did not want to cry in front of him. I inhaled and raised my eyes. "I still feel lost. And if I can't stop the voices in my head—especially that rabbi's—of people saying 'It was meant to be, it was god's will,' I will lose what's left of my sanity."

179

"Yes, that absurd phrase was one most often heard at Terezin and Auschwitz. I once thought it trite or facile, but the camps reduced everyone to an almost childlike begging for answers."

"I'm still waiting for my answer."

"I remember the day when it became so clear to me, when I rejected god forever. It was not long after the murder of Leah and Ottla. I had been interned for a week in a tiny cubicle without food, a bed, anything, not even a hole for my excrement. I was always wet from the water continually dripping into that hellhole."

"How fucking sick." I couldn't think of a word evil enough, but "sick" had to suffice. "I feel like such a self-indulgent wimp."

"Stop. You must know how I feel about the art of comparison suffering." Levi had written that the Holocaust was an emblem of evil and cruelty, which is a chart of human history.

That to deny any individual his or her tragedy is to cheat each individual person his unique humanity; that no human's loss is any greater, in any way more severe, than yours because it occurred in a monstrous fashion or unprecedented number. That Hitler's trying to erase the Jews from history was the same as someone trying to erase your single lineage and history on earth. "There is no need to downplay your pain."

I nodded. I wondered for a moment if he were coddling me.

"Now, one morning soon after I got out of that cubicle, Schneerman and I watched helplessly as a boy who was turning thirteen that week—the time *he* should have been Bar Mitzvahed—who could no longer work, was being taken away to be gassed to death. Schneerman, then this man of no particular faith, looking helpless toward the ashen smoke in the unforgiving sky, touched my shoulder with his skeletal hand. He asked me, 'Levi, it can't get any worse, can it?'

"I removed his hand from my shoulder and told him, 'Adolph, there is one undeniable fact I have learned since the moment I was taken to Terezin: it can *always* get worse.'

"From that moment I knew what choices I had to make and which choices Schneerman would make. I do not know you well enough to know what choices you will make. If you choose to go on, it might get worse and it might get better. I can give you no more wisdom than that. And you will choose to go on or not." There was no emotion, no pleading to live through the pain, promises that it would get better, only his stark truth.

Any sense that I had that he was humoring me was gone.

"You know, I have written of the empty spaces after each one—my wife, my daughter, my siblings, and my friends—was tortured and murdered by the Nazis. That is an easily understood human hurt: how they never leave me and I remain incomplete."

Yes. I remembered that from *Mystical Mistakes*.

"What you have not read is that sometimes I feel like a hologram. I am always whole but pieces of me keep crumbling off. With each person with whom I have shared a smile, a night, a discovery, a sip of water, a train ride to death, a torture, a last drink, a bit of body warmth in the frozen hell we call Auschwitz, a confidence that one has given, a lunch with someone I hardly knew—a piece of me was taken from my whole. Yet in some fashion I knew I remained whole, only seen from a new angle. Complete yet not.

"When, after the war I recommenced my search, my aim was to feel whole without god. Yet god was now impossible so I asked, If not in science and not in god, where?

"I cannot give you my answer the way you give me a diag- nosis for my knees. That is one question no one, no one but you can answer."

"Levi, I understand that and I'm so grateful to you for your honesty." He nodded imperceptibly. I had one more question. "Do you ever feel whole as you once did?"

He only shook his head.

38

182

The Jews, we Jews, erred by claiming the Holocaust as a "Jewish tragedy." By creating a Jewish State with memorials that call attention to, in effect affirm, the truth in Hitler's claims that he would eliminate Jews from Europe and that few non-Jews would care enough to stop him. No doubt, the Holocaust, as evidenced by Hitler's pronouncements in Mein Kampf, *which were proven all too true, issued a moral license for Christians to kill Jews, as well as to kill other Christians, but it did not enforce a contrary moral imperative for Christians to save Jews. The Nazis and their henchmen, and the Allies, who didn't bomb the chambers or railways, proved that all too clearly. What we should have emphasized is that the barbarism signified humanity killing humanity. All humanity. Instead we have retained the gold star of otherness rather than becoming part of the whole, which forced us to live and die outside the human epistasis, servants of the Jewish god, YHVH, who deserted his people rather than becoming entwined in the connective tissue of the greater whole. We remain a word apart rather than a prefix or suffix affixed to the human word.*

—from *MYSTICAL MISTAKES*

39

THE NIGHT AFTER the conversation with Sarah, doubting I'd ever again breathe free of Levi's "ache of incompleteness," I lay in bed and Sarah's soul smell, the ethereal perfume I inhaled that first night and for so many years after, infiltrated my brain like the swift kick of ether. She still lived inside me, and I knew I had to see her soon.

Especially after Matt called me the next morning with news about the new issue of *The Star*. They'd offered us big money to give them an exclusive interview. We'd refused. They sent spies everywhere and found Sarah. The latest issue featured an unflattering photo of Sarah snapped by the same parasite who handed Sarah her summons. The picture caught her in her sweats, hair askew, with no makeup, rushing out of the gym, which ran in their paper alongside the headline: "Sarah Roberts Atones Up." They mentioned Prescott, printed another photo of the massacre and interviewed people who worked in the gym. Damn smart of her to get the hell out of there.

In the following two days, Matt fixed everything in person, no phones, faxes, or emails. He exercised his talents and maneuvers with *shvartz-gelt* with both the rabbi and cemetery director. He made all my arrangements under the pseudonym of Philip Nolan, including reservations at a small hotel on 84th and East End Avenue.

I made it clear to Ludovicci-Lint that there would be no Sarah deposition any time soon. At some point Sarah might talk with her but never to Karpstein, Forman. Her voice implored that Sarah would make a brilliant witness. "No way," I insisted. She sounded displeased, and not altogether convinced, I thought, when I told her I still didn't know the date for the unveiling, and since legally, though it was rare, I could be deposed over the phone from India, I was considering that option. She agreed that all the magazines, not just the *Enquirer* and *Star* paid lackeys to scour court records, computer databases, and hired informants to search for our names. After this conversation, fed up with her manufactured sympathy, I crossed her off my need-to-know list.

Then, all arrangements in place, I called Sarah.

"Safe to talk?"

"After the *Star* article, probably not." Her voice sounded arch and defensive, but that wasn't what I meant and she knew it. "You see it?"

"Heard from Matt."

"I look like shit."

"Fuck 'em, Sarah, really. Anyway, how's this? The first week in January. It's all set if you give the go-ahead."

"Good." I heard the tension drain from her voice. I imagined her posture relaxing, the stiffness in her spine giving way to hope without the need to pretend courage.

I explained the details. No need to explain that she shouldn't tell anyone, including Romey, until the last possible second. We decided not to invite anyone else.

"Ask Matt to book me a room there, too."
Neither of us mentioned staying together.
"Just you?"
"Yes, my mother can stay elsewhere."
So, it was settled.

40

RATISH CALLED AND officially invited me to the dinner on Friday night at the Ashoka Road compound. Disarmed by his insistence that I show up and not wanting to offend him or any Indian hosts, I couldn't politely reject his invitation and, he pointed out, this was an opportunity to meet an "eclectic group of people."

As eclectic as it was rarefied. The gathering included Preeya, Holika's best friend, whom I wanted to meet because Holika spoke of her with such admiration. She was also a confidante and one who shared the same worldview. Preeya had divorced her first husband, whom she married when she very young in an arranged marriage. For a time, she was part of the Indian Diaspora and lived in the UK with her husband. When she left him she returned home, finished her education, got a law degree, and began working with Human Rights Watch and other organizations. If anyone knew about Holika and me, it was Preeya. Holika introduced us and I said a bland but genuine "Very glad to meet you."

"Neil, are you nervous?" asked Holika.

"Feeling a little bit of pre-party paranoia. I didn't know it showed."

"Stick by me." Preeya, a big-boned and stocky woman, with a gentle swish of her neck-length hair and a twist of her small nose ring, reassured me.

The other guests included Summit and his wife who ran a school for the street kids. Alvaro Benigno, a cool dude in dark glasses and full beard, and who, despite the romance of his name, was born in Bayonne, New Jersey. He owned an art gallery in New York but gave it up and opened a prestigious gallery in New Delhi. He lived a gay lifestyle with all of its multiple meanings. His newest artist protégé, Sonia Guptaphya, talked mainly to Begnino and P. K. Bahar. Bahar, the publisher of *Delhi Today*, fortyish with Bollywood good looks, a Cambridge education, a wife and three children, wanted little to do with Guptaphya and rather blatantly chatted up a tall, blond-haired, green-eyed Swedish graduate student doing her dissertation on Tantric ritual. Sharmilla, who worked for Vijay as the head of his charity organization, and her husband, who was a big shot in an Indian venture capital firm, seemed haughty until they started drinking, when they became almost goofy. Lastly, arriving together were Tracee, the anorexic food critic, and another woman. Tracee greeted me with a winsome smile and an airy shake of her delicate hand. Since I didn't know who knew what about her, I didn't ask how she was feeling. Still vastly underweight and pale, she seemed steadier on her feet. I decided to let her call the shots. She introduced me to Anita Gatore, who, like Tracee, knew Holika since childhood. The three of them spent two "wild" summers at a Swiss finishing school. Anita Gatore was the granddaughter of a renowned writer, who the whole country, from the poorest villager to the most renowned pedagogue, knew as "Gatore." Anita too was called simply "Gatore" by her friends.

Vijay, as the others congregated around him in the vast, marbled interior of the immaculately clean and impeccably furnished living room, relaxed in a large red-cushioned arm chair, more like a throne, whiskey glass in hand, face pinkish-brown and blotchy, smile vaguely forlorn, eyelids droopy, already tipsy.

The servants brought us wine, soft drinks, pretzels, chips with salsa, all kinds of nuts, buffalo cheese, yogurts, and Indian-style crudités with tongue-burning spicy dips.

Tracee kept her distance from me, talking with Gatore. Preeya stood beside me and we made simple "How do you like Delhi?" small talk. I spoke in my social-situation bam-bam New York City nervous patter. "I love it. It feels at once so much like New York and at the same time the other side of the world. You have crazed rickshaw drivers. We have wacko bicycle messengers. We both have taxi drivers who're color blind."

"Why do you say that?"

"Cause none of 'em has ever seen a red light." She smiled in agreement. "Really, I do think Delhi represents the future."

"Is that good or bad?" Preeya asked, almost jestingly in a wisp of a voice.

"Not sure. Both, I guess."

"How do you mean that?" Preeya had not been at Vijay's shindig for Charlie. Not her style. I sensed her knowledge that much was rarely as it seemed, which bound her and Holika together as kindred spirits, and which allowed her probing questions to seem more curious than intrusive.

"Because of the population and lack of resources. I think that is a problem that the West is going to have to face soon too."

"One hundred percent right."

"I'm only discovering the multiple layers of Indian life, but the similarities are greater than the differences."

A petite, gray-haired, elderly woman dressed in a plain off-white sari with her midriff showing, peeked into the crowded room from a doorway and then shuffled across the room and slipped out a door that led to a courtyard. She passed as if invisible. I assumed she was one of the servants. Preeya whispered in my ear, "Gertrude's ghost."

I tilted my head questioningly.

"Holika's Aunt Deva. Vijay's wife. She prefers to stay in her own little house on the other end of the grounds."

"Got it."

We were now in "The Pillai House," because Vijay, not Holika's father, was the power broker of the family. Both families hailed from the Brahmin caste but, I was told, a lower *jati* within that caste. Holika's father was born into a long line of scholars and property owners who never held jobs. For years, the family survived on selling pieces of their properties and investments. With almost all of the fortune dissipated, Holika's father married Vijay's younger sister. Her father ostensibly worked in the Pillai family business, but mostly he displayed the meager talents of the dilettante in art and politics.

I'd gotten only a peek at the grounds as Chandon drove up the long gravel driveway. No one offered me a tour of the house or the compound, which took up almost an entire city block and was guarded by the usual high walls and stern-looking bodyguards. Besides this main house, other houses on the compound belonged to Holika's parents. Three smaller private bungalows were for family use and huts housed the dozen or so servants who were always on duty.

Despite the high ceilings and spacious rooms, the house felt encumbered with a sullen sterility, and now I understood why. Ghosts of all sorts, some which could be seen and some which could not, patrolled the hallways. When I went to the bathroom,

189

one of the servants eyed me as I passed a sitting room where Alka and a girlfriend watched American, not Indian, MTV on a wall-sized TV screen while simultaneously jabbering on cell phones.

I returned to the main room, hugged my glass of wine, and found a spot between Preeya and Tracee. I joined everyone who stood listening raptly to P.K. and Gatore face off in a fiery, but not rude, political discussion of Kashmir and the future of India. Each of the billion Indians, regardless of their education, religion, or social station, owned and voiced an opinion on the Kashmir "problem."

Gatore, who wrapped her lissome frame in tan leather pants and a pleated and beaded orange blouse, possessed no shortage of spine or spleen. "No, P.K., India was never really a country. The British forced us into one country for their own selfishness, then two with the Partition, and tried to give us one language, their language, when we have the most beautiful languages in the world." She referred to the English governing style and then the splitting of the subcontinent into India and then Pakistan and Bangladesh. "This should not be and will not be because we have too many states, languages, religions, and customs. The Ossirs have little in common with the Tamils in Chennai and the Moslems in Kashmir and the Communists in Kerala and the Punjabis, and the Christians in Goa . . . and on and on."

P.K., fists clenched, answered with a repressed but obvious volatility, "We *are* a country. We can keep our distinct languages. But all, every child, must be taught his native tongue *and* English to keep up. We must outdo the Americans. Those who control language will control the information, and those who control information will rule the world. Our language can save us or it can doom us. Our peoples and our mutual cultures will adapt, must adapt or we will lose all of our best people."

"Best people?" Preeya seemed to have little patience for those who left India with no intention to return. "Let them go. We must control our population growth."

Vijay shook his right hand limply in the air that held an empty Scotch glass, which a servant instantly refilled. His head staunchly erect. "No, no. You are all confused." Although he spoke heavily accented English with the pauses of someone uncomfortable in the language, in this company he didn't need a translator for psychological reasons. "You do not understand. India will soon be the greatest power on earth and we will not have to speak English. So many times we have been invaded from every direction, from land and sea and no one has conquered us and been able to stay. We never invade anyone. Our inner self-reliance and our unwavering faith are our strengths. We need no one." Vijay remained a firm believer in the post-Independence code of *swadeshi*, where India accepted no help from any outside country. "But the Americans are smart, since the Second World War whenever they send armies they lose, so the smart presidents do not *always* send armies, they are insidious with their power and promises and *their* culture."

"No," said Holika, who, I thought was the only one in the crowd with the temerity to disagree so vehemently with Vijay. "Uncle, nothing they do would matter without having more military men in more countries than any conquerors since Rome. More even than the British. That and their thousands of nuclear bombs *is* their power."

Ratish stepped toward Holika and spit out his words. "And they mock us for being irresponsible for having seventy-five bombs, and entice us with their whores like Madonna and unholy foods like McDonald's, so now we imitate them."

While I debated entering this fray, Gatore answered with

surety. "Yes, it is they, not us or the Pakistanis, who are the most feared and dangerous nation on earth, and when they send their children into battle against an enemy who fights back, they go wild if one hundred of them die, never thinking of the thousands upon thousands they have killed. That's why they prefer to drop bombs on others while they shoot themselves at home. They are so violent with their guns." Gatore expected agreement or snickers. Instead, her jibe elicited the heavy awkwardness of veered eyes, which said to me, "The others know." I held my eyes closed for five seconds, no longer wishing to argue and wishing I'd stayed home. Holika, experienced in a life filled with gaping silences, deftly filled the void. "The food is ready in the next room."

Before I followed the others into the dining room, Tracee spoke softly, "Neil," I turned and was about to speak when we noticed Vijay motioning to me. Tracee nudged me with her elbow; one did not ignore a summons from Vijay. "You must go. If we don't speak later, I will call you in your office."

"Please do."

I took the vacant, red-cushioned chair beside Pillai. He swirled the ice in his refilled Scotch glass, waiting purposefully as I squirmed, before he spoke.

"Dr. Downs, I am enchanted to make your acquaintance. Ambassador Bedrosian is most fond of you, as are Ratish and especially Holika," he paused and lifted his left hand in the air shoulder height and dangled it there, "who so admire your skills."

"They've been really helpful to me. I appreciate their kindness and openness."

Vijay, keeping his spine straight, leaned slightly forward. He lowered this floundering left hand, with its long fingers and gently rested it on my right knee. I sat tensely, afraid to shake it off. His touch felt not so much sexual as creepy as he rubbed his hand ever so slowly in a circular motion.

"Please do not be offended by this political talk."

"No big deal. I agree with *some* of what was said."

"Another time, perhaps with Ambassador Bedrosian, we can exchange ideas." He leaned back and lifted his hand off my knee while his yellowish eyes explored my face, my eyes, and my body language. His voice lost any sense of linguistic pondering. "You see, arguing and disorder in my house disturbs me. I demand civility and respect in my home and from the members of my family. Especially Holika, Ratish, and Alka." He paused. He wiped the saliva cresting in the corners of his mouth with his tongue, which did a languorous dance-macabre before he spoke again. "Because of my situation," he closed his eyes as if to communicate his unfulfilled completion of family duty, "they are my children and I spoil them because I want the best for them." He shook his head slowly up and down making sure I understood.

193

I took my time, not wanting to sound too foolish, but not afraid to sound obsequious either. "I understand completely. I haven't talked much with Alka, but it is obvious that Ratish and Holika idolize you."

He bowed his head in thanks. "Tell me, how do you like India?"

"Because of *my situation*," I paused and he shook his head and we found a mutual meeting point, "I have found tremendous comfort here. The people are so good-natured and warm. And like you, so generous and welcoming. I'm also fascinated and entranced by your culture, but it sometimes, and I don't mean this in any negative way, baffles me."

He leaned forward and touched my knee again, this time a bit less delicately. "Then you'll be staying?"

"As long as I'm welcome, I'd certainly like to stay longer."
I leaned back and his hand slipped off my knee.

"I'm sure you'll be welcome and you will come much more
to understand and adjust to our ways—human nature does not
change—although some things may always baffle you." He
smiled with pleasure at my vexation. "Many have come here
troubled and left renewed. Others, well, it is a shame what happened to your predecessor." His voice did not become threatening, but it beat with a certified assuredness about who had power
here and it wasn't me. He waited ten seconds and then spoke
again. "I need to set a date to come to your office for my semiannual physical."

"Just give me a call." No need to worry that he needed
Schlipssi's approval.

"Have you gone over my records yet?"

I hadn't even seen them on the computer or in the files. "No,
but I will. Is there anything special that is bothering you or is
this a general checkup?"

"At my age there are many ailments of life that bother me,
but nothing that cannot wait and be dealt with in the next few
weeks."

"I'll review your records on Monday and you can call and
come in anytime after that."

He nodded and those liverish eyes, with lids half-closed, dismissed me. He stood up from his chair, a bit shaky, shook my
hand and strolled away, tugging at the bottom of his embroidered,
burnt-red vest. I watched as he made his way to Holika, who
stood in the hallway between the living and dining rooms.
Dressed in red silk pants, a light brown cashmere sweater, and
flat, three-buck red and gold shoes that she proudly announced
she'd purchased at the Dilli Haat market—she could've told a
fashion neophyte like me they cost a hundred bucks and I

would've believed her—and her face lightly made up and hair braided tightly down her back, she appeared quite conservative. Vijay bent over, delicately placed his right hand on her left shoulder and talked in her ear and then disappeared into the recesses of his home. He was not dining with us.

Holika strode over to fetch me. We stood there alone; she touched my forearm with the tips of her polished red fingernails.

"I'm sorry." She apologized almost as if it were her fault. "Gatore had no idea."

"But the others do."

She tilted her head in the mysterious thingamabob motion.

"I was kinda thinking of making an early exit." Between Gatore's and Vijay's intimations, a book seemed a more inviting night's activity.

"No, please, I want you to stay."

"We need to talk before you leave." Holika—maybe she was right about physics—had become my closest, perhaps only, confidante. We'd spoken briefly on the phone two nights before the dinner and I'd told her that I'd made the plan for the unveiling.

"Not tonight. Maybe tomorrow." I understood there were too many people around to expect any alone time. "You must come dancing. It will be fun, and I promise—no more embarrassments. I want you to talk to Summit about his school."

Dancing had not been in my plans. I rearranged my plans.

We went into the dining room. Summit, who was short and bulky with tiny, pointed teeth and tiny hands, with top-heavy tufts of unkempt hair sat on his round head, and he sure loved to talk.

I asked about the possibility of helping out at his school. He didn't jump at my offer. First, we talked for almost twenty minutes. He was Bengali originally from Calcutta, his wife Tamil from a small village outside of Chennai, formerly Madras. After multiple miscarriages, they resigned themselves to not having children. His wife was a Brahmin, he a Dalit who had risen through life through a strong will and education. When they began the adoption process they ran into roadblocks at every turn. He offended sensibilities with his nondeferential attitude. Although they had no preference, they were told the chances of getting a boy were nil. Summit got fed up with everyone and all the crap. He started taking the street kids to his home. Then it evolved into, not exactly an orphanage, but a home where the kids could land temporarily before finding a permanent home, or—and this happened all too often—running back to the streets. Summit said he didn't "give a shit" what these people thought of him. What he needed from them, who were not really his friends, was money from Vijay and press from P.K. That night he had already arranged to have a benefit for his school in Begnino's gallery. And Vijay pledged to give more money through his organization.

I told him that the situation didn't seem so foreign to me, that the same hypocrisies plagued the U.S. That those who refuse to give money for sex education, birth control, or abortions, and who reduce budgets for orphanages while they drive big cars, hate paying taxes and wonder why we have so many young people in jail. Most don't adopt either.

We kept at it until Alka and her friend came bouncing out for the dinner of chicken, minced lamb, chutney rice, dahl, stuffed bread, mustard-seed sauce and beans, stewed tomatoes, and a coconut concoction for dessert. They ran right to Tracee. They wanted to hear all about the new shops in SoHo and on Madison Avenue. Tracee pulled me away from Summit telling

the girls that I was a native New Yorker, while she exaggeratedly bit into a chicken kabob. "Eating. See eating."

The girls screwed up their faces in horror when I told them
I knew zilch about shopping in New York and my favorite activity in India was strolling through Old Delhi.

"I've never been." Alka spoke shamelessly. I looked astonished. "Holika hasn't warned you how dangerous it is?"

"No," I shook my head. I silently impugned her and thought
of the immense divide in Indian society, when suddenly I
smacked into my own ignorance: most of the people I knew in
New York had seen Harlem only from the windows of their cars
and could more easily locate Baghdad than Corona, Queens,
on a map. Alka's warning interrupted my thoughts.

"You make sure you look above and all around you." Alka's
tone, unlike her usual frivolousness, sounded sinister.

"I visited the Red Fort once," volunteered her friend
proudly.

"Which is one more time than I've been to the Taj Mahal,"
I said rather embarrassedly.

"That's a scandal." They gushed with laughter. "We should
get Holika and take you. We own an apartment outside Agra."

What could I answer to these two fabulously innocent and
carefree young women? Sorry, I don't sightsee because that is
a family activity. You do that with your wife and child. Your
son.

"Sure. Any time."

After dinner, except for Summit and his wife, we
caravanned in three cars to a disco located inside the Marriott
Hotel, but with a separate entrance. Like in New York, where I
hadn't been out clubbing in years, a huge throng waited for the
lucky call. P.K. arranged for us to be on the preferred list so they
ushered us right inside. The interior design combined Studio

54 faux hipness, Punk Pogo sweatiness, and Las Vegas glitz. People jammed around a circular wooden bar in the front room, with would-be models, AKA waiters and waitresses dressed in Western garb. Past the bar, in the second, darkened room, guests nestled and inhaled forbidden substances in corner booths. TV monitors hung from the ceiling in the big room, playing either live cricket matches from South Africa or MTV Indian pop videos. An overhead light system modeled on *Saturday Night Fever* swirled colored lights over a dance floor packed with people bouncing and flouncing. The band with sartorial roots in grungeland Seattle and the Lower East Side of Manhattan, led by a skinheaded multi-earringed, tattoo-laden, motorcycle-booted, leather-clad and torn T-shirt rocker, played a pastiche of music: Stones to Donna Summer; ABBA to Iggy; Pearl Jam to techno pop and Tupac.

The primarily Indian crowd, extremely good-looking and adorned in très chic colorful silks and upscale Western "informal wear," swarmed the dance floor and the surrounding tables. Cigarettes were ubiquitous.

By this time everyone, including me, had checked their sobriety at the door. The mood among us, and in the club, brimmed with joy.

Alka and her friend, cell phones in hand, hit the dance floor first. Everyone followed. With the exception of Sharmilla and her husband, no one danced specifically with anyone else. P.K. kept within hand-touching-shoulder distance of the Swedish woman. Ratish, sloshed, danced aggressively with women not in our party and who were with other men. A few times he had to be tugged away by P.K. or Holika. Alka and her friend flirted with many of the men around us. Two handsome Sikhs worked hard to get a one-on-one dance. They bought drinks, many drinks, but got nothing but a hangover for their troubles. Holika removed her sweater under which she wore only a white silk and lace sleeveless top. She reddened her lipstick, let down her hair, kicked off her shoes and shimmied and shook and slyly flashed wry, wet-lipped smiles in my direction. When the band played the chords of Springsteen's "I'm on Fire," Holika and I faced each other for seconds. She slithered her hips and shoulders. As she inched closer then away, her head tossed back in that triumph of hair—my dread of Castor's unveiling, of facing Sarah, of my own duplicity faded away and for the moment I existed in my present and another possible future where I lived in Delhi with Holika and her friends and I emerged a new Neil Downs, engaged in serious talk about social issues with Summit and politics and poetry with Gatore and P.K., and about art with Benigno, who'd invited me to his next opening, and about life and death with Levi. And then, suddenly, the mood, the night, another possible future became blocked as Samaka, surrounded by two bodyguards, looking damn displeased and with the posture of the divine right billionaire, strode to the edge of the dance floor and glowered at Holika. Her eyes closed, her body undulated to the band's cover of U2's "Bad." She ignored the commotion of his presence ten feet away. Preeya leaned over and whispered in her ear. Unfazed, Holika swayed to the song's mesmerizing rhythm, her face stoic, showing neither exultation nor expectation. Under the dark blue light, arms flowing in syncopation, she appeared like a goddess dancing the Tandava. Lifting one leg at a time lightly off the dance floor, spinning in place, she refused to accept Samaka's stare. Her head slowly drifted from side-to-side, denying him. He waited. When the song ended, she opened her eyes wide, giggled, almost skipped toward him and leapt at him for a hug. He caught her, falling back on his heals as his bodyguards kept his balance. He did not grin in ecstasy. He spoke into her ear and

199

without turning back toward anyone, the two of them left the club.

All of us, none too sneakily, had watched the scene. Ratish stood erect holding a large beer stein in his left hand. His pupils whirred with the unfathomable disconnect that I'd seen in psychopathic patients or more frequently in those who had "flipped out" on drugs like Ecstasy or PCP. The sweat streamed down his forehead as he sidled up to me. He spit out the words, "You poor Shmuck." He shifted his body and jutted his head toward the direction of the disappeared Samaka and Holika, "You would *so* be better off without her."

41

HOLIKA CALLED ME Sunday afternoon and
asked me to meet me her at Preeya's apartment at eight o'clock.
I asked if it was necessary to come alone. Her clipped tone and
two succinct words, "not necessary" told me all I needed to know.

Preeya lived in an apartment complex in the Alakananda
section of Delhi where, like so many of the complexes and communities in middle-class areas that couldn't afford armed
guards, the locked gates served as the line of defense against
the hoi polloi of the streets. Preeya, not Holika, schlepped down
the five flights of cement steps and led me up to her duplex
apartment on the top floor. Duplex sounds too fancy: it was two
floors with small rooms and a staircase. With peeling paint on
the walls and water stains on the ceiling, it reminded me of the
cheaply renovated railroad apartment in Manhattan where I
lived for years before I met Sarah. In the kitchen, big enough
for one person to turn at forty-five-degree angles without bang-
ing into a wall or an appliance, a shy woman "servant" named
Meena bowed her head when I said hello, and Holika put slices
of a Domino's Pizza on plates for the four of us. Meena wasn't

your typical "servant," although she came from the Dalit class. Preeya rescued her from her home city of Lucknow, where the woman's husband had "beaten her down like a dog with the threat of worse to come all too likely." The woman's family refused to intervene, so Preeya interceded.

Holika edged her way out of the kitchen, bottle of beer in hand, and for the first time in front of me she wore black-framed glasses instead of contacts. She pecked me on my right cheek. Her usual grand smile and warm welcome were nowhere in the vicinity. The playful banter replaced by a solemn, "Let us sit in the dining room."

Books stacked six feet high served as the dividing wall between the living and dining rooms. Three plants, a pile of floor cushions, a futon mattress, two political posters on the walls, and a wicker chest with a tiny TV and a boom box consisted of the room's entire contents. Past the books, a round wooden table with four folding chairs occupied the space of the cramped "dining" room. Behind the table the only windows, with two cracked panes, looked down into the gated parking lot. On the floor, beneath the windows were two huge satchels overflowing with papers. Upstairs were the bedroom and an office space.

We sat on the chairs and she opened the beer and asked if I wanted a glass. I scrunched my nostrils. The smell of the beer ranked low on my list of sensual desires. "I'm used to not sleeping but it's not the same as drinking and dancing till all hours. After the lights and buzzing in my ears faded, the silence hurt more."

She moved Mahasweta Devi's *Bitter Soil*, which sat on the table, and placed it atop another stack of books. She poured the beer into a glass that she took from a cupboard behind the table.

"Myself, I have had two long nights." Dressed casually in a dark blue T-shirt and baggy jeans and without much makeup, she looked weary with dark circles visible beneath the glasses around each eye and a puffy bag under her left eye. I wanted to touch her eyes and magically lift the weight as if I were some mystic who'd meditated while standing on one leg for thirty years.

Preeya and the young woman carried in the pizza on four separate dishes. After we finished eating, Preeya and the woman each picked up a pile of papers from one of the satchels and carried it upstairs. I offered to help but they refused. Holika didn't move from the dining room table into the living room.

She pulled a cigarette from the pack Preeya had left on the table and held it between her thumb and two fingers. "I know you disapprove." She waited a few seconds, then flicked the unlit cigarette on the table. In one of those odd limbo moments, instead of looking at each other, we watched the cigarette roll to see if it would keep going until it fell off. It hit a plate and stopped. "Neil, this may not be a good time, because of where your life is now, and do not think me insensitive, but it is best because I am not so young and I will need to have a baby—soon. Only one."

She paused and seemed to wait for my reaction to the news, which although we'd never spoken about it and I feared it might be coming, still startled. I cringed and tensed my gut muscles.

"My sister who will forever remain intentionally immature and superficial, will soon be married to some suitor my uncle picks out. Ratish will not wait much longer either. It will most certainly please my uncle and guarantee my inheritance, my heritage." She picked up the beer glass and took a long swallow before speaking again. "I am now formally engaged to Samaka."

I couldn't tell if Holika's repressed yet dulcet tones, spoken through taut lips, were sincerely joyless or if she were hiding her joy so she didn't make me feel worse. Not for what she was gaining but for what I'd lost; what never again would be mine. I uttered a restrained "congratulations." More than that would've been disingenuous. I wasn't proud of my lack of enthusiasm but I wasn't ashamed either.

"I love Samaka in my fashion. I love my uncle. He is the opposite of the demon that his rivals claim. He is a complex man. Many a man would have divorced my Aunt Deva or worse because she could not conceive. He has his beliefs—and they are often pigheaded—but he is faithful to his belief."

"Does your uncle know you're a spy in his house?"

"No," she couldn't deny what she herself had told me, "and yes. One of my long nights was spent with him and Ratish arguing over his involvement with that despicable Hal Burden." She repressed a beer burp so it slipped imperceptibly from her lips. "Do you see those satchels?"

She pointed to them, and I nodded.

"Papers that Preeya and I and others have compiled and are now putting on disc all about the deception between Environ and the government. All this talk of free markets and how it helps everyone is doublespeak. Roberson was right," she smiled in acknowledgment that she had agreed with him. "It gives companies like Environ the freedom to do whatever they damn please. We are trying to stop it, but they have spent twenty million dollars in bribes in the last decade." She picked up the cigarette and twiddled it between her fingers but did not light it. "My uncle claims his involvement will control what they do. Years ago, Siddhartha outlined a plan for solar power plants in the drought-stricken areas that would make them thrive. That's what I want him to support. But . . ." she dropped the cigarette and again it rolled but did not fall off the table. "Uncle made a commitment that he will not try to stop me from doing what I believe in as he has done what he believes in."

The deal with Environ, besides its environmental destructiveness, would benefit a few people and harm millions. Holika would talk of women's reproductive rights, of which her uncle approved. In defiance of Vijay and Ratish, she was also organizing the villagers, speaking with prominent state politicians, working with lawyers to stop the deal that would destroy so many lives socially and deprive the Indian people billions of dollars.

"I hope it all works out as you hope."

"You seem skeptical. We are no different from many families. Just the stakes are larger. I am more concerned for Ratish than for me. Later that night, well, he and I had a more vicious disagreement. He came home drunk again after he had gone out without his driver. He is going to kill himself one of these days." She closed her eyes for a few seconds and shook her head as if warning herself to go no further. "It became unpleasant." She stopped, and almost as a non sequitur, she repeated the family mantra. "It only ended because Uncle awoke and stopped us. My uncle is a patriotic hero, no matter how others slander him. He suffered tremendously, both financially and physically, while in prison during the Emergency."

I didn't need to hear the slogan to understand that Holika loved, respected, and feared Vijay. It was irrelevant and unnecessary to bring up the palpable yet unprovable heebie-jeebie vibes that Vijay sent my way at the party. Or that I saw that her uncle fell into her one large blind spot.

"That's when all of us argued again over Environ. They have to see that because I am getting married it does not change my belief. Ratish believes like my uncle, that they must be able to watch Burden and his people. That if not, they will do whatever they want, and then leave just like Bhopal." The explosion at the Union Carbide plant in 1984 had left thousands of Indians dead, thousands more sick, hundreds still dying years later, and the land seething with toxins. The Indians had tried to get full remuneration but to no avail. All these years later the lawsuits and fighting about who was responsible still rages. "If they are

205

involved my uncle says he will have the power to stop that kind of murderous behavior. He can make sure all is done safely. I think we have to stop it before it starts and not test his power."

Despite the political and familial talk and its importance, I thought that minutes before I wanted to spill my guts about fears of what awaited me in New York. I expected Holika to say, "No more sex," which was fine, but I didn't want to think about her having a child. I pictured her soon-to-be pregnant body, the baby coming out from her. And I felt only the need to listen.

While I envisioned her future, she still felt the need to explain her present.

"You do not have true insight into how hard it is to be a woman in this society, none."

"Or in any society. In America it's hard too. Just different."

"Those differences count a great deal. We have great secrets here of infanticide and men who force their wives to have abortions when it is revealed the child is a girl. If you truly want to know, talk to Meena. But so few can or will talk about it because they become pariahs. We have millions of women now who have climbed out from under the system. But far too many millions—women with college degrees, even—who are still subservient to their husbands. Even for Preeya. Her brothers don't talk to her. Her father refused to have her live at home. Her mother berates her every chance she gets. They consider her a disgrace, not a courageous and brilliant woman." The same could be said of Holika. "Being with Samaka is good for me in so many ways."

"I know and I wish you well. Better than well, the best." Suddenly, I felt such tenderness for her, such warmth without jealousy or rancor. "He has no idea how lucky he is."

"Neil, you remember I told you I never loved anyone as much as you love Sarah?"

"Yeah, but I didn't believe you. Didn't buy it that you were immune to Holika's laws of physics."

She smiled obliquely, signifying her belief in the ineffable physics of love.

"You were right to be skeptical. Because now I can speak of Siddhartha to no one, not even to Preeya. I tell myself that lie and sometimes I almost convince myself that he did not exist, which is what Samaka and my uncle want. That it was a mistake that has been erased." Her tired eyes blinked fast, her small jaw clenched as her posture shrunk and her head tilted down. The inconsistencies of what she had said two minutes before, her secret life, weighed so heavily. I reached to touch her. She held my hand between her two hands. "I could more easily tell them about you than mention his name."

I wasn't too pleased with that comparison. Nor did I want it tested.

"Neil . . ." She gazed at me with such a bizarre spin in her eyes and sideways tilt of her head that I could've sworn she wished, believed for that second, that she talked not with me, but with Siddhartha, "I am doing what I must to do." She reached her right hand to my cheek and barely touched me. I smiled wanly. She took off her glasses and rested them on the table, then leaned her head across the chasm between our chairs and placed her head against my shoulder. I held her hands in mine, feeling helpless and unable to comfort her as she had comforted me.

42

DURING THOSE HOLIDAY weeks, with Holika gone, I wandered as the Diasporic Jew at Chanukah and Christmas seasons. I became a tourist visiting the guidebook suggestions. I still didn't make it to the Taj Mahal. One Friday afternoon I wandered over to the Arts and Crafts Museum. Outside the building, in the courtyard, was a government-run bazaar where, I was told, about half the vendors are permanent and another half gets one month to sell their wares before being rotated out and replaced by a new crop. Just outside the gates were stalls selling foods from all parts of India, as well as Western fast foods. The juxtaposed smells of french-fry grease, curried dishes, beer and sodas, sweet, syrupy fried desserts, and cigarettes coagulated in the winter air. Inside the gates, cubicles and open stalls displayed ceramics, glass bangles, nose rings, moderately expensive and cheap rugs and clothes, papier-mâché jewelry boxes, cigarette cases, puppets, incense, good luck Ganeshas of all sizes and materials, and in this month . . . Santa Clauses. No crosses or menorahs, or baby Jesus or the original Madonna and child statues (yes, but one stall did have posters of the new Madonna), but mini–Santas and "Christmas" gifts. Many in the younger generation of the middle and upper classes in the cities, if not the villages, celebrated Christmas with the hoopla of a party night, more like July 4th than the holy birth of the Most Famous Jew. Far fewer, almost no one, cared or knew about Chanukah, the Jewish holiday of light and miracles that's become the quasi-Christmas for the benefit of Jews living among Christians. Instead, India's thirty million Christians lived among a billion Hindus and Moslems as "the other," so unknown to Christians in the West. In India, I walked and wandered and saw myself again as the other, but different from my otherness in America. More like the invisible but detectable black American who is seen, spotted, and noted, unlike the undercover, already in whiteface Jew in America, where you can't miss Christmas but the day is never yours. Where there are those unsure of who or what you are and who regard you with eternal suspicion until you can be placed. In India, few could take the Christian out of the Westerner. There was no other choice. Even if I hadn't been blond and blue-eyed, they would have marked me as a Christian.

As I strolled along, bundled up in a heavy sweater, the vendors marked me as a potential customer. A slim Kashmiri vendor, who was probably a Moslem, the real Other in India— unlike the Indians I couldn't always tell a Hindu from Moslem—persisted in following and calling out to me: "Best Christmas presents for your family. Best. I promise best prices. You have wife and children? How many? I have three." He pointed to a back stall where a woman, who didn't look old enough to have one child, sat with a baby on her lap and two other children played on the floor beside her. No way to easily explain either of my predicaments, my family or my heritage. "You can leave here without presents for them?" His persistence amused more than annoyed and my Pavlovian reactions kicked in and I decided to buy presents for Sarah.

My family had ritually exchanged presents at Christmas, never thinking it compromised their Jewishness. Sarah and I, and then Castor, continued the gift-giving tradition. Romey labeled me a Scrooge when I refused to allow any Christmas ornaments in the apartment. She scoffed at my explanation detailing the effects of symbols, meanings, and identity. She'd sailed through life believing America existed as an amorphous, yet officially Christian and English-speaking nation, which graciously allowed others to show up and act like European Christians. No matter her mumbled asides, I steadfastly drew the line: no trees and Santas, stockings, candles, or any other commercial or religious icons. No menorahs either, except one year: after Castor started Hebrew school we lit the candles, but he seemed not to care, so we abandoned that idea too.

I was half-heartedly haggling with the vendor when the irrepressible laughter and screams of a gaggle of children from six to ten years old overcame the adult sound of selling. I stopped and watched them for a moment. From behind, I felt a finger tap my right shoulder. I swiveled around, "Hello, doctor!" It was Ratish, effervescent in his greeting. Paint was splattered on his hands, cotton shirt, pants' legs, and sneakers. Standing close on one side and gripping his hand was an adorable young girl. On the other side a young boy held his shirttail. I'd never seen Ratish look so naturally loose. Behind them the children were being led—well, more accurately, leading Summit and his wife, the couple who ran the orphanage out from the building and outside the courtyard gates. These were not orphanage kids but street kids who Summit and his wife tried to gather up every so often. Funded through Vijay's organization and spearheaded by Ratish, the kids had spent hours doing finger painting and making papier-mâché dolls. They also got a hot meal.

"How are you doing?" he asked.

"My best, doing my best. Going to the States for the holidays. Ratish, would you do me a favor?"

"Possibly, yes. Sure."

"Please tell Summit that I would love to help him with the children."

"Is this right for you?" I heard a slight hesitation in his tone, which I felt could be my paranoia as easily as it could have been his empathy.

"Yes, I'm positive. It's a very good thing you do and I'd like to participate."

"That I can do. Yes, it is good, but it is so little. We do this and then they go back to their life." It wasn't as if they were totally neglected. Many of these kids had families who took care of them. Or some form of extended family system. There were laws of compulsory education, preferential programs for them at the universities—yet I knew, as did Ratish, a future free from poverty was unlikely.

The children tugged at him and we bid goodbye. I watched them stream out the gates and then went back to perusing the wares. The vendor, who had slipped invisibly away, came back to my side. I now bought a slew of presents. Not only for Sarah, but also for Matt, his wife and kids, Nurse Donna, Vishnu, Chandon (who told me he wanted whiskey), Charlie and Chrystie—not knowing at all what they wanted or needed.

This vendor, who led me around to all his friends, as he picked up commissions all along the way, offered to give me "a gift—only one hundred rupees" if I took a Santa.

"One hundred rupees is not a gift," I said playfully, getting more familiar and comfortable with the game.

"OK, fifty. For your children!"

"I have no children," I said flatly.

He frowned, upset that he might have insulted me or gotten too familiar. "Oh, then you must take. *Free*. It is a good luck gift. You will have children someday and you give it then. You remember me in India." He stuffed it on top of one of my bags. I didn't object. He smiled triumphantly. I smiled, impressed by his relentless optimism and energy as I, a reluctant Jewish Santa Claus, suddenly so exhausted, strode out the gates. And as I walked to the awaiting car, another of those adorable homeless girls, maybe she was six or seven, maybe she had even been with Ratish's group, strutted over to my side. "Money, please." Instead of money I took the pot-bellied icon from one of my bags and handed it to her. She held it in her tiny hands for a second, not sure if she wanted it or not, then bowed her head to me and scooted away, cheerily yelling something in Hindi while gripping the Santa.

43

CHRISTMAS PARTIES ABOUNDED in Chanakyapuri. There were innumerable cliques in the foreign community and I'd stayed away from all of them—not that I'd been asked to join, but at Christmas I got my share of invitations. Donna, my nurse, and her husband, an international lawyer who worked all over Southeast Asia, invited me to a small cocktail party at their home. "Yes," she told me, their two girls aged nine and thirteen would be there. Donna, who judiciously never mentioned a word to me about Castor, implicitly understood my reticence. "Dr. Downs," despite my feeling that she should call me Neil, she insisted on being professional in the office, "we'd like you to come, but if you don't feel comfortable or aren't ready, I understand."

"Donna, I used to enjoy a good party. I don't mean to be antisocial." I didn't want to explain my wariness after the Donneaux incident.

"People understand. It's just, they don't know what to say, they're afraid to say the wrong thing."

That was our most intimate conversation since I'd arrived, and one of the first acknowledgments that *everyone knew*. I held my breath for a second, accepting my surmised truth as fact.

"As a veteran of many bouts of verbal dyslexia, I often don't know what to say to me either."

She laughed a little and the opening to delve further behind our professional masks petered out and our conversation ended.

I attended their party, a cordial but rather dull affair, which suited me perfectly. I felt duty-bound to make a cursory appearance at the large embassy bash. Feeling entirely out of place, I decided to leave after half an hour. Charlie caught me on my way out. He'd set up a doubles match with him, his son Chuckie, and Chrystie's brother, both of whom were in India for the holidays.

Until we met on the court a couple of mornings later, I hadn't seen Chuckie since the incident in the hospital. Grown into the body of an adult, a year younger than his stepmom Chrystie, he'd already breezed through five careers. He now called himself an "indy, Sundancy-style film producer," with exactly no movies to his credit. He'd certainly mastered the "dude" jargon and inflated sense-of-self spiel, which mirrored Charlie's complaints of Chuckie as an ingrate. I was less than thrilled when Charlie teamed us together on the court, and taken aback when Chuckie started to actually *talk* to me.

"Fully weird, us playing tennis together in India, hey doc?" I was closer in age to him than to Charlie, but his style seemed more MTV than stunted Baby Boomer. "You know, made me think, what happened to your son. Wrote you a letter. I should've been the one who Cobained, maybe if I had, you know—stupid, I guess."

I stood there almost stupefied. I never expected Chuckie to mention or even allude to Castor and my first reaction was to scream, Castor didn't commit suicide, and if it meant, despicable as it sounds, my son would have lived, I wish you had Cobained. But I kept my composure. "Chuckie, no need to apologize."

"Anyway, I didn't have the courage to send it. The world is so fucking, you know, whacked. You know I was cranked at you for years for saving my life."

"And now?"

"It turned out money for me. So, you know, you never know."

Yeah, you never know.

One of Chuckie's earlier careers was as a club tennis pro; he probably should have stuck with it. He moved with grace and hit the ball with both power and touch. After a first set 6-2 shellacking, as Chuckie made a "quick biz call" to someone in the States on his cell phone, I suggested we rotate teams. Charlie, so competitive, glared and roared, "Bullshit. We'll get you." They didn't. The next set was 6-0. I mentioned to Chuckie that maybe he should go easy in the third set. "My father plays to kill or be killed. And he cheats, dude." Chuck continued smashing the ball mercilessly at Charlie, who fumed and looked like he wanted to strangle his racket, but he only flailed haplessly under Chuckie's barrage.

After the match Charlie said that he needed to pass by my office the next day at five. He showed up promptly and alone carrying two folders and an invitation. He tossed the invite on my desk. "Thought you might enjoy this." I read the personal note from Cécile Donneaux, inviting me to the French Embassy's New Year's party.

"I'll pass."

"Wish I could."

Charlie sat down and got to the real reason for a private meeting with me, to talk about Vijay, who decided to put off his visit to my office for now. Charlie handed me the first folder. In it were Vijay's classified medical records containing information omitted from the forty-page folder dating from 1985, which I'd located in the stacks of the file room.

The healers of myth were supposedly gifted with powers to peer deeply into the sickness of the human soul and body and provide cures and comfort. Although we modern healers are often, and correctly, lambasted for lacking bedside manners or compassion, we can diagnose disease and actually cure and prolong life. Vijay's medical chart, the information code no modern healer can do without, gave reason to Charlie's secrecy and underlying sense of urgency.

Each summer, escaping the dreadful heat and rain, Vijay spent two months in Germany, where he underwent his yearly checkup, not because the doctors were superior, but because of secrecy. The previous summer the doctors diagnosed Vijay with multiple myeloma, which is similar to leukemia. It remained dormant but could erupt at any time. He should've been taking monthly blood tests. According to Charlie, he'd been negligent in all things concerning his health since receiving the news. I urged Charlie to drag Vijay to Privat for a full blood workup the next time he visited the farm near Haryana. I'd spoken to the chief doctor there, and he measured A-one.

"Will do, but I want him to see a specialist in the States. Find one. He'll come in for a chat when you get back."

I nodded and contemplated whether or not to ask him about what I saw in the unclassified material: that Vijay allowed his family—perhaps even his wife Deva, certainly friends and foes—to foster the illusion that Deva's infertility was the cause of their childlessness, while he burst with healthy sperm. Untrue. Vijay could have seduced half the women in India and never would he have fathered a child.

I decided to say nothing. If Charlie knew, fine. If not, as he would say, he didn't make the "need-to-know list."

Charlie stuck out his hand and opened and closed it clamp-like. I gave him back the first file. "What you read in these files does not leave this office. Ever. This one, too." Looking slightly contemptuous, he tossed the second file with the name Siddhartha Singh scrawled across the cover, on my desk. "I don't know why you want this. I know you're a covert Trotskyite, and if you want to be a rabble-rouser in our country that's your business. Here, you—"

"I'm only doing research."

"On what? I can protect you when crazy French guys fuck with you. I don't give a shit when you have patients who Schlipssi thinks aren't up to his standards, but there are certain Indian lines even I can't cross." He stood up. "You take as much time as you need and leave it on the desk."

The file contained a series of newspaper and magazine articles and a summary of events of Siddhartha's life. No copy of "The Invisible Burning" manifesto, which told me I didn't receive the full file.

Although he did not appear to be particularly handsome, Siddhartha's charisma sparkled through in the mostly faded black and white photos with the ineffable power and self-assurance that jumped from the photos of Lennon or Martin Luther King.

The two-page summary of his life, which was prepared for readers like me—maybe even for me—talked of a life born into poverty from the lowest *jati*, or segment of the untouchable caste. His father was a toilet cleaner in the home of a middle class and caste lawyer. After his mother died in childbirth when he was four, the family that employed his father adopted Siddhartha and his new baby sister and raised them with all of the privileges embodied in a secular, liberal family. His intelligence, energy, and abilities as a visual artist were so impressive that he entered Baroda, the prestigious university for the arts located in Gujarat. Here he came under the influence of the trendy Marxist professors at the university, but he never fully embraced their philosophies. His bent was toward a more Indian sense of self-reliance and hope. After leaving Baroda, doing his doctorate on the political aspects embodied in the writings of Marquis de Sade, Antonin Artaud, the films of the Marx Brothers and Pasolini, he began to form his ideas on how to revolutionize society through art. He had studied the West but remained every bit an Indian. From these studies arose the Free Radicals, who performed and sang and ranted and painted and introduced conceptual performance art to India. The so-called independent art community and more liberal secular orders resisted and dismissed the movement as childish and unsophisticated. The established male-Hindu power structure, who pooh-poohed his belief that in women lived the future strength and visionaries of India, after all, he too was a male, genuflected into apoplexy at the mention of his name, which pleased him no end. Siddhartha got people's attention.

In the photos of Free Radicals in *Outlook Magazine*, the *Hindustani Times*, the *Times of India*, and dozens of smaller publications that covered the movement a youthful, hair-billowing Holika nearly always stood beside Siddhartha. In the articles and interviews Siddhartha showed off his rare combination of humor and earnestness. Able to quote Brando in *The Wild One*, Gandhi, the Vedas, and Herbert Marcuse with the appropriate sentiment at the right moment.

One week before the launch of the Free Radical Grand March, which would march from the Yamuna in Delhi to the Ganges in Varnassi, Siddhartha locked up his small office in Old Delhi, where he'd held a business "conference" with an unnamed woman. As he made his way toward the bus, which would take him home to his wife, a crazed monkey began throwing flowerpots from a roof. Two people were hit. Siddhartha was one of them. Pots still rained down into the claustrophobic alleyway. One smashed right into Siddhartha's skull. He died instantly. And the Free Radical movement died with him.

I left the folder on my desk. When I returned to work in the morning, it was gone.

44

As a youth I was taken with the resemblance between the theories of the Shekinah and what later came to be called the Big Bang, which spurred my curiosity in Kabbalistic doctrine, where linguistic symbolism and numerology held the key to godhead. If I discovered the missing letters, written in "invisible" ink, I could find the formulae to make those letters become visible and I could discover the hidden god. When I found no words, no science to express the mystery of the madness of the twentieth century, I buried my without, within finding only a deepening belief that higher communication in words without god is impossible. That belief is why I, for all of my disbelief, understand those like Schneerman, who believe in the will and the eventual coming of their silent, exiled god.

After the publication of Chamber, *often regretting I wrote a book that displayed darkness with words instead of light, I stopped writing. I had failed so miserably in my intentions: I made words lie instead of reveal truth. I wanted my words, all words, to be lucid and to lead to a future of hope. I vowed never to betray words again and my fear and hopelessness silenced me. And so, for many years,* words failed me.

—from *THE UNPUBLISHED WORKS*

45

CHARLIE INVITED ME to his Christmas Eve party. He didn't expect me to come and I met his expectations. Rabbi Judah called and invited me to a first night of Chanukah service at the temple with the assurance that Levi would be there. I declined that too. I sent Cécile Donneaux a polite note saying maybe another time. I accepted a Christmas Eve, and the second night of Chanukah invitation to dinner at Levi's house. He lived on the ground floor of the two-story house which he owned. He rented out the top floor.

Levi appeared relaxed when he greeted me. Dressed casually in slacks and a cashmere, button-down, pale-blue sweater over a collared shirt, he wore untinted glasses, which did not make his presence any less forbidding. Walking with the aid of his cane, he showed me around the interior and patio of the modest home. Books in English, German, and Hebrew lined the walls of nearly every room, with the rare books stored inside a glass case. I saw none of his books, publications, or personal photographs anywhere. He became almost effervescent when he showed off his small but impressive and deeply rooted European art collection, which prominently featured a print from Otto Dix, a miniature woodcut from Munch, an original Kokoschka portrait, and a signed and dedicated print from Anselm Kiefer. Classical and jazz records and CDs, filed in alphabetical order, filled a floor-to-ceiling cabinet. The sound system played Samuel Barber's chorale music. He led me to the entrance of his workroom, stopped, and then almost delicately walked into this stark room, with drawn curtains over the windows. On one wall were three reproductions from Goya's *Disasters of War* series. On another wall two framed prints from the *Arbeiter Illustriete Zeitung* newspaper hung opposite his desk. The first was from July 1934, titled "Heil, Hitler" with bullet-filled corpses all around the zealot-eyed Fuhrer. The second from December 26, 1935, and titled in German, which Levi translated for me as "O Joyful, O Blessed, Miracle-Bringing Time," pictured Nazis as angels wearing gas masks and circling above the terrorized/adoring people. Between these two pieces hung a lone rusted metal, one-hundred-and-fifty-year-old key that hung on the wall behind a Plexiglas box—the only surviving key to his former family home in the Jewish quarter of Prague.

I backed wordlessly away and surveyed the computer, printer, and fax machine, which sat on the mahogany desk. He kept his papers stacked neatly on the floor and on a second, large table; cabinets filled with hundreds, if not thousands, of letters surrounded the room. I contemplated this room devoid of books; this external creating chamber of the hell lived within. He nudged me with his cane and led me to the den.

To enter the den we had to walk down three small steps. A twenty-one-inch TV screen hooked up to a satellite dish dominated the room. The furniture felt, well, heavy loaded, muddy brown in color, and without the fluidity and space I'd seen in

Indian homes. It felt like my grandparents apartment. While I took all this in, Levi watched me and called out instructions to the cook.

When Levi invited me for dinner he asked what I wanted to eat. I joked, "Potato pancakes and matzo ball soup." Done deal. He regularly had boxes of Manischewitz soup and potato pancake mix flown in from New York along with other needed essentials. In the dining room, which was adjacent to the den, I eyed an unlit menorah on the middle shelf of the floor-to-ceiling breakfront. "Hannah lit the candles," he said, matter-of-factly.

"Was she religious?"

"Observant." Levi's tone made it clear that there exists a distinction.

He poured me a glass of red wine. I took it and made a   223
motion with my right hand as a toast. *"L'chaim."* He nodded and sat in his favorite chair at the head of a stained wooden dining room table, with a pinkish marble border that looked like the British might have left it behind. He sipped his beer from a frosted mug. "Sit, please."

I did. "I saw Hannah's grave in the cemetery." I asked if he felt any reservations about burying her.

"Of course not," he snorted through his nostrils. "Would I burn her? Cremate her?"

Never. As tattoos were banned in Judaism, disallowing burial in a Jewish cemetery, so was cremation against Talmudic law, and burning would be a victory for hate because it symbolized not the sacred crematoria of India, but the craven chambers of Europe.

"So, when do you leave?"

"New Year's Eve."

"I leave soon after that for Israel." Levi grinned and his yellowing teeth showed, "I am meeting the esteemed Rebbe

Schneerman. He is quite ill. I told him to ask his numerologist
to tell him when he is going to die." He chuckled at his own
jibe as if Schneerman could hear it again. "You know that
Schneerman used my prewar writings on work on tetras and
trinities in *his* writings to reconcile the silence of YHVH with
the hell of Auschwitz? He had no comprehension at all of what
I meant and the implications of Judaism being a faith based
on the numerologies of one and four, the square; Christianity
on one and three, the triangle; and Hinduism on zero and ten,
the circle."

"Yes, I read that essay." Levi first used the phrase "terrible
mistakes of mysticism" in a short essay refuting the writings of
Schneerman. While in the camps, Levi had confided to
Schneerman that using the Hebrew alphabet's letters, which
assigned numerical values to the letters, had spurred some
of his keenest thoughts. In Hebrew the name of Adam has
the same numerical significance of forty-five, a powerful
number in Kabbalistic thought and when broken down (four
plus five) adds up to nine, another powerful number. After
the war Levi had given up that part of his search. Not
Schneerman, who without ever consulting him used his
name to imply that Levi supported his work, which posited
that ACGT, the tetragrammaton of the genetic code, and
YHVH, if one could unveil their secret meanings, would reveal the hidden godhead. Schneerman, too, believed that it
was no mere coincidence that there were twenty-two basic
letters in the Hebrew alphabet, twenty-two X chromosomes
in the male sperm, plus one Y chromosome which equals
twenty-three, and when matched together added up to the
sacred, Kabbalistic forty-five.

"You'd think after I laid into him with all of my power reducing his ideas to gibberish, he'd leave me alone. But no, h

loves me more. He perverted my words and used them to say, 'Levi Furstenblum supports me.' I said no such thing. What I said was that he alone had the fearlessness to write what is the logical conclusion of almost all religious doctrine—Jewish, Christian, Hindu, Moslem—that those in the camps deserved to die for past or present sins." Levi's defense of Schneerman, although he described his ideas as repellent, had bound Levi and Schneerman together again.

"Now he wants me to make a pilgrimage with him to Prague and Berlin, his home city, so we could pray together." A rather unpleasant gurgle climbed out from deep in his throat, which meant "not a chance." He leaned his head forward, pressing his thin, dry lips together. "Have you ever been to Prague?"

He so wanted to hear news of the Prague of which he'd read about. He would have accepted stories of the Prague '68, although I'm sure he would've preferred the Prague of Havel and the Velvet Revolution. Of the cleaned-up Prague with only vague allusions to the Prague of his youth, with no recollections of the jackbooted stomps across the cobblestone, of the ravaged temples serving as Nazi headquarters. Those temples become memorials to 72,000 annihilated Jews. Of Prague with "Kafka cafés" whose owners have never read one word of *The Trial*. Of month-long grand music festivals and hipster hangouts called the Bohemian Bagel. I had no stories to tell.

"No. Been to Berlin. Didn't like it."

"Bah." He sniffed his nose. "Prague, now that is, or was, a beautiful city."

"Why don't you go visit?"

"I am not an apologist. I will not be a smiling Jew used for absolution, like in that insidious movie. I do not want any prizes or gifts sponsored by remorseful-looking children, who then will go celebrate forgiveness." Levi spit out his words with scorn. "In Israel, he and I will meet, reminisce, visit others, but I will not let him use me in any way, not again, to endorse his repugnant ideas. Not even one photo for his newspaper."

He excused himself and gingerly, suddenly painstakingly, it seemed, walked into the kitchen to check on dinner.

My eyes searched around the house again and I realized Levi lived in India, but he had never left the West, Prague, Auschwitz.

He and the cook brought in the soup. He sat down, and while we waited for the soup to cool, he began to discuss my dilemmas.

"So, tell me, is there something else besides the unveiling?" His eyes seemed to open and swallow me up. "Yes?"

"I still can't believe what happened." I fidgeted in place, my hands and arms feeling like uncontrollable extremities. I grabbed the soupspoon and gripped it in my right hand. "I used to be religious in my fashion. I believed in god. In the future. In an ultimate reason. Now, every day, part of me wants to die. Which is better than a few months ago, when every day part of me wanted to kill."

"Wanting to kill is the easy part." So well he understood both urges. He stuck his finger in his beer and stirred the ice cubes for a throat-tensing thirty seconds. "Who do you want to kill? Aren't those children who murdered your son all dead?"

"Their parents . . . and I hate, *hate* myself for saying this—sometimes, my wife." I felt my head and ears become almost feverish, but still fearful of acknowledging my anger.

"Your wife?" His voice quavered slightly with mild surprise; his eyes never wavered as they stared at me. I wished he'd worn his sunglasses. "Is that why she is not here?"

I gulped, hesitated, and blurted a truncated truth. "It came out that she betrayed me."

He shook his head as if to say, Ah-so . . . I see. But he spoke more bluntly. "In your heart you would rather your wife had been killed rather than your child." This was not a question. The accusation petrified me; he knew my inner secrets.

"I, I guess. Part of me . . ."

He interrupted my stammering.

"'*Mörder sind leicht einzusehen*' . . ."

I looked at him, clueless.

"'Minds of murderers are easily understood.'" Levi had cited this quote from Rilke's *Duino Elegies* in his writings, twisting the phrase into another of his controversial challenges to one's heart and one's language: "Minds of *victims* are not so easily understood."

He wrote how easily he came to understand the mind of the torturer, the rapist, and the murderer during his internment. He became excited at the idea of killing his captors, branding them, and having sex with their wives and daughters. After the war, he became sick of hearing the preposterous notion that "We are all Jews." "We are all Nazis" more accurately reflected human history. Understanding what it was like to be in the camps—that terror fell beyond the limitations of most people. The murderers certainly did not understand the victims. Levi suggested as punishment for the thousands, not the few who were tried at Nuremberg, but all who had killed and tortured and watched and guarded and led the imprisoned to the chambers, whether they were Germans, Latvians, Lithuanians, Poles, Croats, Ukrainians, or Czechs, that they be interned for one year as he had been interned. No heat in winter, no change of clothes, no bathrooms, no hot water, barely any water at all, no visiting with loved ones, almost no food. Being magnanimous, he'd allow them to forgo the torture and beatings. At the end of one year they should be released into society on a single condition:

227

they could never procreate. If they had children they had to give them up for adoption. If their wives became pregnant, they could either choose to abort or give the child up for adoption. Many thought he was being ironic.

"You cannot let your murderous desires paralyze you." He dipped a piece of naan bread into the steaming soup.

"Levi, I accept my inner Nazi." He snickered at my psychobabble term. "Though I don't know if I could kill in cold blood. But what I want, I simply want this never-ending, indelible ache of loss to go away."

"I possess no magic elixir," he frowned sympathetically, "that would excise your ache or fill the void. Don't worry about your ability to kill. You can." He breathed heavily. He wiped his mouth with his cloth napkin. "You cannot let your own victimization make you into a torturer."

I nodded.

"Listen carefully," we both stopped sipping our soup. "And I hope this makes sense to you. India gave us, the West, the zero, the idea of nothingness. They have used the zero as a cosmological concept for over two thousand years. In Hinduism, in the cult of Sunya, the essence of nothingness is from where we come and, finally, the ultimate reward. Life is the absence of nothingness. In the seventh century, this universal truth became known to humankind after the Brahmaghupta defined it as a mathematical and algebraic concept.

"Their sense of nothingness is not at all like ours in the West. The end result of life is to return to nothingness. Not like the traditional Western cataclysmic oblivion myth—the word *messiah* did not exist in Hindi or Sanskrit until the Christian missionaries brought it with the Bible. There are those, and I have spoken with them at length, who say I do not, cannot, understand the Indian way. Perhaps they are right." He nodded skeptically. "But in the system of castes I perceive a salvation that, over the centuries, became less transcendent and more Darwinian, more a tool of social control than spiritual. The best ascend and finally reach eternal nothingness—nirvana. In the ideal, I understand it, but this veers from my point.

"In the West, the zero and nothing are the ultimate terror. Even the American colloquialism of 'being broke' means having no money. To have nothing. To be broken." He frowned as if to say bah. "The West has spent centuries trying to negate or transcend the zero and nothingness, which is not possible. For if nothing is possible, then godlessness is not only possible, but probable. I accept this. There is no ultimate reason for existence, only chaos and what comes next is nothingness. Absolute nothing. I do not consider myself a nihilist. I have faith in nothingness. It is a wonderful feeling, in which I embrace the barbarian in myself, the cruelty in being a part of the human race. I accept my being as part Nazi and a creation of European culture, which has given the world TNT, the guillotine, the gas chamber, and the atomic bomb. I don't forgive. I never forgive. Those who say they forgive but don't forget are liars. But *I understand*."

I bowed my head, feeling quite sullen and inadequate.

He stared at me, with those pupils that sucked you in like vacuum tubes leading to the metaphysical void. "I don't tell you to understand those boys who are killers or the parents who may or may not be responsible, but understand your wife. You will not have tranquility, but you must have less hate, hate that is filling your void. And hate kills like no other emotion."

46

Epistasis is the biological term, which science best defines as that nothing is simple and everything depends on everything else. It's an essential precept that humankind must accept as a philosophical truth. We must accept and acknowledge our interconnectedness without demeaning, simplifying, or undervaluing our differences and individuality. We must live in the space, which maintains our uniqueness and our oneness in a Cosmological Epistasis.

—from *THE UNPUBLISHED WORKS*

47

ALTHOUGH I'D FLED New York for India to be alone, to be deaf to the world around me, in the week before I returned to New York, India ignored me all too well, as my apprehension over returning home became almost unbearable. My insomnia increased and the few hours I slept were fitful and plagued by nightmares. Not only my thoughts but also my behavior became obsessive. In a move reminiscent of my parents at their most ridiculous, I packed and repacked my suitcase time and time again. My waking hours became daymares, fraught with anxiety and dread.

Sarah called me from Romey's on Christmas day. Romey began making noises about the size of the phone bill. I said I'd call back, but the bill was only a pretense for Romey's orneriness. I heard her yell, "What's the big deal? He doesn't celebrate Christmas anyway." Knowing we'd see each other soon, we decided I shouldn't call back. Best left to do our talking in person.

Holika, gone down the path of her life's calling and then joining Samaka, didn't contact me. Charlie and his family vacationed in Pune. I didn't feel comfortable calling Levi. He'd given me his x-rays, MRI reports, and all the needed material. We left it that I'd call him when I got back. I got tipsy one night with Chandon, who rhapsodized about childhood and his idolized mother, who lived in the foothills of the Himalayas. He and Vishnu planned to zip off to their home villages the minute after they dropped me off at the airport. One evening I marshaled my defenses and called Ludovicci-Lint to inform her of my impending arrival. She insisted on a face-to-face meeting at her office. I didn't tell her the exact date I was coming, leaving, or the day of the unveiling. I did make an appointment. The conversation helped my paralytic funk not one bit.

So, it thrilled me out of all proportion when Tracee called and asked if I'd like to meet for dinner.

She suggested Kwality, not far from Connaught Place. The pinkish-hued decor of the drapes, blood-red tablecloths, and bright lights seemed like a Bollywood set for a restaurant. Tracee thought the owner preferred this style to impress the tourists with the cleanliness of his establishment. He proudly gave us menus and bragged about the "quality" of his chef, ignorant of Tracee's professional acumen.

Tracee showed up decked out in a jade-colored sari, gold earrings, much makeup, an amethyst necklace, a nose ring, and bangles on her wrists and ankles. A bit flashy, I thought, but if it made her feel better about herself, why the hell not? She shook my hand with her bony hand, which felt damn cold. Bad circulation. She chose a table in the back corner and sat with her back to the wall. She ordered a vast assortment of appetizers. She certainly appeared heartier, which begged the question, Was the anorexic critic on a new diet? "No, no, I've started writing a monthly column for Bahar's magazine. And better makeup, lip botox implants, and laser surgery can do wonders even for someone with a death sentence." Before I could lecture her, in between bites and comments—"too much cumin, can't taste the mustard seeds"—she told me that she fainted again right after her return to New York, in the offices of *Cosmo*. "What a scene. The editor either wanted me fired because I was on drugs or given a raise so I could afford a therapist." A friend, who knew her diagnosis, dragged her to a specialist where she underwent a battery of tests. Her T-cell count remained over one thousand. She suffered none of the usual symptoms of oncoming full-blown AIDS. After more sessions with this doctor, who insisted she did not have a "death sentence," she changed her diet from one "where 90 percent of my calories came from cigarettes, vodka, and diet pills." She even began practicing yoga. She had her limits, "Aerobic exercise is not in my past, present, or future." She decided not to start her on a protease cocktail yet, only a regimen of vitamins and supplements.

233

As she sipped her vodka, her voice lost its "gimme a break, don't kid me" drollness, dropped a register, and hissed out with a surreptitious intimacy. "What do you think of Holika's engagement?"

Not sure of her motive I waffled, "Good, I guess. What do you think?"

"Oh, we are playing the answer-a-question-with-a-question American game, are we?" She shook her head. "I smelled the way you two practically screwed on the dance floor." She twitched her nose from side to side. "Don't deny and don't worry. No one else noticed. They were either too drunk or too self-involved."

The waiter brought my Kwality Chicken and Tracee took a dip of the sauce with a piece of garlic naan bread. Tasted excellent to me. She rolled the small bite around in her mouth. "Indians are good at Indian food, leave the creamed sauces to the French. Now, you were getting ready to deny something . . ."

I cut her a piece of the chicken. "Try this, it's very tender." She stabbed it with her fork. "What I was going to say doesn't matter anyway."

"Maybe."

"What's that mean?"

She took her fork, with the chicken hanging off the edge, which reminded me of a Francis Bacon painting, and I started to lose my appetite as she pointed it directly at me, almost accusing me of some unspoken error of judgment. "My opinion is that Vijay is not as he presents himself."

"What's that have to do with Holika's engagement?"

"You are naive." She took a gulp of her vodka, which still supplied an ample amount of her calories. "Has Vijay regaled you with his tales of the jailed patriot?"

"No, but plenty of others have."

"It's bullshit." She looked suspiciously around.

"I have a feeling the reason I've heard is not your reason."

"You are right there, Doctor. Pillai started out by selling treasures from his own and his wife's family. Then in the early 1970s Pillai smuggled artifacts and treasures from our museums, from our temples, and from other desperate families, and replaced them with fakes. They finally caught and jailed him months before the Emergency."

Tracee used the word *our*, which didn't surprise me at all. Her speech, her education, many of her attitudes reflected her American side; her inner-self boasted of Indian pride.

"He received amnesty when the Emergency ended. Almost everyone did. Then he created this myth around himself, making speeches and writing articles, but he also kept his money and he became oh so legitimate and started Indya Petrochemicals." She stuck her left index finger in her mouth as if she were going to try to make herself wretch. From anyone else this would've been a childish gesture, but from Tracee it made me nervous. "Be cool, doc. I was never a puker. I'm telling you deadly serious stuff here—think I'm gonna ruin this with a scene? Got something stuck in a molar." I laughed and nodded. "So few people remember, and the longer it goes the more the lie becomes accepted truth and everyone fears him. But there are those who will never forgive him and his partners for selling out our country."

The story reminded me of Sarah's maternal ancestor Mawbridge Brockton. During most of the Revolutionary War he sold munitions and supplies to both sides. As the tide began to favor us future Americans, Brockton arranged a commission for himself as a Colonel in the Colonial army. After the war he used his status to make a fortune. Fatefully, the only legacy left to Sarah from that long-spent fortune was her middle name and a listing in Daughters of the American Revolution.

235

"How do you know all this?" I asked, slightly suspicious.

"You remember what I said my husband's family did?"

"Sure," I nodded. They were importers and exporters of Asian art. Art historians. They'd know.

"Does Holika know all of this?"

"She knows what she knows, interprets how she must, and then, like all of us, believes what she believes." That told me nothing but my instinct said she must know. "You must be discreet. Many who you think you can trust you can't." She smiled beguilingly.

"I'm trying to learn that. I trust Holika."

"Did she tell you she was married before?"

"To Siddhartha Singh."

Tracee nodded as if to say "So, things got that far, eh . . ." She took a bite of a spiced coconut salad. "Nearly *parfait*—both Siddhartha and the salad. I admired him. We all did. He loved people. Especially women. Siddhartha believed the women of India would rescue us from the patriarchal superiority."

I was slowly forming a picture of Siddhartha, whose charisma belied a cunning and practical mind that understood the complexity of the male–female relationship in India. Tracee's veins became visible through her pale skin as she explained his vision.

He believed even the worst woman beater or berater could be changed if educated correctly. Siddhartha believed in the women of India much more than the men. No one was more disappointed in Indira Gandhi than he. I think her failure turned him even more radical. He also understood the irony of his being male, but he seemed to know women would have to carry on his work.

"So, sounds like you knew him well?"

"Yes, he mentored many of us." She squirmed away from the table and leaned her back against the pink cushion of her chair as the waiter served me a conventional dessert of chocolate cake and a honey-dipped fried banana for Tracee. She sighed, but she cared less about Siddhartha than Holika, now more than ever knowing she'd trusted me, and who Tracee felt an almost maternal need to protect, yet whose flaws she didn't soft sop. She whispered even more softly than when she'd put the truth to Vijay's lie, so I had to lean across the table, our heads coming within six inches of each other. "I love Holika. When we were young she acted more like a sister to me than my sisters. Now, well, we have suffered some distance." She needn't explain the never specifically understood divides and fissures that arise between once close friends, where beyond the divide, the closeness exists unblemished. Tracee, her hazel eyes unblinking, insisted that I get her message, "Holika has the capability to act with incredible willfulness. Given the chance, she will do great things for India. But she thinks that she is more powerful and crafty than she is. What she's doing now is so courageous, but also dangerous." She sat back, her posture straightened with pride.

"Is it that dangerous to tell women about birth control and that they don't always have to listen to their husbands?"

"Yes, that is more dangerous than you can know but . . ." She paused and her eyes said, Do you know *this*? "But that is not all she's doing."

"Yeah, but she also asked me not to speak of it with any-one."

"I am not anyone. Holika thinks she holds Siddhartha's mantle and she is fighting Vijay and the Americans. That's why I think she's marrying Samaka—to get his help."

I thought of Holika's admonition when we first met—noth-ing in India is what it seems. I didn't know how right she was, or how much she had risked by trusting me.

Tracee's voice stayed firm without any scintilla of doubt as she described how, yes, Vijay believed he could sway Samaka to his side and have Holika married off to a future ally at the same time.

"Why are you telling me this?"

"People you think are your friends are not. You need to beware of everyone, and please, be careful for Holika." She sat back while the waiter filled her glass with white wine.

I needed no more warning. Not that I supposed I needed to hear it. A supposition that got support when Holika called me.

"You prepared?" I heard the swagger of contentment that enters a person's voice when all life is going well.

"You love that question."

She laughed in a voice bigger sounding than her small body.

"I got my ticket? Yeah, but . . . no, . . . How're you doing?"

"We had a productive trip. Mostly peaceful." I thought I heard her light a cigarette and take a puff. Then came a long pause, an exhale of air, and a question I never expected. "Neil, you are not a scoundrel are you?"

"I sure hope not."

"No, you are not. Do not *behave* like a burner either . . ."

"I'm not sure what you mean, I wouldn't ever . . ." I felt compelled to defend myself. It would've been bullshit. I stopped. She didn't mean literally. The silence drifted in between her warning and my acceptance of my "inner Nazi."

"You must do your best to understand Sarah."

"Yeah." I sighed.

238

"Please, call me when you get back. I will give you my cell number." She wished me a better and happy New Year and then she was gone.

The conversation left me feeling even emptier. I needed to purge my inner space of anger, yet at that moment my gut and my id overflowed with the dreaded fever of purgatorial anticipation. I wanted so desperately to feel even the illusion of control over my future—I had carefully planned all external-world goings and comings and meetings—yet, what I needed to control lay far beyond my powers. When Chandon dropped me off at the airport on New Year's Eve, I began the long journey home.

48

AFTER ALMOST TWENTY hours of flying and sitting in the Paris airport, I neared home. Still wary of the stares of a teenage girl and her mother who boarded in Paris and sat beside me but had the grace to remain silently voyeuristic. I had assumed but never really understood the power of the media before, which I had learned too well in my "fifteen minutes" of notoriety. No matter that I had rejected it, many had seen my face, and even if they couldn't place me, I was in the vast consciousness of faces that make up the celebrity gallery that has become the world's common sign language.

My body creaky and weary, I inhaled and tensed my spine when the plane finally touched down at Kennedy Airport. Always before, when returning home, I felt invigorated. Revivified. Knowing Sarah and Castor awaited me were the best gifts in the world. No gifts awaited me that day, only the driver from the car service who Matt hired to pick up "Philip Nolan." At least my changed visa status came in handy and I didn't have to wait on any lines.

The car sped over the decaying roads leading out of Kennedy Airport to the great American highway that passes through the poorest areas, yet is built to blinker the poverty and squalor. The car radio, tuned to the all-news station, reported that there had been seven murders in the city during the New Year's period. When Charlton Heston's recorded voice began to bellow his defense of handguns, I asked the driver to change the station. He looked at me in the rearview mirror. "I got a CD for people coming in to New York. Should I play it?" The disc jockeys I'd listened to since childhood were spinning platters from radio heaven, so I said, "Sure." He flipped in the CD and Leonard Cohen's existential drone sang of taking Manhattan and what everybody knows.

The Van Wyck Expressway was empty on this New Year's Day, unlike the rancorous trips in bumper-to-bumper traffic to relatives in Brooklyn on Jewish holidays when it seemed like all of New York was Jewish, and we showed up late and everyone sounded as bitter as horseradish. We whizzed by Shea Stadium and the Queens of my childhood filled with reddish-gray rows of apartment buildings, now housing thriving Korean neighborhoods, but the memory uprooted childhood ghosts where lived the quiet crimes of ugliness that surrounded us. Where the best, uninhibited ambitions lay crushed among a maze of fractured dreams, wasted marriages, and unwanted babies. I shut my eyes as we passed the Northern Boulevard exit, which could lead to where Castor and my parents lay under the ground. Past LaGuardia, and the excited Manhattan chill that always snaked up my spine when I glimpsed the Empire State and Chrysler Buildings, turned to the chill of terror as we crossed over the Triboro Bridge. Below, to the north, existed the shame of the cancerous marrows of shrunken buildings of the South Bronx, which worshiped the holy towers of the

American heaven across the Harlem River. A heaven beyond the reach of my belief, if not my pocketbook.

We got off the FDR at 96th Street and headed over to the hotel in an elegant brownstone run by a family of French people on 84th between East End and York Avenues. The smell of croissants and coffee seeped out from the office decorated with posters by Manet and Cézanne as I registered under my pseudonym. The husband-owner gave me a message from Sarah, who'd called to say that her plane was delayed, but not canceled, because of a snowstorm in Chicago where she and Romey had to switch planes. She'd be in, she hoped, later that evening.

I fell into bed and watched the news. With reports warning of potentially unsafe drinking water, rolling blackouts on the entire West Coast from San Diego to Seattle, and a snippet of an interview with Hal Burden of Environ lecturing about the need for more oil drilling and nuclear power, I thought, Geeze, am I in India or America? I switched off the TV and dozed until Matt knocked on the door late that afternoon. He brought me warm clothes, a suitcase full of mail—he'd already sorted through the hate screeds—and pastrami sandwiches, potato knishes, and Doctor Brown's cream sodas. I couldn't finish my food, so Matt, who was five-seven and stocky with a mammoth appetite, knocked off my half-uneaten sandwich. While swilling the last of his Doctor Brown's, he asked the question that had remained on his tongue for months, "So, Mr. Liberal, you still got people?"

"Yeah," I shrugged, "no excuses but my hypocritical frail humanity." My remembrance of my determination not to fall prey to the easy sense of deserving "people," seemed so far away at the moment, when all I felt was humanly frail.

He smirked with uncensored satisfaction. "C'mon, let's walk." We headed out for a twilight stroll in Carl Schurz Park beside the East River. The icy wind ripped off the river and my ears felt like they were being sawed off, and I wished I'd worn the hat Matt brought for me. We walked north toward Gracie Mansion. I asked how much extra this *shvartz-gelt* unveiling was going to cost me. Matt smiled churlishly, "Not a cent. We struck a deal with a guy I know from BCA Rugs. The temple's getting all new rugs and draperies."

"That's it?"

"The 'temple,'" he cleared his throat histrionically, "includes the rabbi's house at no extra cost."

I laughed at his affable relationship with human corruption. Then Matt asked the only question that seemed to matter to everyone but me.

"So, you still love her?"

"Yeah, but you got a discount for trusting duplicitous spouses?"

"Nope. Can't afford to."

Matt proudly and rightly proclaimed himself one of the great skirt chasers and catchers of his time. On his gravestone he wanted this epitaph: For a little guy he had the biggest thing and the most money. When he got married he and his wife understood the unwritten clause in their prenuptial agreement: he'd screw around quietly, and she'd spend his money lavishly.

"Want to hear why?"

"Nope, I know why." My answer made no impression on his wheeler-dealer mentality, where "no" only meant, "Keep going."

"When I turned forty, which you'll see is no fun, I got myself the gift of two two-hundred-buck-an-hour hookers for the night."

"And your point?"

"Lust never sleeps. It only closes its eyes."

"Who're you, Neil Young's rewrite man?" Behind my flippancy, the toughness of the statement burned.

"Sorry, man."

"No need."

"Sarah called me a bunch of times so she could talk to me to be near you. She always sounded like she wanted to confess something but she never did. I believe that she did it once and only once."

"Sometimes I believe, sometimes I don't."

We strolled on, passing dog walkers, lonely solo walkers, and couples holding hands. A tall blond woman smiled flirtatiously at Matt and he shot a slanted half-smile back. If he hadn't been with me, he would've talked to her. He couldn't help himself. He didn't bother to try to hide his lusts the way most married people repress their secret desires. I'd seen glimpses and more in so many of our friends and acquaintances relaxing boozily in restaurants or lolling down the street. My own infrequent hot flashes passed in and out of my blood without a serious desire to act on them. I was satisfied with Sarah. And Sarah—I figured the same went for her with me. As we walked on I thought about the time when we went to see that movie where the woman screwed Redford for a million bucks. During dinner with another couple, Sarah joked she'd "do him in a second for free." I'd laughed. We all did. Big deal, I thought, everyone fantasizes and what woman wouldn't fantasize about him or someone like him? As Matt stopped, and I stopped alongside him, I decided that it was no joke and I should've seen Jeremy Riegle coming. He was the Redford of the art world.

Matt leaned against the iron hand rail and pointed to Roosevelt Island.

"Look. What do you see?"

243

I thought not of what I saw but of what Castor would've seen: a land, pristine and unbuilt. Once we walked through an American Indian exhibit at the Museum of Natural History with the proudly sculpted Indians in their canoes, welcoming Mr. Hudson. Castor looked at me and not Sarah, "Dad, did you ever imagine how beautiful Manhattan must have been when there were no buildings and it was all green and forest?" Came my embarrassed answer, "No, I haven't."

"I see a dirty polluted river with damn scary currents and a run-down island with putrid buildings. You?"

"Possibility. New buildings. Hotels on the island. That's my dream." He spit over the handrail into the river. "I don't claim to be any damn psychologist or understand human nature beyond greed and ambition, but you gotta come to terms with Sarah so you can dream about saving the fucking poor people of the world from early death."

Everyone kept telling me to try to understand, be generous, make peace. Was I prepared? No, I thought, no fucking way. So I told myself until the second Sarah knocked on my door and I felt her agonized shiver as she awaited my greeting, as I felt Castor so much in her and I hugged her with a wild flood of joy and remorse and . . . All talk, all thought of talk vanished. We stripped and fell into the king-sized bed as if somehow this merging would erase all doubt. Her cherished soul smell, her body, her sweet-honey taste—her love smothered me. I nestled my head against her body, nestled between her breasts. I moved to enter her, drive the past into oblivion, and emerge into a future, a renewed, forgiven NeilSarah, and then the fleshy tip of my hard cock touched her wet vagina—and my cock collapsed. Without hesitation she slipped down my body, taking me inside her warm mouth and I got hard again but she did not make me come. We needed me *to be inside* her—and then, my cock fainted again.

I started to move to go down on her to see and hear her pleasure, but she stopped me with a tug on my hair. Shook her head. This was no macho, drug- or alcohol-induced failure.

I rolled over and tried to cradle her in my arms, but she pulled away from me and lay on her back.

"Sorry." I muttered feebly. I held her hand in mine. With the other hand I wiped the salty tears leaking from her eyes.

"I guess you were right not to want to see me yet."

"No. It's not . . ." No words could alter my inability to enter her.

"I suppose we need to talk . . . but, can you listen?"

"Yeah."

"I made an appointment with Debbie for tomorrow morning. I need you to come with me."

The unorthodoxy of a couple seeing the same therapist who cared for one of the spouses didn't bother me. I'd met Debbie and thought she could be semi-impartial. Her presence might inhibit words, once said, never to be taken back, from spewing unguarded from our ids.

"OK. Whatever you need."

Sarah got up, dressed, and went to her room where she unpacked and showered. My body clock was way off, but she wanted to get some food, so we trudged to a coffee shop on the corner of York and 86th. I'd been there hundreds of times with my parents, then with Sarah and Castor. As if time had not progressed, Sarah and I ordered a turkey burger and a Greek salad sans anchovies, on which we went halfsies.

For the first time she asked me about Levi. Until now, for reasons I didn't know, she hadn't wanted to hear about him. When I mentioned going to the Delhi temple, she perked up. She knew how distasteful I had found the idea of organized religion.

"It was crazy—I almost liked being there with all those people. But I'm not going back. I see Levi outside the temple."

"So you two are buddies now?"

"I wouldn't go that far. But we share something and he has shared his insight with me. What I've discovered is what I call my 'inner Levi,'" I half-laughed and she raised her eyebrows at the corniness of the phrase and knowing my cynicism about half-baked pop therapies, "my need to understand my basest instincts and accept them. We talked about the caste system and he equated it with how, in some ways, the Untouchables were treated in India with how others have used Jews and how the Israelis and the Palestinians use each other. How everyone needs a scapegoat."

"You mean *those* kids or us?"

"I mean me."

"And I am yours?"

"Maybe, yes, you were. Sometimes. Sarah, I *know* you have not one second of blame for what happened to Castor."

She didn't look at me but at her food. As she played with her salad more than she ate it, and I wondered if she were going to mention Riegle, she hit me with more unexpected news.

"I decided to have a show at the beginning of March."

I listened as she explained the gallery owner, Barbara Kugliani, arranged the show as a benefit for Women Against Guns. Before I could even attempt to object, she stopped me cold. "I need to do my art. I have to fill this emptiness with something. I'm not my mother who fills herself up by shopping." Sarah never fell into the consumerist trap that the more shoes you owned, the better your shot for inner peace. "I have nothing else now. I need to do more than just feel terrible." How could I argue against that reasoning? She understood the consequences of the attention as clearly as I did. "Maybe," she opened her eyes wider, blue with a wash of inconsolable red, "I have to use this tragedy to help. Somehow."

She did not ask, knowing the answer, for me to come back for the opening.

"Done?" She nodded and I paid the check. We walked back to the hotel and quietly, awkwardly, without a kiss or a hug, parted with only a fleeting touch of our hands.

49

There are those who think the greatest historical calamity of the twentieth century is Soviet Communism, a heinous philosophy that denies god and misunderstands man. Unquestionably, it is an immeasurably tragic, yet historically inevitable mistake. Which is, as the late Andre Amalarak has written, and I agree, doomed to the trash bin of history, because it not only denies god, but also denies the ego and the id of individual and collective humanity. This is the opposite of Nazism, which embraced the ego and freed the collective id.

Freudian psychology, which was born in Austria as was Hitler (which was no accident, in the midst of a sexually, socially repressive, and orderly society) opened the Pandora's box to the id. Which in effect were the godless Nazis unleashing the id of an entire continent—where all rules and order were broken and the threat of both earthly and cosmic retribution annihilated.

The mistake is to think that a rational philosophy can be made to control and define an irrational force. It cannot. Now that the evil has been released, been acted upon, in no way can it be returned to its box. Evil can only be contained but never, I fear, elimi-

nated. Thus there will be more genocides, more horrific wars in the name of god, race, and country, and new isms that in the end, whenever it will be, the last id will be standing.

My unsuccessful mission has been the need to find words to express the unsayable. To warn, as I tried to warn in Chambers, *of the invidious power of words spoken by those who signify the baseness of humanity. I retain this slim hope: that there will come those more equipped, whose perceptions find power in words to express the evil and find the good that will free humanity from itself. Because in the end, I believe, it is not that words failed me,* but I, who failed words.

—from *THE UNPUBLISHED WORKS*

50

THE NEXT MORNING we taxied over to Debbie's office on 90th Street between Columbus and Amsterdam, a small cubicle with cheaply made bookshelves, a desk, one closed window with the blinds drawn, and a pervasive musty smell. All the bad smells of rancid thoughts piled so dense that no air freshener could erase them. Debbie sat in her shrink's chair, feet up on the ottoman. Sarah and I sat beside each other but not touching, on the off-white, foam-cushioned couch with softer pillows. Two generic blue tissue boxes, each with one tissue hanging out, rested on each arm. Debbie, a small woman in her mid-forties with short, neck-length auburn hair flecked with gray, thick glasses, and wearing a shaggy off-white turtleneck sweater and long tan skirt, was all business. We exchanged extremely brief pleasantries. I stared at Sarah and she at me. I thought it would be hard to start. I was wrong.

"OK, tell me what I did to make it so easy for you to run to Riegle? Was I a fool for ever trusting you?" I detested the bitterness I heard in my voice.

"Neil, do you trust me?" Debbie interjected in her nasal Long Island accent. I wondered if I hadn't been set up.

"How do you mean? If you're on Sarah's side? Yeah, I think so. Would you lie to me? Don't think so."

"OK, I will work with that. Let's start with this. Sarah never betrayed you with *anyone*," behind her glasses, she held her brown eyes open wide without blinking. "Please let her explain."

I thought she meant before Riegle. I appreciated her use of the word "betrayed." I believed her.

Before I spoke, Sarah let forth what seemed like a prepared statement. "You were the best, you read my moods, supported me in my career, understood my relationship with my mother, you were the best father . . ." She sighed and as she talked, rotated her wedding band around her finger, which she too had not removed. "Do you remember what we talked about when we went to the River Café for our anniversary?"

"Yeah." An odious silence filled the room.

On the Saturday three weeks before the murder, over dinner, and out of nowhere, she asked what I thought about having another child. To be kind to myself, in the guise of bluntness, I reacted like a callous asshole. For so many reasons, we'd always agreed on one child. My mind hadn't changed. Some of her friends, who missed having kids in their twenties were now having kids, so I thought this question arose from some midlife-crisis last gasp toward a receding youth before the onset of menopause.

"Neil, how do you feel about that now?" Debbie called me on my monosyllabic response.

"I haven't, can't think about it." I turned to Sarah, "Because of that, you slept with Riegle?"

"No." She paused, glanced at Debbie for reassurance, and then stared at me. "I never had an affair with him or anyone else. It's more complicated. You never noticed how upset I was." She seethed with anger and anxiety, violently twisting and twirling her hair with her dexterous artist hands. And I grit my teeth wondering what the hell she was talking about. "I was pregnant."

"What? Oh, fuck." I whispered, jolted forward. Debbie, making an almost anti-therapist handbook move, took her feet off the ottoman, sat up straight, and shook her head trying to shut me up. I began to sweat, feel faint. In the haze of my own inner voice I heard my own words: working with Doctors Without Borders, traveling as two adults, she could exhibit in Europe and we could hang out, and at forty-one it might be too hard, less than a 30 percent chance for her to get pregnant and have a healthy kid even with fertility drugs. How could I have been so wrong? How could I have never noticed? How did I not listen to the exactness of her words when we were alone in the room in Matt's house? And then as I relived all of my justifications, I reheard her words, "I was pregnant," and I heard echoes in the innuendoes of that sanctimonious radio announcer and his question about an abortion that I didn't know about—and he did.

"Why didn't you tell me before? I thought we talked about everything?"

"I ask myself that everyday. Maybe because you would have said, 'Have it.'"

She was right. I needn't say that aloud. "And what did you do—and what'd that have to do with Riegle?"

"Nothing, nothing at all. I was at his apartment that afternoon because I had the abortion early that morning, and even after a couple of hours in the hospital I felt tired and I didn't want to go back to our place alone and you don't believe this, but Jeremy is a good friend and can be trusted so I called him and I didn't tell him why then, but I said I needed to go to his loft to rest, I didn't want to go home until you were there—I wasn't going to the opening and then. I've been everywhere on this with Debbie."

I imagined she and Debbie had examined every bit of minutia about why she'd kept this secret. The why of her own internal betrayal. Why she mistrusted me so deeply. I wondered if she found the answer she wanted and still could not tell me. I imagined the sessions analyzing her mother's mean-spirited sneakiness, her first-strike maneuvers against all her ex-husbands. Her scoundrel father's disappearing act, which culminated in Sarah's self-flagellating fear of growing up deceptive and irresponsible. But it seemed like bullshit now and had nothing to do with us. No, this was about Sarah and me. No doubt they'd dissected why she couldn't trust me enough to say the words: "I am pregnant, I want to keep this child." I still couldn't imagine why she never could tell me *the truth*? Had I become so selfishly distant? So lost to her inner desires? I didn't want to hear the answer. Not then. I was afraid of my own inner truth.

"Neil, mostly, I think I didn't really want the child, and I was angry and relieved when you reacted so disdainfully, that I made up my mind to do it and blame you and then . . ." She spoke haltingly, taking deep breaths. "Neil—your face."

"What? What?"

"My god, don't look so sad."

I tried to make my face remain impassive, but Sarah knew me too well and saw my pain.

"That is why I thought implying I had an affair would be easier than the truth and then after, then I couldn't tell you, you wouldn't even look at me after, you so instantly believed that I'd have an affair and I was so damn hurt and then so pissed off and then each day it got harder and—"

253

"Sarah, I, I'm so, so sorry . . . I hate myself right now. How could I have been so blind?" I slipped down on the couch; my body feeling boneless. My hands grasped the edge of the cushions. Sarah's shoulders drooped toward me. Abruptly, she sat up. The tissue boxes were getting a workout.

Debbie let us sink into our silences, where we stared straight ahead, no longer looking at each other and my mind obsessed on Sarah's torment and circuitous rationalizations. In my obtuseness about Sarah's moods and Sarah's refusal to accept that she didn't want another child—because of my outright male ego-idiocy we betrayed our own sacred words. Inside, I screamed: Why didn't you tell me? Why didn't Debbie help you to tell me? Why'd you carry the burden of mourning the unborn fetus alone? I questioned my anger at her for not being in the hospital when Castor died. My fury because I'd been denied the truth behind the truth. I trembled at the answers to those questions, which so fucked up any sense of my stability.

Debbie interrupted the quiet. "Because the circumstances are so urgent, the time seems so limited with me, the situation so unique—we haven't even talked about Castor—you just need to let yourself talk and start to tell me, tell yourselves what you want. You won't be able to answer that today. You both need time to understand your anger and sadness. To let the interior mechanisms of your emotions work themselves out. This may take a long time."

"Seeing Sarah now, knowing what I know now . . ." I reached for Sarah's hand. I held it limply in my damp palm. I turned to her. My voice shaky. "I feel like such an asshole. Everything I never wanted to be. My only constants were you and me and Castor. Until, what, an hour ago, I believed we wouldn't be having this conversation if Castor had lived." I shrugged, as much an Atlas sag of my shoulders as of helplessness. "But I need to make it up to you somehow. Repair what has been broken if I can. We can." And yet, as I spoke those sentiments, which I meant with every part of my being, questions and contradictions of need still clawed at my insides. "When were you gonna tell me?"

"While I was at Jeremy's I'd made up my mind I had to tell you that evening. But . . . I can't think of what would've happened. Only what did happen and about the future."

"That's where we part—not one day, shit, one hour has gone by when I haven't relived that second, what could I have done—when I looked down at my hands, his bleeding body, and then the next second . . ."

"And you think if I had told you before it would've been different?"

"I don't know. I used to think the Buddhist schtick about the tiniest stick in the stream that could change oceans but . . . there were other sticks."

"Castor was shot by four sick individuals. Nothing you or I did or didn't do could've changed that. I love you. I can't imagine the rest of my life without seeing and talking to you the way we used to. I need to understand why I didn't tell you. I need you to help me understand. I need that back. I made two huge mistakes. I don't want to make a third."

I wished I had time when we left the office to gradually grasp how Sarah struggled, how we broke our word with silence, how she believed in her heart that if I'd said, "Sure, let's have another kid," there'd be no need to discuss redoing time, meditate on our time ending. Debbie was right—our, my, choices needed time. Time I didn't know if we had.

255

51

WE HURRIED BACK to the East Side, unluckily getting a taxi driver with a good memory, who recognized us and asked for our autographs on the bill printed out from his meter. We obliged rather than argue, and asked him not to tell anyone he'd seen us. Thankfully, I'd asked him to drop us at the corner of 85th and York instead of at the hotel. At the hotel we met with Matt and a real estate broker connection of his whom he'd chosen to handle the sale of our apartment. Neither of us could ever live there again. We agreed not to go by the apartment. Before I'd left for India I'd packed up many of my belongings which I didn't take with me, and left them sitting in the apartment. The broker knew someone we could hire to put them in storage. The few mementos I wanted could be saved or sent to me. Sarah, who, for the moment, had decided to stay at Kugliani's house in the Hamptons while she prepared for the show, had time to decide when she could go back inside the apartment. Maybe she'd go with Romey after the apartment sold but before the final closing date.

Then came the meeting with the lawyers. There were over nine ongoing lawsuits surrounding the massacre. We had refused to take part in any of them, although we were considering joining the one against the gun manufacturers.

Everyone in the antiseptic Park Avenue and Fifty-seventh Street office of Grubman, Green, Lint, and MacAlister looked TV-commercial scrubbed clean. All the furniture, carpet and painted walls seemed newly varnished. I wished I had some Delhi dust to sprinkle like the anti–Tinker Bell.

A receptionist asked us to sit briefly in the waiting room.

Ludovicci-Lint, not at all as I pictured her, overweight with big bones and older, over fifty, wearing a gray suit, short, cropped hair, a weathered, hard face, and a slow earnest gait came out to meet us. "Dr. Downs and Ms. Roberts, please come this way." Gravity, rather than pleasantness, eked from her voice. We followed her into the conference room. John Linscombe sat at one end of the hockey-rink-sized table where magazines, blue binders, folders, reams of papers, and law books filled half the table. He sniffed and wiped his nose with a handkerchief before he shook our hands. "Sorry, allergies." He stood over six-foot four, with tortoiseshell glasses and prematurely gray curly hair, framing youthful facial features; he could've been anywhere from twenty-seven to forty. He had perfect white teeth, too many of them.

On top of one stack I spotted the newest issue of *Teen People*, with a cover headline, "The Stuyvesant Massacre: Beyond the Tragedy." I felt a perverse compulsion to look inside. I picked it up. There were interviews with kids who survived. I came to a one-page essay written by Mary Sweedlow, the girl who Castor pushed to the ground and covered up. I read the blurbs, "I know why I am writing this, I don't know why so many people care. It feels so invasive." "In the night when I go to bed, I keep the light on because I still see Castor's kind face and I touch the scars where two bullets passed through his body and into mine."

Mary had written a letter to us saying she'd wanted to come to the funeral but understood our desire for privacy. I'd sent her a brief note of thanks. After scanning her story, I asked for her phone number, which they had, and placed the magazine back on top of its stack.

"OK, why is it so essential for me to be here?" I was in no mood for lawyerly dissembling.

Linscombe poured us each a glass of bottled water while Ludovicci-Lint spoke with measured calculation. "Aside from a desire, because personal contact helps, we have offers from "60 Minutes" and "Dateline" for you to appear, which might be helpful."

"No. Never."

"OK." Ludovicci-Lint shifted her left shoulder back and her right shoulder forward and then reversed the shoulder positions as if she were cracking her back. "The Skirpans are not the finest caliber of people and it's important you know who we're dealing with."

Linscombe handed us each a red binder.

Ed and Nicky Skirpan, who'd divorced five years earlier, found new togetherness in this lawsuit. She had taught in the New York public school system for twenty years before being reprimanded for the fifth time. The last for calling her black students "lows and prims," a code for lowlifes or low IQ. After that incident, the Board of Education transferred her to work in their offices in downtown Brooklyn. Ed Skirpan, an alcoholic, had owned a plumbing business in Howard Beach, Queens. It'd gone bust and he now worked odd jobs.

Ludovicci-Lint had compiled pages and pages of information on the killers; I stopped reading.

"What's the point of all this? I don't care about these people."

Ludovicci-Lint and Linscombe flashed one of those quick, silent-movie ominous glances while Ludovicci-Lint did the talking. "The Skirpans are after only money."

"So, you want me to pay them to go away? Will that make me culpable in some manner? I won't sign off on anything like that—"

She didn't even let me finish. "The hospital wants to make a settlement. The Skirpans are willing to take $100,000. We think we can get them down even lower. It's peanuts."

"No." I'd sign nothing that gave any implication that I'd acted improperly. "This is insane. How the hell did I become the guy on trial?"

"It's not only you they're going to put on trial." She clenched her left hand around a pencil. A massive diamond ring glistened on her forefinger. "It's going to be damn dirty."

"What?"

She hesitated. Linscombe tapped his feet on the carpeted floor.

"G'head, gimme the worst," I said as I saw Sarah's neck begin to spasm. "No, wait."

I leaned over to Sarah and asked if she wanted to leave the room. If I should stop them right there.

"No. Tell us what you *think* you know," she ordered.

Linscombe spoke in a monotone voice while staring at me. "We have verified Ms. Roberts visited the office of Dr. Julie Stone on the morning of the shooting. Later that day," he moved his gaze to Sarah, "after being out of phone contact for hours, you made a call from the loft of Jeremy Riegle."

I felt sick. Sarah looked sick. Unsure if they knew what occurred in Stone's office, her neck twitched and constricted so deeply that I thought she might have trouble breathing.

Ludovicci-Lint took over. "We can only presume if we know this, so will Corricelli of Karpstein, Forman. We need to know if there was something going on, if they can prove that all those calls made to find Ms. Roberts, that her visit to Stone's office and Ms. Roberts' absence distracted you, Dr. Downs."

"They have a chance?"

"Not to win. But it might not get thrown out, which before I was sure it would be, as frivolous. Which means it will go to trial. Depositions. Money. Investigations. It will get ugly. The Skirpans, Corricelli and his partners at KFC deserve each other."

These two worked for the hospital and insurance company and would sell me out in a second. My stern refusal to admit any guilt reversed itself suddenly and entirely. "Settle."

"No, Neil. You said you'd never ever give in and you'll be forever tainted."

Ludovicci-Lint stood up, "Should we leave you two alone?"

"No," I stood up. My knees buckling. "We're done. Settle the damn thing. I want all of this over." I placed my hands flat on the table to calm myself. "But if I read the merest hint of any bullshit that has no basis in fact about my wife in any paper, even *The Enquirer*, I'm coming after all of you somehow. Slander. Libel. Breach of attorney–client privilege. Let me tell you, I will be one sympathetic witness. Somehow you fix it that whatever you *think* you know stays inside this room."

"We can't guarantee that. We need to know certain facts." Linscombe squinted at me. I wasn't sure what he was trying to convey. "People like the Skirpans and KFC are completely immoral."

I didn't look at Linscombe. Ludovicci-Lint was the partner, the big cheese sniffer.

"This is the only *fact* you need to know: I acted as a doctor without any prejudice or knowledge that Bobby Skirpan killed my son until after that day was over." I glanced at Linscombe who paled and drank a sip of water. "They want their money. You manage it. You want me to cooperate? I can do that. One of the best decisions I ever made was paying an extra out-of-pocket premium for supplementary malpractice insurance aside from what the hospital paid, so you need me to sign off on any payment or agreement. So far I have not hired a separate lawyer and I've asked my insurance company to cooperate with you. That can all change."

Linscombe let out a discernible, "Oh, shit." He knew how much trouble I could cause them. That anything they agreed to would be flawed, maybe useless without my cooperation and the cooperation of my personal insurance company. When Matt had negotiated my settlement with the hospital he made sure I retained that right.

"Now, do it. Please."

I despised them although they were only doing their jobs. I despised Karpstein, Forman and the Skirpans. I despised myself. My black hole of hate felt insatiable, sucking in all my good air. Except for Sarah. Right then, I didn't hate her at all. In the elevator, I looked at her. I ached for her sadness. I put my arm around her and hugged her close to me.

"Neil, I want you to think about this. You only gave in so I wouldn't be humiliated."

"Sarah, I don't give a damn about humiliation. I want you

and me to be left in peace. That's how we decide. We'll never get beyond all of this until this bullshit is over."

I understood why the families of the others who were murdered kept on with these lawsuits, magazine articles, books, and TV programs. Some for greed. Most because this kept their children alive. I couldn't exist that way. Castor was dead. For me to go on, I needed to let my son die. Again.

52

THE DAY OF the unveiling was the worst day of my life. The murder and the funeral hit with such unexpected speed that I remained in shock for weeks, still disbelieving that Castor could be dead. The saving release of chemicals in my brain refused to let me fall into catatonia or immediate clinical depression. Not so the unveiling, which lurked over each day, each week, clawed inside me for months. When it came, my body ached, my insides bled, my heart hurt. It was pure pain.

I wanted time to run faster or to stop. I wanted, like a child, to wail, "Go away!" Of course, time did not stop and the hellish visions did not end. During those few days before the ceremony, I ate but had no appetite. I slept but did not feel rested. I don't remember checking out of the hotel and the car picking up Sarah and me. I don't remember that Romey already sat in her fur coat and hat emotionless in the car when it arrived. I don't remember the ride to the cemetery. I don't remember the photographer hiding in a nondescript car across from Castor's grave; I only remember that the photo showed up the next day in the tabloids. I don't remember seeing Matt and the few friends and cousins whom Matt, with my permission, invited at the last minute. I do remember seeing Castor's best friend, Drew, and Mary Sweedlow holding hands with other friends whose names I couldn't recall. I remember Mary hugged Sarah and me and we hugged her as if she were our child.

I do, in some haze, remember the rabbi sermonizing about how we are god's jewels on loan to this world and Castor, a unique jewel, was now returned to god. I remember his phrase "Life is only part of a longer, unknowable journey, and Castor's journey on earth was cut short for a reason. As part of God's unknowable plan."

I remember glaring in disbelief at the headstone of my son: Barry Castor Downs.

I remember, against my will, picturing the four faces of those who killed my son, and wishing they were alive to suffer in life and not in death.

I remember I halted, knelt, and placed stones on the graves of my parents, Zohar and Bernie, and I felt a moment's relief that they had not lived to bear this weight. As I tried to stand up, I felt my body lose all motor control, becoming woozy. I thought I heard my mother's thunderous cadences, "I told you Not to send him to that school. But he's safe with ME now so Act like a Man, a mensh, a husband to your wife like I raised you!" I almost laughed inside the dizzy pain at her ability to make me feel even guiltier from the grave, as if she could've saved Castor, and made me act correctly—all in two short phrases.

I remember Sarah and Matt held me up, as the hovering inner voice passed, and we bonded like a molecule of water, becoming one in a vapor of tears.

I don't remember the car dropping us off at a new hotel on Lexington and 87th. I don't remember Sarah and I checking into separate rooms. I remember ending up in her room, so exhausted we lay down on the bed. Fully clothed. Then we slept. I remember when I awoke I felt her hand on my cock, which yearned for her like it never wanted a woman before and I knew I was ready and would not fade. I remember fearing my words couldn't promise what my heart couldn't give, so I remained silent; still our needs transcended words and we fell into each other's cavern of pain. She needed my tender touch of love as I dreamed her whisper of hope as truth. With eyes closed and tongue tucked into my ear, she begged for what we both wanted so damn bad as we made love. With my tempered breathing, I released the acrid mix of the angry male exercising the vengeful power of the penis, the tangled intellectual guilt of accepting primitive lust and the love of a husband who wanted to please his wife.

265

In the inner quiets of my comings—feeling clean air, I exhaled and urged my seeds to answer her plea.

53

Trans, Sub,
AB-, ent, -los, un-, ver-,
-less, un, ab-, trans-

Prefixes and suffixes. Words, yet not words. Bleeding with mean-
ing. Part of the larger whole. We are like prefixes and suffixes, part
of the whole. Alone and incomplete unless we become one with
the whole.

    From the moment of the newborn's first cry evolving into the
young child's grunts and groans of yearning we speak in our lan-
guage of need. With more grunts and groans begin words. Some
languages sing of the loss. Others only syllabify and emphasize.
All are insufficient to the task of defining the first smells. The
unknown echoes becoming familiar voices. The infiltration of col-
ors becoming emotion. Virgin forms emerging as the tactile chords
of love. The sounds becoming words. All becoming language. The
child's world, like the universe as inexplicable gaseous mist becom-
ing the hard, knowable, and secure markers of the mystery hidden
in the meaning of words, which still ache of incompleteness. Sound

of something missing. Do not fill the void. The yearning from the womb. For the mother and father. For the mate. For the child. For the unanswerable. For certainty. For the ache of emptiness which is filled by the search for the silent gods.

—from *THE UNPUBLISHED WORKS*

54

AFTER THE REVELATIONS in Debbie's office, the disputatious meeting with Ludovicci-Lint, and the unveiling, it seemed perhaps irrational that Sarah and I would fall into each other as we did, yet at the moment it felt natural. In the late morning we awoke wondering, What now? If that was a one-time final goodbye fuck or a merging of love leading to a future together, we both needed time to reflect, to absorb the possibilities of being together again. Had that night given Sarah a graceful, exonerating exit? Her actions gave no indication to the implicit, but unspoken question. We spoke little about the new truths we heard in Debbie's office, we needed to let the emotions and acts find their place in our hearts and heads, become comprehensible. At last we agreed she'd come to India after the show, and we'd try to rebuild the trust and love that had been so good for so many years and somewhere, even before I knew, turned against us.

On her way to Kugliani's Hampton's home, Sarah went with me to the airport, where six months before I'd gone alone. I'd left New York then feeling like a metaphysical paralytic cemented in a Beckett-like static time, aching for my own death as the silent blip . . . blip . . . blip . . . on the monitor of my mind played and replayed the known vision of my son dying, and the unknown image of my wife screwing another man. Denying I was searching for anything but silence until Levi exposed my empty denial, that begged the question, What do you search for after there is no longer a search for god?

That day, no less laden but hating myself less, less lost but not yet found, still godless and faithless, still a walking dialectic—loving Sarah and newly befuddled and furious at Sarah, missing Sarah, wanting to be with her forever and never see her again, but wanting less to die myself, we parted—and as the 747 lifted off and the spires of Manhattan and the pyres of Brooklyn and Queens and New Jersey merged into a sunset sky of pink and gray, wounded yet scarring, with a quixotic mix of hope and despair, and an odd, unreasoned belief that a future existed beyond Castor's death, my gut told me that I was leaving New York, where forever I would be from, for the last time when I could call The City my home.

55

UPON MY RETURN to New Delhi with a suddenly different past, I wandered into the future of the known and an unknown and found answers to questions I had never asked. For what transpired in that future, now past, appears in my present like the disjointed flickering images of rapid-eye-movement dream sleep spliced with the slow motion, frame-by-frame replay of events eternal and ever-changing. More than ever the frailty of perception becoming truth in words haunted me. Haunt me still as I tell you now of my last months in India, which began with being confounded by Sarah's distrusting silence, with my search for "why" unanswered, with my unbelief in god no less certain. During that plane ride I questioned over and over again how I never sensed Sarah slipping away from me. Of how easily I embraced the falsity of her implied actions, for she never once spoke the condemning words. Of what I should have done but did not.

The tormenting speculation quieted as I jostled my way through the crowded airport where I found relief in the cacophony of sounds—a massive taxi strike and the chaos it created suited me still. Vishnu found me and we hustled through a near-hysterical mob. The technicolored saris and turbans felt so uplifting after the dour black and gray tones of New York in winter. The children's euphonious voices struck at my empty ache, and amidst the crush of sensations I resigned myself one more time to forever missing Castor's tranquil gaze.

Vishnu informed me that Chandon no longer worked for me. When I asked why, he refused to say anything but made a swift motion with his semiclosed fist, thumb sticking out, and a tilt of his head as if he were swigging alcohol, before looking askance. At home I met Pankaj, who replaced Chandon. He was older, mustachioed, and spoke better English. He didn't seem the type who'd sling down a beer while giving me Hindi lessons.

I left two messages on the voice mail of Holika's cell phone. I called Charlie and left a message with his secretary; I needed to set up a tennis date and make plans for Sarah's visit. I'd finally see the Taj Mahal.

Charlie didn't answer my message immediately. Instead, Schlipssi called and told me not to leave before five-fifteen on Thursday, when Vijay had scheduled his appointment. Almost apologetically, Schlipssi informed me about impending trouble at AIIMS, the best and second busiest government-run hospital in New Delhi. One of the "C"-class workers had beaten up a doctor because he refused to treat his wife ahead of other patients. A melee ensued and the "C&D" workers, meaning the low-caste workers, were threatening to blockade the hospital. As a favor to the government, the International Hospital at Chanayakpuri would be used for emergency purposes. Schlipssi asked if I'd volunteer in the evenings if they needed me. Of course I would.

When Holika called from Udaipur, she seemed in a bit of a tizzy. Neither serious nor banteresque, she recited her itinerary:

a few more days in Rajasthan. Then off to Bangalore to see Samaka and then back to Jodhpur. Hesitancy entered her voice, "Neil, I am almost afraid to ask . . ." I didn't give many details but she sung out in elation when I told her Sarah would be coming. "That should give you some optimism."

"I wouldn't go that far. And you?"

"I must remain optimistic. I have other obstacles to deal with. Because of the to-do at AIIMS, the residents who are obligated to help have begged off. Cowards."

"I can ask Charlie to let me come for a weekend or something."

"Oh, yes, I am sure he and Chrystie would escort you to the first plane."

"Maybe if you or your uncle ask him."

She paused. "There are problems," she dare not explain them over the phone, "and you did not come to India to become tangled in our lives or politics."

No, I hadn't. But India, its people, and its culture, at first almost voyeuristically, captivated me. Then it absorbed me; caught me in its intimate grasp of a billion pairs of hands. India could be loved and reviled in the same breath, but never ignored. Even when I tried. Holika's subtle reference made it clear I shouldn't mention our conversation when Vijay, who treated me with his usual politesse and underlying sense of purpose, arrived exactly on time on Thursday.

Donna and I did the EKG, chest x-ray, and took new blood tests, a stool test, and a PSA test. The test results, which he brought with him, showed a grade-two myeloma that indicated it remained in a "smoldering" state. As I examined him, his body draped in the gown, the visibility of his rib bones, knees, and spine betrayed physical frailty. My touch was by no means scientific, but his bones felt soft, perhaps a sign of the disease's progression. He didn't claim any symptoms of osteoporosis.

Once he dressed and took a seat in my office, we discussed advisable therapies for the myeloma. I suggested a regimen of low-dosage gamma globulin IV once a month, which could be augmented with chemotherapy and administered in Delhi. I recommended he go to Rockefeller University in New York or the University of Oregon at Eugene. Both were experimenting with onogene therapies and the use of Thalidomide specifically for his condition. A donation to the research program would guarantee his acceptance.

"I will make the donation and perhaps next year I will go." He waved his right hand in the direction of the future and the West, as if he were waving bon voyage to a neighbor who'd stayed too long.

273

I frowned. Dubious. A year seemed an awfully long time for a condition that could turn in a month—and kill him if left untreated.

"No, I have much to do this year."

"The positive reason-to-live attitude can serve you well, but you should try to get there this summer during your vacation. Maybe there's a program here. I can investigate for you, if you like. Germany probably has a program."

"No, no I am so busy this summer with Indya Petrochemi-cals." Although he mentioned no specifics, I nodded my head in understanding at this rare allusion to his business affairs. "Power is the key to all—information and nuclear power are keys to the future of India." He crossed his legs in an almost relaxed fashion, and folded his clasped hands on his lap. "Your power as a doctor is the information you possess."

"I try not to think of it in those terms." I didn't want to admit it but I also thought he was right.

"Think it or not, you conduct yourself as one who is aware of his power—unobtrusively perhaps, but certainly." His eyelids drooped to half-mast, reaching the tops of his pupils. "We both know you have power in what you know about me—and I must request that you not tell my nephew and nieces of my condition."

"I wouldn't. I can't."

"*Would not* and *cannot* are words that I do not accept as having full meaning."

"I *will not* tell them."

He nodded at my expected acquiescence. "I do not want Holika to get so overly anxious about me." He took a monogrammed handkerchief from his pants' pocket, folded it

in a triangular fashion and blew his nose. "I feel sure that Samaka will take care of her." He folded the handkerchief and put it back in his pocket.

I saw no benefit to impolitely question why Holika needed anyone to take care of her. "Yes. She seems quite pleased."

"Pleased, yes. Now that my children are taken care of," I wondered if he hadn't arranged marriages for Ratish and Alka as well, "death does not feel unwelcoming."

His voice did not break or reveal any inner fear. His sincerity only emphasized the contradictions of so large a personality. "May I speak openly?"

"Of course," I said, more noncommittally than my words implied.

"It is no secret that you came to India because of death. I am not foolish enough to believe anything I say can bring you peace, but as I picture my bodily life ending each morning before my meditation, I think of the words of Bhagwan Krishna." He stared at me across the desk with a beatific calmness, with his hands pressed together in front of his chest. "'He who is born must die;

he who dies is sure to be born again. The inexorable circle of lives and deaths goes on. You are getting worried about a phenomenon, that of death, where there is no loss.'"

He closed his mouth and breathed out from his nose before he spoke again. "I am prepared for death. If it is to be, a better life awaits. If not, then not. The loss, for there is the loss of those who are left behind, is not for those gone elsewhere."

The conviction of his transcendent certitude, with his life's mission of dharma so inextricably meshed with his formidable, earthly Darwinian survival skills, left me in awe. More than someone like Hal Burden, who was so transparent, Vijay emanated a complex sincerity in his beliefs. I had no doubt Vijay believed he lived and acted in the best interests of his family and his country in accordance with his principles. He would insist that what either of us thought was incidental, for his final judgment rested in the beyond.

Before he left to see Athol Fugard's *The Road to Mecca* at the National Theater, he invited me to a cocktail party at the prime minister's official residence the following week. "A special celebration between your country and mine. Holika and Ratish will be there."

That piqued my curiosity. I eagerly looked forward to talking to Holika in person.

The embassy coordinator for the party contacted me. Not allowed to go alone, he assigned me to a car with other members of the embassy staff. Soldiers paraded up and down the street. Vines and shrubbery covered a metal gate that surrounded the official home. We parked the car inside the gate and then a soldier led us along a garden path and through a security check that paled in comparison to security at New York nightclubs. Because terrorist actions from many factions were not uncommon in Delhi, I almost hoped there were hidden sur-

275

veillance cameras. The soldiers made a big deal of searching the bags of the women.

After walking down another path, we came to an expanse where banquet tables filled with hors d'oeuvres ringed the outer edge of the lawn. The Americans, both the men and women, unaware or uncaring of Indian custom, intermingled on line in the usual banquet style—first come, first bite—while the Indian women waited for the men to finish being served.

On the far right of the grounds a tent, covering about two hundred and fifty chairs, flapped in the wind. Milling in the crowd on the circular lawn I recognized Hal Burden, Chrystie, Alka, and the Donneaux. No Charlie. No Holika. Soon Charlie, Ratish, and Prime Minister G. B. Sowat, surrounded by his surly bodyguards, strolled out from the residence. Still no Holika. And she never came. It didn't take long to understand why: this gathering celebrated the consummation of the deal between Environ, Indya Petrochemicals, and the Indian Government Power Authority. No matter her reasoning, Holika's absence displayed defiance or disrespect. I wanted to speak with Ratish but he motored around so fast, like a barely-in-control stock car, that no matter how I tried I couldn't catch his attention.

I exchanged one unsolicitous glance with Olivier Donneaux. He and Cécile maintained their distance. I avoided making eye contact with anyone whom I didn't know. I stuck by the embassy people who took advantage of this time to ask both obvious and arcane medical questions. I didn't mind.

Chrystie gave me extra minutes on her air-kiss clock, inquiring in a stage whisper how was I "coping" and if she could help with anything, which impressed the other staffers who considered her the Queen of Aloof. I heard a few catty asides aimed at Chrystie because of her black dress, a color that, to many an Indian, signified bad luck. A fixture on the "People" pages of the Indian newspaper and magazines, she posed for pictures in her tight V-neck gown with a string of pearls around her neck that would've sunk the Titanic. I watched Charlie as he eyed Chrystie while she flitted from guest to guest. In his admiring gaze, I saw his pride in her youth and beauty; in her new gift to his immortality in their daughter, Heather; in his virile need that heard her voice assure he was the greatest fuck of all time; in his belief in her hidden depth. Under that crepuscular winter sky, in her briefest glance back at Charlie, not her studied party smile, but in the tender blink of her eyes, the speed with which she strode to his side and squeezed his hand when he looked distressed—I saw the unveiled mystery of love stained by duplicity and felt the dread of the stains upon Sarah and me, of words unspoken, deeds undone, of duplicities deeper than adultery, and what others saw that we did not.

Aides started to round us up to sit for the speeches. Head down, I started across the lawn kicking the perfectly cut grass with the tip of my shoes, feeling perversely envious of Charlie and Chrystie, when Ratish stopped me.

"Doctor, so glad you could make it."

"Me, too." My eyes peered into his, which had buzzed insanely on the night of the dinner and dancing, so empathetically outside the Arts and Crafts Museum, were so intensely focused and burned with a triumphal gleam.

"Holika asked me to tell you that she is sorry she has been unable to see you. She became ill with a stomach ailment and had to remain in Bangalore. When she comes back we should all go out again. I think everyone had a great deal of fun."

"I know I did. My wife is coming and I'd like her to meet all of you."

"Excellent!" He glanced over his right shoulder as he heard Vijay calling his name. "A good friend of ours has just opened a disco at the Taj Palace. It's one of our finest hotels. Have you ever been there?" He opened his eyes a sliver wider and his neck stretched slightly forward. He didn't gloat, but the question could've ended with the word, "Check."

I nubbed the grass with my foot trying not to give away this new fluttering in my gut. "Yeah, one night," I gritted my teeth, not so much for me as for Holika.

"Well, I hope you enjoyed it." He moved to my side, no longer facing me as Vijay, with his almost bunny-hop stride, reached us. Trailing behind him, lolling at his own pace, came a pinkish-skinned man, with a gaunt face, thinning gray hair, a crooked nose and bad posture, his spine seemed in serious need of a chiropractor. Vijay introduced James Grimes, former ambassador from Great Britain to India. He'd recently arrived in Delhi to serve as the representative of the European Energy Council. Vijay spoke in English. "This is Dr. Downs, the superb physician at the American Embassy." We shook hands and then Vijay turned his body about thirty degrees, just enough so I felt like an intruder. "And this is my *son*," Vijay massaged his nephew's right shoulder with his left hand, "Ratish."

An aide came by and whisked them away for the speeches.

I sat in the next-to-last row as the wind crackled through the electric microphone and speakers. Charlie, a master of saying nothing, mumbled twenty of the most insipid words possible. Burden stood stiffly in his gray suit, looking tight-lipped and so sour. I'd recently read an article about Burden, in which the prep-school-nicknamed "White Rat" gave up a life of drinking and debauchery at age thirty-five, when he returned both to his religion and to his duties in the family oil-drilling business. In later years, he formed Environ. He did not make a speech. Next came Vijay, who, smiling proudly, spoke in Hindi. Aides passed out an English text of his speech to the audience.

When he reached the end of the prepared text, he switched into English and spoke extemporaneously.

"People like the honorable Prime Minister Sowat, Ambassador Bedrosian, Ambassador Grimes, and Mr. Hal Burden understand the future where India is America, and America is India and India is Europe. They understand the nexus of the new democratic order, which, as we inaugurate this future, I say to our critics who proclaim that we have no rights to dam rivers, undo older dams, and build power stations, who say that we are against nature—I say, 'Untrue.' We stand as one under the vast guidance and wisdom of Krishna. Let them recall that in Bhagavad-Gita, 5.19, it is written, 'They have conquered nature . . . Therefore they are established in Brahman.' That is my true goal. To follow the way to Brahman."

279

Once more, I almost accepted that Vijay's motives arose from genuine spiritualism; then I glimpsed his partner, Hal Burden, who also posited himself as a god-loving man, who believed man should and could control nature, which gave me great pause.

Lastly came Prime Minister Sowat. He had a Big Daddyish *Cat on a Hot Tin Roof* heft and gave his brief speech in Hindi.

Immediately after the speeches, two young journalists from the Nehru University newspaper cornered Burden. At six-foot two and fat, his hulking mass kept the student journalists at bay. He consciously looked down on them as he grumped out a few words. I inched closer and heard his voice, as moist and dirty as day-old New York City sludge, which echoed the sound bite heard on public television noncommercials, "Environ aims to be the energy source for the new century divining new ways to bring the environment safely to the world." He broke away from them, his pale face, callous. The young Indian woman yelled after him, "Can you please tell us how you feel about the legacy of pollution and displacement this project will have on the future generations of Indians?" He curled his thin upper lip with scorn. Burden pointed with his stubby hand to his spokesperson. "He is here to answer all questions." Interview over, Burden about-faced, surrounded by his bodyguards, and marched down the path that led inside the prime minister's residence to attend the dinner for special guests.

I took a taxi home and resumed my new evening activity of reading the bag load of mail Matt had given me. I answered many letters, giving weight to the most heartfelt and lonely. I still didn't want any anonymous person to know my where-abouts so I sent them to Matt who mailed them out. One of the screeds got by Matt's censoring. It enlightened me about the Web site memorial to those "heroes Bobby, Linda, Mitch, and Rusty." I passed on that invitation and sent the missive to Ludovicci-Lint.

Ray Esperenza sent an apologetic letter. Each handwritten word weighed down with guilt over his "hatchet man actions. I should've told them what I thought of them. Told them to stuff their damn job." In September, he had quit St. Vincent's and taken a job with a clinic in East L.A. Him, I wrote back, posting the letter from New Delhi, saying I thought the hospital admin-istration acted scandalously, but business is business and he needn't explain anything.

After reaching my emotional limit with the letters, I went to the desk in the dining room where I'd finally succumbed and plugged in my laptop. The embassy set up a special account for me. I gave the email address only to Matt and Sarah. She and I wrote often. Sometimes we wrote of the little events that danced around the pain. Other times, the words arrived as direct hits from the darkness of the nightmare.

I read her latest email:

Neil, today I feel more lost than ever. I saw Debbie this morning and I know I will never understand why I didn't tell you before—I wonder about myself. My grandmother used to say we're all born with at least one cardinal sin in our bones. She said my mother was a born liar, which is nothing compared to what she said about my father—on his best day she called him a charming liar. Most of the time she called him a stink-bag bullthrower and thief. Is that my sin? No matter what I do, did I inherit their liars' genes? I don't ever believe I lie but I feel somehow dishonest. I used to think that I could will away all my bad traits just like I used to believe that I could will myself to become a famous and successful artist, and Christ, what made me "famous" is my greatest pain and I had no part in that at all. I never believed that I had so little control over my life. Now, I feel like all I'm doing is waiting. Love, Sarah

281

I read and reread her words and then I answered.

Sarah, We're both waiting now. All I want to do is live without hurting anybody, which is much tougher for me than it sounds. I say things that I don't intend to hurt, but do, and that is my cardinal sin.

It's so typical of my screwed-up worldview now, where, whenever I say never, it means in about five minutes. Because our positions have reversed, I need you to come here soon. I feel so alone, and with each word I write I feel my sadness pouring out of me as I feel your sadness pouring into me when I read your words. There seems to be an endless refilling. I wish we could pour our loss into some garden of grief.

But then, even if we could, what rests in the bleeding silences between words in these emails? I must have done something to make you distrust me that I don't even know about. Maybe you don't either. I fear silence as much as I fear your words or mine. I don't know what to say but will hope we will find the words when we are together again.

love, N

Sarah had been my best friend and I had no replacement. I needed someone to talk to about her, and now about what Ratish probably knew about Holika and me. Maybe Matt or a therapist I could trust. Or Holika. Or Levi, who was still in Israel. Maybe Charlie. When we met a couple of days after the Environ party for what we hoped would be become a twice weekly tennis match, I was changed and already on the court. "Downsie," he yelled with that frat-boy jargon that sounds ridiculous from anyone over the age of thirteen. I frowned. I never joined the Boys 'R' We crowd and he dropped the faux buoyancy before giving me the requisite shake of the hand that would feel like a patronizing pat on the back. "Sorry I'm late." "No problem," I said, but I realized what I already felt; we could never be true confidants. Although he tried. When I'd told him of Sarah's impending visit, he grinned and wiped his crooked, filmy teeth with his index finger. "That's good. Real good. It didn't seem right you two splitting." Yeah, to me either, but I'd never told him what I thought had happened and I felt no need to now.

As he stretched, he casually dropped a bomb on me. "I need to know how long you plan on staying."

I had no quick answer. I mumbled, "No plans to leave. I guess whenever you say go, I go." I jumped to the conclusion that somehow I'd offended Vijay.

"No rush. Just prepare yourself. This isn't official yet, but I'm retiring by the end of the year, maybe even in the fall."

"Congratulations and thanks for the tip." I knew he wanted to leave. I never thought it would happen that soon. I gave him the info on Vijay and my advice as his doctor, that Vijay see a specialist.

"I'll talk to him."

"So that it's no breach of my confidentiality, please ask him how it went before you let on you know."

"Finally catching on, Downs. You'll be a diplomat yet."

He promised to give me information on whom to contact about where to stay when Sarah came. Give us introductions. His name guaranteed access to the finest accommodations and shrines throughout the country.

"Oh yeah, some staffer in Washington contacted me about The Presidential Medal of Freedom. One of those good-guy medals."

"That'd be a capper for your career."

"Not for me—for you. For your work during the crisis." He couldn't hold back his ironic condescension. "The *people* love that crap."

Yeah, a dinner and speeches where truly heroic events become schmaltzy bathos. That appealed to me about as much as a guest appearance on one of those shock-jock radio shows.

"I don't want to sound ungrateful, but give it to someone who actually acted like a hero."

"Sure." He didn't give a damn.

We split two sets, both in tie-breakers, before he zipped off to a breakfast meeting. I wished I'd thought ahead about where to go, what to do next. I wasn't ready to either leave India or go back to New York. If not New York, where? I was no wanderer—lost, yes—but I needed routine. As much as I wanted or thought I could handle it in my post-Castor world, I didn't possess the talents for anarchy that an unstructured life demanded.

My uncharted life got another jolt when Schlipssi strode into my office later in the week. He did his best to sit nonchalantly in the chair on the opposite side of the desk.

"Are you still in your Father Theresa mode?" I thought this attempt at "humorous" camaraderie referred to the AIIMS problems.

"Possibly. Why?"

"Because of that bull at AIIMS, they settled the strike issue but the doctors who have been helping Mr. Pillai's niece won't go. Same with the doctors she's used in Jodhpur. You up for a trip to Jodhpur in two days?"

"Sure. But I'll need some guidance."

"Pankaj will take the train a day before you. You will stay one night in Jodhpur. Then go to the villages. Friday night flight out. Tuesday a.m. flight back here for work."

"I thought Ms. Bedrosian didn't want me doing any extra-curricular work."

"I have no knowledge of any such request. The ambassador told me personally to brief you on this." He stood up, ready to leave.

"Hey, any chance I can get Chandon back?" I hadn't wanted to bug Charlie with something so trivial, but I felt partially responsible for his dismissal. "I don't care if he drinks a little. I'll pay him out of my own pocket."

"Not my department, but ask me again when you get back."

Later that day a messenger brought in a list of my flight times, of whats and wheres. I'd do examinations, vaccinations, prescribe antibiotics. Maybe give a talk on hygiene. Holika, or whoever, would translate. I'd have no assistant.

I emailed Sarah that I'd be leaving Delhi for the weekend and why. I'd told her about my failed attempt to work at NDP, and the immense shortage of doctors in the villages, who, despite promises to the ministry of health, never fulfilled their obligation and that left so many public facilities functioning improperly. I warned her that if she didn't hear from me, she shouldn't worry. I didn't know if email were possible from the villages.

In my search for friends, I'd called Tracee. We'd made plans to meet on Saturday night. I called her to cancel. When I ex-

And the Word Was

plained why, she managed only a flustered, "Oh, OK." She called me the next morning at my home.

"I'm going to the States for treatment soon. Can we meet at lunch time today?" She picked Rajghat, Mahatma Gandhi's cremation site located inside the park along Ring Road, which also held three other cremation sites of noted modern Indians. Across the street from the park, along the banks of the Yamuna, thousands of people lived in "unauthorized" slums.

Pankaj dropped me off in the parking lot filled with dozens of tourist buses. Tracee waited by our designated meeting spot, her hair tied in a ponytail, her body under a long cotton green dress, and a denim jacket hanging loosely on her shoulders. Slightly tinted, designer wraparound sunglasses masked her eyes.

285

She gave me a hug.

"Why the mid-day siren?" I felt swallowed up by the tourists streaming around us.

She spoke softly as we veered off the main path leading to the monument. "I finally told my mother."

I waited to hear more. Nothing came. "That's smart, I think."

"Me too." Her thoughts jumped ahead in a desultory fashion as we maintained a slow, quiet pace across the park. "I have this feeling that you and Holika will remain friends for a long time. Much longer than I—"

"Look, you can live—"

"Maybe, but that is not what I mean." She spoke now with a deliberate focus. "You know many people thought Siddhartha's death was no accident."

"I bet."

She sighed. "Is it OK if you hold my hand?"

"Sure." I saw goose bumps pop up on her neck and forearms. Not from any chill in the balmy, seventy-four-degree air.

"They were right."

Not saying any more yet, Tracee and I strolled down the entryway to the well of the spartan monument area. I lip-read some of the most well-known sayings of Gandhi, in the thirteen official Indian languages carved into the sandstone walls that surrounded the black marble monument. Children romped, people snacked and sipped drinks. Frolicked.

Tracee led me out from the monument well and we sat on a cement bench. From above, we watched the crowds. Cautiously, she revealed what happened on the afternoon of Siddhartha's death. Sighing between words, she explained that she and Siddhartha "had maintained an intimate friendship for years." I said nothing indicating I'd read Charlie's report about Siddhartha's "business conference" that day, only that I understood their relationship.

She left the office before Siddhartha and drifted in and out of the shops on the way toward where she'd parked her car. While browsing in a silk shop, she heard gunshots mixed with the splattering sounds of crashing pots and panicked screams. She'd been around enough guns—her family were expert hunters—to distinguish the unmistakable snap of gunfire. She tossed the silk fabric aside and ran toward the gathering crowd. Fearing the worst, she approached the body. In the commotion she got close enough to see his body face down, blood spilling from his neck and back. Alongside him lay another limp body. Everyone screamed in a rage of confused voices: "Monkey Man, Monkey Man!" shrieked the loudest while pointing upward. Tracee, shaking her head, let out a dark cackle. Yes, she'd seen a crazed monkey, but monkeys aren't assassins. Not yet. The "Monkey Man" screamers were hired by the killers to cause a distraction. From behind the walls and portals of Old Delhi the killer had fired the fatal bullets. She backed away from

Siddhartha's body. She heard one more shot. The police, who "happened" to be in the area, destroyed the "crazed" monkey. She fled, sure that someone would discover their affair, uncover her presence in his office that afternoon, and come to question her. While she mourned with Holika and hundreds of others, she waited. No one ever came.

For years, she told no one. Finally, after she got married she confessed to her husband, who didn't care one iota about the murder, only that she'd slept with Siddhartha. He never forgave her for that transgression.

She shivered and I felt her need for confirmation that she had chosen correctly by keeping quiet.

"It only would've hurt Holika and tarnished Siddhartha. No one could do a thing. I know that."

We began to circle the lawn back to the parking lot.

"Holika must know. Now is the time."

I thought she wanted me to tell Holika, but no.

"That is too brutal a favor to ask. You must be careful, too."

"Me? I'll be OK." I felt arrogantly safe, an American, who would bother me, a friend of the ambassador? I had a better chance of being killed during a random shooting back in the U.S.A.

A group of young boys kicking a soccer ball and flinging a chewed-up Frisbee stampeded across our path. I felt an inner wish to smile at the scene, which both seemed so right and so out of context, but Tracee coughed. Her thin body shook. The pollution could undo the lungs of the healthiest person. At least I hoped it was only the pollution.

"Holika is blind when it comes to her family. And I fear you are blind to Holika."

I reassured her that I would be watchful, but suddenly, after we bid goodbye, not sure when I'd see her again, I felt less than safe. When I flew into the nighttime darkness of the Blue City on a rickety jet, I felt less safe still.

Pankaj, not Holika, met me when the plane arrived a bit after ten. He hired a taxi, which sped through eerie, quiet streets to the family home of the personal polo pony trainer to the Maharajas and English governors who lorded over India for centuries. Joginder, the grandson of the last trainer, turned most of the house into an upscale pension, greeted me as if he knew me. Perhaps, in some fashion, he did because Holika and Preeya, who'd checked in earlier and already gone to bed, must've given him some information. He addressed me boisterously as "Dr. Downs." As he escorted me to my room he pointed out the photos of the esteemed Maharajas in their polo getup, the many Hollywood and Bollywood stars who'd stayed there, and the saddles and strops the governors left behind.

He informed me that Holika and Preeya expected me to be ready at 6 a.m. After a lousy night's sleep, I was awakened by Joginder's knock on the door. Still groggy, I met Holika and Preeya in the dining room. Both were dressed in saris, Preeya in pink and Holika in a combination of dark and deep reds. They each had placed a *Tilak*, the powdery colored third eye, on their forehead. Preeya shook my hand. Holika issued a stilted "Thanks so much for coming," and then we kissed cheeks with all the plastic intimacy of inept actors. Over coffee, lots of coffee, and toast with jam, I mentioned that she looked healthy. For good reason, she'd had no ailment. She'd purposefully boycotted the prime minister's dinner—this she had no problem saying in front of Preeya. Everything else of a personal nature, including any mention of Sarah, remained off limits.

At 6:45 an Ambassador car pulled up with Holika's driver at the wheel. Pankaj drove ahead of us in a van with supplies to the first village.

With the three of us in the back seat, Preeya in the middle, we made a detour. Holika and Preeya decided I couldn't visit Jodhpur without seeing Mehrangarh Fort. They were right. The immense edifice towered over the early morning streets clogged with the usual cars, minitrucks, buses, and an excess of elephants, camels, and oxen-driven carts; Jodhpur seemed more divided by modernity than Delhi, and not just a pre-Information Age society, but also a pre-Industrial Revolution society. More women drove their own scooters and weren't simply backseat riders. Yet, when we got stuck in traffic more people gaped into the car examining me. "Cyber cafes" abounded, but were no more than shops with one computer stuffed between candy bars, sodas, bottled water, Band-Aids, envelopes, pens, incense, cigarettes, and all sorts of ninety-nine-cent-store items. I marveled at the turbans, half of which seemed larger than the men wearing them. Preeya explained how the method of tying and specific color of each turban had special significance to the Rajasthani.

From below, the fort, built in 1459 by the Rathore Dynasty, which controlled the area, still looked impregnable—a natural outgrowth of the arid brownish-red dirt mountain top. We parked at the bottom gate and began the four hundred and fifty foot chug to the top of the fort. A street barker scurried up to me wanting some cash to unleash his cobra-versus-mongoose routine. I shook him off with a scram-like wave of my hands. There were few non-Indian tourists and no other Westerners that I saw who weren't with a bus tour. With two Indian women by my side, the inquisitive stares—more from older women— often bordered on disdain. The children, the teenagers wanted to touch me, shake my hand like I was some kind of rock star. Some came close and then backed off.

This man-made structure and the panoramic cityscape of hundreds of houses painted a pastel Matisse-swimming-pool

289

blue, as dreamy as a Dibenkorn painting, knocked me out. The city evolved from first only Brahmins painting their homes until now, when virtually the whole city adopted the color. When we reached two tents covering the outdoor space in front of a marble temple, the smell of incense and smoke disseminated into the air. A bell gonged every time an offering was completed. The majesty of the achievement seemed to falter with each gong as Holika's suddenly impatient preen displayed disdain for the prayers and rituals.

Soon began a journey down roads that made a brakeless roller coaster seem safe. No pavement, no signs, no speed limits, and blind turns around hilly roads with only a honking horn between us and decapitation. We passed women parading in carnivals of color with two-foot-round pewter and copper bowls filled with water balanced atop their heads, or toiling on their knees in the near-barren fields, and shepherds, trucks, and animal-drawn carts teeming with people.

As the careening car slowed down, Holika perked up. "This village is atypical. Himmat, well, you will see, he is remarkable."

She didn't exaggerate. Born a poor low caste Rajasthani, Himmat spoke broken English, French, and German—all of which he'd taught himself. He ran the village business of weaving and selling handmade carpets called dhurries. All seventy members of the village shared the profits equally. He had a computer, but had wanted the money spent on other items. I asked why. His sinewy body stiffened. "As I asked the government representative, Can a computer make it rain? Make kerosene? Give us milk? Bring us electricity? I am trying to use it to earn money for those things but that's why half the village still farms and the others make rugs." He would get more cows, oxen, sheep. He handed me a brochure of his business, which the Pillai Foundation printed for him. He sold me two rugs—and I mean sold, he took both American Express and Visa. After I picked out the colors, which I thought would please Sarah, he promised to make them "personally." I would've loved to watch Matt and Himmat dueling over deals.

I began the examinations in a large, wooden meeting hall because unlike the mortar buildings or huts, it had large windows and better light and an electric generator, with Holika by my side. No fiery speeches needed here. "Himmat is with me all the way," she told me. "He has vision and authority. He looks up and sees the sun and sees the power of solar energy without needing a Ph.D. His people will participate in the grand march."

Himmat introduced his two daughters, a three-year-old and an eighteen-month-old—both needed full sets of immunizations. He whispered to me in English that he vowed to have no more children. Holika, looking exasperated, talked to his wife about birth control. Himmat, breaking with tradition, had decided to use condoms. His wife, it seemed, wanted to keep trying until they had a son. I wasn't sure who was going to win that argument.

It took all day to finish. So many needed a specialist or more treatment than I could offer in so cursory a fashion. Almost everyone needed to see a dentist. Jodhpur Public Hospital owned some of the most modern equipment in the world. Anyone who got there had access. Getting there was the key. Unlike other villagers, Himmat would make sure his people got to Jodhpur as soon as Holika secured a bus for transportation.

As we readied to say goodbye, Preeya took out a disposable cameras. The people crowded around and she took pictures. Himmat "made me a gift" of a one foot by one foot dhurrie with a dark blue border, green inset, and a red star-shaped design. Preeya snapped a photo as we embraced, each clasping one end of the dhurrie in our hands.

56

LEAVING THE VILLAGE my emotional mix of guilt, ignorance, remorse, and, above all, confusion reminded me of the young Orwell, who served in the British army in Burma, and felt compelled by the sly contempt of the Burmese, and his "duty," to shoot a poor elephant. I wondered if behind their mask of gratitude and smiles, some of the villagers didn't think of me more like the self-satisfied and phony Levin in *Anna Karenina*, who worked in the fields for one afternoon and discovered his kinship with the peasants, before retiring to his mansion. Instead of a mansion we ended up at a former palace. Pankaj and Holika's driver dropped us off inside the high-walled gates and disappeared. To where, I had no idea. I only knew, abracadabra, they'd reappear the next morning.

Inside the grim walls, leaving behind wild dogs, sewerless streets, and impoverished homes of another small town whose name I never knew, we entered a world apart. A luxurious palace-turned-hotel with peacocks as common as New York pigeons, a large pool with mini-temple structures in each corner and fragrant gardens. I wished I could've sent my bedroom, with one exception, back to America: the smooth, slate-tiled floors, the marble two-foot-high bed frame with a marble framed cushiony sofa built into the foot of the bed. Chairs covered in black velvet cushions were placed around a small, hand-carved wooden table. Large windows opened into the courtyard. The exception was major—a five-foot painting of Ganesha with swastikas on each hand spied down from the wall across from the bed. When I lay down for a nap before dinner, I kept glancing up at the image. Backward or not, it creeped me out. I asked for an extra sheet and covered the painting.

We ate dinner beside the pool. Holika, Preeya, and I ordered a bottle of red wine to wash away the images of poverty and unhealth and to allay the guilt. After dessert, Preeya excused herself. Finally, we could talk.

293

Holika blanched when I confessed my new reality, which didn't change the fact of Castor's murder. "Is that better or worse?"

"Better, I think."

She allowed me the space to unload all the swirling and contradictory emotions I'd kept inside since my return, which always came back to Castor.

The waiters wanted to finish cleaning up and go home. Holika gulped her coffee. "Let us go talk in my room."

"Not a good idea."

"Why? Afaid you might lose control?" A mischievous gleam replaced the placid seriousness.

"That's not all I couldn't control."

I made a motion with my eyes to a circle of wooden chairs across the grounds, through an open gate in the adjacent courtyard. She dabbed her lips with a napkin. We nodded our thanks to the waiters.

"Ratish knows." I whispered as we made our way through the gate.

"Oh, fuck." Her complexion first paled. Then reddened. I told her about the exchange at the prime minister's home.

"He *more* than knows." She violently dusted peacock feathers off the chair. Then pounced her small body onto the cushion of the seat. I sat in the chair at a ninety-degree angle to hers. "My uncle is adopting Ratish. He will be his legal son." The staggering repercussions of such a manipulation gave Ratish complete and ultimate control of the private Pillai family fortune and the Pillai Foundation, which relegated Holika to no more than salaried functionary who would need Ratish's approval to get funding for her projects.

"Please do not say anything. I understand what I did not see." There was a cold fury in her calmly stated words. She did not want to discuss the nature of her uncle's deception. I decided that silence was the best answer.

"This adoption is so painful and real. That ceremony meant nothing. All blather and pomp. It is corporate maya, an illusion they hope will become reality, but Siddhartha taught me not to underestimate the people. And I have weapons. The choice is if, and how, I use them. I have decisions to make and I am not sure of my allies beyond Preeya. If you are worried about him telling Sarah, do not. He cannot feel that confident and invulnerable yet."

"I have to tell Sarah. Not sure when. Before or after she gets here. What about Samaka?"

"Are you kidding? No, it is better left unsaid for now." I understood her reasoning and I'd understand his reaction too. "The situation is tender. My uncle did not tell him about the adoption plans until it was a fait accompli." Vijay had manipulated not only Holika, but Samaka. "My uncle is not a good enemy to have."

"I've heard."

"Challenging him and Charlie, not even Samaka wants to do that. I need his help to get past the gatekeepers in the government and the influential press. Between Charlie and my uncle, no one will really go for the throat."

"Charlie?"

"Your friend Charles Bedrosian is for Charlie Bedrosian first and second and third." I wanted to defend Charlie but Holika didn't give me the chance. "Do you know that Chrystie is on the board of Environ and has been given, in her name, over three million dollars worth of stock in the last three years as payment for *her* services?"

295

All too much became clear: Why Charlie couldn't afford another divorce—the hell with philandering and love. Why he arranged for Hal Burden and Prime Minister Sowat to give interviews. Why he wanted to retire so soon.

"Do you have proof?"

"Yes. We have friends inside the embassies and we accumulated records, emails, faxes. All that one needs. Our courts are tied up. Our big press is under wraps and so is yours. We cannot get anything done in your country. We have been told that is not illegal anyway."

"We have many levels and differing sympathies for corrupters in the States. Legal and illegal."

"I also know that it was Charlie who aided my uncle in his 'trading' our treasures years ago."

Her unsentimental admission proclaimed, "I am aware of the lie of the Vijay myth." Of course, it became clear Charlie, who fell into my blind spot, as a mid-level assistant ambassador in India during the seventies, made it possible. She waited for my answer to her implied question.

"Tracee sort of told me."

"I thought she might have."

"Holika, today totally screwed with my head, I've hit overload."

"Me too. Suddenly, I am exhausted."

She leaned forward and so did I. Inches from each other, we didn't touch. Our intimacy as friends now unquestioned, we hit the wall of strangeness because, no matter my love for Sarah and her commitment to Samaka, and confused, driven, and guilt-ridden by our desire, we knew we couldn't. Understanding, accepting, not denying the amoral impulses of the id, the amoral desires of the body and not acting on them, we sat there not moving, our eyes meeting, experiencing some kind of out-of-body sex with no climax.

I got up and slinked off to my room, my body feeling like a vial of viscous fluid.

57

Twenty-first century physics will continue to revolutionize life as
no other "discovery" has revolutionized the world. Twentieth cen-
tury physics did not create what did not exist. It only brought the
notions to consciousness. The quantum phenomenon defies simple
dissection in the lab; the idea of which is to break down in order
to understand the pieces through the whole. The sum parts are
whole, yet not whole, yet the whole is whole yet not. Uncertainty
not only can lead to truth, but is truth. Concepts once thought
universal are not; above all, we will learn that information can
be transferred faster than the speed of light. It is my hope that we
will see that the universe is not only three dimensional, but mul-
tidimensional. If we exist in the implicate order that implies the
universe is a hologram, that would solidify my theories of a cos-
mic epistasis. This gives substance to my feeling both unwhole
and part of the mosaic of the hologrammatic web that is the uni-
verse, and explains why I felt a kinship even with my torturers.
This idea will not require the mystical leap of faith. It will be a
provable truth. Truths that have always existed, as gravity existed
before Newton and time bending before Einstein. New truths will

be found that merge the seeming *contradictions among these constructs.*

What has already changed is our consciousness of these laws and thus the need for a language to express this new reality as we enter the era of the quantum id, where we are all one in good and evil.

—from *THE UNPUBLISHED WORKS*

58

IN THE MORNING, after breakfast, I asked the
office manager if he had email access. He did. We tried and tried
to get on line. No luck. Soon we had to leave.

Himmat's village might've appealed to those revelers in the
mythical Jeffersonian agrarian utopia built upon the backs of
slaves, because his seemed more honest. Not so the next village.
We drove into the village and a group of women and children
sat segregated from the men under a group of trees. A small group
of men, the council leaders, sat in a teashop. Parminder, a col-
lege-educated woman who had returned to help in her home
state, waited for us. She would translate and help out.

"Some people here regard me as a terrorist or a succubus."
Holika warned me. She needn't have worried. The people were
kind and glad to see me. All had been set up for me in the usually vacant medical offices that Nehru planned, and many were
built, for all villages. Now most stood deserted. The government
tried to insist, with inconsistent success, that all resident doctors do time in the villages where 600 million Indians lived. It'd
been over six months since any doctors had come through.

Even before I started, four fifteen-year-old boys cut ahead of the selected order. Parminder translated. One of them happily informed us that he'd be married in May. I couldn't believe either his age or his future. He looked much older, already with a full moustache and puffy, weary eyes. He wanted advice. How to guarantee a son. If he should go to Delhi to look for work. How to get to America. Since he'd broken both his arms in a fall and they'd never healed properly, I doubted his body could withstand the heavy lifting in the kind of work he might find in Delhi.

With so little modern equipment, I felt myself drowning in helplessness. The amount of coughs, skin rashes, malnutrition, dysentery, and lice, and, at the same time, the relative health of the people astounded me. Three years before a severe drought, followed by a week of monsoons, followed again by scorching heat, produced a scourge of malaria, dengue fever, and leptospirosis, which devastated the village. Despite my sophisticated knowledge, without the technology that served as extensions of my hands and sight, I was no better than a third-rate shaman. What those boys and others wanted, I could not give. Doctors once were emissaries between gods and humans, blessed with spiritual powers of healing. Those medicine men knew little of science, surviving on their insight into minds and hearts. Now we save with science and most doctors no longer have the sensitivity to give a damn about the spirit and hearts of men and women. I lacked the faith or prescience to answer so many questions worthy of a seer.

More than a seer was needed to deal with the problems of the higher caste Indians, who refused to be examined in the same building as the Dalits. I left that problem to Holika and Preeya, who decided that I'd see the Dalits in a different building the next day.

As soon as we got back to the palace, even before I showered, I tried to get online. It took five minutes but I got through and read the email we'd both been waiting for.

> Neil! It's happened! I'm pregnant! I felt it that night. I did. I couldn't tell you because you think that is such nonsense but *I felt it*. I waited longer to take the test but it's true. I took the test as soon as I got your email but you'd already left when I called.
> Love, Sarah

Almost disbelieving the words, I teetered outside. I saw Holika, showered and changed into jeans and a T-shirt, bent over the flowerbed by the pool. In reaction to my mother's unrepressed hollers, I usually avoided loud outbursts in public. I couldn't contain myself. "Hey Holika, com'eer, quick! You gotta read this!"

She scooted across the lawn and read the email. She clutched my arm, then quickly released it. "This is wonderful."

None of the cell phones were working, so I asked if I could use their phone to call the U.S. The operator couldn't get the international connection to go through, so I wrote a quick email saying I'd call her as soon as I got a good phone and that I'd be on a plane back to the U.S. ASAP.

Unwilling to give up, I tried again after dinner and got her. The connection crackled like the "get me an operator" phones in old movies.

"It's me."

"You got my email?" For the first time in almost a year, I heard the confident Sarah, the Sarah who believed in herself.

"Sarah, have you checked your HCG levels?"

"Don't start nagging. Everything feels good. I'm seeing Stone again next week." She'd seen Stone after I left, for different reasons. Stone agreed to eradicate all computer and handwritten records indicating that Sarah ever visited her office that day in May.

"OK, as soon as I get back to Delhi I will get in gear and be back in no time."

"You don't want me to come after the show?"

"Not a good idea."

"Neil, I'm *fine*. Indians have millions of babies every year."

"It's not that. I'll be back in Delhi Tuesday and I'll call you."

Physically depleted, mentally shaken, and at the same time invigorated with anticipation, unwilling to process all I'd seen and heard, with one more day to go, I had a celebratory drink with Holika and Preeya and went to bed.

The next day felt immeasurably long with examinations. The Dalits were much less healthy than the Brahmins. Holika and Parminder spoke with the men on the need for birth control. With the women, they subtly brought up the taboo subjects of infanticide, abortion, and birth control. She told me that some women, especially in the middle classes, were using abortions as a tool to make sure they got a male child. She had to convince them not to be afraid to confront their husbands.

I gritted my teeth, felt a pang of recognition slice though my guts, but smiled obliquely signaling my understanding. What she didn't know was how terrifyingly familiar that sounded to me. How much I wished I had *listened* to my wife. How much more, even then, I too needed to learn.

Later in the hall Holika gathered everyone together and ran a ten-minute documentary on the Bhopal disaster. With the power of that video she won many to her side and she looked pleased.

The three of us took the Tuesday morning flight back to Delhi. Vishnu picked me up and we went straight to Chanayakapuri. I called Charlie. He'd taken off for the south. I left an urgent message with his secretary, who refused to tell me when he'd be back.

He called around four. I told him the news.

"Good work, supersperm. You'll love being an older father. Avoid the mistakes of the first go-round."

Mistakes I never got the chance to make.

"Can you wait 'til next Monday to make plans? You don't have to be there yet. You have months."

Yeah, sure, but I wanted to get going. Even Sarah, ready for the show and not in her usual frenzy of drying the last pieces ten minutes before the opening, seemed blasé about when I got back. Any reasonable time after the opening, which, because of the publicity, she knew I didn't want to attend, suited her.

Levi, who'd returned from Israel, left a message with Donna. I phoned him the next day. His tone dour, he didn't want to gab. Schneerman had died. The trip sapped his patience and strength. He mentioned that he'd been back a week and still felt fatigued. He preferred not to come to the office, so we made plans to meet at the International Center for lunch on Saturday.

I arrived at the restaurant before him. The maître d' showed me to his table. When Levi arrived, I watched his struggling steps, while his recalcitrant demeanor refused to acknowledge his pain. He sat down, nodded, and grumbled "hello" from behind his tinted glasses. Quickly, he ordered a beer and so did I.

His face remained devoid of excitement or relief when I told him the good news: He needn't go to the U.S. The head of the Lenox Hill Hospital hip and knee replacement department, Dr. Ranwat, went to Bombay's Breach Candy Hospital once a year to do knee replacements. His credentials were as good as you could find anywhere in the world.

Levi remained stoic, unwilling to hear my supposed bad news. Then I mentioned that I wanted Sarah to meet him some time. No reaction, so I blurted out, "She's pregnant."

Skepticism crawled on his closed, dry lips. He sniffed with his suspicious nose.

"It's mine."

His lips parted. He pushed himself up from his seat, came to my side of the table, cupped one hand on each of my temples and kissed me on the forehead. Before this, he'd never even shook my hand. I'd never even seen him touch anyone. His smile turned sanguine.

He returned to his seat and we toasted with our beers, "Mazel Tov." He gulped his drink and ordered another. Now, he wanted to talk. "You had a much more fruitful trip than I."

"I'm sorry about Schneerman."

"Don't be. Our friendship was one of irreconcilable differences and shared laments. We didn't agree on much, but we agreed it is important to die correctly. I helped him die correctly."

It didn't seem appropriate to ask what he meant by that.

"After all I did, some of his followers wanted to ban me from his funeral. Until then, I didn't even want to go. The same foul jackasses who wanted to burn, *burn*, not ban, my books. Can you believe it?" The Israeli right wing had eviscerated Levi for years. The Jewish establishment in America went from celebrating him as a hero for *Chamber* to branding him a traitor for *Mistakes*.

"Is that why you stopped writing?"

The era of good feeling over, he eyed me with his withering scowl, "Who says I did?"

"Well, uh," I phumphered.

"You want more answers from your Jewish guru?"

Sorry I asked, I shook my head. He clasped the beer glass in his arthritic left hand. He gulped down the beer and then thumped the glass on the table. He reached and picked up a napkin. He gently wiped the condensation off the glass. He took off his shaded eyeglasses and meticulously cleaned them with the damp napkin. Then he tossed that napkin on the table and picked up a clean napkin and dried the glasses before he put them back on and glared at me.

"I stopped publishing. There is a difference." He held his breath, burped into his fist.

"OK, then." Feeling a what-the-hell boldness I pushed for an answer, "Why'd you stop publishing?"

He paused, signaled to the waiter with a shake of his hand not to bring our food yet. "I stopped writing. Not because of the reaction. I accept silence or condemnation. I appreciate accolades. But writing, serious writing, imperils or embraces the beyond. It is an act ignited by despair but signaling hope for a future. I no longer had hope for the transcendent beyond. I certainly had no hope for this world. Then I decided, at Hannah's urging, that it was imperative that I find a future. What I found is what I've written."

"Will you publish it?"

"Not in my lifetime. No."

"Any chance I can see it?"

"You, you are an American?"

My eyes and neck did a double take, looking behind me as if someone else must've sneaked up behind me. "Um, yeah . . . yes."

He laughed. "Very good. You have a plastic face."

"Thank you, I think."

"You also have hope, a sentiment for which I have no interest. You Americans are hope fiends."

Not sure if he was joking, I half-smiled.

"America has hope for what you can do in this life which is superior to hope for a better life in the next nonexistent world. The American Dream, which is now the world's dream, presents itself as a dream of freedom when it is truly the dream of an empire. I found its essence to be narrow and self-righteous. To be an oppressive dream. Too much hunger for the tangible. Not the dream of what you cannot measure, feel, touch. That is why I left America. Too many *things*. What is needed is not hope for what you can have, but what you can give, for what is beyond measure, not beyond life."

His condemnation pierced; for all that happened from the Gypswitch lawsuit to the massacre, and belief that somewhere we had gone horribly off course, I still believed in America, the idea of America, the *hope* of America.

"Neil, perhaps you are the right kind of American, at least," he grinned showing his teeth, "I will allow myself to hope that for you. So yes, you will see it sometime in your future . . ."

Future, where, yes, I now had a future that so soon became a forgotten past—where the pain of Castor never left, but began to subside into the haze of memory. Where I awoke in the morning without feeling the burden of failure. Where I lived without the fear of impending doom. Where I emailed Matt and Ray with the good news and they emailed back with thrilled-for-Sarah-and-me congratulations saying how much we deserved a break. Where I met Holika for lunch and talked of her new position as an outsider. Where she'd met with Tracee. Yes, she often wondered if Siddhartha was murdered. More frequently as she got older and more cynical. Yes, she knew he fooled around. No, she never suspected Tracee to be one of his consorts, and she could not, at least now, forgive her former close friend. Where she could never directly confront Ratish, "That is not the best way with him. I have time to change my uncle's mind and I will succeed." Where I asked, Why worry about him since Samaka is loaded? She did not want to be dependent on Samaka's money any more than she did on Ratish's beneficence. Where I hinted that because the press so desperately wanted to talk to me, I might be able to help her. Where I looked into the faces of the street children with aches and empathy for them and not for me. Instead of envy and pity, I fed off their boundless energy. Where I asked Donna sincerely about her daughters. Where I played tennis with Charlie while I kept silent about his illicit machinations and confronted the quandary of personal loyalty versus the need for the greater good, and I questioned if, and how, I could help Holika. When he slyly eased out the question, "You enjoy your vacation to another world with the Mistress of the Good, the Unwashed, and the Needy?" I shook my head. "Nope," I gave my guy-like answer, "it was fucked up." He didn't want to hear that "enjoyed" didn't capture the upsetting complexities of such an incomprehensible world. Where Charlie and I made plans for my leaving and we jested about my being sixty when the kid was twenty, which was nothing compared to him being eighty when his daughter Heather turned twenty. Where I emailed Sarah how much I looked forward to a new job helping the abandoned poor in America.

Where I would raise a child into the beyond of my life. Where time seemed to move faster than the speed of light and Sarah and I again knew what each other thought before we spoke or emailed. Where Sarah and I, not in remorse but in restrained euphoria dared dream of again being one, of loving unconditionally in a future brimming with hope.

Where those ten days of pregnancy appear as a cruel ten-second yet never-ending mirage in time stopping with one broken word—

"*Ne-il.*"

Terror vibrated in the falling timbre of Sarah's voice, "I've started spotting. Bleeding. It's getting heavier by the hour."

"Look, it could be nothing but go to the ER and have a blood test and a sonogram. Call Stone and get your previous HCG levels. Then get them done again in twenty-four hours. They should be doubling. Call my cell anytime."

"You sure it could be nothing?"

"Yes, I'm sure. Now go. And call me anytime. Please."

It's clear by now I don't believe in premonitions, but, despite my reassurances, somehow I knew. The future turning into a failed past enveloped me. The weight of bad air expanded inside me.

Looking for words to stop my internal hemorrhage of hope, feeling evermore diasporic, I wandered the streets, walking and walking until I ended up at the Jewish cemetery. The Indian family recognized me. I guess they didn't have too many visitors, but I exuded heaviness and they stayed away. Even the dogs stayed away. I knelt by the grave of young Rachel. I placed no stones on her grave this time. Just sat there. Melancholic and defeated. Imagining Sarah alone, watching the pregnancy test turn positive, elated yet unwhole, because I wasn't there. Frustrated, unable to reach me, unable to celebrate because I wasn't there. Working on her paintings, waiting for my confirmation and hearing nothing, because I wasn't there. Suddenly spotting, tense. Afraid, questioning what to do because I wasn't there. Bleeding the life away with no hand to hold. Because I wasn't there. Again.

I needed to leave. Immediately. Not the cemetery, but Delhi. I'd seen women come into the ER, lose their babies, and then lose faith in their bodies, themselves. I'd seen blankness in the faces of inert husbands and I knew I had to be by her side to say I understood, touch her with love. I saw that those who suffered and could never again conceive rarely recovered their sense of self. If I didn't go back, I'd be lost to Sarah forever.

Through the side gate that led to the temple I heard the voices of a group of people and Rabbi Judah came through with a tour group of American Jews. He waved to me and I waved limply back. I knew it was rude, but still, I got up to escape. I couldn't talk to him. I'd reacted too slowly. I heard his small, sputtering steps behind me. He reached and patted my shoulder with his hand. I turned around. "Dr. Downs," my desolation unhidden, he actually sputtered rather than spoke without halting, "Do you need to talk?"

"No. Thanks, but no." What could I say? I didn't believe in god. That I came here to be around death.

I mustered an incongruous, "If I'm here, maybe we will have a Seder and invite Levi." Passover was only weeks away.

"Yes, that would be fine. Quite fine."

The idea of attending any Passover service, no less making a Seder, seemed absurd. The world seemed senseless. Mean.

59

My last years have been consumed by two opposing beliefs—one that humankind has lost the war within itself, between good and evil and the fact that we are all part of the hologrammatic universe, which is completely neutral, which has no influence in the individual everydayness of life. This understanding that the universe is randomly unfair and that we are at war with the consciously amoral id, which, as did quantum physics, renamed the order of the universe. This renaming did not discover rape, murder, or genocide. It only gave it a new frame, half an understanding, which enabled evil to become justifiable and orderly as concentration camps, and coldly scientific as atomic weapons. Neither naming gives order or reason to the random horrors that abound.

We lack the language to define, contain, comprehend, and transcend this godless world. If we are conscious, sentient beings capable of "feeling" information in a manner faster than light, then the connected "spirit" between every living being does exist. It is these dichotomies, the rift between the sentient and the drive for conquest and what lies beyond the pleasure principle, the ultimate reasonlessness of tragedy or euphoria, that gives no responsibility to god that I find irreconcilable and yet necessary. I believe the rift can only be transversed through a pure language that does not yet exist.

—from THE UNPUBLISHED WORKS

60

I STOPPED AT a nearby STD and called the embassy. At first the operator refused to patch me through to Charlie's home; she couldn't interrupt his "crucial" meeting without cause. Finally I got Schlipssi to give the go ahead to pass me through. Charlie got on right away.

"'Z up, pops?" His tone said the meeting couldn't have been that crucial.

"I hate to bother you, but I have to talk to you tonight." My voice cracked.

"You OK?"

"No."

"Come on over."

I got a taxi. He met me in the entrance foyer.

"Charlie, I have to go to New York, like now. For at least a few days." I explained why. I said I'd try to come back with Sarah. If he could wait for a replacement for more than a week or so that'd be great.

He slung his arm over my shoulders as if he wanted to say something, do something, but this kind of fundamental loss landed in the center of his emotional impotence. "I'll make a call and you take the 7 a.m. plane to New York. Take as long as you need. The army boys can handle it." I felt newly shitty, a different shitty, because I'd considered betraying him. "You do what you have to do."

I called Sarah's various numbers. No answer anywhere. I left messages everywhere saying what time I'd be in at Kennedy. Charlie fixed it so I got a diplomatic first-class seat. I called Holika on her cell phone—and caught her in the middle of dinner with Ratish and Vijay. "Please come after. Tell them why. It's OK." I didn't want to be alone.

She arrived around ten. I still hadn't reached Sarah or Matt. I didn't want to think about what was happening to Sarah and my inability to help her. I preferred to talk about what Holika called her "family conundrums." At dinners and gatherings everyone acted as if there were nothing amiss and her brother and uncle's unmentioned manipulations weren't reducing her to the invisible and irrelevant. I prattled on in a stream of non sequiturs, packing and repacking, while Holika curled up, shoes off, in the comfy bedroom chair. She listened empathetically after making us some herb tea, until I said that Charlie had really come through. She uncurled her body, jutted her jaw, clamped it shut.

"No. What? Say it," I continued folding a sweater and stuffing it in the suitcase as my posture stiffened defiantly.

"I don't want to argue with you tonight."

"Maybe, I need to argue."

"OK, if you like. You think Charlie is your friend. He is not. He is quite devious. Even to the point where tomorrow Pankaj or Vishnu will report that I arrived here at 10:06 and exactly what time I left." Of course, Chandon got canned because he lacked reliability as a spy. "Getting you a ticket? That took one

phone call. About my 'conundrum' with you, my brother is a
fool. My uncle and Charlie are too sly to show their cards too
soon, I can tell you. I think Charlie would have preferred we
stayed together in Jodhpur."

"What?" I thought the paranoia might be getting to her.

"Think of what you know. How we met."

I went over it in my head: Charlie introduced us on my first
day in Delhi. Then pushed us to get together whenever she came
to visit the embassy. He'd coordinated my trip to Rajasthan. He
probably thought he'd give it a shot and if something happened
he was getting me laid and compromising Holika.

"This is not important now. I hope you two come back, but
if not, I am sure we will meet in the States."

"Yeah, I'm sure I'll be back some time. Maybe soon. I
haven't even seen the Taj Mahal." I finished packing and
wanted to lie down for awhile. I walked her downstairs where
her bodyguard paced outside the car. We stood on the street
where no one could hear us; her paranoia had won me over.

"Holika, you might have less time than you think."

She didn't understand and scrunched up her nose and
shook her head.

"Your uncle has a form of leukemia." I didn't need to be
specific. "It is serious and he is not taking care of himself."

"How long?" Her voice sullen, concerned but unwavering.

"Months if it turns, years if he treats himself."

"Charlie knows?"

"Yes."

"Are the records in your office?"

I nodded.

"I will protect your confidence." She glanced at her bodyguard. "I must go."

I watched the car pull away and then went upstairs, took a Valium and slept for five hours before I began my most unwanted trip back to New York.

At the stopover in Dubai, I called Sarah. Still got the machine. Kugliani knew nothing. I called Matt, who kept muttering, "Oh shit, man, oh shit, man." I asked him to find her and gave him the vitals about when I'd be arriving. He had a meeting that could last for days, "puttin' together the team to start developing a landfill deal, outside of Paris on the Seine!" It didn't seem like he could pick me up.

I got in and saw no Sarah or Matt. I spotted a sign that read "Philip Nolan." Matt had hired a car and the driver had instructions to take me to Kugliani's family house in the Hamptons, a smallish, sub-million-dollar job on the bay, not the ocean.

Sarah had left the door unlocked and a light on in the hallway. Peter Gabriel's "In Your Eyes," played on the CD boombox upstairs. I set down my bags in the living room and taking two steps at a time, ran up to the bedroom to find Sarah sleeping. Light peeked out from behind the bathroom door, which was open a crack. Afraid to disturb her sleep rhythms, I didn't turn off the music. On the night table, beside the bed, I saw a half-filled glass of water and two bottles of pills: Tylenol with codeine and Xanax. Still plenty left in both of them. I watched her sleep. I took off my shoes and tiptoed into the bathroom in the corner of the bedroom. She stirred. I stood in the bathroom doorway. Her head slipped sideways off the pillow as if she lost power over her muscles. I froze. Her delicate complexion, with almost imperceptible freckles around her eyes and beneath the hairline, looked ghostly as she flinched and blinked, then fully opened her too widely set apart eyes. So deeply blue with streaking comets of green that glistened in the shadowy light, yet

315

looked so . . . so gone. I saw her as Castor. As I had seen him die. Abruptly, she jumped in place and sat up and my body unlocked.

"Geeze, Neil, you scared me. How long you been here?"

"Few minutes."

"Someone could've killed me. If only. . . ."

"Don't say that."

"OK, but . . ." Her naked shoulders sagged. "It's good you came."

"Not soon enough."

Her silence told me what I didn't want to hear.

She tottered as she stood up to put on her bathrobe, I grabbed hold of her and we embraced. She needed to use the bathroom. With the door only half-closed, dulled by the drugs and disbelief, she related her last thirty-six hours. "The asshole doctor, a woman no less, said it would feel like a bad period. Either she has some damn horrible periods or she's a quack. And her breath stunk of bananas and onion sour cream." Sarah's sense of smell remained as acute as her bleak humor. I heard her stand up, a delay of a few seconds as she blew her nose, which filled from the unending well of tears. Then came the flush of her blood, and the last remnants of our unborn child still leaking from her body mixing into the vast sewer of shit and piss.

She wobbled back into bed. I sat by her side. She held my hand.

"I felt like I was dying."

I closed my eyes. I didn't want to say it: Part of her had died.

I washed up, turned off the light, and got in bed. Sarah gripped my arm; soon she fell asleep. I lay awake for an interminable number of hours, fearing the clarity of sunlight where began an unofficial period of mourning. One we could share together as we had not mourned together after Castor's death.

The next days passed with Sarah coma-like, still disbelieving that she did not feel death inside her. Not comprehending how the world could be so uncaring. Her constant expression asked, What did I do wrong? Between the vaults of despair erupted unbridled anger. An anger that lashed out at me for the simplest indiscretion. One morning, she yelled for five minutes because I put too much milk in her coffee. I got another blast for watching a hockey game while she slept. Her hormones raged. Her body still expected to be pregnant and though it was only a symptom, her moods constantly shifted. Some moments she wished to be alone. Others, I could never leave her side.

I understood her anger, her rage at me for leaving and knew I had to accept it. I didn't try, not then, to explain that if I had not left for India those months ago, no matter how cruel it felt, I could not have been there now. But that knowledge kept me almost sane.

We watched lots of TV, which dulled Sarah better than any tranquilizer. We took somber walks. Talked too much of the past. Some about Levi. I described India, the travels to the countryside, the whole *mishegos* of the Pillai family, Charlie, and Environ, leaving out the details of my relationship with Holika.

Matt called. Romey called, barely able find the emotional depth to say "sorry," incapable as ever of showing empathy, not offering to come visit or asking if we wanted to come there. Calls came from the few friends or acquaintances who found us. We didn't want to talk to any of them. We rarely answered, letting the machine take all the calls.

We made an appointment to see Debbie the same day we were to deliver the last two paintings, which Sarah had finished before the miscarriage. Sarah had picked up our six-year-old Toyota station wagon that had been stored at a friend's upstate home. When I cleaned out the trunk to load the paintings, under

317

a pile of bubble wrap, an old sheet, and an oily cloth, I found a pair of his mud-stiffened socks. They must've been there since Sarah and Castor went hiking in the Catskills two summers before. I had the urge to drive the car into the bay and leave it there. The session with Debbie felt tensionless compared to the session weeks before. Now remorse dominated. No resolutions existed beyond recognizing the anger and loss of the last year. Sarah decided she wanted to perform a ritual of letting go. I knew that idea was what made her Sarah. Despite all that happened, the ideas of some unseeable, eternal spirit joining the universe, so infused in her paintings, is also what kept her alive and sane. As soon as we got back to the Hamptons she began sculpting a small papier-mâché figure and a larger wooden pedestal. She tested it out to see if it would stay afloat in the bay. It did. If it made her feel better, that was good enough for me.

It made me feel better to indulge my compulsion to drop our load of new problems on Ludovicci-Lint. I wished I could do it face-to-face. I couldn't, so I called her. She gasped when she heard the news. Quickly, she reined in her emotions.

"I'm sorry. I had a miscarriage myself before my child was born."

"We're going to leave New York, maybe head back to India when Sarah is ready."

In the space between my words and hers, she factored this news into her equations. "We can work with that. I have great news."

Sure you do—you can undo time.

"The Skirpans got greedy. They upped their price rather than headed down. We assume they have the information."

"And that's great news?"

"Yes, because I will crush them with delays. Make them spend money. Extend discovery. Or I can end it fast. Bonnie

Graper, who is a good woman, gave us her daughter's diary. There is an entry that says she and Bobby Skirpan, one night when they were high, boasted to Ed Skirpan when he was plastered, what they were planning and he laughed and told them to go head, nail the effers. The DA would start salivating if he got his hands on that. The judge, too." Ludovicci-Lint's voice almost bubbled with the froth of her victory. "When I finish with those losers, they'll wish they'd never left Howard Beach."

"That doesn't mean they won't go to the papers."

"This is how it will play out. They don't want the DA to see the diary. I can make it disappear. That finishes them. Corricelli isn't stupid. He pulls any shit and I'll be at the ABA before he learns how to pronounce 'disbarment.' And I assume that Dr. Stone has expunged all evidence from her records."

319

"Yes. Someone might be able to find it, but she never put it through the insurance, so it'd be tough."

She kept talking. I tried to absorb the enormity of Ed Skirpan's silence. I wanted to call the bastard and let out one long howl of rage.

Sarah reacted with a listless shrug to the "great news" about the lawsuit. She remained skeptical that some greedy lowlife wouldn't sell the gossip. Caring what anyone thought now seemed even more trivial. I obsessed on Ed Skirpan's irresponsibility—one word from him and . . . How different our future. Skirpan's irresponsibility made me rethink my Indian dilemma. I asked Sarah her opinion. At first she barked that she didn't give a shit about Charlie or India. Then later, more reflective, she apologized and gave me her usual smart advice. "Call the hairdressers," that's what she called Ludovicci-Lint and Linscombe. "See if the offers from the *Times* and "60 Minutes" still holds and when you're ready, go for it. It's the right thing to do. Charlie can take it. If not . . ."

Ludovicci-Lint seemed astonished that I would seek publicity now. "Not yet," I told her, but maybe in a month or three.

What was the right thing about my other Indian dilemma—when should I tell Sarah about Holika? Each time I came close it was as if she knew and somehow stopped me. And I thought of how she had tried to tell me her "secret" and somehow I had stopped her. And I thought of the duplicity of which I'd so wrongly accused her and of my secret. I thought about scheduling another session with Debbie, or one with only me, but I still felt, no, not yet, and although I was haunted by the secret Sarah had kept, the speed and weight of events outpaced my ability to confront her, feeling that it would doom us. I told myself secrets had their place and time and eventually I had to tell her. First, we needed to survive the next weeks.

Whether or not to attend the opening became another contentious choice. In my completely male hypocrisy, I didn't want to see Riegle. Rather injudiciously, I asked if he was coming. "Of course," came her blunt answer. "It's not him but so many others I can't face. I hate putting on my opening face."

In the end, we went and the evening passed in a blur. Sarah handled herself marvelously. I hadn't seen her new work and her description failed to convey its power. Magnificent abstracts of fiery reds, yellows, with precise understanding of the blank space of canvas, of white and black, of the universal feminine shapes of the mandala and triangle, breathed with the mythic symbolism of life and death. The president of Women Against Guns gushed over the poster: a fading mandala-bull's eyes of muted blues, with blood-red splatters from corner-to-corner forming an X and "Stop the Killing—20,000 Gun Deaths Every Year." WAG, not wanting to exploit Sarah, held the press conference to unveil the poster earlier in the day.

Kugliani invited the press and, unlike any of her other openings, this time they came. I harbored no illusions that the paintings would've been shipped back the day after the exhibition ended with a "thank you" and a churlish smile, if the show hadn't sold out, which it did. A first for Sarah. Amazing what a little notoriety can do—the slew of reviews in *Art in America*, the *Village Voice*, and the *New York Times* crowned Sarah Brockton Roberts as an "art presence." What should've been the culmination of twenty years of struggling toward a meaningful art and recognition left her feeling almost hollow, wondering if the praise were false.

Sarah, awakened from her scattered state, handled the crowd and questions with nobility. Most of which had nothing to do with art or the Second Amendment. Instead the give-and-take went like this: "Did Patricia Field, the noted downtown designer, donate your dress?" "No, W.C. and Mrs. Fields designed this for the Comedy and Cookie section for Ross's Dress for Less." "Are you writing a book?" "It's taken me this long to become a decent painter, what makes you think I can write?" From Callie Finn, a network newswoman came the capper, "You must miss your son terribly. How do you feel tonight?"

That last question sent her to the back room. We didn't stay for the dinner.

Driving back, instead of the usual yentaing about who honestly liked it, who showed up, who bought or didn't buy, who acted like a jerk, who was so zonked they didn't make any sense, who tried to promote their own career, Sarah dozed on and off. When she fell asleep, I put on the Knicks game. That dulled my senses and I hoped I had handled my one-minute eye-to eye meeting with Riegle in a way that would satisfy Sarah. I thanked him, told him how much I appreciated his friendship and support. Before a deep discussion ensued, two young art groupies tugged him away, and my inhaled gut released itself.

When Sarah awoke, she punched the button that turned off the radio and stared vacantly out the side window at the dimming lights of the suburban monuments to the American Dream. As I slowed down, and exited from the Long Island Expressway, she turned and faced me.

"I need to get the hell out of here. Soon."

"OK, whatever you say."

She reached over to the dashboard and turned up the heater.

"I owned one last hope that I could will myself pregnant, that I would know if something was wrong in my body. Just like I couldn't believe I sensed no danger for Castor. It was silly. Stupid. I know nothing."

I hated this admission. From the day we met, Sarah's optimism, her drive for life had inspired me to believe in myself. To believe I served the good by working in the ER. I so desperately wanted to give her back that hope.

"Where do you want to go?"

"India sounds far enough away to me."

We agreed to get out of the U.S. before those conjoining holidays of Passover and Easter—a holiday she remembered fondly from early childhood when she painted and hid eggs, and when she "secretly" bought Castor chocolate bunnies. I "secretly" liked them plenty, too.

The next day I made the plane reservations and called Schlipssi, who secured Sarah's visa within twenty-four hours.

The evening before leaving for the eleven o'clock flight, in the icy twilight I lugged a rowboat out of the garage and down to the sandy beach in the backyard that led to the bay for what I feared might be a morbid or maudlin ritual. Sarah gripped the doll-like sculpture in her gloved hands. I rowed out about four hundred yards. I doused it with lighter fluid; set it in the water. Sarah knelt silently as she tossed matches into the bowl-shaped pedestal until it caught fire. I watched as we sat together holding hands—thinking that we must let go of the past, of what can never be, my insides feeling so empty, amidst my silent tears and Sarah's sobbing and shivering body held close to me— as it quite beautifully flamed and flickered orange and yellow, reflecting in the water under the moonlit night before it faded unnamed, and merged into the sea.

I rowed to the shore. Sarah never once looked back to see the last dying ashes.

A day later, we landed a hemisphere away.

Sarah, like most first-timers, exhausted from a day of flying, was ill-prepared for the volumes of humanity that accost you the second you get off the plane. She threaded the gauntlet through a phalanx of bobbing, smiling, and hissing faces. Her bedazzled eyes, agape mouth asked, You like it here? Is this the right place for us now? Yes, it was.

While I went back to the office, Sarah slept for almost two days. Donna informed me they'd chosen a doctor who'd be there right after the holidays. Schlipssi messengered over a document with all the details, along with the information that Pankaj had been reassigned and not replaced. We didn't have to move. The new doctor had a wife and three kids, so they'd secured a house for him. I'd "transition" him in and myself out. I could keep the house if we wanted to stay and pay rent. I didn't hear directly from Charlie, who was "preoccupied." His secretary prepared all kinds of possible travel plans for us: Kanha National Park. The sacred city of Varnassi and the temples of Khajuraho. A trip through Rajasthan. Of course, two days at Agra to see the Taj Mahal.

Rabbi Judah had called Donna the day after he saw me in the cemetery. Donna told him of my family emergency. He called again right after we returned and invited us to attend a Passover Seder at his home. I doubted we'd make it. I asked if Levi attended these celebrations.

"It is hard to say. Like Elijah, I always have a place for him, but one never knows when he will come or go."

"How about the Donneaux?" He gave his windy explanation that meant yes. "I'm sorry then." Sarah did not need that kind of scrutiny.

I wanted to call Levi, but more from him than anyone else I wanted to withhold the news. When Sarah felt stronger and became more acclimated we'd invite him for dinner. Maybe even with Holika and Samaka, and if I could swing it, Chrystie and Charlie.

I reached Holika in Bangalore. She'd be back with Samaka for the huge Holi party at the Pillai farm. Holi, the festival of color, marked the joyous end of winter welcoming of spring fest, where the crowds light bonfires and squirt paint at each other. She surmised it would be a good, problem-free occasion for us to all meet. We discussed little else. Sarah had read about Holi and wanted to go.

A bit refreshed and looking for newness, Sarah and I ventured into the streets. The teashops, the markets, the huts and Coke stands, the beggars and tent-dwellers, the clothes and smells, and the music of Delhi life took her right out of herself, exactly as I hoped it would. The wildlife often fascinated her and also upset her; so many animals appeared maltreated —sacred cows eating and choking on plastic bags mixed in with the garbage. She tried her best to keep a blind eye to the waves of children, which was damn near impossible. I saw the remorse creep into her eyes and could only hold her hand tighter. I kept

her away from Old Delhi and some of the poorer colonies, because Sarah, with her innately positive and serene nature, bat-
tling one-too-many corrosive blows—from an unloving mother
to an uncaring world to, at best, an oblivious husband—never
connected with her "inner Nazi" and I didn't want her to. We
shopped for cheap clothes in Janpath. She bought pajama-style
pants for a dollar, Buddha bags for a quarter, shoes for two
bucks, shirts for me for another dollar. She found a handmade
paper store where she spent two afternoons marveling at the
high quality and low price. At night we took in a few Bollywood
movies—no understanding of Hindi necessary to get the plot,
as it never varied much. The over-the-top acting, the inserted
music videos, which were a choreographic mix of nineteen-
forties musical kitsch and MTV quick-cut editing enthralled us.
She loved the food and we ate out often.

One evening we strolled over to a restaurant in Hauz Khas
village that served some of the finest *dhosas* in Delhi. We ran
into Alvaro Benigno, whose gallery space was nearby. I introduced Sarah. His eyebrows arched high above his glasses. "Oh,
I didn't know your wife was *that* Sarah Roberts." He kept his
head in the New York art scene, reading reviews, getting the
lowdown on the hot shows and the dirt.

He asked us to join him. We did and he filled us in on the
art supply stores at South Extension, and offered to introduce
Sarah to "other" Delhi art world honchos and artists. It didn't
take long until he suggested giving Sarah a show if we stayed.

"Maybe. I can't make plans now," Sarah answered diplo-
matically, while she kneed me under the table. We weren't
out of the restaurant two minutes when Sarah declared the
Gossip Line now open for business. A good sign, I thought, as
she explained that six years before, Benigno skulked out of
town in one of the biggest art-world brouhahas in years. He

325

owed the government thousands in taxes. Hadn't paid his rent or his artists either. Bryce Kanyon, a punk rocker turned installation artist, and now, yes, gallery owner, took an ad out in the *Voice* warning Benigno that if he ventured below 26th Street, he'd rearrange his profile into a found object piece of public art.

Gosh, I loved the rarefied splendor of the art world. It made dealing with Charlie almost charming when he sauntered into my office on Holy Thursday. Finally, a slow time for him before Good Friday, Holi, and Easter. I thanked him for arranging our travel itinerary. He sloughed that off with a half-wave of his hand and ambled around the office, while I organized some files. "Even though it's not your holiday, maybe Sarah would like to join us for Easter supper." I would've wagered big shekels that Charlie had no idea Jesus was leading the Passover Seder at that Last Supper. "Chrystie would appreciate it."

Chrystie wanted to meet Sarah. She even called and volunteered to take Sarah shopping.

When Charlie relaxed himself in what I considered my chair behind my desk, I sensed the purpose of this visit extended beyond cordial Easter egg hunts and shopping sprees.

His voice dropped to a gravelly register, "You ever let anything slip about Vijay's problem to Holika?" His head shook, admonishing me before I answered. "You two became quite close."

"You introduced me to her."

"We all make mistakes." He tapped his fingers against his thigh.

"She asked me. I denied it. She called me on it. Friends of hers at Privat told her. She wanted my opinion. I told her he needed to do something and soon."

"You should've told me."

326

"I found out the night I left for New York—after I saw you." I assumed someone told him she came by my home. "Charlie, I don't know who knows what in this place. I'm guessing—but are all the phones bugged?"

"Not all." His chuckled but his face didn't laugh.

"Charlie, I'm cool about this," I lied, feeling completely uncool, "but Vijay is letting himself die and Holika loves him and does not want him to die.

"Not yet anyway." Love never interfered with Charlie's business decisions. "I once told you to watch where you step in this country. I meant it. Friendship will only take you so far."

"Hey, I know who my friends are. And me, I'm trying to survive. I just need to help stop Sarah from drowning. I'm not into any internecine wars. Filial or otherwise."

"That's all I needed to hear."

Sarah had no desire to get festive with the Easter Bunny known as Charlie Bedrosian. I wish getting away from Passover and that ineffable missing of my parents and family would've been that simple. On that first night of Passover I wished I had accepted Judah's invite, Levi or no Levi. For no matter where I was, I could never escape the yearning, yet childish feelings that spurted from my gastric juices on the Jewish holidays. The semiannual get-togethers of jealousies between siblings and cousins, where I cherished being an only child as they squabbled over who would lead the Seder, which Haggadah, the Seder prayer book, to use—English or English-Hebrew, and who would ask the fabled Four Questions. My father, a religious blank page, always rolled his eyes as my uncles or cousins kvetched and quibbled, when he wanted to say, "Let's eat." And my mother, no latent repository of spiritual sacredness, but in search of family harmony, would snake-eye stare him to shut up and be patient. Why I missed that is beyond me, but I did. And so much I missed my son.

Since it was also the night of Holi, not a good night to be out on the streets, Sarah cooked a dinner of pasta with a mutton meat sauce. Good Jewish food. Zoned out, I lounged on the couch, half-reading the new issue of *JAMA*, half-watching an American series about a bunch of calorie-deficient female lawyers and their neurotic male counterparts—both composed of more plastic than Barbie and Ken dolls, yammering over some inanity—helluva Passover show, when the phone rang. Not my cell phone, so I assumed it was the wrong number.

"Mr. Downs, I am sorry to disturb you and I am aware you are experiencing a less than happy time." I recognized Rabbi Judah's high-pitched, anguished speaking voice, which often left no room for commas or periods so you could slow him down with a question. Only this time, I had no questions. Not four. Not even one. My legs gave out for a second and I half-collapsed to the floor. Sarah saw me and yelled "What?" absolutely panicked. I mouthed, "Levi's dead."

Earlier that evening Levi swallowed a few dozen Darvocets and Vicodins, the pills that I had prescribed for him, using beer to wash them down. Then he turned on the gas oven, lay down on the kitchen floor, stuck a pillow under his head and placed the hundred and fifty year old rusted key from his family home in Prague on his chest.

In his last act of the unbroken spirit, his last spit-in-the-face to his dead god, to his pious-posturing torturers, to the legacy of Schneerman, like so many Holocaust survivors unwilling to let others make the decision, Levi chose the elegiac weekend of salvation and sacrifice to die correctly.

I regained my composure and promised Judah I'd be at the funeral on Sunday morning.

"I'm so sorry."

I turned off the TV. "It's OK. I'll miss him, but it's what he wanted." His was a death, if not a life, that I could understand.

"Are you upset you didn't call him?" She motioned for me to sit beside her.

"No. It's better this way." I couldn't say that I wanted to re-member him almost glad, with a glimmer of the innocent hope he denied, kissing me on the forehead rather than hearing the harsh disappointment, which certainly would have overtaken him had I told him there would be no child.

Sarah touched me, rubbed my back like she used to rub Castor's.

"You still want to go to the party?"

"Damn right." I didn't want to sit around and brood one more day. "I want to get shitfaced blind drunk. You OK with that?"

"That might do me some good, too. Or might make me dive into a fathomless lake of wallowing self-pity."

"Don't worry. If you need to, you need to, and we're now here to catch each other."

61

For so long it puzzled me why John placed the most important naming in the New Testament in the past, rather than the present tense. Now I see that he, like Jesus, born a Jew, perhaps unconsciously, perhaps slyly intimated that the natural progression from polytheism to monotheism is to a world beyond god. The command in John 1:1 that the "Word was God," placed god in time, rather than being time or transcending time. This comes in stark contrast to John 4:24 when he commanded: "God is spirit:" I now interpret this, as a god who killed his son and did not assure eternality, but ended the dream of immortality beyond time while bequeathing the "spirit" to us. Our responsibility is to allow that spirit to thrive within humanity and within time.

—from THE UNPUBLISHED WORKS

62

THE NEXT DAY we dressed in shabby clothes,
sneakers for me, flip-flops for Sarah, a baseball cap for me and
a straw hat for Sarah. Vishnu had the day off, so one of the Pillai
family drivers picked us up. The traffic so light, this might've
been the only day I could've driven in Delhi. During the night,
revelers splattered paint everywhere—threw colors, as the Hindus called it—on streets, signs, walls, traffic lights, cars, elephants, and dogs.

The party was in raucous sway when we arrived, and soon
we, too, were bombarded by the colors. A good portion of the
hundred or so guests pranced around already drunk and high
on *bhaang*, a thick concoction of dried fruits, milk, almonds,
couscous, aniseed, and a generous helping of marijuana. It did
not look too tasty. Sarah and I had given up pot years ago when
she got pregnant with Castor. Watching people act like human
Easter eggs didn't entice us to start again. Vodka and beers suited
us fine. I set about on my mission of getting soused.

Sarah kept close to my side. I introduced her, and I'd never
have believed this, to so many of the guests whom I knew.

Sharmilla and her husband, painted like two Druids, brought us two vodkas. Benigno, with his new boyfriend, and Sonia Guptaphya invited us to try some *bhaang*. We declined. P. K. Bahar had brought his wife to the party. Gatore and Preeya and several of their friends talked together in one circle. No Tracee. I'm not sure she would've been invited now anyway, but she'd already left for New York. Ratish prowled around like a commando. Alka and her friends danced and laughed, with their ever-present third appendage—the cell phone. Vijay stayed inside, occasionally peering out from the balcony with a single dollop of red paint, the color for married people, on his forehead. He preferred to drink quietly with a few older compatriots and business associates. A DJ played Indian music. Servants manned the barbecue pit.

I pointed out Samaka and Holika to Sarah. She playfully called him "cute." About Holika, she remained mum. When Holika spotted us, wearing paint-sopped jeans, T-shirt, and her hair multicolored, with her limbs loose, she practically skipped toward us with a glass of *bhaang* in her right hand. I introduced them. Politeness echoed in their voices, but they did a wary, gladiator dance while exchanging cliched pleasantries. Holika asked if I'd heard about Levi. She'd heard about it on the news. CNN placed the "suicide of the controversial and reclusive" Holocaust writer between spots on the meaning of Passover and the sprightly preparations for the White House Easter Egg roll.

Samaka ambled over as we spoke about Levi.

"You knew him?" Samaka might've been the only sober person at this bacchanalian fest.

"We met a few times."

"I'm jealous. I saw him speak once when I was at college." He puffed on a cigarette and courteously blew the smoke away from us. "You know, I must thank you for something."

"Oh?"

"Because of you, Holika has finally stopped calling me 'Shmuck.'"

Bad timing. She put her arms around him and cooed, "You are my Shmuck."

"OK," he took the glass of *bhaang* from her, "no more for you and I may have to get a drink or this party will become untenable."

Ratish sneaked up behind Samaka and Holika and smeared paint on their heads. Samaka didn't look too thrilled. Holika shook a playful fist at him before he rushed off and smeared it intentionally on Preeya's right breast. She slapped him across his face. He smeared her other breast. She slapped him again and stomped away. Sarah and I watched mystified. Although many looked disgusted, especially Samaka, no one said a word.

We ate the food, though hesitatingly at first. The dust from the industrial dye in the paint drizzled down like colored mist seeping into your skin, the ground, the cups and plates, the food and barbecue pit. After a few drinks, we just said the hell with it.

Almost everyone offered advice on what to do and see in Delhi and where to travel. We got a half-dozen dinner invitations. In a quiet moment, I explained the "Shmuck" reference to Sarah, who seemed awed by the magnitude of the Pillai family wealth.

Fulfilling our pledges to let go, we drank and, at first, watched others dance and party. Soon, Sarah, cautiously, and I began to dance. It was so hard for her to let go. After about an hour of dancing without a break, we plopped down in seats at a table under a gas heater and lamp, which we needed as the sun set and it got cooler and darker. Holika, coming down off her high, and Samaka, who seemed genuinely interested in my impressions of India, sat with us. Ratish bullied his way onto half the chair with Holika, who frowned, annoyed. "Get your own chair." He placed her hand in his mouth and puffed on her cigarette. "I thought you are claiming we should share everything as sister and brother." He didn't want, or wait for, an answer. "Are you having a good time, Madame Downs?"

"Madame Roberts. I kept my own name. And yes, I am."

"Shit, another one. You will be perfect to join my sister's cause to free the women of the world."

"It's a good cause."

"Hmm. Yes." He eyed Sarah almost a little too lasciviously. "Are you are an admirer of my sister's first husband, Siddhartha Singh? He taught his disciples the virtues of free sex."

Holika squirmed in her half of the seat. She put out the cigarette. "Ratish, they care not about the history of my life nor do they need an Indian civics lesson."

Sarah's lips pursed into a small pink knot, a sure sign that she was getting fed up with Ratish's boorishness. "I know nothing of Siddhartha Singh, but I'm certain nothing in life is free— especially sex."

Ratish guffawed. His eyes gleamed with the same freakish madness I'd seen when we went to the club. He'd undoubtedly done *bhaang* that night too. "Dr. Downs, I detect that your wife is one willful woman."

"I prefer the words independent and determined, and I wouldn't want her to be any other way."

"What about you, Samaka? You think nothing is free in life?"

"Just speech, even when it is offensive." The perfect jab, which set up his goodbye punch. "And you have misread Siddhartha. I disagree with much that he did during his too short life." Samaka stood up and affectionately caressed his hand through Holika's hair. "But he taught the need for unconditional love, not free sex."

"Maybe. He also believed," Ratish stared directly at Sarah, while he nudged Holika with his elbow, "we should unconditionally love *their* women," he paused and gazed at me, "not they, who should love ours."

"Now you've gone from the inane to the insulting. It is not worthy of you," Samaka answered. He kept improving by the second. "Would you two like to join me for a walk?" Samaka's implicit question also warned Holika, who behind the paint looked livid, to deal with Ratish. We got up. Ratish yelled after Samaka. "You have no idea of my worth."

"I apologize for him. He cannot handle his liquor or his drugs. Unfortunately, we do not get along."

"It would take much more than him to upset me." Sarah put her hand in mine.

"I am sure." He took off his glasses and tried to clean them with his T-shirt. "Damned paint." Sarah gave him a clean tissue from her pants' pocket. He nodded his thanks. "I hope this doesn't sound intrusive, I too am a bit less level-headed than my usual self, but India can be a remarkable place for healing."

"It's the people," I said. "So many have been good to me. Holika has been a great friend, I mean great friend to me during some awful times. The night before I left, you know," he nodded grimly, "if she didn't sit with me I might've lost my mind."

"Yes, she told me. But this is too serious. Holi is a day for fun."

Samaka found small talk difficult. He shared his ambitious ideas on the absolute need to reach the millions of people living in India's villages. He believed in technology, the way others believed in gods. As one of the creators of the technological world, he believed in the necessity of India becoming a nuclear nation. He didn't convince Sarah any more than he convinced Holika, but he made a better case than Burden or Vijay. I would love to have seen a debate between James Roberson and Samaka.

After a twenty-minute circle of the grounds, we returned, Ratish's antics forgotten. Instead we found a distraught Holika inside the house. She'd washed her face, which, even with the residue of color, looked ashen. She'd tried to reason with Ratish, asking him to behave with their guests and slow down on the pot and drink. He answered with a curt, "You are boring me, sister. Ta-ta." Making a loud scene, he got up from the table, embarrassingly announced his departure, grabbed another glass of *bhaang* and a bottle of Scotch, trotted to his car as if he were taking a victory lap, slammed the door shut, revved the engine, and skidded away. Alone and without his driver.

Samaka comforted her. "Ratish has done this before. I will send a man out to look for him."

On a bit of a down from what had been a good time, we offered our thank yous and bid goodbyes. During the car ride home, Sarah nestled her head against my shoulder and closed her eyes. At home, in a post-party, semidrunk, not yet hungover cloudiness, Sarah got in the shower first. She called me in to wash the paint off her back. "I see why you like it here. You've started a new life without me." I didn't see her face but she sounded intense.

"And it's going to be even better with you."

"Maybe." The hot water flowed, felt good as I scrubbed her back. "Do you ever look at me without seeing Castor?"

"Of course," my words had no weight. They looked so similar and not only physically but in their body movements and facial expressions that I "saw" him all too often.

"I wonder if you could ever again love me the way you did. You will always look at me and see the future you won't have and I don't know if I can live that way."

"No, it will change. Everything is already changing." I hoped the same was true of her; that she could look at me without seeing what I had denied her. "You need me to do your back?" I handed her the soap. "Sarah, I'll do whatever it takes to make this work." I moved under the water and then she scrubbed me clean. She reached around and began to wash my chest. Then, for the first time since the miscarriage, we made love. An almost solitudinous, remorseful love. As she gripped me tighter, I felt Sarah sobbing as she came.

She didn't want to speak anymore that night. Ask any more questions. By the time I finished washing my hair and brushing my teeth and got into bed, with her head tucked between two pillows, she slept lightly. She awoke for a second, grasped onto my forearm, as she had for so many years, and was asleep again in seconds.

At around 5 a.m. the phone rang. I thought it was a call from the States, and in a daze I answered it. "Neil. I am sorry but please can you and Sarah come quickly to the compound?" I recognized Holika, her voice hoarse, her tone somber.

"What? Why?"

"There has been a terrible incident. Please, the two of you must come now. Bring Sarah. A driver will be waiting downstairs."

I didn't ask any questions. Sarah, too, had awakened, and as we dressed, she questioned why Holika wanted her to come. I shook my head. The driver, as usual, volunteered no information. We approached the compound and Sarah, with her acute sense of smell sniffed smoke in the air. Immediately, I thought they needed me as a doctor. I pressed the driver for

337

some answers. He reluctantly volunteered that there'd been a blackout and one of the kerosene lamps had caught on fire. Inside the gates, we could see and feel the haze of smoke. The driver dropped us in front of the main home. A fading, not quite familiar odor wafted in the air. Holika came quickly outside to greet us. The left side of her face was swollen and there was a cut below her eye, her clothes were sooty and frayed and a shawl hung loosely, wrapped around her neck. A young girl, maybe ten or eleven, Holika called her Sita, her face petrified, clutched the waistband on Holika's pants. In a raspy rush of words Holika explained what happened.

"Ratish is in the hospital. In the burn unit. He is alive. But I asked you here for a reason." She didn't look down but at us as she squeezed the girl's hand. "I must tell you fast and you must decide now. I came back to Delhi when Ratish never returned to Haryana. Samaka went to his family home. I fell asleep and awoke when the electricity went off. The emergency generator had started so I went outside to turn on the primary one and I saw the lamplight in his bungalow. I was still so furious at him for his vile behavior. I went directly to talk to him. Only he was not alone." She glanced down at Sita. I understood right away. Sarah still looked confused.

"I told him I was taking her to Summit's and began to untie the ropes on her hands and he attacked me. He was so drunk and high and he started strangling me." She stopped still incredulous at her brother's actions. "And I smashed him with a kerosene lamp. The kerosene spilled out, mixing with the paint and he, he ignited into this . . ." She paused and held her breath before exhaling and speaking simultaneously. "And he began screaming like I have never heard." She was now crying as she spoke but did not acknowledge her tears. "I jumped up, grabbed blankets off the bed, and Sita and I, we wrapped him in the blankets and then sped to AIIMS."

Suddenly, Vijay, pale and sunken, still believing in politeness and propriety, began to walk toward us. Holika, with Sita still holding onto her, rushed to his side, held him, and escorted him back to his room. Sarah looked at me quizzically. Before I could answer, Holika quickly returned to us and said what we could see for ourselves, "He is crushed. I could not let him stay at the hospital. Samaka is there now."

She didn't need me to help Ratish. The Indian doctors had saved him. He remained in critical condition, inside a burn tank, and if he survived, it would be months, maybe years, before he recovered. If ever.

Holika thought she'd gotten to Sita before Ratish raped her. She told Holika that Ratish forced her "to do things to him," but she bit him and that's when he tied her up. She said what was now too clear to me: this was not the first time he had done this.

"You want me to examine her?"

"No. I wish you to take her home. Now."

Startled, it took me a few seconds before I fully absorbed her intention. Sarah tilted her head, her body jumped and then clenched as if she'd been punched in the gut.

"I must tell you that she cannot read or write or many other things you might expect. I need to know now. I must get her away."

They could not hurt Holika. What could Ratish say about the girl? He found her lurking in his room? The truth could certainly hurt him. Holika, in an odd way, was protecting her brother one last time.

Sarah, still somewhat bewildered, wanted Holika to be clear. "What do you want from us?"

"She has no place. No one. I can fix much. Charlie and my uncle can fix the rest so you will have no problems leaving the country. If you want I will send over a woman tomorrow who speaks English and Hindi to help you until you leave."

Sarah and I glanced at each other, then one more time at Sita. Wordlessly, with a slow closing and opening of her eyes and a quarter-inch nod of her head, she agreed.

Holika bent down and spoke to Sita in Hindi. Her shawl slipped down as she stood up and I saw bruises and abrasions on her neck.

"You need to get that looked at," I said.

"No, it is nothing. I will have it checked tomorrow."

"No one will ever know what happened here, will they?"

She didn't answer. We would read about an accidental fire at the Pillai Complex in the papers. Luckily, the bungalow was constructed primarily of cement and marble and only a few items caught on fire before the dozen or so servants, ever on duty, in seconds were out of their huts in the far corner of the compound and doused the fire.

I reached my right hand toward Sita. "Please mister, sir." Her voice small but firm, she did not move. She told Holika in Hindi that she could walk on her own. Taking tiny but confident steps, she led us outside. Holika needed to get back to the hospital. I gingerly hugged Holika and so did Sarah. She got in her car and it pulled away. We got in our car and Sita reached for Sarah's hand, which she took. Sarah seemed almost as afraid as Sita. In the car, Sita practically tucked herself into Sarah, whose sideways glance told me doubts buzzed in her head. "Later. Let's talk more later," I promised.

Still unable to sleep in what would've been Castor's room, I slept on the couch. In another few hours I left Sita and Sarah sleeping together in the master bedroom. I had to attend a funeral.

A huge crowd, five hundred people at the minimum, showed up at the cemetery on this Easter Sunday. Indian intellectuals, Moslems and Hindus, Communists and Capitalists. Physicists from the universities. Correspondents from the local and international press. The Israeli ambassador. Cultural attachés from at least thirty embassies. No Charlie or Chrystie. The owners of bookstores and restaurants that Levi frequented. Neighbors and strangers. For a crotchety old loner, he sure had plenty of friends.

I couldn't get near the closed casket. From one of the dozens of baskets of flowers I pulled two white roses. For what I hoped would be the last time I sat by the grave of Rachel Mulemet and placed the roses, not stones this time, on her headstone and bid her goodbye.

Long ago Levi advised Rabbi Judah on how to conduct the ceremony. Judah acknowledged that Levi wanted no prayers, no shivah, no eulogy service at the Habitat Center. Judah didn't listen. All were being arranged. He prayed in Hebrew and English and asked us to pray along. I couldn't. I never even mouthed "amen."

To close, Judah did recite the lines Levi had chosen from the German-Jewish poet, Heinrich Heine:

> No one will sing a Mass
> No one will say a Kaddish
> There will be nothing said and nothing sung
> On the anniversaries of my death.

The service done, I hung back, letting the crowd pass me by. From behind, a pale-faced Cecile Donneaux tapped me on the shoulder. Automatically, I said hello. She wanted to keep the conversation going, "confessing" how much she'd miss

Levi. She moved into gear and started making excuses that her husband often acted too zealously. I stopped her.

"Forget it. I'm leaving India."

"Us, too. Next month. Back to Paris," her two-year tour finished. "Did you hear about the accident at the Pillai's?"

"Yes. Why?" I didn't trust her motives.

"No, no, I am not speaking as a journalist."

"OK. Then this conversation is officially off the record?"

She nodded. I thought this might be a way out of my dilemma.

"You want to get mitzvah points?" I asked.

"Yes, if I can."

"Next week, call Holika. Vijay Pillai's niece."

"Are you sure that would not be intruding at a bad time?"

"More than sure, only you never heard it from me." I shook my head solemnly.

"Yes, of course."

The petite, almost toothless older lady, who had greeted me the first time I came to the temple tiptoed up and stood about five feet from us until we finished.

"Please. You are Mr. Doctor?" I nodded. She pointed inside and I followed her into the back room of the temple. Piled on the table were twenty bound copies of Levi's unpublished writings. "One. For you." I felt like one of the anointed.

Levi made provisions for the book to be published one year after his death. He had established a trust while in Israel that would donate the proceeds from his books to designated charities. The Delhi Temple was one of them. After all his rants about Jewish monuments, Yad Vashem, the Holocaust memorial in Jerusalem, would inherit his papers. In life and death, no one would ever figure out Levi Furstenblum. That's exactly how he wanted it.

I hustled back to the apartment, hoping to get a few hours of sleep. No chance. Charlie had called. Sarah said he sounded like one pissed off ambassador because I didn't answer my cell phone. He insisted that I meet him at one o'clock in the library at Chanyakapuri.

While Sarah cooked me an omelet, she let me know she needed to talk about Sita. I thought, it all came too quickly. We knew nothing about this abandoned child and the hell of her life that would become an essential part of our life. The hazards that lay ahead. The questions of her health—emotional and physical. What we knew did not augur well. "Sarah, I know we need to talk and if this was all too fucking fast, please just say so." She sat beside me as I shoveled the food down. It was already 12:30.

"No, I want to do it. I'm afraid if we do this and something goes wrong . . . I'm frail, Neil. Really frail."

"I know. So you and your needs come first. I'll do whatever you decide is best. Be selfish for yourself." I kissed her goodbye. "Wish me luck with Charlie."

"Forget luck, what can he do to hurt you? Fire you? I'll be here when you get back."

Once there, I scurried up the stairs to the library where Charlie talked on a cell phone. From the neck down, dressed in a polo shirt, khaki trousers, and new sneakers, Charlie looked like a proud papa ready to loll down Fifth Avenue with Chrystie and Heather in the Easter Parade. From the neck up, his teeth clacking, his complexion red, he looked like a cobra ready to swallow its prey whole.

He hung up and we moved to the balcony that overlooked the courtyard, which was virtually still and free of people. He leaned against the cement pillar, acting more like he held up the building than the other way around. I stood in the corner, arms folded across my chest.

343

"I had a most unpleasant conversation this morning with Samaka Abhitraj. I want your version of what happened last night. No bull."

I gave him a rundown of the events as I knew them.

"Christ. And that's the girl you and Sarah want to adopt?"

I'd omitted any mention of adoption, only that we'd taken her to the safety of our house, so he knew plenty already. "Maybe."

"You aware the hell a kid like that can give you?"

"Same hell as any kid. I'll give her a full workup. Take all the tests. Get her the immunizations. Can you fix it?"

"Sure, sure. It's gonna cost you even with my help."

"Go for it."

"OK. I got bigger problems. Medically speaking, is Ratish done?"

"Forever? Can't say without seeing him, for now," I stuck my head forward and crunched my shoulders in a who knows motion, "I'd say he's lost to you. Even if he recovers, I don't think Vijay will forgive him. In his way, he is quite moral."

"In his way," he scratched his right eyebrow, then rubbed the back of his neck with his right hand, "Vijay needs to get his house in order. We spent years clearing the way for this deal. Next week Burden is bringing the Environ board members."

"Then you best keep Vijay healthy." I decided to state the obvious. It cost me nothing. "Holika will do everything in her power, which is now considerable, to thwart you."

"That little cunt . . ." He caught himself too late, his harshness too evident. "What did you see on your trip?"

"She can cause you problems."

"Can? She already has." He moved away from the pillar and closer to me. "That's really why I kept her around." Charlie, like all good diplomats, followed the maxim "Keep your friends close and your enemies closer." I'd been moved to the enemy camp. "She's told anyone who will listen about Chrystie and the stock. She's trying to get this to the courts."

Feigning ignorance, I practiced the art of the nondenial denial. "I know nothing about nothing. I'm a doctor."

Charlie didn't buy it. "What about you and Holika and your significant others? That solved?"

With that question, Charlie dropped all pretense of selflessness. As a Cold War diplomat, I figured he worked on the premise that mutually assured destruction maintained the peace.

"I heard that there's no statute of limitations on embezzling national treasures out of India."

"Sure, Downs, you're one dumb doctor." Charlie smirked, baring his crooked teeth, almost in admiration. "You think about this adoption deal. If you want it, I'll get it done in a week or two. Then our slate's even and you stay dumb. Your word?"

His threat had eliminated much of my guilt about talking to Donneaux. When he stuck out his hand, I stuck out mine and we shook, in what now felt like a paltry and meaningless gesture.

"Not another word." I sure hoped Cecile Donneaux's word was good and she would talk to Holika and keep me out of it because from that moment on, I could never talk to her or anyone else.

When I got home I found no Sarah or Sita. Only a note. Holika had come over and they "went out." I lay down, exhausted. In less than fifteen minutes, I heard the rumbling in the living room.

They'd gone shopping for Sita and bought her a pair of jeans, T-shirt, and sneakers, and when I saw her, I breathed a sigh, as she smiled proudly. Holika, looking drawn and beaten up physically and emotionally, asked for some tea. I plugged in the electric kettle. She gave me the update: they'd flown Ratish to the special burn hospital in Bombay. She'd never seen Vijay so moribund, but every suggestion that came to her head appeared silly. The next morning, the whole family, including Samaka was flying to Bombay.

I served the tea and Holika let hers cool as she got up and rooted around in her handbag, started to take out her cigarettes and then, remembering who she was with, put them back. Her staccato-like movements made me nervous. Then she blurted out, in a much less articulate manner than usual, the reason for her visit. She felt like she'd put us in an insupportable position. She couldn't think of any other alternative. This was our chance to renege.

"No, you did right." Sarah spoke with calmness, and looked with reassurance at Holika. "It's going to be hard. I'm worried and have doubts, but I've thought about this all day and I want her to come if she wants to go with us."

In Hindi, Holika asked Sita, who sat on the floor beside the couch, if she wanted to stay with us. Her usually taut face grinned and she nodded her head enthusiastically, "Please, mister."

"Good." I heaved a sigh of bad air and inhaled good air. "Not so good is Charlie. He's going to war with you now."

"At least that means he knows I exist." She sipped her tea. "All I need is time."

"Charlie knows that too." Because Holika would be distracted with Ratish and Vijay, I'm sure he planned to move fast to push the deal further along where it would be tougher to stop.

Sarah, never a fan of Charlie's reassured her. "You can't let your guard down with those types."

Holika needed to leave. Sarah suggested I walk out with Holika, and in the gesture, she told me *she knew*. I sighed. Sarah and Holika hugged each other. Outside, Holika reached for a cigarette, but didn't light it. "Well . . . I hope this is good for you. And for Sarah. You both deserve something good."

"Yeah. I hope. Go ahead light it, I can handle it for two minutes." She did. "Holika, what really happened in the bungalow last night?"

"What do you mean? It's exactly what I told you."

"I saw your neck. Something doesn't seem right. It won't matter, we still want her."

"Ratish, maybe he was going to kill me. If Sita didn't . . . when she hit him like that, she saved my life." She spoke without emotion as if still in disbelief at her brother's debased madness and I knew I'd guessed right about who'd actually picked up the lamp. "It is better if she is not here when Ratish recovers."

If he recovers, I thought. "We'll be back. Sita will have to get to know her country. And I still have to see the Taj Mahal."

Out came a forced smile, a commitment to speak by phone and we said goodbye and she was gone.

When I came back inside Sarah was fixing up the extra bedroom for Sita. Before she took her into the shower, she admitted her fears. "Neil, I hope I can do this."

I hoped my surety would overcome her doubts. "I hate to say this because I hate prognostications, but it's going to be good." I needed to go get some sleep. "Think about it 'til we have to leave and if you can't, no questions asked—ever—and I call Summit. Sarah, I think we need to talk about some other things that happened in India over the last few months." I wanted to confess about Holika and me.

"No need."

"Are you *sure*?"

"*Yes.*"

The next day I began making plans for us to leave India. It took longer than we hoped to get all the paperwork and plans straightened out. In some ways that worked better. Sita, although generally healthy, needed every shot imaginable. In those few weeks she became more comfortable with us and started to learn English. Holika, who after all the turmoil, and Vijay's decision to treat his myeloma, was making big plans for the Grand March and contemplating a run for Parliament.

On the day we left Delhi, in the wake of the oncoming squalid heat, Holika dropped us at the airport and the three of us boarded the plane as a family.

63

Where we once found god, we must now fill the empty soul of the
living heart; we must find love without the smell of vengeance and
hate; a poetry for the songs that have not yet been sung, a canvas
for the visions that have not been seen, a language for words that
have not been thought.
    The word that was god is silent.
    We are the word that is.

I leave you now from a city built on the desert. A city built on
the backs and brains of many cultures. A city overflowing with
people. People crammed into too-small one-room apartments and
estates bigger than a city block. A city with languages I don't understand. A city that can be brutally hot in summers and without rain for months on end. A city with a dead and poisoned river.
A city with vast wealth and immense poverty, a city where the
rich hide behind gated mansions and the homeless wander abandoned on the streets. A city where I now work in a clinic with
the poor and underfed: the people who need me.

I wish this were an end where I could guarantee what the future holds for Sarah and Sita and me, that we will be together a year from now. I can't. We are of the known past and unknown future. As we live beyond, in the past, dreaming of a mystery unsolved, some days I feel Sarah with me always, together with the vital and thriving Sita, who is loved simply for being our daughter Sita. And I see us as NeilSarahSita. Other days I see Sarah wandering alone in the horizons of time grieving for her lost children—born and unborn, fading into the New Mexico twilight, or sublimating her pain under the spell of New York celebrity—yet always weeping over Castor's grave, moving not forward or beyond. For her nightmare does not go away, recede, close down—never able to lock the chamber of memories that is Castor, where an offhand remark, a child's cry, a smell, a rush of color in a thought or dream recalls the life she cannot have—and I hope the unconditional love from Sita and me is enough.

Arbitrary though this ending is, it is too a beginning in this finite world of the word, where the least articulate mumbler to the most able versifier is in possession of the same interminable ache. Where we crave solutions to the mysteries, solutions that are nothing more than placing a period at the end of the sentence. For as each new sentence, each new word, each new letter begins in hope of a new life, a new response, a new question, a new mystery, a new choice, I begin again as I will end.

My name is Downs. I am a Jew. I belong to the human epistasis.

I ache. I search. I love.